FLAMEKEEPER

Other books by TW Lawless:

HOMECOUNTRY

THORNYDEVILS

BLURLINE

DARK WATER

FLAMEKEEPER

TW LAWLESS

CAMPANILE
PUBLISHING

Published by Campanile Publishing
www.twlawless.com

© 2019 TW Lawless

The moral right of the author has been asserted.

A National Library of Australia Cataloguing-in-Publication entry has been created for this title.

    ISBN 978-0-9942651-6-6 (pbk)

    ISBN 978-0-9942651-7-3 (ebook)

Cover design by Golden Orb Creative: www.goldenorbcreative.com
Cover image by Yuganov Konstantin used under licence from
    Shutterstock.com (photo ID: 48124753).

Text design and production (print and ebook) by Golden Orb Creative.

Edited by Linda Nix AE of Golden Orb Creative.

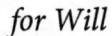

for Will

CHAPTER ONE

One am. Fort Bragg, North Carolina. 1972.

THE HOUSE WAS DARK EXCEPT FOR THE GLOW OF A SMALL PORCH light. In the car pulled up out front, Sergeant Antonelli switched off the car's ignition. Apart from a cat wandering around the front yard meowing frantically, the house was quiet too. Earlier, base dispatchers had received a call from a neighbour saying that a loud domestic was occurring at 540 Castle Drive. The two military police officers now getting out of the car had been sent in response.

The cat followed Antonelli and Corporal Thorne to the front door. Antonelli bent down to pat the cat curling past his ankles while Thorne knocked on the door. When there was no answer, Antonelli tried to peer in through a small gap in the curtains, but could see nothing.

'Looks like they ran out of steam again,' Thorne remarked.

'How many times has it been this week?'

'Two.'

'So much for the shrink.'

Thorne knocked three more times. The cat had disappeared.

'I don't like the look of this. Let's check out back.' Antonelli unclipped his pistol holster.

'Yeah. They usually answer the door.'

They crept around the side of the house to the back. Antonelli held his pistol in his right hand and tried the security door with his left. It was unlocked. Now Thorne unclipped his holster. He stood back, legs apart, knees slightly bent, his pistol raised in the firing position. Antonelli checked the back door. It was also unlocked.

'Ready?' Antonelli mouthed.

'Yeah.' Thorne nodded.

1

Antonelli quietly opened the door and flicked on the kitchen light. The cat was sitting on the table. Everything seemed in order, except for an open drawer. As soon as the two moved towards the table, the cat jumped off and ran out the back door.

'How did it get in? It didn't come in with us.'

'There must be an open window.'

'Let's check the living room.'

From past visits, Antonelli had a general understanding of the layout of the house. It was a typical Army home: uncluttered, neat as a pin, unpersonalised. He and Thorne crept towards the adjoining room, stopping once they reached the open doorway. Antonelli looked back at Thorne and nodded. The interior of the living room was completely dark. He signalled he was going to turn on the light near the doorway.

He tensed as he flicked off the safety on his pistol and raised his other hand towards the switch. He could sense danger. It had a scent; he could smell it. He had done two tours of Vietnam as a scout and had survived. His senses were as sharp as a cat's.

Thorne was in the firing position before Antonelli hit the switch. Their eyes adjusted to the flooding light and were quickly drawn to a large stain on the rug near the coffee table.

Antonelli's eyes darted around the room, ears straining for the slightest noise. He pointed his pistol towards a blood stain the size of a large salad bowl. 'Fresh blood.'

'Got you covered,' said Thorne.

Antonelli inched towards the stain. When he was nearly on top of it, something caught his eye. It was wedged between the coffee table and the sofa. 'We have a body,' he called.

At first, it was hard to distinguish whether it was male or female. The top half of the body was dressed but the shirt was soaked in blood. Antonelli squatted. He could make out deep gashes to the chest and throat. The victim's eyes were open, terror still etched in her heavily disfigured face. His own eyes glanced beyond the sofa. It was then he noticed the bloodied ice pick.

'A female. Stabbed multiple times.' He reached down to feel for a pulse. 'She's dead. She has no pulse.'

Thorne hesitated.

'We have to check all of the rooms,' said Antonelli.

'Should we wait for back-up?'

'We may not have the time. The perp could be still here.' Antonelli pointed towards the hallway. 'Check the bathroom and bedrooms. I'll cover you.'

Thorne turned on the light and inched along the hallway, while Antonelli stayed behind. He knew the next room to the right was the master bedroom. Thorne attempted to turn the door knob. It was locked.

'You want me to break it down, Sarge?'

'Wait.' Antonelli sidled down the hallway with his back to the wall, his pistol covering the rear. He double-checked that the door was locked. This wasn't war and he was mindful that they were about to damage Army property. 'Got you covered,' he said. 'Kick it in, Corporal.'

Thorne holstered his pistol, took hold of the door knob and with one shoulder barge, forced the door open. He stumbled through the doorway and then righted himself, as Antonelli clicked on the light.

Thorne gasped. The wall behind the bed was a bloody mural. His eyes followed the spray up over the ceiling and back down the opposite wall. He fumbled as he pulled his pistol out of the holster.

'What the fuck!'

A naked man lay spread-eagled, face up on the bed, his bloodied throat gaping open. Thorne was frozen. 'Come on. Get it together,' said Antonelli, pushing past him. He stooped over the body. 'It's Captain Donnelly. Throat's cut from ear to ear.' He noticed the Gerber knife lying next to the bed. 'He sure wanted to die. See here? There are also vertical cuts to the wrists.'

Thorne started to retch. He took out his handkerchief, pressed it to his lips and swallowed hard. 'You think he killed himself? No one would slash their own throat. No one sane, that is.'

A smile flickered across Antonelli's lips and was gone. 'He was in 'Nam.' He felt a breeze ruffle the curtain. The window was open. 'That's where the cat got in,' he remarked. 'But the door was locked, so there must be another window...'

Thorne was now wiping his forehead with his handkerchief.

'Pull yourself together, Corporal Thorne.'

'I'm trying, sir,' he stammered.

Antonelli looked around. There was no sign of anyone else in the house, no bloodied footprints, no strange noises. 'Call emergency,' he ordered.

'Don't you want to secure the rest of the house first?'

'Never question an order, Thorne. Just call emergency. Now.'

The phone was on the kitchen wall. Thorne returned the way he had come, holstered his pistol again and dialled, while Antonelli returned to the body in the living room. 'Tell them to send CID also.'

Thorne was already talking to the operator; his voice was strained. He replaced the receiver with shaking hands and joined Antonelli. 'Can you tell who it is?'

'I think it's Mrs Donnelly. By the feel of her, she hasn't been dead long.'

'And the captain?'

'I don't know. The blood's still draining. Probably died not long after her. Or before her. Maybe she took her time dying.'

Thorne had turned pale. Unlike the sergeant, he hadn't yet done a tour of Vietnam. He was trying not to look at the body.

'You'll get used to it,' said Antonelli. 'Maybe.'

'You think the captain did it?'

Antonelli stood up and wiped his fingers on his handkerchief. He shrugged his shoulders. 'Oh, sure, he may have done it all right, but I don't think he was responsible for this, if that's what you're asking.'

Thorne looked puzzled.

'Easy,' Antonelli explained. 'He gets fucked up in 'Nam and comes back crazy. He goes back home to his wife, only he's changed. And they fight a little—okay a lot—until something inside him snaps. And it snaps good. And now 'Nam's killed the both of them.'

Chapter Two

Low Library, Columbia University, New York City. 1992.

PETER CLANCY WAS ON HIS BEST BEHAVIOUR. HE'D PROMISED Stella. It was her day and that made him need a drink more than ever.

Stella Reimers was in the next seat, looking more like a flight attendant than a Pulitzer Prize-winning journalist. It had been a difficult few weeks for Peter since the announcement of the winners of the Pulitzer Prize and, to top it all off, Stella had invited him to the luncheon ceremony. It would have been unsporting of him to refuse, so here he was—the only Australian in a roomful of Americans— nursing a lemonade and a bad mood and sitting at a table alongside eight strangers (mostly journalists and spouses) and Stella.

She looked like a winner, from her neat chignon all the way down to her shiny, black Munro pumps. Peter, on the other hand, felt like he'd been pressed and folded at gun-point into an ill-fitting suit. The shirt collar cut into his neck and the tie was as tight as a noose. He felt ridiculous.

Yes, Stella had been nominated for the best investigative journalist award for breaking a story about a British paedophile ring. It had been huge. But it had been Peter's story. The same story he had worked on during his time at that oily rag of an English tabloid, the *Star Gazer*. The same story that destroyed his relationship with Ruby, the sweetest, most beautiful woman he had ever met. The same story that had almost cost him his life.

Stella had brought it all together and found the missing pieces that made it water-tight, but it was his story and it should have been his byline. Peter wasn't listed as a co-author on legal advice, and therefore he could not be considered as a nominee for the Pulitzer

Prize. Unable to publish the story in the United Kingdom, Stella had carefully steered the story's publication in the United States. And now she was reaping the benefit. And Peter had come along to the Pulitzer luncheon as her handbag.

Minus a drink, he'd already sat through the chairman's speech. He was getting thirsty. He wished he'd tucked his trusty old whisky flask into his suit pocket for sustenance. But that would have ruined the line of his jacket. Even handbags have standards.

He thought about the speech he had written for the award for which he wasn't nominated. *To all my fellow journalists, I have one thing to say. Fuck you!* He needed a drink. Was there enough time to summon the waiter?

'You look nervous,' Stella said, tossing him a glance as he shifted uncomfortably in his seat.

'I don't know why. I haven't won anything.'

'Still hurting, hey?' She took hold of his hand and squeezed.

'I'm fine. I'm glad you won. Truly. Happy for you. Very happy. That's what my therapist said I should say.' He smiled.

Stella pretended to slap his face. 'You know I'm eternally grateful. The story wouldn't have seen the light of day without you.'

'Well, without your efforts, I guess the story would have been buried forever.'

'I'm sorry that you never got the credit you deserved, but try to think of the good you've done for all those victims. You helped bring their story into the public eye.'

'Sending some politicians and celebrities to prison equals a good result. I know that. Evil bastards.'

'Do you ever wonder how Ruby Manzanoni is coping?' she asked.

'I haven't given her a thought since I flew out of Heathrow,' he lied.

'That's good,' replied Stella.

He watched a group of people return to their seats and considered leaving the luncheon in favour of a long, slow pub crawl. He mumbled something about how his story—their story—had relaunched one starlet's career, until his voice faded away.

'I know it stings, but you know it's also yours,' said Stella.

'Really? Since we're spouting platitudes today, I'm the wind beneath your wings.' Peter felt the nausea rise up. 'Still, I can't help feeling that I wasn't rewarded for all the hard work and the near-death events.'

'I already offered to split the prize money with you. I'll let you hold my certificate.'

'Can I babysit it when you're not home?'

'Can I trust you?'

Peter laughed and was still wondering if there was enough time to drift away before the chairman of the board announced Stella as the winner of the prize for a distinguished example of reporting on international affairs. The certificates were neatly piled on a table adjacent to the rostrum.

'Oh God. We're up next,' Stella spluttered nervously.

'Have you got your speech ready?'

'This isn't the Oscars. You don't get to speak.'

'Well then, in case anyone asks you later, remember to thank God, diazepam and Jim Beam. That should just about cover it.' He paused. 'And me. Don't forget to thank me.'

'Stop being such an asshole, Clancy.'

'If you had let me get drunk...'

The chairman looked bored. 'We come to the prizes; the real reason we're here...' He flicked open a sheet of paper and stared at it for an eternity.

Stella squeezed Peter's hand so hard that he winced. She looked as nervous as a nun in a brothel. Where was the normally cool-and-collected-take-no-bullshit-or-prisoners Stella?

'The award for a distinguished example of meritorious public service by a newspaper goes to...'

Peter tuned out. He watched the editor and a select group of journalists from the *Sacramento Bee* collect their medal and pose for photographs, and felt sick. It should have been his day in the sun but, instead, he'd handed Stella a cash bonus and a job for life. It wasn't fair and he couldn't be magnanimous about it today. Maybe in a few years' time the sting would subside, but not today. *It's not the Heart of Melbourne, it's not even the Walkley, it's the fucking Pulitzer!*

Stella was holding her breath as the chairman lifted a lazy finger towards his glasses and pushed them back onto the bridge of his nose. Peter looked away as the announcement came. 'Stella Reimers of *The Washington Post* for *Dark Secrets in Britain's Corridors of Power: Exposing the Whitehall Paedophile Ring.*'

By the time Peter looked back again, Stella was already clutching her certificate. She was beaming right at him.

Yes, she deserved it, he thought. She'd worked her guts out all of her career. She had more battle scars than any other journalist he'd ever met. *There'll be other stories. There always is.* He watched her graciously accept the applause. He watched her pose for photographs. His name may not have been on that prize but he'd finally done a story that really mattered. *I wish you were here, Ruby, to share this. Wherever you are I hope you are well. If I could have saved you from all of the pain, I would have.*

Peter embraced Stella when she finally returned to her seat.

'Thanks,' she said. 'I'm in your debt now. You think Bob would have liked it?'

Bob Connelly had been the irascible, hard-drinking, *Melbourne Truth* editor, Peter's mentor and Stella's one-time love. 'Of course he would have,' Peter replied.

'What would he have thought of this place?'

'Nice lunch but where's the party?'

'Precisely. Let's get the fuck out of here.'

There had been a champagne celebration at *The Washington Post* the day of the announcement, but the party didn't really start until Stella and Peter got back to DC. Staff from the *Post* and anyone else that mattered in Washington's media world were at Stella's apartment. It had been a long time between celebrations for Peter. He hadn't had much cause for a party since leaving England. Now he was going to let his hair down.

Let's teach these Yanks how to party... Peter grabbed a can of beer and ripped off the tab. He was about to scull it in one until he looked around the room. The others were sipping wine and nibbling at their canapés. He was in rarefied company. Possibly for the first time in his life, consequences mattered more to him than the icy beer in his hand. This wasn't the time to embarrass Stella or himself. This was a great place to get contacts. He needed a more stable, lucrative job. The life of a stringer was a disorganised hand-to-mouth existence. He was also getting tired of a voice at the other end of the phone calling him any time of day or night and asking, 'You available?'

Peter had been staying with Stella since his unannounced arrival in the States. Stella hadn't only pushed to get the story published, she'd also given him a place to stay and sorted out his visa. Without her pulling strings he would have been sent back to England. Even counting the Pulitzer, he still owed her favours for the rest of his life. So, no dancing on tables or sculling contests allowed. Only lively, droll chit-chat and the occasional song were the order of the day.

By the second hour, moderation had dropped out of the window like a piano. The Americans had more than met Peter's measure. He watched a well-known political reporter tap dance on Stella's coffee table while wearing a bra on his head. Whose, he couldn't say. Stella didn't mind, since she was right up there as well, doing the same with a large bourbon in one hand.

Maybe Peter was getting old or his liver was packing it in but it was after ten and he was going to crash. To make matters worse, he was going to do it alone.

'Where are you going, Clancy?' Stella shouted as she stumbled off the coffee table. 'You're not skipping out on me, mate. Where's that hard-living liver of yours going in such a hurry?'

'I need a sleep,' he replied.

She grabbed him by the arm. 'What the fuck is the matter with you? This is your party also.'

'I'm just tired. I think it's all caught up with me.'

'You're going to bed alone? Just take a moment to look around you.'

'No thanks. I'm going monk for a while.'

'In that case, I think it's a good time to talk.' She took Peter's arm and led him into the bathroom and locked the door.

'No coke for me, thanks,' he joked.

'I gave that up years ago.'

'What's this about, then?'

'Can you keep a secret?'

Peter laughed. 'You're asking a journalist to keep a secret?'

'I'll rephrase that. Off the record, this is between you and me.' She paused and stared him in the eye. 'This will come as a shock to you, but I've taken a job in San Francisco.'

'But you've just won a Pulitzer Prize for the *Post*. Why would you leave? That'll piss them off more than a little. '

'I could care less. This is a more lucrative job. I'm going to be heading up the news department at the *San Francisco Daily* and I'm also going back to my hometown.'

'I always thought New York was your hometown.'

'For a long time it was, but San Fran is where I grew up. I figure with each year that passes, I'm closer to retiring and this Jewish girl ain't getting any richer or younger. It has great weather and it's more relaxed. It'll be a nice place to grow old. A few more years in this game and I'll be set for life. I'm getting tired, Peter. I'm not tired of chasing stories, I'm just tired of all the bullshit.'

'I wish you well, Stella, I really do. I'm going to miss you a lot.' Peter smiled. 'When do you leave?'

'I'm giving the *Post* two weeks' notice.'

'Since you're not going to need this place much longer, I could take over your lease.'

'I don't think so.'

'Why not? I should be able to afford it if I get someone else in.'

'I left out one tiny detail. I'm hoping that you'll be coming with me.'

'I like you, Stella, really I do, but I don't know...'

'Relax, I'm not proposing marriage. I realise how much missing out on the Pulitzer meant to you. As part of the negotiations, I got you a chief reporter position in the news division. If you take it, you'll answer directly to me.'

'But I've only just arrived here. I haven't even got used to driving on the right-hand side of the road yet.'

'Well, you're the finest crime reporter I know. You'll cover the same stories, just in a different country. Are you up for it?'

He hesitated. 'It's come as a bit of a shock. Can I think about it?'

'Yeah, you're right. It's just that I got the feeling you were sick of the freelance crap. This job is well-paid and it sure beats working at gossip rags. The *Daily* is the third biggest-selling newspaper in San Francisco.'

'Third?' His brow furrowed. 'That's a little low.'

'The *Daily* is a well-respected paper but it needs a kick in the ass. It's a little old-fashioned, a little too conservative for my tastes. I know for sure, with your help, I can make it number one. Do you need to know any more than that? Never figured you to walk away from a challenge.'

'I was aiming for the *Post*.'

'Nothing doing. Take it from me, the *Daily's* on its way up. Make up your mind quickly because I have to tell them tomorrow.'

Peter looked at himself in the mirror. He looked tired. He needed stability in his life. He felt like he had never fully unpacked since he left Collingwood. Did he still have the fire? Was there still enough mongrel left in him? Stella's face was hopeful. 'Shit, you've put me on the spot.'

'That's how you've always liked to do things. You're the guy who hops a plane to England on a whim and then turns up at Dulles without the right visa. That's you all over.'

'Impulsive? Me?' He had no ties to Washington DC and he was dreading the winter. 'How much does it pay?'

'A lot more than you're making now. How's five hundred a week sound to you?'

'Shit. I was making more than that at the *Truth*.'

'Five-fifty?'

'Better. I'll do it for six-fifty a week plus medical insurance. I deserve a decent job.' Peter knew his worth and he knew that, along with her Pulitzer, Stella had bargaining power.

'Just as well I got you seven hundred, then. So it's a deal.' Stella laughed. 'What took you so long?'

CHAPTER THREE

San Francisco, California.

PETER DREAMED OF A TRIP ACROSS AMERICA IN A FAST CONVERTible but Stella, ever keen to have her feet on the ground as soon as possible, insisted that they take the red-eye instead.

Stella had already leased an apartment in Dolores Street, overlooking Dolores Park. She was happy to share with Peter until he had settled into life in San Francisco which, as he figured it, would be measured in days. He already knew all about Haight Ashbury, cable cars and Alcatraz from popular culture. If he was a fish out of water, he was going to be a lungfish: he wouldn't need water to breathe.

On his second day in the city, he and Stella headed into the offices of the *San Francisco Daily* on Mission Street, near Union Square.

'You know where to go?' he asked as they bustled up 16th Street towards the station.

'Aside from having grown up here, you mean? Yeah, I was interviewed there. I haven't met all of the staff, but I know the lay of the land.'

They got off at Montgomery Street Station and walked the remaining few blocks.

'Nervous?' Stella asked him as they rode the elevator to the *Daily*'s offices on the ninth floor.

'Not really.'

'You should be.'

'Why?'

'I told them you were an asshole.'

'Why the hell would you tell them that?'

'I've done you a favour. They respect assholes here.'

Stella checked her makeup in the mirrored wall as the elevator door opened. Her face suddenly hardened and her heels click-clacked as they crossed the lobby. She swung open the door confidently and they strode into the newsroom together.

Peter stifled a gasp. It was the quietest and neatest newsroom he'd ever seen. The reporters were all at their computers typing feverishly. A few noticed them but didn't offer any greetings. The only sound he heard was the clatter of keys being struck. He felt like he had walked into a classroom during an exam.

'There's something wrong,' he remarked as they entered a corridor. 'This is way too sterile. Newsrooms should be more Petri dish than autoclave. They're robotic. Not one of them said hello.'

'We're not here to make friends, Peter. We're here to make this paper number one. Remember that.'

Further along the corridor, they were met by a well-dressed woman. It seemed to Peter that she had traded youth for makeup a long time ago.

'Hi,' the woman burbled. 'I'm Beverley. I'm your secretary, Mrs Reimers.'

'I'm Ms Reimers, please remember that. Mrs Reimers doesn't exist. This is our new chief reporter, Peter Clancy. Mr Clancy and I would like two strong black coffees.'

Beverley blushed. 'I'm sorry.'

'Don't tell me, coffee isn't part of your job description.'

'No, Ms Reimers…'

Peter watched Stella stare Beverley down and felt a tinge of pity.

'Well, it is now,' she said. 'Oh, and can you also bring me the newspapers for the past week?'

'Yes, Ms Reimers.'

Beverley turned to leave.

'Hold on, I'm not finished yet.'

'Yes, Ms Reimers?' She blushed again.

'I want all the reporters in the conference room in twenty minutes.'

'Yes, Ms Reimers.'

'Thank you. And where is the conference room by the way?'

She pointed. 'Just down the hallway to the left.'

13

'Thanks, Beverley,' said Stella, opening the door to her office. She walked past a large desk to the window and looked out.

'Nice view,' said Peter.

'Don't get used to it. We won't have time to admire views.'

There was a rap on the door. Peter turned around. The man in the doorway was dressed in a light grey suit, with matching hair and tie.

'Hi. I'm Frank Styles. Welcome to the *Daily*.'

Frank was tall and thin, and probably in his fifties. Peter quickly deduced by his dress and demeanour that he wasn't a reporter.

'Frank is our editor-in-chief.'

'How are you, Stella?'

Stella smiled. 'This is Peter Clancy,' she said.

Frank shook his hand. 'So this is our whiz kid. Welcome aboard. Stella says you're the best reporter she's worked with. You must be good because she wasn't going to take the job without you on board. She was firm about that. That's some compliment coming from a Pulitzer Prize-winner.'

'That's very flattering.'

'So, how do you like San Francisco?'

'Well, I haven't had much of a chance to see the sights yet, but what I've seen reminds me of Sydney.'

'Yes, I hope to travel there one day.'

Stella was already rearranging the desk drawers.

'It must feel good to be back home, Stella.'

'I don't think I mentioned it, Peter, but this is where I started.'

It must have slipped your mind, he thought.

'Great days, weren't they?' said Frank.

'I have many fond memories of this paper and this city. When I left the *Daily*, it was number one and it had been for many years. My intention is to make it number one again.'

'That's the spirit. Who remembers the runners up?'

Peter shrugged. Frank was bland. He reminded Peter of boiled custard.

'So,' Frank asked Stella, 'when are you meeting the reporters?'

'In ten minutes.'

'Good. Mind if I'm there?'

'Of course not.'

'See you then.' Frank Styles closed the door after him.

'He's more politician than editor,' said Peter. 'Softly, softly. A bit grey, like his suit.'

'Frank's retiring soon. He gave up when he had his second heart attack. He was a great reporter in his day. He once received a letter from the Zodiac Killer wanting to meet him. It was probably lucky for him that the Zodiac was a no-show.'

'That case has always fascinated me.'

'Well, you'll either have to ask him about it or wait for his memoirs. Apparently, he's going to write a book on it.'

'So, you've always kept in touch with Frank?'

'Yeah, we're old buddies.'

'I don't think he likes me. Not that I could give a shit. If I'd wanted to be popular I would have become a game show host.' Peter hesitated. 'Does that mean you'll get his job?'

'Whoa there, Clancy, you're getting ahead of yourself.' She slammed one of the drawers shut and stood up. 'First things first.' She went to her door and called out, 'Beverley. We're still waiting for that coffee.'

Peter laughed. He suspected that Stella was just getting started.

CHAPTER FOUR

Daily conference room.

PETER STOOD AT THE FRONT OF THE CONFERENCE ROOM NEXT TO Stella and watched the reporters file in. Most of them were men barely pushing forty, all white, and only two of them were female.

What a boring bunch. They look more like teachers than hacks.

To a man, they looked suburban. They were school pick-up, nine-to-five people. Most packed in at the back of the room; the two women and a handful of the men sat down. Aside from the occasional cough, they were silent. Eyes down, no one looked towards the front.

Stella was laying out the past issues of the *Daily* on a table in front of her.

'They look uncomfortable,' Peter whispered in her ear.

'So they fucking should be.'

Frank Styles drifted in and stood in front of them. 'Good morning, boys and girls.'

I've got it all wrong. I've regressed seventeen years. I'm back in high school and Franks Styles is the bloody headmaster!

'I'd like to welcome two new members to our team. Stella Reimers is joining us as news editor and Peter Clancy as chief crime reporter. Please join me in welcoming them to the *Daily*.'

Only Frank clapped.

'As you already know, Stella comes to us fresh from *The Washington Post*. She's a Pulitzer Prize-winner and she and Peter will be bringing a wealth of experience to our great paper. I am confident that she will be the catalyst that makes the *Daily* the number one selling newspaper in San Francisco again. Since I will be retiring at the end of the year, I will be taking a less active role in the daily functioning of the paper. Stella will be taking over some of my duties.'

Peter watched the shockwave ripple through the room.

'So she will be the one to impress. I know you each have it in you and if we work together as a team, we'll be number one. It's going to take a lot of hard work but I know we can do it. Now I'd like to hand over to Stella Reimers.'

A few claps. Stella winked at Peter and stepped forward. By the time she reached Frank's side, she had her unleash-hell look.

'Thank you, Frank. As I watched you coming in, I asked myself why most of you were standing at the back of the room like frightened schoolchildren. I'm not going to attack, at least not yet. Come forward and grab a seat. Sit.'

She took a drink of water, as the seats slowly filled and the grumbles subsided. She looked around the room. 'Are you happy working here?'

No one answered.

'No one's talking? That's very unusual for a bunch of reporters.'

She stood in front of one of the reporters who had just taken a seat and was suddenly regretting it.

'What's your name?'

'John Travers.'

'Are you happy working here, Mr Travers?'

'Most of the time.' Travers looked around the room for support.

'Really? Most of the time. What about the rest of the time, Mr Travers?'

The door opened and another reporter hurried in as Travers took an audible breath and tried to relax.

'Sorry,' said the reporter. 'I was… The interview I was doing took longer than expected'.

'And your name is?' Stella asked.

'Ben Shapiro.'

'Mr Shapiro, if you're ever late for a scheduled meeting again, you're fired. Understand?'

'Yes, Ms Reimers.'

'Unless you're interviewing John Lennon direct from heaven, or hell, or wherever else he happens to be, you have no excuse for missing a meeting. You got it? Good. Take a seat. And that goes for the rest of you. Where were we? Mr Travers.'

'Yes?' he squeaked.

'Yes, you said you like working here, most of the time. What's wrong with the rest of the time? You hate the coffee? You work too hard? The stories are boring? The boss's giving you a hard time?'

'I'm just speaking for myself, you understand, but the other papers always seem to be ahead of us. That's what I dislike particularly.'

'Thank you for that honest insight, Mr Travers. I'm glad you said that, because I totally agree. I can tell you why they are ahead of us. The simple formula is, they're filing more hard-hitting stories which are selling more papers and therefore attracting more advertisers. If we don't have eye-catching stories, reporters will have to be laid off. I don't want to have to do that, but if we go any lower in the circulation figures, I'll be forced to.'

Some of the reporters at the back were shifting uncomfortably. Peter grasped the tail-end of a comment that finished, *what would she know?* and glanced at Stella. From her face it was clear she heard it too.

'What would I know? What would I know. Let me see... Here's what I know. I started working at the *Daily* as a cub reporter back when it was number one in this city. Since then, I've worked in major dailies in New York, London, Singapore, Hong Kong and Washington DC. Not to mention a short time in the Antipodes. But seeing as you're all journalists, and since you're so good at research, you should already know all of that.' Stella took a measured breath. 'Now for the ugly truth. The *Daily* runs a poor third these days. I find that unacceptable. They say your heart always remains true to your first love, and for me that's the *San Francisco Daily*. That, in a nutshell, is what I know. The question is, what do you all know?'

The room filled with silence.

'No one brave enough to answer, huh? How are the others getting the best stories? Don't just sit there like stunned fish. Speak up. '

'We have a good relationship with the mayor's office,' one of the female reporters piped up.

'The police chief likes the *Daily*. That's a fact,' another reporter added.

'And so we're all about law and order, city hall, respect the police, Mom and apple pie? Why aren't we selling lots of papers, then? Why? Because it sounds like the people you're looking after are biting us on the ass,' said Stella. 'Let's ask our new chief crime reporter. What do you think, Peter?'

'You don't get good stories schmoozing the establishment. They're not your friends. They only have one angle—theirs. I always go to the people on the street. Love it or hate it, fear and uncertainty sells papers. That's the reality.'

'But,' a reporter spoke up, 'we know our audience. It's largely white middle class. They like to know that there is order and their homes and kids are safe.'

Stella laughed. 'For a moment, I thought Ronald Regan was talking.' She went to the table and held up a newspaper and looked at it. She dropped it back on the table, and continued on until she got to the third newspaper. 'These aren't headlines, they're deadlines. They're prescriptions for insomnia. Where are the stories on crime? When I read the *Daily*, there appears to be hardly any crime and the police have it all under control. I grew up in this city. I worked at this paper for ten years. San Francisco is a criminal city. It was founded on crime. Where are the stories on the large gay community, the ethnic minorities? This city is not all about contented, straight, white folk.'

'That's not how we want to portray San Francisco. Stories like that will only scare people. To me, it sounds unethical and immoral.' The voice came from a reporter at the back of the room, his face beetroot red.

'And your name is?'

'Ben Sanders.'

Well, Mr Sanders, I have news for you. The other papers are already doing it and they're doing it well. If you want to write tourist brochures, I wish you well.'

Sanders stood up and stormed out of the room.

'Anyone else wish to follow Mr Sanders?' Stella thumped the

table. 'It's time you all pulled your fingers out of your bloated ass-holes because change is coming. You may not agree with it, you may not like it, but it's coming and you'll have to be fast and ambitious to keep up. I don't want any slackers or complainers on my team. So, I will give you the opportunity after this meeting to come to my office and tender your resignation. I want all my chief reporters in my office in ten minutes. Thank you.'

Frank and Peter clapped as everyone else stood up quietly and headed for the exit.

'Thank you, Stella, you've let them know right away how you operate. They'll get used to it. You'll be a breath of fresh air for this tired old girl,' Frank remarked. He sighed and looked at newspapers spread all over the desk and floor. 'I did my best. It's different times now I guess. I wish you well. My door is always open.'

'This paper wouldn't have even lasted this long without you at the helm,' said Stella.

'You're a flipping hurricane,' Peter quipped.

'Enough out of you, Clancy. You're the one who will be leading the charge so I hope you're ready to show these reporters how to get a hard-edged lead.'

'When do we start?'

'After I listen to the resignations.'

'I reckon four,' he said.

'I reckon less. We'll see. Winner has to shout.'

In the end, there was only one resignation and one early retirement. The *San Francisco Daily* was ready for a change.

CHAPTER FIVE

Castro District, San Francisco. 1975.

'YOU SAY YOU HEARD LOTS OF SCREAMING IN THE ALLEYWAY WHEN you were passing by? What's your name?' Officer Garcia asked.

'Paul Branson.'

'So, Paul Branson, when you heard all this screaming, why didn't you call 911?'

'Well, the police don't like going near the Castro,' he replied.

Earlier Branson had flagged down Officers Garcia and Malone's squad car on Castro Street. They had only stopped when they thought they might run him over.

'Don't get lippy with me,' Garcia said. 'We have better things to do than arrest a bunch of screaming fags.' He looked Branson over. He was a typical Castro clone: jeans, combat boots, tight t-shirt and full moustache. It made him sick. 'So, do you know who or what was causing the commotion?'

'No. I don't. I was just concerned.'

'Just what we need, a community-minded fag.'

'Excuse me, I pay taxes. Those taxes pay your wage.'

'Okay, knock it off. In the alleyway down there?' Malone pointed. 'You said you thought it sounded like someone was being killed?'

'How do you know what it sounds like when people are killed?' Garcia guffawed.

'I was in Vietnam. Yes, that's what I said.'

'Okay. We'll check it out.'

Malone grabbed a flashlight from the squad car. 'Stay with him,' he said to Garcia.

'Great,' Garcia replied. 'As long as he doesn't try to proposition me.'

'You're safe with me,' said Branson. 'Besides you're not my type.

Don't worry, gay's not catching.'

Malone held up the flashlight and proceeded carefully along the alleyway. Apart from graffiti and garbage hoppers, there wasn't much to see.

'Anything?' Garcia called.

'Not so far.'

Malone continued down the alleyway. He stopped next to a caricature of Richard Nixon painted on a stucco wall. Below the words, *Jail to the Chief*, a large bundle of rags caught his eye. He tapped them with the toe of his boot. He expected the rags to fall apart but there was something heavy and hard under the pile. As his eyes adjusted to the dimness of the light, he realised the rags were clothes, and the viscous ooze to which they were stuck was coagulating blood.

'I have a body,' he called back. 'Possibly deceased. I'll check.'

He gave the body another tap. There was no response. Then the torso fell backwards, revealing a skirt lifted up high and bloodied panties pulled down to the knees.

'Deep cut to the throat. Female, I think. I can't tell yet.' Malone knew that this area was a well-known haunt for transvestite prostitutes. He shone the flashlight on the face and crouched down. 'Holy shit!' he yelled as he stepped backwards. 'Holy shit!' he repeated. 'We've got a real sicko down here.'

'What is it? Are you okay?' Garcia took his revolver out of his holster and rushed down the alleyway, as Branson followed.

'I'm fine but get homicide on the radio.'

'What is it?'

Malone glanced back at the victim's face. He felt the nausea rise in his throat. 'A dead transvestite,' he began. 'It's a dead transvestite with a... He's got a dick in his mouth. Possibly his own.'

Branson gave a wry smile when he saw Garcia lean against the wall and vomit.

CHAPTER SIX

Tenderloin District, San Francisco. 1992.

'WELCOME TO SAN FRANCISCO'S WORST SUBURB,' CHAD MULROY said as he stepped onto the sidewalk, narrowly missing a rag-covered man who was having a seizure in the gutter. 'Bad drugs, I guess,' he added.

Peter looked up and down the street and smiled. For a moment, he was back home in the Collingwood badlands. The Tenderloin was San Francisco's festering open sore, a mass of faded high-density buildings covered in signs that advertised everything from rooms to rent to Vietnamese cuisine and strippers. The street was teeming with San Fran's flotsam: drunks, drug addicts, drug dealers, the homeless. It was a symphony of hopelessness.

'Nice. The dark side of the American dream,' Peter said.

'This must be the place.' Mulroy noticed two uniformed cops standing outside a building with external fire stairs, below a hoarding advertising single rooms for rent. 'Do you want to do the talking?' he asked.

'I'll let you do it this time. You need the practice,' Peter replied as they walked towards the cops.

Mulroy took a deep breath. It wasn't that he was new to the game; in fact he was a newspaper veteran of ten years. He just hadn't been getting out and working the street lately.

'You can't get the lead if you don't see it bleed,' said Peter.

'Hello, officers,' said Mulroy. 'We're from the *Daily*. We heard on the scanner there's been a double murder.'

'Pimp and his lady got themselves shot. The john must have gone crazy when she couldn't put on the condom. Nothing that interesting.' The officer sniggered.

'You should have stayed in the office,' the other officer added.

'That's it?' Mulroy looked at Peter for help.

'Mind if we go up and take a look?' Peter asked.

'No, we can't let you up there. Second floor is a crime scene.'

'That's interesting,' said Mulroy. 'I'm sure the Chief will be interested in hearing that.'

'Yeah? How so?'

'Well,' took up Peter, 'when our boss had dinner with Chief Gibson just last night, the Chief told her that the police and the *Daily* will be working closely together to curb the surging crime rate in this great city.'

'He said that?' The cop looked at the other.

'Just last night. Over a plate of fresh oysters at the Marriott Marquis.'

'You're bullshitting us.'

'No, that's the truth.' Peter got his cell phone out of his coat and started to punch in numbers. 'You want to talk to the Chief or my boss?'

'Okay. Homicide Inspector Belinski is still there so don't get in the way. He'll bust our balls if you overstep,' the first officer said. 'And just so you know, if there's trouble, you better call the Chief.'

Peter stopped punching the cell. 'We owe you a drink,' he said.

Mulroy followed Peter up the dimly lit stairs. 'You know that I could have got you in a lot of trouble.'

'You didn't, so why worry,' Peter replied. 'Good, I see light.' He sniffed. 'Vietnamese food. Love it. Just like Collingwood.'

'Where?'

'Collingwood. Victoria. Australia. You've heard of Australia, haven't you?'

'Kangaroos, outback and shit? Yeah I've heard of it.'

'Well, I used to live in Collingwood. Part of Melbourne. Lots of Vietnamese there, too.'

'All I can smell is human piss back here. Fancy using the stairs as a urinal.'

'Love it. Just like Collingwood.'

24

As they climbed the last few steps, they heard a man and woman shouting.

'I hope they're not killing each other,' said Mulroy.

'If they do, that's the splash.'

By the time they stepped onto the landing, the yelling had reached fever pitch. The inspector was standing in the doorway of one of the apartments, trying to question a Vietnamese woman. She barely reached his armpits, but it was clear that the inspector was getting nowhere and his face screamed frustration. The woman was more than twice his age and a third of his weight. He looked like a giant next to her. The apartment next door to hers was sealed with police tape.

'Clancy and Mulroy from the *Daily*,' said Peter as she attempted to slam the door. The inspector held it open with one hand, while a uniformed officer stood nearby. They all turned to look at Peter and Mulroy.

'How did you guys get up here?' the inspector asked.

'This is a crime scene, reporters aren't allowed,' said the officer.

Mulroy started to turn back.

'I might be able to help you out there,' said Peter, pulling Mulroy away from the stairwell. He turned to the old woman. '*Chào bà. Tên tôi là Peter. Tôi đến từ các tờ báo.*' He noticed that the old woman relaxed her grip on the door knob.

'*Chuyện gì đã xảy ra?*' she replied, gripping the door knob again.

Peter reached into his wallet and pulled out a ten dollar note and handed it to her.

'*Người già,*' she said as she pointed to the taped door.

'Older man,' he translated.

The old lady chattered as if to a friend until Peter signalled for her to slow down. She resumed speaking slower, miming what she was saying.

'He had a limp?' Peter asked.

She nodded. 'Daddy, Dad, Dad,' she shouted.

'Who said Daddy?'

She stopped and reached for the door again. Peter pulled another ten out of his wallet.

25

'*Cô gái.*' She pointed at the other apartment.

'The girl,' Peter repeated.

'*Diễm,*' the old lady whispered.

'She was a prostitute?'

She nodded yes. 'God bless 'Merica.' She smiled as she looked at her money and slammed her door.

The inspector sent the officer downstairs to check on the other officers. 'Holy shit,' he said when the officer was out of earshot. 'The girl's father may have killed them?'

'Maybe. See, Inspector, money speaks in my world. In your world, that would probably amount to corruption.'

'Homicide Inspector Jerry Belinski. I don't much like your style, but that sure saved me a lot of pain and hard work.'

'Anything to help the police.'

'Where did you learn Vietnamese?'

'I haven't learnt it. I just picked up a few words at a Vietnamese restaurant I used to go to in Melbourne.'

'I guess you think that means I owe you one.'

'You reckon we can have a look at the crime scene? Grab some photos?'

'Do we have to?' Mulroy stammered as he glanced at the taped door. 'Haven't we got enough?'

Belinski shook his head. 'I can't take you in. You can't cross a police line.' He swung open the door. 'But I suppose I couldn't do much about it if you were to get a photo or two from out here while my back is turned.'

'Take a good, long look at a real crime scene, Mulroy. How else are you going to get a feel for the story?' Peter grinned.

Chapter Seven

Next day. Stella's office.

Peter peered over Stella's shoulder at the headline story in that day's edition: *Tormented father confesses to murder of daughter.* The strapline read: *What every parent needs to know. The tragic story of an average family torn apart by drugs.* The byline was all his: Mulroy didn't even get a look-in.

Underneath the headline was a high school graduation photograph of Sally Anderson, a pretty girl from a small town in the Midwest. Next to the photograph was another of the bloodied apartment minus the bodies. Below that were mug shots of Sally and her pimp boyfriend, Cory Carr.

'What a tragedy,' Stella said. 'I wonder what makes a dad kill his own daughter? The police chief called to congratulate us on the story and he particularly mentioned you. Apparently, you helped them catch him.'

'That would be the first time the police have ever said anything complimentary about me.'

'You might want to take advantage of it. It could make life easier for you. You hit on a great angle by the way; you've given crime a human face.'

'Yeah, that's all well and good, but I'd like to hand the reins over to the other reporters once I've brought them up to speed.'

'And what would you like to do?'

'More in-depth investigative stories.'

Stella leaned back in her chair, rubbing her forehead.

'Something wrong?' he asked.

'Christ, Clancy, you're starting to give me a frigging headache.'

'Maybe it's just a hangover.'

'I barely drink anymore. I've seen what it's done to you.' She shook her head. She reached into her drawer, took out a pack of aspirin and swallowed two tablets, washed down with a swig of coffee.

'So, what do you think?'

'About what?'

'Me stepping back and doing more in-depth stories?'

'See what you're doing? Now you're giving me dementia... Wait until the circulation figures come out and, once things have improved enough, I'll think about it. Until then...'

'But...'

'Don't argue with me, Peter. If these figures don't go up, then you, I and a whole lot of other really good people will be losing our jobs.'

'Okay, but I just don't want to wait too long. You know how good I am at the hard-edged stuff.'

'I never figured you for a FIGJAM, Clancy.' She paused. 'I suppose a cure for a really bad headache hasn't made the long list of everything you're so great at.'

FIGJAM. Fuck I'm Good, Just Ask Me: the acronym had become popular in reference to a Collingwood footballer. It momentarily made Peter smart. He watched her massage her temples and replied, 'Not yet, Stella, but I could work on it.'

CHAPTER EIGHT

A few months later. *Daily* offices. 1993.

PETER WATCHED BEVERLEY OPEN STELLA'S OFFICE DOOR AS
quietly as she could while simultaneously carrying an armful
of mail. Moments later, Frank Styles walked in, his eyes darting
around like a squirrel on the lookout for an eagle. Peter recognised
the signs. They were universal. The quarterly circulation figures
were in.

With some luck, the figures would show the *Daily* breathing
down the necks of the *Chronicle* and the *Examiner*. He was growing tired of finding the human face of crime. Sometimes crime just
had an evil face. Period.

'Are the figures in today?' Mulroy asked from the next cubicle.

'Yep. It's the day of reckoning. You'll hear Stella screaming either
way, so get ready,' he replied.

'How will we tell which is which?'

'If it's bad news, you'll probably hear something being thrown at
the end of the screaming.'

'Thanks for the warning,' Mulroy said. A moment later he added,
'You seem to know the boss pretty damn well.'

'Okay, Mulroy, so what are you implying?'

'Nothing.'

'Bullshit. You're wondering if Stella and I are a couple.' Peter
laughed. 'You think I only got this job because I'm fucking the boss.'

'Well, are you?'

'We're a couple all right. We're a couple of old hacks with a thirst
for a good lead. That's it. Now, how's the story on the nightclub
shooting in Chinatown going?'

'I was talking to Belinski about it. He thinks it's gang-related. If he's right, I imagine the locals will be reluctant to talk. They could think their lives are at risk.'

'We'll get down to Chinatown and talk to them anyway. Take a photographer with us. I'm sure your immense charm and charisma will get them talking.'

Mulroy spluttered. 'I'll leave that one to you.'

'Let's have a chat with the Chinese Chamber of Commerce first, then we'll follow up with Tommy Lee at the Dragon's Den. He's a good source. While we're there we may as well have lunch. I hear it has the best dim sum.' Peter settled back into his chair just as screams erupted from Stella's office.

'I hope it's good news,' Mulroy said.

'I don't hear anything smashing so far.' Peter smiled. 'It's a good sign.'

The door flew open. Frank emerged first with no sign of the squirrel. Instead, he was grinning like a prairie dog. Stella was holding a sheet of paper and still hollering. Even Beverley allowed herself a smile.

'Number two,' Frank announced, 'we're number two.'

You bloody beauty. You pulled it off, Reimers. Now we can talk.

'Long time since we've had a celebration in this place. I thought we'd given away all our bottles of champagne,' said Frank. He picked a bottle up from the floor next to Beverley's desk and popped the cork. 'To Stella, who singlehandedly saved the *Daily*.'

A moment later, the line of reporters snaked down the hall, their glasses and coffee cups waiting to be filled. After two glasses, Frank's cheeks finally had some colour and he'd given the champagne dispensing duties to Peter.

'Thank you to everyone for stepping up to the plate,' said Stella. 'Now is not the time to get complacent. Number one is in our sights. Keep those stories coming.' She took a sip and called Peter over. 'I didn't want to say it publicly, but a lot of this is due to you. You're filing some great stories.'

'Thanks, Stella. I've put aside the old, I'm-not-worthy Peter. He's long gone and you can tell anyone you want. I know I can spin a great yarn, even if I can't kick arses quite as well as you. That's why the paper is going to be number one. You're the expert when it comes to arse-kicking. I'm your ace reporter. Now can we talk?'

'In my office in one hour.'

CHAPTER NINE

'SO, CLANCY, WHAT ARE YOU GOING TO ANNOY ME ABOUT?' Stella asked, taking a final sip of champagne. 'I much prefer whisky. What have you got?'

'I want to do a retrospective. Crime in San Francisco, then and now. Where are we headed?'

'Ah ha. You're determined to solve the Zodiac Killer case, aren't you? You think there's an award in it for you.'

'Well, that's only one of the stories I've looked at. There are a few unsolved crimes in San Francisco I want to work on.'

Stella leaned back in her chair and stared at the ceiling for a moment. 'I don't think people will be interested. The past belongs in history books, you know that. We work on a twenty-four-hour news cycle.'

'What if I bring new evidence to the table? What if we can solve some of these crimes?'

'Clancy... you're a great reporter but it's not what the people want right now.'

'You know what they say about history.'

'Leave rotting corpses the fuck alone?'

'Those who cannot remember the past are condemned to repeat it.'

Stella sighed. 'So what's this really about?'

Peter hesitated. 'I feel like I need a break from the everyday routine. The guys seem to be up to speed now. It's been non-stop mayhem for the past five years for me.' He stared out of Stella's window towards the courthouse. 'I'm burning out... I only have myself to blame.'

'Do you want some time off?'

'Shit no. I feel I can do big things here.'

'That's good to know. You're my right-hand man. I need you.' Stella pulled out a flask of single malt and poured two glasses. She handed one to Peter. 'I know you've been on an emotional roller-coaster. I'll only give you this advice: you can't get involved with a woman every time you research a big story. That will wear you out.'

'Yes. I'm over it. No more women for a while and,' he continued, pushing back the glass, 'I'm also cutting back on drinking.'

'Now's that's taking it too far. I don't want you becoming a boring old man. Just cut back on the women.' She reached into one of her desk drawers and pulled out a folder. She took out a black and white photograph and dropped it in front of Peter.

He picked it up and glanced at it. He recognised it at once. '*Life* magazine, a couple of years ago. I remember it. David Kirby, dying of AIDS, surrounded by his family as he takes his last breath.'

'You want to take a break from the daily beat,' said Stella. 'So, what do you know about AIDS?'

'Only what I've read. I try to stay current on issues, even if they don't directly impact my work. I haven't done any stories on AIDS. It hasn't been on my radar.'

'You don't have a problem with gays, as I recall.'

'Of course not. Remember, Concheeta was a friend as well as a source back in Melbourne.'

'Yes. Hard to forget a six-foot drag queen.' She took back the photograph and looked at it. 'If one photograph can capture a moment and move people to think differently, this has to be top of the pile.'

'So what's this got to do with what we were talking about?'

'Wouldn't it feel good to do a story like that? A story that captures the human side of AIDS?'

'It depends on how you do it.'

'When AIDS is portrayed in the media, it's all about the blame-game. It's got nothing to do with Middle America. It's a gay, IV drug user disease. But we know it's not.'

'Doesn't the *Chronicle* have a gay reporter on staff, who deals with the AIDS issues?' Peter asked.

'Yes, but the *Daily* has barely mentioned the AIDS epidemic. It makes us look homophobic. Do you know AIDS is the biggest killer of young men in the United States right now and we've barely given it a mention? San Francisco has a huge gay community that we're not giving a voice to.'

'What does Frank think about this?'

'I've talked him into it more or less. You know, I eventually get my way.'

'Of course you do.'

'If you can come up with something that makes people aware, makes them sympathetic, you'll get the attention you want, Peter.'

Peter shook his head. 'Crime is my niche. Why don't you get one of the other reporters? Maybe someone gay?'

'It doesn't matter. I want you to take a middle ground on this issue. It's not all about gays with AIDS, it's about people.'

'I still think I'm not the best qualified.'

'You only broke that story in London because you cared about the victims. You've come into this place as an outsider. You have no preconceived ideas. That's great. Perhaps, we could also look at the opposing views about AIDS.' She thought for a moment. 'We'll see how this story goes. I'll call the editor at the *Bayside Journal*. Let them know you're coming.'

'Who are they?'

'They're the local gay newspaper. They've done some great stuff on the AIDS epidemic. Some of their stories were syndicated. The editor's name is Raoul Amos.'

'I haven't said yes yet.'

'It'll be great. Amos apparently doesn't suffer fools. He's also a big gay activist.'

'Nice. I can't wait to meet him.'

'Don't sound so reluctant, Peter, it doesn't suit you.'

'Is this newspaper ready for this story?'

'That's my call not yours, and I say it is. It has to be. We're on the precipice of a new millennium and there's no time like now. We have to stay current. There's nothing as sad as a tired, old, worn-out hack still filing yesterday's news. It's a chew-you-up-and-spit-you-out world. You have to stay current.'

Stella had the better of him. She knew how to push his buttons. 'I'm no hack, you know that, but I'm too tired to argue with you. You're a bloodhound, Stella, and I have to trust you. If you say this could change my career, I believe you. Set up that meeting. Raoul Amos, ready or not, here I come.'

CHAPTER TEN

Lincoln Park, San Francisco. 1975.

INSPECTOR CASPAR STRODE TOWARDS TWO UNIFORMED COPS standing near a group of shrubs beside the lake. 'What have we got?'

'Woman was out walking her dog early this morning when she came across a body lying in the shrubs,' Homicide Inspector Killian replied.

'Male or female?'

'Male. Sorry. I need a coffee…' He looked at his notebook. 'Aged probably early thirties. Dressed in business attire. He had money and receipts, but no identification in his wallet. He had a card for a gay nightclub in his pocket. Theft obviously wasn't the motive.'

'Anything distinctive?'

Killian snapped his notebook shut. 'The body has been mutilated.'

'Like those two in the Castro? Christ.'

'Looks pretty much the same. Throat's been cut, the penis severed and placed in the victim's mouth. Hands have defensive wounds.'

'So he's spreading out. Maybe getting too hot for him in there.'

'I suspect the victim may have come here with the killer.'

'Christ. In all my thirty-two years on the force, I've never come across shit like this. What's the world coming to? Back when I started, people killed their wives or their husbands and warring gangs killed everyone else. Now there are sickos out there who kill people for enjoyment,' Caspar said. He was due for retirement in three months. He followed Killian to where the body lay. Caspar looked at the two uniform cops. 'Are you guys all right?'

'We're fine.'

He crouched down. 'This is all I need on a nice, sunny day,' he murmured as he lifted the sheet covering the body.

He shook his head as he looked the body over. The body was drenched in blood, his pants pulled down to his knees, his penis still in his mouth. 'I'd say he was killed five to seven hours ago. My theory is that the victim may have been a closet gay who came here with the killer. That explains why there's no ID on the victim.'

'Or somebody stole it?'

'And left the cash behind?'

'We'll talk to the people at the nightclub,' Killian said.

'Good luck with that. None of them want to be found out by their wives or girlfriends.'

'I can only try.'

'This is all I need. The Chief is going to go apeshit when I mention this latest killing to him. The Zodiac Killer made us look like a bunch of incompetents, and we don't need another serial killer on the loose in this city, even if he is just killing faggots. I don't need another ulcer before I retire.'

'We'll get a breakthrough soon. I'm confident we can contain this.'

'You got a lot to learn, Killian. You only made inspector this year. Leave the PR to the Chief. You don't want to stay awake at night doing his job for him.' Caspar placed his hand on Killian's shoulder and left it there. 'You remind me of a colleague of mine. I worked with this guy twenty years ago. He was a good inspector, idealistic, ambitious just like you.'

'What happened to him?'

'He blew his fucking brains out in his garage five years ago.'

CHAPTER ELEVEN

Bayside Journal offices, Ninth Street,
San Francisco. 1993.

RAOUL AMOS SHOOK PETER'S HAND WHEN HE ENTERED HIS OFFICE. His grip was firm. Peter hadn't expected that.

Amos was rail-thin with a beard and a set of blue eyes that looked way too big for his face. Peter immediately felt overdressed in his jacket; Amos wore faded jeans and a t-shirt with Freddie Mercury's face emblazoned on it.

After they sat down, Amos went back to rolling a joint. 'Help yourself,' he said as he pushed a bag of marijuana across his desk. He stuck the joint in his mouth, lit it and inhaled deeply.

Peter coughed. 'No, thanks, I'm fine. I experimented with marijuana once or twice, but I didn't inhale. I didn't like it much. I have enough trouble with alcohol. Isn't smoking that illegal around here?'

Amos chuckled. 'We don't see the cops much in these parts. That's good in some ways, bad in others.'

'So, which do you prefer?'

'It's kind of nice to have them around if you have a message to get out there. There's nothing like police brutality to get you into the mainstream. If we could just get the National Guard involved. Apart from that I have no particular use for them.'

'But there has been a lot of violence directed at gays. You can only take so much.'

'No worse than the past. The violence on the streets is still there, but now they don't stab us in the back as much. They're more savvy. Now they try to erode our rights from the pulpits and the legislature.' He laughed briefly.

'So can you give me some examples of homophobic violence? Any major stuff?'

Amos tutted. 'Shame on you, Peter Clancy. You're getting distracted. I've heard you have trouble controlling the crime bug. That's a bad addiction to have. You want straightening out. That isn't why Stella sent you here, is it?'

'I'll keep the crime bug thing in my back pocket.'

He took another drag. 'They're going to legalise this shit one day. Hopefully, before I die.'

'Does that go into the same category as curing AIDS?'

'I intend to see both happen. Ever the optimist, that's me. If I wasn't an optimist, I'd already be dead. You just have to keep pushing and making noise. And smoking joints.'

'You have a clear view of the future without the AIDS epidemic hanging over people's heads.'

'I heard you were good.' Amos laughed. 'Straight to the jugular.'

'No, I'm more of an ankle biter. If you heard that from Stella Reimers, she's a little heavy on the flattery.'

'I read the *Daily*. I read your stories; they certainly smack of injustice and the human condition gone down the toilet. There's too many sewers blocked with the downside of the human condition.'

'Thanks.'

Amos stubbed out his joint. 'You know the *Daily* was the most conservative paper in the city—possibly even the west coast. That must be like Russia not being communist anymore. I salute you.'

'We have to stay in touch with what's going on around us.'

'You have to or you might catch something from *those* people. If you can scare the folks in the suburbs, they'll be throwing money at AIDS research and harassing their politicians on a daily basis. I get where you're headed.'

'If we can give a bigger voice to those who have AIDS, politicians will sit up and do something about it. I think I'm that good that I could put the issue on the dining table along with the mashed potatoes.'

Amos didn't answer immediately. 'You know I've had national papers, television networks, the international media, all beating a path to my door. All of them have attacked us like we deserve this. They've had a real us versus them attitude. They want to take their photographs of dying gays just so they have clear confirmation that we're evil gays.'

'We know it's more than that.'

'And you're the first straight journalist who has not mentioned AIDS and gays in the same sentence. That is admirable.'

'I didn't come here to judge or condemn. That's not a journalist's brief.'

'So you're after one of your famous flushed down the toilet stories?'

'No, I want to delve into how people are surviving and facing their deaths, in a sense. How do they pay for treatments, how do people with AIDS deal with stigma and losing their jobs, where do they live?'

'I know just the place, if you fancy a trip to the other side.'

'Where to?'

'Ambassador Hotel. That's in the Tenderloin. You should know of it. Isn't the Tenderloin one of your favourite haunts?'

'Strangely, I don't.'

Amos crossed the room, picked up the phone and talked for around two minutes. He hung up. 'I'll take you there on one proviso.'

'What's that?'

'No photographers. I don't think the residents are ready for the paparazzi yet.'

'Maybe they'll want to be photographed.'

'No photos and no real names. Hank doesn't want it turned into a freak show.'

'Hank?'

'Hank... Henry Wilson is the manager. He's the nearest thing to a saint I've ever met.'

Amos led Peter out the back to the carpark. Peter stopped in his tracks, staring at Amos's car.

'What's the matter?' he asked. 'We don't always drive Honda Civics.'

'It's a Mustang GT 390!'

'Same model that Steve McQueen used in *Bullitt*.'

'I loved that movie. No, I loved the car chase scene. To be honest, the rest of the movie was shit.'

'I bought the car for the same reason. I just wish I had the guts to wind it out to one hundred and ten like Steve did.'

'Is it better to go out fast driving a Mustang with one hundred and ten on the dial or die a slow death in a wet bed?' Peter ran his hand along the Mustang. 'Nice wheels.'

'I think you've been doing crime for far too long. You're starting to sound a little like Raymond Chandler. The Ambassador is going to be a welcome change.'

Chapter Twelve

Ambassador Hotel, Tenderloin District, San Francisco.

PETER STEPPED OUT OF THE MUSTANG AND LOOKED UP AT THE Ambassador Hotel. It reminded him of a six-layered cake with piped frosting.

'Still a grand dame in a sea of decay,' Amos said as he locked the Mustang.

'Impressive. I half-expect flappers to Charleston out the front door.'

'That's precisely the right style. A crime aficionado like you should know that this is where Miriam Allen deFord used to live.'

'This is the place? I read some of her books.' His eye settled on two guys in torn track pants looking at the car. 'Is the Mustang going to be here when we come out?'

'I'll ask Hank if he can spare someone to watch over it.'

Peter followed Amos into the foyer of the hotel and thought he'd wandered into some kind of eccentric hospital. Amos knocked on the manager's office door, as Peter glanced at the people sitting on the couches and chairs pushed next to the windows. Some were chatting, but most stared out of the windows. Some were skeletons clad in parchment, others looked as healthy as anyone walking down the street.

Two men were sitting in wheelchairs near a door marked 'medical center'. A nurse came out and pushed one of the men inside. As the door shut, Peter heard them laugh as they shared a joke, even though the man could only laugh intermittently between jagged breaths.

'They,' said Amos, 'are some of the residents.'

'They all have AIDS?'

'The hotel is very exclusive; it's the only way you can get in here.'
Peter tried to smile.

'You looked shocked.'

'It's confronting. I'm sorry.'

'Well, I hope you channel some of that emotion into your story.'

He noticed a woman sitting away from the others, holding a baby. She was probably still in her early twenties, yet took all her strength to hold the child. 'Who is she?' he asked.

'I'm not sure. Hank will know.'

Just then, the manager's door opened.

'Hank,' said Amos. 'This is Peter. He's a reporter from the *Daily* here to do a piece on you.'

'Hello, Peter, please come in.' Hank was a handsome, if weary-looking, man. From his balding head and the creases around his eyes as he smiled, Peter estimated his age around fifty. Hank closed the door and pointed them towards two chairs.

'Peter Clancy, the king of crime tabloid, meet Hank Wilson, the Mother Theresa of the Tenderloin,' Amos announced with a flourish.

'Who would have thought? Who can we thank for the epiphany?' Hank took a sip from a coffee cup on his desk and grimaced. 'Cold.' He put it down. 'Do you want coffee? I'll get some for all of us.'

'Black please, no sugar,' said Peter.

'Cream and two,' said Amos. 'I like mine as sweet as your fine assistant.'

Hank turned to the young man who was typing in the corner of the office. 'Simon, you heard that?'

'On my way,' Simon replied.

Hank watched him leave the room. 'Sad story. One among the many in this place.'

'He has AIDS?' asked Peter.

'Of course,' Hank replied.

Amos offered around a pack of cigarettes and they both refused. Amos took one out and lit up.

'I hear that Stella Reimers is the new news editor,' Hank said.

'Yes, they snaffled the winner of the Pulitzer Prize. That's a coup for the *Daily*. Let's hope it now keeps an open mind on AIDS,' said Amos, puffing.

Peter leaned forward. 'I want to do a human interest story on people who have AIDS. The people will be anonymous, of course. I'd like to know what their life was like before they contracted the disease, what's happened since and how the Ambassador has helped them.'

'Every single person here has a tragic story to tell,' said Hank. 'It would fill a book. If I had the time… Without the Ambassador, without the work all our fine volunteers are doing, all of the residents would be living and dying on the streets.'

'What prompted you to want to set up a hotel for AIDS victims?'

'Well, I've been a gay activist for many years. There was a need. I had to do it. I'd heard the horror stories, the inhumane treatment of human beings. It made me want to do something about it.'

'What were you told?'

'Oh, too many to list.' Hank paused. 'Some examples. A loved one not being allowed to be with his dying partner. Hospital staff leaving a patient to lie in his own shit for days on end because they were too afraid to change him. And it goes on.' He sighed. 'So I set up this place. We have twenty-four-hour nurses, volunteer carers and a doctor does a clinic once a week. We have various support groups here. We're one big family.'

Simon returned with the three coffees and placed them on Hank's desk. Peter picked up his coffee and hesitated. Hank and Amos exchanged glances.

'People thought you could catch AIDS touching someone,' Amos said.

'That's crazy,' said Peter, sipping his coffee. He looked at Simon. 'So, what did you do before you came to the Ambassador for treatment?'

'I was a fashion designer,' he replied wistfully. 'No, I'm still a fashion designer. When I get better, I'll be going back to it.' He went back to his desk and resumed typing.

'It's not about your last days around here,' Hank said, 'it's about the life that's left. The new treatments are prolonging life, but we could do with more money. We need all the positive press we can get right now.'

'I'm here and I'm willing to help.' Peter took another drink.

'Where do you want to start?' asked Hank.

'Simon, would you be willing to talk to me? Do you want to be in the newspaper?'

Simon swivelled his chair around and clasped his hands. 'Do I get my photo taken?'

'No. No photograph and a fictitious name.'

'That sounds very secretive. Can I talk about my fashion label, though?'

'Well, that's up to you. People might be able to work out who you are.'

'And I care because?'

'You want to go on the record? Then of course you can,' Peter said. 'Photo too, if you want.'

'Great. I'll go and put on a better shirt.' He left the office.

'What about the girl with the baby out in the foyer?'

'That's Gina. She hasn't been here long. You can but ask.'

'You're going for the Madonna and child,' Amos observed. 'Such pathos.'

'I'm pulling out all stops.'

'I'll ask for you,' Hank offered.

In the end, Peter interviewed them both. By the time he'd finished he was wrung out. He asked Amos if he wanted to go for a drink and they found themselves in a wine bar near Union Square. It was nearly empty. Amos picked out two bar stools at the far end of the counter.

'What are you drinking?' he asked.

'You choose. I don't usually drink wine but I'll drink anything right now,' Peter replied.

'Taken aback by it all? But you're the king of the tabloid.'

'Crime is one thing, but when people are ostracised because of a medical condition, that's something else. I have a problem with that. I thought the world had moved past that.'

'But human ignorance has a default. When we feel threatened,

45

we blame anyone who's not like us. We're still medieval peasants at heart.' Amos caught the attention of the barman. 'Two glasses of Australian chardonnay. In honour of your homeland.'

Peter liked chardonnay even less than he liked wine generally. It was a silly, pretentious drink for women who thought drinking spirits was beneath them. He didn't tell Amos.

'You could weigh up opposing views on AIDS. It might be interesting.' Amos watched the barman pour out two glasses.

'I'm not sure about that. This is a great stand-alone piece.'

'What about all things in balance?' Amos said as he raised his glass. 'Cheers, to the success of your story.'

'I think the saying's all things in moderation. Cheers,' said Peter. He took a sip. 'Well, that tastes like grandmother's piss, but if it has the desired effect, who's to complain?'

'About those opposing views,' Amos continued. 'You're probably thinking I'm asking you to interview the Catholic Church or some similar big, anti-gay, anti-AIDS outfit, but we've been getting a lot of attention from The Ten Commandments Church.'

'Ten Commandments? I think I broke at least five of them today,' Peter replied.

'Well, in this church they like to think they dutifully follow all ten, plus I believe they have another few to spare.'

'What are the members of this Ten Commandments Church doing?'

'Well, they frequently have demonstrations in front of our office and at other gay venues. They have assaulted our staff on occasion. The list goes on and on,' Amos replied. He took a drink of wine. 'I see what you mean, although I wouldn't classify it as grandmother's piss exactly. It has a more refined bouquet,' he laughed.

'Perhaps I should air the opposing view. If I do it right, it will show them up for what they are,' Peter said.

'I'd like to think so. They deserve all of the negative press they can get.'

'How big is the church?'

'In the thousands, but growing.'

'Not so big.'

'But here's the kicker, my friend. The church has political influence: at least one senator. Does that make you more excited?' asked Amos.

'I'm listening. My interest is heightening. Tell me more.'

'Let's not ruin a good night by talking about those wretched folk here. I have a file on them in the car that I'm willing to share with you.'

'But only after I order a round of whisky,' said Peter pushing his glass away and pulling out his wallet. 'I can't drink this shit.'

CHAPTER THIRTEEN

That evening. Stella's apartment.

'YOU KNOW, I REALLY SHOULD NOT LET YOU COOK.' STELLA WATCHED Peter splash pasta sauce onto the kitchen counter top as he stirred the pan. She grabbed a towel and mopped it up.

'Don't you worry about that,' he said. 'I'll clean up. You know you can't resist my spag bog.'

'Spaghetti ragu,' Stella corrected. 'Keep that up and no one will understand a word you say. Plus, they'll accuse you of being an illegal immigrant.'

Peter poured himself another glass of wine. 'I hate wine, but it gets the job done. One for the cook and one for the pot. You want another one?'

Stella drained her glass and shook her head. 'No more for me. And I don't think you should drink and cook. You'll set fire to the kitchen.'

'More for me, then.' He filled the glass nearly to the top.

'I thought you were cutting back.'

'I'm having a night off. I've been a good boy.'

'Don't go on a bender now. I need you to be at the top of your game.' She grabbed the bottle of wine and shoved it in a cupboard. 'Enough.'

'The Ambassador Hotel was a challenge.'

'How so?'

'Well, I expected to see people wasted from AIDS. I knew that. But it isn't easy to listen to how they got there. It was like they were society's garbage. Society was saying, you deserve to die from this disease because it's your lifestyle. You're unclean. It's the modern world's version of leprosy. You get what I mean.' He took a drink.

48

'You have to be detached or you won't make it. I know that story in London really hurt you. I know things with Ruby ended badly. But you have to heal. You'll go under, otherwise. I've seen good reporters succumb. I won't let that happen to you.'

'I'll be fine. Even Peter Clancy has sad days.'

'Are you up to dealing with the other side of the issue?'

'Of course I am.'

'The vitriol that comes out of the anti-gay groups will amaze you.' Peter nodded.

'But we'll talk about that tomorrow.'

He kissed the top of Stella's head. 'Thanks for being there when it mattered. You know, if we both get desperately lonely, we can always marry each other,' he laughed.

'Marry you?' she said as she pulled away. 'I'd want to kill you at the wedding ceremony.'

'Forget I said that. It's the grog talking.' He gave the sauce another stir and turned down the pot of boiling water. 'By the way, I still want to do those articles on unsolved serial killings.'

'Are you still going on about that?'

'It's fascinating. You might give me a hand when you get time.'

'The public's moved on, Peter. All they care about is the immediate and how it will affect them. After that, they don't give a shit. I learned that very early in my career. Drop it.' Stella went to the cupboard, grabbed a fresh glass and the wine bottle.

'Having second thoughts?'

'You're a bad influence.' She took a drink.

Peter grabbed two plates. 'Hungry?' he asked.

'Put mine in the oven. I'll eat later. I want to work on something.'

'Okay. I forgot to let you know. I've started looking for my own place.'

'Don't be in a hurry. Who will I argue with?' She finished her drink and disappeared into her bedroom.

Chapter Fourteen

Next morning. *Daily* conference room.

Stella was passing around a set of papers. She had summoned Peter, Shapiro, Mulroy and a journalist named Clark for an impromptu meeting. It was early, and Peter hadn't quite recovered from the cabernet the night before. He still wasn't used to drinking wine. By the time he arrived, the others were sitting around the table drinking their first coffee of the day.

'Peter thinks we should get the opinion of an anti-gay group,' she said, 'to balance the piece he's writing.'

'So, who's the winner?' asked Clark.

'The Ten Commandments Church.'

'Why them?'

'Raoul Amos has named them the number one gay hate group in the city.' Peter poured himself a coffee from the pot on the desk and sat down.

Mulroy picked up a sheet from the bundle and started to read. '*The Ten Commandments Church. We preach American values and family morals. We fight to preserve America as a Christian nation unto God.* Et cetera, et cetera.'

'Doesn't sound that far out there,' Shapiro commented.

'Keep reading,' said Stella.

'*Our aim is to reclaim San Francisco from the dark forces destroying our city and turning our children into homosexuals, prostitutes and drug addicts,*' Mulroy continued aloud.

'I think kids watch too much television these days,' Shapiro said.

'Put them in the military,' Clark commented.

'*AIDS is a message from God. The pestilence is upon us,*' Shapiro picked up. 'Sounds like Sodom.'

50

'Isn't that where Lot was turned into salt?' Clark asked. 'Not much worse than the shit I heard at the Catholic school I went to. *Don't listen to Pink Floyd or look at a woman with bad thoughts.*'

Peter scowled. 'It was Lot's wife, actually,' he said under his breath.

'You or the girl? With the bad thoughts?' asked Shapiro.

Mulroy laughed. 'It's consensual, I suppose. That's where all the trouble starts… with bad thoughts. One minute you have bad thoughts, the next minute you have a wife and kids.'

'Okay fellas,' Stella interrupted. 'I know it's early but I want some serious comments from the peanut gallery.'

Shapiro put down the sheet of paper. 'We don't have to give people like this any voice. Giving them airtime debases the AIDS epidemic.'

'Point taken', said Stella.

'Why don't we just go and interview the Catholic bishop? We'll get the same kind of response.'

'On the contrary. If they are more extreme, it will carry more gravitas,' said Peter. 'Do you know of any neo-Nazi groups in the city?'

'I don't think you'd be achieving anything by interviewing The Ten Commandments Church.' Mulroy shook his head.

I'm surrounded by fools and Stella's blind to them. 'You might not see it, Mulroy, but I do. I want to look into the church and this senator who supports their cause. If the *Journal* says they're number one on the hate scale, then that's worth putting into the story.'

'I wouldn't bother with them.'

'Stella, surely you see my point, here. Put them next to the piece on the Ambassador, and they'll look out of touch and callous,' said Peter.

'How big is their congregation?' she asked.

'In the thousands and growing.'

'Well, they're not going to be taking over the Castro and burning it to the ground anytime soon.'

'Don't give them a voice.' Mulroy leaned back, shaking his head.

Peter felt like wiping the smirk off Mulroy's face. 'C'mon guys.

You're missing a trick, here. What do you think, Stella?'

'I say, leave it for the moment. Your story is going to have a big impact without giving a little homophobic church a viewpoint.'

Peter had given it his best shot. 'Okay. I hear you. I don't agree with you, by the way, but I'll drop it... for the moment.' He stood up. 'And you, Mulroy. You have a lot to learn, so if I need an opinion, I'll fucking give it to you.'

'Knock it off,' said Stella.

Chapter Fifteen

Two am. Carpark, Castro District, San Francisco. 1975.

'Another Slasher killing, Officer?' Homicide Inspector Killian yawned as he approached a VW Beetle.

'Looks like it. It has the same profile. Victim's throat's been slashed. Pants pulled down.'

'And his cock?'

'Intact. The killer may have been disturbed.'

'Great. Can't stomach a severed penis right now. Do we know who disturbed the killer?'

'There's a man who claims he was waiting for a friend. He was waiting for this friend of his at the end of the street. He heard the disturbance and tried to intervene. He's in the squad car.'

'Probably selling his ass. A lot of sickos around here.'

'Do you want to talk to him?'

'Yeah, yeah. But let's get this over with first.' Killian looked at the VW. Both doors were wide open. The body was sprawled face down on the road, next to the driver's door. There was blood spatter all over the inside of the Beetle. It was heaviest on the windscreen. 'Looks like a slaughterhouse. Did you find the weapon?'

'Nothing.'

He lifted up the sheet covering the body and squatted. 'Same wounds. The hands have multiple defensive wounds. One of the hands has been pierced right through and one of the fingers on the other hand's hanging by a thread. This guy sure put up a fight.'

'The Slasher would have had his work cut out for him. The victim was a big guy. I'd say over six feet.'

'So that gives us an idea of the Slasher's probable physique.'

'The Slasher was at least the same size, maybe bigger?'

'Good in theory. So, he may not be a mincing fag. Any identification?' Killian dropped the sheet.

'According to his ID, he was John McGraw. Seems he worked in an advertising firm in the city. Wife and kids. There was a photo in the wallet. Why the hell does a married man want to go cruising?'

Killian shrugged. 'Beats me. His wife's gonna get two shocks this morning. You know, some people would say the Slasher's doing the community a service. I think I'll talk to that witness now.' He walked back to the squad car where a uniformed officer was watching over a man in the back seat.

'What's your name?' asked Killian.

'Alamo Egan.'

'From Texas, huh? I heard they hang queers in Texas.'

'Why do you think I live here?'

'Aren't we the lucky ones. The dregs of society. Why don't you stay in Texas?'

'Can I go now?'

'Not yet. I have a few more questions.'

Egan turned his head and sneered.

'So, Egan of the Alamo, what did you see?'

'I already told the other pig.'

'And now you can tell me.' Killian leaned in, grabbed his collar and dragged him out.

'Police brutality,' Egan cried as he thudded to the ground.

'No, that's disobeying a lawful command and resisting arrest,' Killian growled. 'Get up, fag.'

Egan slowly got to his feet and leaned against the squad car.

'Up straight!'

He straightened himself up and looked at his grazed hands.

'I know you're involved in this, and I want you to tell me how much.'

'I wasn't involved. As I already told you guys, I was waiting for a friend.'

'We'll see. Accessory to murder.'

'I heard someone yelling and then I saw a man running from the car. The driver got out of the car and collapsed right there.'

'What did the guy who ran away look like?'

'He was too far away for me to see properly. He was tall. I'd say six two, maybe six four. Short hair.'

'White, black, young, old? '

'He was white, maybe late thirties.'

'Then what did you do?'

'I ran after him for a little while but he was too fast.'

'And what did you do then?'

'I came back to the car and checked the body.'

'Was he still alive?'

'No… no.'

'How did you know?'

'What the hell? He wasn't moving and his throat was slashed right open. I thought that meant he was dead.'

'Take him down to the station,' Killian said to the officer.

'Can't you let me go? I've told you everything I've seen.'

'We need a statement.'

'But I've told you everything I know.'

'We'll see.'

The officer grabbed Egan by the arm and pushed him into the back seat of the squad car. Killian heard footsteps coming towards him and looked around. The uniform cop flicked his flashlight in the direction of the footsteps.

'Susan Banks. I'm a private investigator.' A young woman was shielding her face from the flashlight beam. 'Do you mind?'

'What in hell's name is a PI doing here?' said Killian.

'I've been tracking someone for his wife. I heard there'd been a murder,' Banks said, 'from a birdie. Who are you guys?'

'I'm Homicide Inspector None-Of-Your-Goddamned-Business and this is Officer John Doe.' Killian looked Banks over and shook his head. 'A freaking female PI, who is too young to be out on these streets alone at night without her mommy. What in hell is this world coming to? You did say PI not PA?'

'Yeah, yeah. That's right. A freaking female PI. So, Inspector… Should I call you Goddamned or Business? Is this a Slasher killing?' she asked.

'Slasher killing? Where did you get that? Is that like Jack the Ripper or something?'

'I heard from that birdie that there has been a series of gay killings. They've all had their throats slashed and their penises shoved in their throats. Not very nice.' She paused.

'You better get that birdie of yours a cage. What's it to you anyway?'

She continued, 'Maybe my client's husband is in the closet. Maybe that's what she's asked me to find out for her. So, do you think it's the same person doing the killings? With the Zodiac still free, does that mean there is another serial killer loose in the city?'

'Where do you get off, lady? There's no such thing. Go home and take something for your overactive imagination.'

Banks peered at Egan sitting in the back of the car. 'Who's that?' she asked. 'A witness perhaps? Can I talk to him?' She tapped on the window. Egan started to shout something back.

'Christ. Get her out of here!'

The officer grabbed Banks's arm. 'Sorry lady.'

'You can't do this; I'm allowed to be here. I know people. I got friends who write for the *Chronicle*. Do you want to see a headline about police brutality tomorrow?'

'You go right ahead. The Chief will make sure you won't be sticking your ugly, gay-loving face in our business again.'

'Oh, this isn't over, Inspector, not by a long shot.'

'Yeah? You're lucky I don't arrest you too. Now, get the freak out of here.'

CHAPTER SIXTEEN

Daily conference room. 1993.

'CONGRATULATIONS, PETER,' SAID FRANK STYLES TO THE assembled reporters. 'The piece on the Ambassador's been syndicated. It's gone national.' He smiled as he watched the reporters clap. 'I knew we were onto a major story. Well done. NBC wants an interview,' he added.

'Do you want me or Peter to take that?' Stella asked.

Peter wondered why she'd even offer. He stood up. 'Thanks, Stella, but I wrote the article. I'll be doing the interview.'

'Okay,' she said slowly.

'Thanks, Frank,' Peter added. 'A few more like that and we'll get to number one before you know it.'

'Yes. We'll see...' Frank adjusted his tie and looked at Stella. 'Okay, Stella, I'll let you carry on with your morning conference. I'll handle the interview myself.'

Peter watched Frank leave. 'I didn't know he was a glory seeker.'

'Maybe he's becoming aware of his legacy,' said Shapiro. 'Or he wants to control the message. Frank doesn't like ruffling feathers too much.'

'Okay. Can we stop the theorising and get on with the job at hand. What have we got today?' Stella rapped the desk with her knuckles.

'The usual assortment of muggings, break-ins and robberies,' Mulroy read from his notebook.

'A ten-year-old girl was shot in a convenience store robbery last night. That could make a good lead.'

'Is she dead or alive?'

'The hospital says she's critical. She was shot in the head when the robber opened up in the store. Killed the shop owner, the girl's dad was injured.'

'Why would you take your kid to a convenience store at night?' asked Mulroy.

'The kid was hungry?'

'Okay. Let's show some empathy here. A child got shot. Imagine if it was your child... Peter? Do you want to take it?' Stella asked.

'No. Send Shapiro. He's ready for the big time. Mulroy and I are still following up some stuff on the gang war in Chinatown.'

'What's the update?' she asked.

'Chinese Triad's involved. Arrests are imminent. I've got a source. We're nearly there,' Peter said.

'Okay. So, Shapiro, you do the convenience store shooting. Happy with that?'

'I can see the kicker right now: *Child Shot in Store Robbery*. That says it all. Should I get a photo of a bloodied teddy bear?' he asked.

'That's taking it too far,' Peter replied.

'So, that's settled. The other reporters get whatever's left,' Stella said. 'Let's get writing.'

Peter had only just settled back at his desk when the mail clerk dropped a bundle of letters on his lap. 'What the...?' He looked at the neat pile.

'They're all yours. Enjoy,' the mail clerk said dryly as he moved on.

'Is that fan mail?' Mulroy peered over the partition.

Peter was already opening one of the envelopes. 'I have a feeling they'll be connected to the Ambassador. The lunatic fringe loves me.' He unfolded the letter that was inside and read it aloud. '*To Mr Peter Clancy, I hope you burn in the fires of hell...*' He screwed up the letter and threw it in the waste basket. 'I've already been there and it wasn't that bad. Although, the coffee was cold and instant.' He opened another. '*Thank you, Peter, for the wonderful story about the residents at the Ambassador Hotel. Your approach to the issue was truthful and sincere... with deepest sincerity, Mother Theresa.*'

'Are you for real?' Mulroy laughed.

'Mother Theresa and I go back a long way. She can drink me under the table.' He grinned. He put the letter back in the envelope and picked up another. It was padded. 'It smells,' he said, sniffing the envelope.

'Maybe you should get security to have a look at it. It doesn't smell like a bomb, does it?' said Mulroy, standing up.

'No. More organic. What does a bomb smell like anyway?' Peter placed it against his ear. 'I can't hear any ticking.'

'I don't know about ticking. Wouldn't it smell like gunpowder? I don't know. Maybe you shouldn't open it.'

Peter opened the seal. 'Bloody hell. It frigging reeks!' He grimaced and turned his face away.

A reporter five desks away complained.

Peter pinched his nose and peered inside.

'Return to shitter?' Mulroy joked.

'Not from one of your disturbed girlfriends is it, Clancy?' someone quipped.

'Thankfully, it's only dog shit in a plastic bag. And there's a letter attached.' He slipped the letter out of the envelope and opened it carefully. 'Just as I thought, it's not from an admirer. *May you perish in the flames. May your private parts be removed and burnt. Repent. If you cherish your life, you'll do no more stories on these anal worshipping abominations...* I can't read the rest. Too smeary.'

Mulroy shook his head. 'That's gross.'

'Think I'll mail it on to an ex-boss,' Peter said as the complaints died down.

'Are you worried about these letters?'

'No. Why should I be? You're not doing your job properly unless you attract criticism. Rule one of investigative journalism: if shit arrives in mail, don't let it hit the fan.'

Mulroy laughed. 'You're so cool with all of this. I wish I could be the same.'

'You don't want to be like me. Even I don't like what I do sometimes, but I get the job done. You can learn some tips off me, but make the rest up on your own.'

'Okay.'

Something he had said had been resting uneasily for the last couple of days. Peter knew that bad blood was better off out in the streets and not in the newsroom. 'By the way, I apologise for chewing you out at the conference.'

'I think it's one of the best stories we've done this year. Maybe you were right about the church.'

'It's done. I've got better things to do.' As the words left his lips, Peter's phone rang. 'Yeah, what is it?'

'Well, that's a fine hello to your old Mustang buddy,' Amos replied.

'Is it about the story? Happy or pissed off?' he asked.

'Mostly happy, but you didn't cover the opposition. That came as a surprise.'

'I got vetoed. I wanted to do it but I was overruled.'

'That's a shame because they're demonstrating in front of my office right now.'

'Any violence?' he asked.

'I'm looking out of my window. They're just holding up placards with the usual *burn in hell* messages; they're shuffling around like a bunch of well-drilled zombies. You have to laugh; one of them has *infrormed* written on their placard instead of *informed*... Bunch of fucking morons, if you ask me. They do this every time the mainstream press gives us a positive story. The morons get jealous when we get any attention.'

'Let's see what we can do.'

'That sounds evasive, Peter. Are you going cold on the idea?'

'No. We'll get there.'

'I'll be here when you change your mind. And by the looks of things, I won't be alone.'

Peter hung up. 'Did you hear that?'

'Most of it. He's very loud, isn't he? Should we go or pass it on?'

'Leave it. It's just a peaceful demonstration. I think Amos is trying to get maximum publicity out of all of this.'

'Your call.'

'Come on. We're going to the *Dragon's Den* for what you guys call dim sum and we call yum cha back home. We're meeting someone.'

'Who? One of the gang members?'

'You'll see.'

Chapter Seventeen

Midday. Dragon's Den, Chinatown, San Francisco.

Belinski was already at the restaurant when Peter and Mulroy arrived. He was seated in a booth next to a decorative ginger jar four feet high, eating a steamed pork bun. The owner, Tommy Lee, was hovering near the crayfish tank.

'You good today, Mr Peter?' Tommy asked.

'I'm great.'

'Your friend is waiting for you. I know him. He is a good cop, cleaning up the scum in Chinatown.'

'Thanks.'

Tommy glanced at Mulroy and then back at Peter. 'When is a handsome guy like you bringing a girl to see me instead of an ugly man?'

'Been there, done that. Taking a well-earned break,' Peter replied.

'Shame. If it's all about work and not enough play, Mr Peter will get very dull. If things are not working, maybe you need a Chinese doctor to fix you up?'

'Thanks, Tommy, I'll remember that.'

'You couldn't wait?' Peter said to Belinski as they sat down.

'Who's that?' asked Belinski, pointing at Mulroy with his chopsticks.

'This is my associate,' Peter replied. 'He's learning. Mulroy, Inspector Jerry Belinski.'

Belinski put down the chopsticks long enough to shake Mulroy's hand. 'I only wish I'd come to this place earlier,' he said, taking another bite. 'Thanks for the invite. This sure beats hotdogs and French fries.'

A waitress pushing a trolley of food arrived. Peter peered at the baskets as she presented them, picked out four, and ordered a couple of special dishes. Moments later another waitress arrived to take the drinks order.

'Just a beer,' Belinski said, 'I'm working.'

'Scotch,' Peter said. 'I need more grain in my diet.'

'A soda,' Mulroy ordered. Peter looked at him. 'So little time, so much more to do. Have you got some more information on the gang war?' he asked Belinski.

'Nothing you probably don't already know. Three dead, five arrested, the rest have gone underground or hightailed it back to Hong Kong. I'd call that a good result.'

'Yeah, we already have that,' he said sulkily.

Peter placed his arm across Mulroy's chest. 'Whoa, there, I'll do the talking. This is about something else. Let me do the talking, you listen and keep everything you hear quiet. We don't need anyone stealing our thunder. Got it?'

'Sure. Is this about the unsolved murders, you're always talking about? The Zodiac Killer?' asked Mulroy.

'Not the Zodiac; a big dead end there. Besides, I don't think he's that interesting. But along the way I discovered another cold case—a serial killer who killed more people than the Zodiac Killer. I've been talking to Jerry about it. It received very little press and the San Francisco police—no disrespect—don't seem to have a great desire to solve it.'

'None taken. San Fran police back then were a law unto themselves. Some think that was the good ole days but I think you have to move with the times. I studied criminology at UCLA. I like to think I'm a different breed.'

'I've been looking into this serial killer who they nicknamed the Slasher. What a frigging maniac.' The waitress arrived with their drinks and Peter lifted his scotch and took a long swig. 'This guy was around in the mid-seventies. He picked up his victim, then took him to a dark place, cut his throat and lopped off his genitals. I'll tell you the rest when you're not eating.'

Mulroy shook his head and slurped his soda as Belinski pulled files out of a briefcase.

'Do you want to look at the photos? Think you can stomach it? It will be a good education,' said Peter.

Belinski opened one of the files and passed along a photograph. 'That's the first known victim.'

Mulroy wiped his mouth. 'Interesting.' He was still looking at the photograph when the waitress returned with two large platters of food. She glanced at the photo and quickly looked away.

Belinski waited till she was gone. 'Others are more graphic than that.'

'I'm fine. My mom's a doctor.' Mulroy picked up a dumpling and bit into it. 'So the victims were all gay, hence the inaction. No one came forward fearing they'd be outed. So the case was buried.'

'Yes.'

'Unless there's some new information, how is any of this remarkable?' he asked.

'That's it in a nutshell,' Belinski said. 'Strange. When Peter ran this by me, I didn't know much about it, but I've been looking at the files and I found something.'

Peter put down his drink.

'I've looked at all ten victims' profiles and I...'

'Ten victims? And nothing ever made the papers?'

'And that's exactly what makes it newsworthy,' said Peter.

'I ran the photographs of the autopsy by someone I know at the Medical Examiner's office. He couldn't be totally certain as he only had photos to look at, but he thought the wounds were caused by a Gerber Mark Two knife. They were commonly used during the Vietnam War.'

'A Gerber? Why did he say that?'

'Because it's a double edged blade: this knife has pointed edges on both sides of the wound. It usually means the initial entry cut is spindle shaped. '

'You said that you thought this killer was in or had been in the military? Is that why?'

'Or it could just mean that he purchased the knife from an Army surplus store,' Mulroy observed.

'True, except that one victim survived.'

'What?' Peter was dumbfounded. 'How and why was the investigation shelved?'

'He gave a description and his name. He wouldn't swear up to it,' Belinski said. 'No one did anything more about it. He was probably married, influential or well-known, I guess.'

'But...' Peter began.

'He gave his name as Anthony Mayberry. I've looked at records but I can't find anything. He doesn't exist, if he ever did. It may have been an alias.'

'This is going nowhere.'

'Mulroy, you're not listening. You need to hone those senses of yours.' Peter polished off his scotch and motioned to the waitress for another.

'I've looked at this Mayberry statement over and over, and one thing really intrigues me. Mayberry said he was talking to a young woman in Figaro's before he left with his attacker.'

'Figaro's? It's not open anymore,' Mulroy interjected.

'It was a popular gay bar for men in the seventies.'

'What would a woman be doing there? Could she have been a trannie?'

'A trannie?'

'Transvestite,' Peter explained. He slapped Mulroy on the back. 'That's what we'll have to find out, huh?'

'She may have seen the Slasher?'

'Possibly. I don't know yet.'

'Any description of her?' asked Mulroy.

'Mayberry said she was a pretty young girl who looked like she was waiting for someone. She asked lots of questions. They talked until he met his attacker then they left the bar. She followed them and she saved Mayberry's life.'

Mulroy scratched his head. 'Why would she follow them?'

'Was she someone's girlfriend? A wife?' Peter was thinking aloud. 'Maybe she was a private detective. Or a trannie.'

'Can't you guys look into it?' Mulroy asked.

'The Chief won't allocate anyone to it. He thinks it would be a waste of resources.'

Mulroy chuckled. 'You want us to look into it.'

'I think you've hit the nail right on the head.'

'I don't know that there's a story in it.'

Peter passed one of the platters to Belinski and helped himself from the second.

'Geez, Mulroy, where did you say you studied? Where's your sense of adventure? You want to be an investigative reporter then you're gonna have to do some investigating.' Peter laughed as he picked up his chopsticks and tucked into the Peking duck.

CHAPTER EIGHTEEN

Bayside Journal offices

'THE NATIVES ARE GETTING RESTLESS,' AMOS OBSERVED, GAZING out at the group of demonstrators. Even as he and two staff reporters watched, they were growing appreciably in number and in voice.

'I hope they're not going to get violent,' one of his colleagues said. 'I don't see many police officers to keep them in check.'

Amos turned to the receptionist who was standing frozen at his desk. 'Lock the doors!' he ordered. 'Now!'

'Aren't we the popular ones? I'd say there are two hundred of our most loyal fans out there.'

'Can't you ever be serious?' one of the reporters said.

Amos was looking nervous. 'I thought the mainstream media would be here.' He looked at the phone. 'Where are you, Peter Clancy? Isn't there anyone out there who gives a damn or don't we matter anymore?'

'I'll call them again.'

Four police officers were trying to hold the crowd back from the office door, as a few of the demonstrators, wearing scarves to hide their faces, pushed against them. Suddenly one of the officers lost his balance and tumbled backwards. While two officers linked arms and waved their truncheons, the third directed pepper spray at one of the demonstrators. The officer caught some of the spray and collapsed to the ground, covering his eyes. The others headed towards the door.

'Get ready, boys, here comes the Hitler Youth.'

As Amos spoke, a rock smashed the front window, leaving a neat hole. To his relief, the rest of the window held together. The officer who had fallen got to his feet, grabbed one of the masked men in a head lock and threw him to the ground. Another demonstrator already had a rock in his hand, ready to aim at the door, when he was pepper sprayed.

Amos watched the crowd turn its anger towards the police. He listened to the wail of police sirens as another police contingent arrived. Within seconds, they were pushing the crowd back away from the pavement and into the street. A television network car pulled up.

'Too little, too late. The party's over, fellas.' Amos watched them setting up.

'You're a publicity whore. Is that all you care about, Raoul?'

'Oh, really? I'm a publicity whore? Think about it,' he replied, 'if we don't grab the news, we don't elevate our cause. And then they'll let us quietly die. Do you want to quietly die?'

'Fuck you, Raoul. What's going to kill us first? AIDS or these people?'

Amos looked at the reporter and felt like shaking him. 'Do you really think those are our only choices? How about neither?'

'I'm a realist, unlike you. There's no Oz at the end of our rainbow, Raoul, you'd better face it.'

The reporter had to go. If Amos had the chance, he would fire him tomorrow, but for the moment, the paper needed stability.

'Don't be so fucking defeatist.'

CHAPTER NINETEEN

Figaro's nightclub, Castro District, San Francisco. 1975.

SYLVESTER HAD TAKEN A BREAK AFTER PERFORMING HIS FIRST set of the night. He had just gone to the toilet and was adjusting the wad of socks he used to create the illusion of a cock and balls. It was a busy night; Sylvester and his band, *The Four A's*, were always a big draw at Figaro's. The place was packed and the vibe was electric.

The bar was packed two deep. Patrons hollered for drinks, cavorted with their lovers or lit up their first cigarettes. Looking right out of place, a pretty blonde leaned against the bar, sipping a bloody Mary and trying to blend into a place where it was wall-to-wall, floor-to-ceiling men. She and Sylvester were possibly the only two real women in the joint, and she was the only one who was obviously genuinely female.

Blending into the background wasn't really working for the blonde, but she had a line in case someone asked what she was doing there: *Capitol records. I'm in A&R. Just checking out Sylvester. Isn't he great?* But she was a predator after prey. She took a taste of her cocktail, nibbled on the celery and thought this was a bad idea.

'Are you hungry?' A man who looked like an off-duty business-man was laughing. Aged about thirty, he was dressed in a jacket and an open white shirt with a couple of buttons undone at the top. The blonde thought he had something of James Dean about him. *What a waste of a good-looking man.* He pushed a cigarette into the corner of his mouth and lit it.

This Ivy-League-James-Dean hybrid didn't look that unusual here. She looked around at the crowd shoehorned into the bar—there were splashes of denim, sequin and leather mixed in with the suits—and answered his question. 'Yeah. I missed lunch.'

'Cigarette?'

'No thanks,' she replied.

'I heard your line,' said the man.

'And, do you like it?'

'I used to work at a record company back when we believed rock-and-roll was going to be the start of the revolution.' He exhaled the smoke in a thin stream. 'Back in the sixties. That was a great time. Best time for music.'

'Is that so? I'm not really A&R. I just wanted to see Sylvester. No one else wanted to come with me. I just work in an office.'

'I thought so. I still like your line.'

The blonde smiled and offered her hand. 'Susan Banks. Pleased to make your acquaintance.'

The man shook it. 'I'm Tony. Tony Mayberry.'

'Is that your real name? Only it sounds kinda hokey for someone like you.'

'Maybe it does and maybe it's just my real name.'

'Well, perhaps I shouldn't have given you my real name after all.'

'You can trust me. I won't tell anyone. I'm good at keeping secrets.'

'Of that,' said Susan, 'I'm certain.'

'Can I buy you a drink?'

'Sure. Another bloody Mary. Skip the celery this time.'

Mayberry caught the attention of one of the barmen. 'Bloody Mary, no celery. Straight bourbon.'

'Here by yourself?' she asked.

'I'm waiting for someone.' Mayberry checked his wristwatch.

'A date perhaps?'

'Wow, Susan, you ask a lot of questions.' Mayberry grinned. 'But that's good in your game.'

'Oh, I'm sorry. Wait, you really think I'm an A&R rep.'

'If you're not, you should be. Ask the question. Be direct. I like your style.'

Mayberry took his bourbon and swallowed a mouthful, looking around as he drank. Then he checked his watch again as Susan went back to sipping her bloody Mary and studying the crowd.

She watched a clean-shaven, tall man with a crew cut pushing through the crowd like he was heading for a touchdown, and it seemed that she and Mayberry just happened to be standing in the end zone. She noticed he wore a dark, corduroy suit. 'Looks like the Forty-Niners' quarterback has finally arrived,' she quipped.

Mayberry smiled. 'Thank goodness, he's here. About time.'

'So,' she said, studying the man's face, 'that's your date? I'm sorry.'

'No need.'

The man pushed into the space between them, looking right through her, and put his arm around Mayberry. Susan felt a shiver run down her back. His eyes were steely blue and cold. 'I'm glad he's on our side,' she muttered to herself.

'Richard.' Mayberry smiled and kissed him on the mouth.

Richard pulled away and glanced at Susan. 'She isn't with you, is she?'

'No, she was checking out the band.'

'I see.'

Susan turned away and drained her bloody Mary, ears straining to catch their conversation.

'You look great, by the way,' Mayberry said.

Richard grabbed him by the collar. 'Hey. You want to get out of here? Let's go somewhere quiet. I don't like this music much.' He grabbed Mayberry's hand and started to push back through the crowd.

Susan thought of her last liaison. It was the same old routine; they'd meet somewhere quiet for dinner, go back to his place, screw, then he'd talk about the shit that was going on at his work. He wasn't just a great screw but also a great source of information— valuable in her line of work. Her folks wouldn't have been pleased to learn of her pre-marital activities, but whose folks would? He wasn't ideal, but they would have accepted him had she introduced them to each other. At least the guy was successful.

The big case of the moment involved the Slasher. Her lover had told her of the Slasher's unique parting gift. *What a sick fuck!* He told her that the police wanted to keep the case quiet. It was a bad secret to tell someone like Susan. He said that nobody really cared if there were a few less gays in the world and, anyway (worst of all), the police couldn't catch the sonofabitch. She suspected that the Slasher might have been one of theirs but, then, she wasn't in the SFPD.

Her lover had called her once and told her that a gay guy had been murdered in a back street in the Castro. Some male prostitute had seen a man running from the scene. Perhaps she'd gone too far by turning up at the scene minutes later. It was an important lead, and she always followed up leads, no matter how tenuous. Her appearance at the scene hadn't gone down well with the cops and she'd been hauled over the coals. What the hell, she wanted to crack the case. She was ambitious. She wasn't going to do the same old thing for the rest of her career. Then her lover froze her out, for fear of being discovered as her source. All he would give her was a vague description.

It seemed to Susan that the Slasher probably picked up at Figaro's and two other popular gay bars. This was a hard way to crack open a case, but she suspected a fissure had just appeared. She put down her glass, grabbed her purse and pressed through the crowd, not really knowing where to go.

Should she just go home, call for help or solve the case herself?

She was too ambitious to go home. She asked one of the doormen if he knew in which direction Mayberry and Richard had gone. The doorman pointed down the left side of the street.

'Listen to me,' she said. 'I believe one of the men may be in serious danger.'

The doorman waved her away. 'How do you know that, lady? They looked happy to me.'

'I'm a private investigator. I've been tailing one of them.'

'You? A PI?' The doorman chuckled.

Susan pulled a twenty-dollar bill from her handbag and slipped it to the doorman. 'Can you call the police if I haven't returned in ten minutes?'

'In ten minutes?'

'Ten minutes. Don't forget.'

'Okay, lady. Whatever turns you on.'

She continued along the pavement, growing more cautious as

the street darkened and the crowd dwindled. She glanced in at the parked cars, hoping to see the two men. She unzipped her purse and gave the .38 revolver a reassuring pat. Her lover had gotten it for her. She left her right hand in her purse.

A narrow alley led off from the left-hand side of the street. One afternoon as her lover slept, she had slipped away and read the case file and she knew that this alley had been the scene of a previous murder. She gazed down it but could only make out a dumpster about fifty yards away. She was reluctant to go in there. She knew she had to.

Susan withdrew the revolver from her purse and stepped cautiously into the dark alley.

Just as she approached the dumpster, she heard a muffled cry. She couldn't be certain but she thought it was a man. She flicked off the safety and pointed the revolver in the direction of the dumpster. 'Who is that?' she cried. 'Who's there?'

There was another muffled cry and the crash of trash cans.

'I'm armed and I fucking know how to use this gun!'

'Help. He's trying to...' a male voice cried. A trash can rolled across the laneway.

'Mayberry?'

Susan caught a glimpse of a shadowy figure moving from the side of the dumpster and the gleam of a knife blade as it was caught in the moonlight. She ducked to the side, caught the heel of her shoe and tripped. She felt herself hitting the ground. The pistol was luckily still in her hand. She fired blindly towards the shadowy figure. She heard a cry.

'Fucking bitch,' a male voice yelled.

She felt someone kick her in the back.

'Help me,' cried Mayberry.

She fired again but the bullet ricocheted off the alley wall. The shadowy figure had gone. She could hear someone running down the alley back to the street. She stumbled to her feet.

'I'm bleeding,' Mayberry called.

'I'm coming.' Susan staggered towards him. She saw a flame flicker from a lighter.

'I'm here! Help me please!'

Mayberry lay beside the dumpster with his body propped up against the wall. He was holding the cigarette lighter in one hand. His other hand was covered in blood.

'He's slashed your hand right open. I'll try and slow down the bleeding.' She tore the scarf from her neck and wrapped it around Mayberry's hand.

'He tried to cut my throat.'

'You're safe now.'

'It was Richard,' he said.

'I thought it might be him.' She stopped speaking when she heard sirens. 'Help is on its way.'

Mayberry tried to stand up. 'I've got to get out of here. No one can know about this. I'm married with children.'

'You'll bleed to death if you don't get help.'

'Please don't tell anyone. Please. Promise me. My life will be ruined.'

'I won't tell. I promise.' She placed her hand on his shoulder.

He appeared to relax slightly. 'How did you know?'

'I've been trying to track down a serial killer. I'm a private investigator.'

Mayberry groaned and dropped the lighter. 'What the hell? I'm finished. It's all over. My job, my family… I wish the fucker had completed what he set out to do.'

'You don't mean that.'

He attempted to stand up again. 'The police can't find me here.'

'Sit down. I promise you. I won't tell anyone. You're just another victim except you survived.' She saw lights at the end of the alley and heard voices coming closer.

'Please!'

'I swear. I don't know you. I've never even met you.'

Mayberry slumped backwards as the pool of blood grew. 'Yes. Leave it at that.'

CHAPTER TWENTY

Stella's office. 1993.

'WHERE WERE YOU?' STELLA SHOUTED, AS PETER ENTERED HER office.

He closed the door. 'In Chinatown, exactly as I said.'

She fingered the stress ball on her desk. 'I tried to contact you, but your cell was switched off.' She gave the ball a final squeeze and threw it at him.

Peter picked it up off the floor, put it back on her desk and resumed his seat. He hadn't seen Stella at home most of the week. She was up and out the door before he woke and never back before midnight. *She's going to burn herself out.*

'So, why all the yelling?' he said.

'Raoul Amos called to tell me that there was a demonstration in front of their office. He said he'd also tried to call you four times before he called me.'

'But that's just routine for them.'

Stella was shaking her head. 'It was peaceful for about five minutes before it turned ugly. Their windows were smashed and the police were assaulted. And worst of all, we weren't there when it all happened. By the time I could send someone, they were mopping up. We missed out on the lead story of the day. I hope that makes you feel bad.'

'But we were following up the gang war story. Belinski was giving us an update on the arrests.'

'Never bullshit a bullshitter. You had that information days ago.'

Peter shifted on his seat. 'Now you're going to tell me you called Belinski to check out what we were doing?'

'I did. Two days ago.'

'What? You don't trust me?' Peter was fuming. What was it with people and management? *You're either one of the people or you're not.*

'No. You were going behind my back. What were you really doing? If you were goofing off, I'll fire you and Mulroy.'

'You can't do that.'

'Try me.'

'Shit, Stella. Okay, I was asking Belinski for information on the Slasher murders.'

She shook her head. 'You can't let it go, can you? You want to be the reporter that caught a serial killer.'

'Well, if you trusted my judgement, you would have let me run with it. I always trusted your judgement. How do you think we've survived in this game?'

'But I told you to drop it. That should have been the end of the matter.'

He looked at her. Fatigue was etched in every wrinkle. 'Okay, okay. I don't agree with you but I'll drop it. You're the boss.'

'Yes, I am. And never forget it.'

'What do you want us to do then?'

'You should count yourself lucky that I'm not assigning you to the court reporter's position and Mulroy to the mayor's office.'

'I really don't want to walk the beat all the time. I don't want to be just an ambulance chaser.'

'The AIDS epidemic is the main issue in this city right now.'

'But we can't keep doing stories on people dying from the disease. Eventually, it will turn people off.' He changed the discussion. 'I haven't told you what happened over lunch. It was interesting what Belinski dug up.'

'How's that?'

'There was this one guy named Mayberry who survived an attack.'

'Really.'

'He told the cops about some girl he met in a gay club. What would a girl be doing in a gay club anyway? She said she was a private investigator.'

'She wanted to catch someone's husband in the act? Or maybe she wanted to have a good time without some sleaze bag hitting on her. Who knows. Who cares.'

'She apparently followed him and the Slasher when they left. She saw them in an alley and fired a gun...'

'Enough of gumshoe detective shit, Peter. I'm frigging busy.'

'Maybe it's because...'

Stella interrupted him again. 'Enough already. Peter, I have the finger on the pulse. The trouble with you is that you have your finger up your ass. Insult intended.' She sighed. 'Now that you've got that off your chest we can talk about a real story. There's been a recent rise in anti-gay rhetoric and violence all led by several right-wing Christian groups.'

He frowned. Hadn't they had this conversation before? 'But you didn't want me doing that piece on The Ten Commandments Church, or have you forgotten?'

'I didn't want it done as a companion piece to the Ambassador. Now it's become a story we need to cover, and I'm not just talking about The Ten Commandments Church. The stakes have suddenly gone through the roof.'

'They're probably certifiably insane folks who like to wear hoods. You're okay with the fact that this will give them a voice?'

'Timing, Peter, is everything. Leave the decisions to me. Got it?' She pushed out her chair and stood up. 'If you weren't the best reporter on staff and Mulroy wasn't the best up-and-comer, there would be a different outcome.'

Thanks for the vote of confidence. He never considered himself to be sentimental, but her words stung. 'Is that all?'

'I want you to go to the *Bayside Journal*. After you've gone down on your knees and apologised to Raoul, I want you to do a major investigation into the rise of anti-gay sentiment in the city.'

Peter was silent for a while. 'I don't want this to get between us.'

'This? We both have a job to do and that's to make this paper number one again.'

'Even if our friendship suffers?'

'Stop taking it personally, Peter. Nothing is going to stand in my way of achieving that goal. Do your job and we'll be fine.'

He looked at his outspread hand in his lap. 'I think for the sake of our friendship, I should move out.'

Stella didn't miss a beat in her reply. 'I think that's a good idea.'

CHAPTER TWENTY-ONE

PETER SPENT THE NEXT FEW DAYS SCOURING THE ADVERTISEMENTS for somewhere to rent. Working and living with Stella had made him claustrophobic. He needed his own space. He was getting the same feeling he'd had back in Melbourne when Michelle had insinuated herself into his life. He always thought it was his fear of commitment that caused him to push people away. Now he suspected it was his fear of proximity—he just couldn't bear anyone getting too close, even if they were mere friends.

He realised that Stella had also withdrawn a bit, to give him some room, until he secured a place of his own. When their paths did cross, he tried hard to be as amicable as always. Something jarred. He hoped that time would heal that and they could get back to being great mates again. He'd already ruled out a third of San Francisco for being too exclusive and another third for being totally unsuitable.

While he searched, he visited Amos again. They talked for a while about the best localities, the lunatic fringe, The Ten Commandments Church and the piece that he and Mulroy were going to craft about the *Bayside Journal*'s woes.

'If you cover this, I warn you, you'll attract the attention of the loonies.' Amos slid open his desk drawer, took out a pill bottle and popped one in his mouth.

'I like a challenge,' said Peter, raising his eyebrows as Amos took a sip of water and swallowed.

Amos followed Peter's gaze. 'Oh, don't worry, sweetheart, that one's legal. So, where were we? Oh yes. You're a crazy bastard, aren't you?'

'I'll go as far as anyone else to get a good story.'

'Huh. As will we. You know we monitor their preachings, or

whatever you want to call their barking rants.'

'You have someone who attends their church?'

Amos nodded. 'We have someone inside.'

'Can I talk to them?'

'The answer is no.'

'A rough identity? Male? Female?'

'I can't tell you that. It's a covert operation. Gays do the CIA thing really well except we dress better. Let's leave it at that. And before you ask anyone else here, I'm the only one who knows their identity.'

'What can you tell me about the preacher?'

'He calls himself Pastor Zachary Gatting.'

'Do you know much about him?'

'He came out of the Bible Belt around two years ago, preaching and hollering like a wired-up carnie. He had a vision from God, and God had told him that San Francisco was a sinful place and needed to be saved. Why didn't he go to Detroit? That place needs saving more than San Francisco. Leave us the fuck alone.'

'Do you know much about his personal life? Any perversions, addictions?'

'None so far, except he hates us.'

'Family?'

'Gatting has a wife who applies her makeup with a trowel and two kids straight out of the Hitler Youth. His wife likes to sing, but a cat would have more talent. I've heard that the kids join in sometimes and make it worse. They're just a humble, God-bothering, all-American family.' Amos laughed.

'What does he preach?'

Amos pulled out a bag of marijuana from his desk drawer. 'Do you want a joint or coffee?'

'I'll stick to the coffee.'

After he lit his joint, Amos flicked the button on the desk intercom. 'Coffee order. Black, no sugar. Thanks.' He took a drag and exhaled in Peter's direction. 'I had so hoped you'd be a stoner.'

'You were saying?'

'Well, he says that all gays should be refused medical treatment, jobs and education. They should not be served in shops. What next? A concentration camp out in the Mojave Desert?'

'So he's going more extreme.'

'Yes, he's telling them what they secretly want to hear. His parishioners are increasing.'

'And Gatting has political connections?'

'That's right, Senator Terrence Richardson. Republican senator for California: anti-gay, anti-women, anti-abortion, anti-immigrants and anti-anything connected with human rights. How can anyone be so hateful?'

'Anything known?'

'Can't find anything yet except he was an alcoholic and God saved him.'

Peter wrote a few hurried paragraphs in his notebook and snapped it shut. 'Will you share the information?'

'My colleagues are reluctant, but what are colleagues for if you can't argue with them? If it helps brings the church undone, I will gladly share.' He extinguished his joint and placed the butt in the ashtray. 'Your paper has a circulation of four hundred thousand and we have thirty thousand. We rarely get national coverage. It's simple math, isn't it?'

'I'll see what we can do. We'll probably do a piece about the attacks.'

'Whatever you do, please don't compromise our informant.'

'I'll be very discreet.' Peter stood up to leave.

'What about your coffee?'

'Don't worry, Raoul, I'll get it to go.'

Chapter Twenty-Two

PETER WENT FROM THE *JOURNAL* BACK TO WORK VIA A SMALL, semi-furnished apartment in Dogpatch, which seemed to fit most of his exacting criteria. *Door? Tick. Bathroom? Tick. Somewhere to eat, sleep and—if I'm ever that lucky again—fuck? Tick.* He was going to let the realtor know later that day that he would take it and move in at the earliest opportunity.

He checked up on Mulroy and found him dozing over his computer after, Peter supposed, having spent much of the night writing the first draft of his memoirs. That done, Peter decided to drop a bombshell on Stella.

'You want to what?' she said.

'I want to go undercover.'

'I really think sometimes you've chosen the wrong profession. Please tell me it doesn't involve your crazy cunning kit.'

'Sadly I left that behind in London. But, good news: I'm putting together a new one. An American edition.'

'What did I do to deserve this?' Stella rolled her eyes.

'See, that's my dilemma. How does one dress and act when visiting The Ten Commandments Church?'

'I wouldn't get too ahead of yourself, Clancy. I haven't even approved your idea yet.' She smiled. 'Anyway, I'm never been to a church service, period. I've more of the lapsed Jewish faith.'

'I was raised a Catholic and I still don't know. I'm stuck.'

'Watch one of their TV channels. That will give you an idea how they do things. What the latest evangelical fashion trends are.'

'I want to get into this church and find out if anything is going on.'

'So,' Stella hesitated, 'what are you proposing? If it involves a wheelchair and a miraculous cure, I'm not allowing it.'

'The wheelchair sounds like a great idea. I might keep it in my back pocket. I'm thinking I'll go there as a new parishioner, just arrived from Australia. The thing is, if I take Mulroy with me, they may think we're gay.'

'It's not a place where you'd hold hands,' she laughed.

'I would like to take a small recorder and a hidden camera, though.'

'I'm pretty sure you'll be searched. Those people don't like outsiders. I wouldn't chance it.'

He was certain that squaring up to the Russian underworld trumped a bunch of churchgoing Americans, homophobic or not. 'I want to find out what they're doing first-hand. I don't want to rely on information that comes from the *Bayside Journal*.'

'You're not going to let go this stupid idea of yours, are you? Amos is a good source; you don't have to infiltrate the church to get a story.'

'Well, you wanted a Peter Clancy investigative piece on this church and you're going to get a Peter Clancy investigative piece on this church.'

Stella sighed. 'How's this idea: you and I both go to the church. We just pretend we're a happy, normal God-fearing, gay-hating couple. It's as simple as that. No need to go all James Bond, is there?'

'You'd be happy to do that?' He was stunned. Since she'd become his boss, he'd forgotten how ballsy she could be. 'If we win a Pulitzer, this time I won't be going as your handbag.'

'Deal. Besides, it's good to get out of the office occasionally,' she said.

Peter chuckled. 'It's a long time since I've been to church.'

Chapter Twenty-Three

The Ten Commandments Church, Oakland, California.

PETER LOOKED OUT OF THE PASSENGER WINDOW AT THE BUILDING beyond the tall, wire fence. The building dazzled in brick and brass, exactly like a new penny. The morning sun glinted off every carefully placed angle, giving the impression of rays emanating heavenwards from the roof. Stella stopped the car by the enormous gate and waited as the line of cars ahead turned right.

'Wow. It looks like a shopping mall but with a cross on top,' he said.

A man dressed in an orange vest waved at them.

'Not too loud, Peter,' she replied as she watched the parking usher's hand signals and tried to understand them.

'I just didn't expect the church to be that big.' He wound up his window and sat back as Stella inched the car forward.

'I call them Walmart churches.'

'I like that,' he replied.

'Remember to smile. Show them the white of your teeth,' she hissed.

'I'm smiling.'

'Full of the Holy Spirit, remember?'

'My mouth is hurting already.'

'You're the one who wanted to go undercover.' She stopped her car and waved a thank-you at the parking usher. He tapped on the window. 'Let me do the talking.' She wound down her window and smiled.

Any moment now they'll be onto us. One suspicious look and Peter was ready to leap out of the car and make a dash for the gate.

'It's always good to welcome new worshippers to our church,' said the usher, returning the smile. 'Are you ready to hear the good word of Pastor Gatting?' He wrote down the car's registration in a notebook as he spoke.

'Hi there. We're Faith and Christian Noble,' she said. 'My husband and I have just arrived from Australia. We've heard so many good things about Pastor Gatting we just had to come and see for ourselves.'

'Then, welcome to you both. Please park your car safely and make your way inside.'

When the usher was out of earshot, Peter sniggered. 'Faith and Christian Noble?'

'I got carried away.' Stella nosed the car into a space at least a hundred yards away from the church.

'What were you thinking? You've watched too many of those shows. I'm starting to worry,' Peter murmured.

'Just remember, we've just arrived from Australia. We have to blend in, so no laughing or they'll be on to us. No stupid comments during the service, either.'

'Mind if I drink, Faith?' Peter grinned.

'God help us,' Stella replied as she pulled out the key.

They squeezed past the rows of cars and strode to the front entrance of the church. The ushers at the top of the stairs held metal scanners, scanning people as they passed. Occasionally, they stopped one of the faithful to check a bag or to search a coat pocket.

'There's more security here than a bank,' Peter spat out of the corner of his mouth.

'Shut up, Christian.'

One of the ushers stopped them as they passed. 'You're new to the church?'

'Ah-huh,' said Stella, nodding and smiling as widely as she could.

'Praise the Lord, we've just arrived from Australia,' Peter said. 'We've heard so much about Pastor Gatting.'

'That's nice to hear. I'm sorry, sir, but I have to search you.'

'Go right ahead,' said Peter as the usher patted him down. 'Never been searched going to church before.'

'Evil comes in many forms. There are some who don't like to hear the truth.'

'Yes, Satan works in mysterious ways,' Peter replied.

The usher looked perplexed for a moment. He rummaged through Stella's purse and asked Peter to empty out his pockets. Peter tossed a few coins and a set of keys into a tray and turned his pockets inside out.

'You may enter,' the usher finally said.

They continued into the cavernous hall. It was theatrical: seats set out in sections, criss-crossed by aisles and all sloping down towards a central stage. They found seats in the middle of the congregation, high enough to maintain a good view of their surroundings and close enough not to miss any of the action.

'So far so good,' Stella whispered in Peter's ear.

The woman next to Peter craned towards him, trying to listen in. 'Yes honey,' he said loudly, 'I can't wait to hear Pastor Gatting.'

He looked around him and two things immediately caught his eye: the congregation were all white and the stained glass windows were the largest and cheesiest he'd ever seen. In the centre of the biggest pane was the image of a man with shafts of light projecting from his head towards the clouds above. *Is that meant to be Christ or Gatting?* Whoever he was, he was flashing an enormous smile filled with dazzling white teeth. Peter stifled a laugh and looked around. At least five hundred people sat in the auditorium—some in prayer, others chatting and a few singing—all eagerly anticipating the pastor's coming.

The stage was decorated with a single wooden cross suspended from the ceiling on an angle and backlit, so that it seemed to descend from a golden heaven. There was band equipment all over the immense stage. He watched the ushers setting up the drum kit and testing the sound system. A sound engineer sat behind a mixing board in a booth at the back, earphones on, looking humourless. Peter prayed silently for Jimmy Page, John Paul Jones and Robert Plant to appear.

He was adding a miraculous, Lazarus-like return of John Bonham to his prayer when the lights turned down and everyone jumped to their feet and began to cheer.

'Are you ready to rock?' he screeched in Stella's ear as they stood up.

'Shut up!' she replied.

The band started to play while the backing singers belted out what sounded to Peter like a rock ballad, except that it was about bibles and redemption instead of booze and rock-and-roll. The cheering from the congregation was deafening. After that song finished, the band played the 'Star Spangled Banner' and everyone sang.

'Was that the opening act? Is there more?' he said.

'Peter, just shut up!'

The auditorium lights dimmed and the cheering increased along with the stage lights. A spotlight picked out a woman in the centre of the stage. She was dressed in a high-necked, full-skirted frock with sequins. Her hair was bleached blonde and stacked on her head like a wedding cake. Her makeup was plastered on so thick, it made it difficult to work out her age. She looked like a grotesque interpretation of a country and western singer.

'That must be Mrs Pastor Gatting,' he remarked to Stella.

'You mean Gretchen Gatting,' she replied.

'I reckon if her makeup ran, we'd all drown.'

The woman beside Peter elbowed him. 'Isn't she just the most beautiful disciple of God? When she sings it's like God sings through her.'

'Really?' he responded.

Gretchen Gatting lifted the microphone from the stand. Her accompanist played an introductory flourish on the piano and Gretchen started to sing. 'When evil comes, we fight together, we rid this world of Satan's followers. All who sin burn in hell's fire. They will burn, let them burn. God punishes all the sinners, and the righteous go to heaven.'

The woman nudged him again. 'What a beautiful gift from God to be able to sing and write your own songs. I have all of her records, you know.'

'It's moving me to tears.' Peter wanted desperately to cry out in pain but he knew he couldn't. He felt like the tines of a fork were being scraped across his brain. He looked at Stella. 'Help,' he grimaced.

Stella wore a thousand-yard stare. 'Ditto.'

86

Mrs Gatting sang a more up-tempo song next, with similar themes of the certainty of an agonising death for all who opposed the teachings of Gatting. Her fervour intensified, as did the crowd's. It was reaching a feverish crescendo. Just then she ripped a cord from her waist and the skirt of her dress ballooned out to reveal the stars and stripes in sequins. The effect was astounding.

'Glory to God and our great nation!' she enthused as the crowd went wild.

After Gretchen Gatting left the stage, the congregation sat down again and the ushers began to pass wicker baskets around.

'I think it's donation time,' Peter said to Stella.

'Funny, I was thinking more Moses in the bulrushes by the size of that basket.'

'They're expecting some big donations. Have you got any money? Aside from loose change, I haven't.'

'Well, that was quick.' She reached into her bag and pulled out a note.

When the basket reached them, she added twenty dollars to the mound of notes. Peter noticed that they weren't small denominations either: there were hundred-dollar bills in amongst the tens and twenties. After the collection, the lights dimmed again and the congregation rose to their feet. The floor shook. Several people ran towards the stage, where ushers stood to prevent them from climbing up.

'It's him, it's our saviour!'

The woman raised her hands and gabbled something that he couldn't understand. Others did the same, but none of it sounded like language. He'd never experienced anyone speaking in tongues, although he'd always assumed that it would be intelligible. This was pure babble.

'Preachermania?' he whispered to Stella.

Search lights swirled around the auditorium as a trumpet heralded Gatting's arrival. A chorus of angels took over as the man they'd gathered to hear pranced onto the stage. Clearly, he'd never taken a vow of poverty. He reeked of new money and bad taste in a sharply tailored suit, white handkerchief in the top pocket, burgundy suede shoes and a greased duck-tail that Elvis would have envied.

Peter estimated that Gatting was probably in his fifties, but his energy belonged to a teenager. An usher handed him a golden mike as some people stood to get a better view. A couple collapsed in the aisle and others appeared to pass out near the stage. A handful of ushers rushed over and helped them to their feet while the remaining ushers locked arms in front of the stage. It was Altamont Speedway, except this wasn't 1969, Gatting wasn't Jagger and Peter hoped that the ushers weren't Hell's Angels.

From his vantage point, it was pure theatre. Peter felt like chuckling. Gatting moved across from stage left to right, waving and acknowledging the crowd like a seasoned performer. As the applause died down, he pointed to a man who was standing near the front. Peter tuned out while Gatting recited a prayer studded with thees and thous, calling on God—on Jehovah—and on the anointed one to use him as their vessel on earth today.

He pointed at the man again. 'I…' he began, but his voice failed to fill the auditorium. He glared at the sound engineer, 'I sense your pain. I sense you have suffered much for God!' He motioned the man to come forward and for an usher to help him. As the man shuffled forward, Gatting continued. 'God hears you. He hears each one of you. He knows what's in your heart and in your prayers. He is here to heal. He is here right now. Can you feel Him?'

'I feel Him,' cried a lone voice.

'Can you feel Him?' repeated Gatting.

'I feel Him,' shouted several more.

'Can you feel Him?'

This time the response was thunderous. 'I feel Him!'

Gatting went to the edge of the stage and placed a hand on the man's forehead. 'Are you ready to be healed by the Holy Spirit?' he asked.

The man seemed to be weeping. 'I am,' he replied. 'I am.'

'We are all God's children. What's your name, child of God?

'Zebediah. They call me Zeb, Pastor Gatting.'

'Zebediah, why, that's a good, holy name. What is your suffering, Zebediah? Tell everyone, don't be afraid, speak up.'

'I have rheumatoid arthritis,' he replied. 'I am in terrible pain all the time. The doctors say they can't do anything for me.'

Gatting looked down and placed both hands on Zebediah's head. 'Almighty God, the Maker of all things, I beseech You to give me the power to heal this child of Yours. I ask You to free him from the darkness and from his suffering. I implore You to heal this man now and free him from the sin that binds him to this illness.'

He pushed down on the man's head with so much force that Zebediah teetered forward and Peter half expected his neck to snap. Then he stumbled backwards and fell limply into the arms of the ushers standing behind him. They placed him upright, as he regained his senses. Moments later, he was crying and kissing Gatting's hand.

'I can't feel any pain! None at all! For the first time in twenty years,' Zebediah cried. 'It's a miracle!'

The congregation loved it. Gatting took out his white handkerchief and wiped the sweat off his forehead. He sipped from a glass on the pulpit. He repeated the performance another three times and returned to the middle of the stage. The lights dimmed. Gatting bowed his head momentarily and then slowly raised it.

The woman next to Peter gasped. 'It's the Holy Spirit! Can you see it?'

Peter shook his head.

'The sermon is coming.' She glanced at Peter and Stella. 'I pray that God helps you understand every precious word of faith from Pastor Gatting.'

'I wish I had a Dictaphone to record this,' Peter whispered to Stella.

'I wish I had some diazepam to give her,' she replied.

Gatting began with measured words. 'When I was called on by God to come here some years ago, I knew I had been called here for a reason. I knew that it was God's will that I undertake His very difficult mission.'

He returned to the pulpit and took another sip. Peter wondered if the liquid was water or something significantly stronger, but decided against sharing his thought.

'At first, I believed it would be certain suicide to go to San Francisco and I prayed about it every day. I said to God, "Lord, if it is Your will that I lay down my life and die for You, then I am ready, Lord, only say the word." As y'all know, I am—we all are—every true believer amongst you is—the servant of the Lord, and like any good servant we must do as his master bids. And so God said to me, "Leave your home, son, and go forth to San Francisco and there you shall find your true calling." And I have faith in God, but I questioned Him. "You want me to come to this modern day Babylonia, to march straight into the belly of Satan?" Isn't that what Jesus Christ was asked to do? In my anguish and in my doubt, I said, "God," I say it again, I said, "Lord, are you okay?"'

The congregation laughed.

'I said to God, "I am honoured, Lord, but there are others far more qualified, far more brave, than Zachary Gatting."'

The woman next to Peter stood up. She threw open her arms and yelled, 'No! It's you! You are the chosen one!' as others cried out 'Amen!'

Gatting waited for the *amens* to subside, and then smiled. 'I got down on my knees and prayed for eight hours straight. Imagine that. Eight hours. My legs were numb, my tongue blistered. Then, at the point of collapse, I saw a vision. It was God himself. He came to me in a shaft of dazzling, white light. I said, "I am only a common man. Why have You chosen me?"'

He was silent for a while. He strode around the stage. 'Imagine that. I'm talking to God Himself and I'm asking Him why, of all the people in the world, He has tasked me with this mission.' He scratched his head. 'And then God replies. Yes, folks, God spoke to me as He did to Moses and to Noah and to Lot and to so many before me. He said, "I am displeased with San Francisco. It has become a city of sodomy and depravity. Only you can rid the sin from the homes and from the streets. You must go to that place. You must not question me anymore. You must obey my every word and every instruction that I give to you and to your followers. If you follow me, the Kingdom of Heaven is yours. If you disobey me, I will punish you in the fires of eternal hell.

You will burn and burn in perpetual fire." Wow, not much of a choice, huh?'

The congregation tittered. They were spellbound, hanging on every word.

'Of course,' he resumed, 'I replied with a yes. How could I refuse? Thanks be to God. Hosanna in the highest! It was all made clear to me.'

After a significant pause, the congregation erupted in applause.

'The Lord then told me what I had to do. I was just like Moses on the top of Mount Sinai, receiving the ten commandments. I was humbled by God's trust in me. See, folks, if you have faith in God, He has faith in you. I didn't receive any tablets but I received the word direct from the Lord. He told me to gather all those who believe, all those who want to be God's warriors. He told me to seek out those brave enough to rebel, those faithful enough to fight, those upright enough to rid the world of prurience and depravity. The homosexuals are an abomination unto God.'

Peter looked at Stella who was pale with rage.

'They are worse than the basest animals on earth. They cry like hyenas and debase one another like baboons. AIDS is the punishment for their sins. They must now accept God's punishment. I have heard the word of the Lord and it compels each one of us to stop the evildoers.'

The congregation began clapping again. Among the *amens*, Peter heard someone cry out, 'They must die!'

'It's not enough that the sodomites flaunt their depravity, they ask for help from our government. Hollywood is filled with homosexuals trying to convert your children. The gay-loving liberal press promote their cause. They are all helping them. But who is helping us? We are God's soldiers, we are fighting for righteousness, but no one is helping us.'

Stella was squirming. Peter knew they had to wait until the end of Gatting's ravings, no matter how uncomfortable.

'AIDS is proof of God's wrath. We must fight the homosexuals. We must stop the spread of their disease and their immoral teachings. Our children cannot be exposed to these evildoers. If we don't stop them, we will also incur the wrath of God, just as surely as God destroyed Lot's wife. If we don't stop them, their disease and their ideas will spread. And where will it end? First, they will be demanding the holy sacrament of marriage to each other and then they'll be marrying their animals.'

From their left, someone yelled, 'Stop the fags!'

'This is a war and we must fight to preserve our American Christian values, otherwise we are doomed as a civilisation.'

He paused, picked up a towel and wiped his hands, dropping it on the edge of the stage. A woman darted forward, took the cloth and placed it to her own face.

'Your faith,' he said to the woman, 'is rewarded.'

Peter felt the anger rise in his stomach. *Who the fuck does he think he is?* He sat back in his chair, hands gripping the armrest so tightly that his knuckles blanched.

'We must stop the people who support them by whatever means God grants us. We must support those who are willing to put up their hands and fight their pro-gay laws in our government. Men like Senator Richardson over there.'

A spotlight lit up a man who stood and waved.

'Senator Richardson, a loyal child of God. A great man you are, Senator. You are willing to fight with us in the trenches, to stop this spread of this idolatrous doctrine.'

The senator sat down again.

Gatting continued. 'Once the sodomites are rounded up and taken away, God's will shall be done. But first, we must fight to withhold the health care funding that slows their God-ordained punishment. We must stop them being educated, stop them working, stop their immoral lives. The day they became faggots, they gave up their right to live like the rest of us. We must protect our children. Onwards, Christian warriors, onwards.'

Most of the people leapt to their feet. Gatting mopped his forehead.

'I want to get out of here. I'm feeling really sick,' Stella said. 'It's the Nuremberg rally all over again.'

'We can't. They'll be onto us,' Peter replied.

Gatting motioned the congregation to sit down as the collection baskets went around again. This time, the donations supported the fighting fund. Gatting pronounced a final blessing, raising his hands over the crowd. As Gretchen Gatting sang, her husband slowly left the stage.

'Adolf has left the building,' Peter said.

'Let's get the hell out of here!'

They hurried back to their car, ahead of the crowd that stayed behind to witness the departure of the Gattings in their limousine.

Stella wasted no time steering the car out of the carpark. 'My parents only barely escaped Nazi Germany. Most of their relatives were exterminated because of shit like this. My God, these people will be gassing gays if they ever gain any power. What on earth is Senator Richardson thinking?' She exhaled loudly as they cleared the front gate and turned onto the road. 'Anyone stand out to you as an informant?'

'No, but I don't think they would wear a t-shirt saying *I am an informant,* would they?'

'We need to talk to Raoul again. We need more information.'

'I'll talk to him,' Peter replied. 'He must realise that only a large newspaper has the muscle to do a wide-reaching exposé.'

'We need a co-ordinated plan. We need to push his informant.'

'Do you want to pay them?'

'Whatever we have to do.' Stella pulled over and rubbed her head.

'Are you all right?'

'I keep getting these migraine headaches.'

'Have you been to a doctor? You should see a doctor.'

'I haven't got time to go to a doctor. Move across, you're driving. I'm seeing double right now.' Peter ran around the car to the driver's side as Stella manoeuvred herself into the passenger seat. She clipped her seatbelt. 'And remember, we drive on the right.'

CHAPTER TWENTY-FOUR

JACKIE HAMEL HAD STARTED AT THE BOTTOM OF THE TEN Commandments Church's pecking order, but she had just been happy to be part of the church, no matter how lowly.

Having drifted from church to church for years, she had met many evangelical pastors: some who had their own television networks, most with private planes and gated compounds resembling gaudy palaces. It had never occurred to her that there was any hypocrisy between the love of God and the love of luxury. The preachers were all simply doing God's work. They had these luxuries because God wanted them to have them. That Whore of Babylon, the Catholic Church, displayed its wealth for everyone to see. The evangelical pastors weren't corrupt because they preached the true word of God, but none of them had filled the void in her, so she had kept trying churches on for size, waiting for the perfect fit.

The Gattings were different; this church was telling the truth and she would have cleaned the toilets if it meant being close to the Gattings. She felt next to God when she was near them. It was so overwhelming that she often broke out in tears and songs of joy. She had become a volunteer from the first day, handing out the hymn sheets and helping the infirm to their seats. She quickly gained the Gattings' trust and graduated to holding back the fervent worshippers. She hadn't yet cracked the inner sanctum of the Gatting organisation, but she scored invitations to their home for church functions.

She would have gladly set fire to herself, had the Gattings asked her to. Hearing their message had changed her life. She thanked the Lord for bringing the glorious Gattings into her shattered existence.

For a while the adulation was mutual. Gretchen Gatting called Jackie her gift from God. Jackie had been helping set the church up for a service, when she walked past the grand piano and felt the urge to play it. Long ago, she had been a professional pianist, and she had even co-written a Grammy-winning song for a crooner she never much liked. Jackie had never wanted to be a famous musician—she just wanted to be an accomplished musician. Music was everything to her. Something told her that day that she had to play, although she hadn't played the piano since her husband had left her ten years before.

Even when they had fallen in love, the piano had always been in the background. Her husband joked that she would have taken the darn piano on their honeymoon if she could have. After a couple of days of not playing the piano, she had begged the hotel manager if she could play theirs. When she told him, her husband had smiled and said, 'You'll never change, so stop trying to. You are what you are.' Together, on that hotel piano, they wrote a song about their love but, after four years, the marriage fell apart. It hadn't been an easy marriage, but then, which marriage is? He was what he was: plagued by self-doubt and an inability to love her completely. He left before the winter set in.

Her world had shattered once he'd gone, and the music in her had died. She couldn't play without breaking down. Her life had become empty, dark and silent until she had joined The Ten Commandments Church.

That morning, on a whim, she had sat down and played. Her fingers had danced over the keys like they had never been away. She had hummed along to the tune she was playing until she had heard Gretchen Gatting's voice.

'I'm sorry,' she had said, closing the lid.

'Don't let me interrupt you.'

An hour later, she and Gretchen had written their first song. Another year passed and the pair had recorded an album. Every member of the congregation had bought a copy, guaranteeing a runaway success. The money they had made had gone straight to the church.

She felt at times that the Gattings were envious of the other, more successful evangelical pastors. It was written on their faces. She had once overheard a loud argument between the couple about why they didn't have hundreds of thousands of parishioners, like the others. Gretchen had said that they were too soft; they needed to push Christian values. After that everything changed. Pastor Gatting's sermons had become more hardline, more punitive towards adulterers, abortionists and gays. Especially gays. People flocked to hear his hate-tinged sermons as if he was the Messiah himself. But in the back of her mind, Jackie always wondered, would Jesus Christ preach condemnation like that? He reached out to the whores and the lepers.

The answers Jackie needed weren't coming from Pastor Gatting. All she heard these days were words of hate. The Gattings had been her salvation and music had become her escape, but she was haunted by a secret that she could never tell anyone, not even her beloved Pastor and Gretchen Gatting. How could she? She would have been shunned by the church. Only she and the music would ever know her secret.

Then she discovered what Gatting and his associates did every Thursday afternoon, and that was too much for her to bear.

She wanted to talk to the only person she had ever really trusted. So, Jackie Hamel picked up the telephone and called her ex-husband.

CHAPTER TWENTY-FIVE

Ranchero Motel, San Jose, California.

AMOS STOPPED THE MUSTANG ACROSS THE HIGHWAY FROM THE Ranchero Motel. It was as nondescript as its name suggested. The garden featured a wagon wheel, some cacti and a windmill: a bad seventies western in the middle of suburbia.

Peter unbuckled his seatbelt and wound down his window. He checked his watch. 'Ten to twelve.'

He noticed the *Daily's* photographer pull up in a late model Ford Explorer a few yards away. Larry Bruce waved when he saw them. 'Nice place for a stakeout,' Peter remarked.

'My first.' Amos smiled. 'I knew I'd make investigative reporter one day.'

Peter chuckled and settled back in the seat. He liked the Mustang and it seemed especially appropriate in the circumstances. 'Although you're more Steve McQueen than Dustin Hoffman in this car.'

'Steve McQueen. Now he was a man's man.'

Peter looked at Amos and laughed. He grasped Amos's meaning but didn't take it further. He reached behind him and grabbed a shopping bag.

'Gee-zuz!' Amos gasped as Peter removed the contents. 'A porn moustache and a Doris Day wig?'

'I'm going undercover. It's part of my cunning kit.'

'Cunning kit? Tell me you don't use it privately for bondage and sadism. You're a sick man.'

'I use disguises, so I can… blend in.'

'In that? Where exactly would you blend in? A convention of seventies newsreaders? Last time I tried wearing a disguise, the cops beat me up.'

'No, it's so I won't be recognised by Gatting.'

'How would he… You went and checked out his den of hate, didn't you?'

'Stella and I did. I wanted to get a feel for the place.'

'And what feel did you get from it?' Amos asked.

'It isn't like any church I've been to before.'

'I went there once as a demonstrator and they beat us up at the front stairs. Just be careful. There isn't a lot of Christian forgiveness in that place, they're more the stoning-and-sacrifice kind.'

'I've noticed.' Peter tucked his hair into the wig and stuck on the moustache.

Amos laughed until he snorted.

'How do I look?'

'Shit, you look like a serial killer or a dead member of a rock band.'

'I'll take both as a compliment.'

Amos noticed a limousine with blackened windows pull into the motel. 'He's here.' He started the car.

Peter checked his watch again. 'It's twelve. He's very punctual.' He waved to Larry Bruce.

'So where is Inspector Belinski and his posse? I can't see them anywhere,' Amos remarked.

'I hope they're here. Belinski called me this morning to say that it was going ahead.'

'We can't do anything until they go in.'

A few minutes later another limousine slowed down to turn into the motel's driveway. This time, the windows were clear.

'Holy shit,' Peter said. 'The senator is one of the guys in the back seat.'

Amos clapped his hands. 'It's going to be a great big party.'

Peter looked up and down the highway. 'Where is Jerry? I can't see Jerry anywhere.'

Amos switched off the engine and scowled. Another five minutes passed as Peter debated getting out of the car and taking matters into his own hands. He had unlatched the door and was about to swing it open when a Ford transit van pulled into the Ranchero Motel.

'Here comes the entertainment,' Amos sniggered.

Larry Bruce was now parked adjacent to the motel across the highway from them. He was out of his car and looking at Peter, holding his hands up in frustration. Peter imitated his gesture.

'It's ten after twelve,' Amos said. 'What happens if the cops don't show?'

'I guess the show is off and we get out of here. Or...'

'Or?'

'We could go in ourselves,' Peter said.

'Are you totally crazy? They'll beat the shit out of us.'

Peter pulled out his cell and punched in Jerry's number. It rang out. 'He isn't answering,' he said angrily.

'What do we do?'

'Five more minutes, then we'll call it a day.' He watched the minute hand on his watch creep around the dial. Three minutes passed. Then he heard a car horn sound twice. His head swivelled towards the noise. 'At last. The cavalry has arrived.'

'Where the fuck are they? Have they come by helicopter?'

Two squad cars and two Chevrolet Tahoes in a tight procession suddenly turned into the motel driveway, blocking the entrance. Amos started the Mustang and revved it hard. Peter gave a thumbs up to Larry Bruce as Amos threw the car in first gear, pushed down on the accelerator and spun the Mustang around into a u-turn.

'Try not to kill us, Raoul,' Peter said as he hung on tightly, 'this isn't a bloody movie.'

The Mustang crossed onto the other side of the highway and stopped across the driveway of the Ranchero Motel. Larry Bruce was already there. His camera was locked and loaded.

Peter darted out of the car, and they ran towards the police cars. A cop saw them, pulled out his service revolver, propped his elbows against the car and pointed it at them.

'Stop!' he ordered.

'Press,' Peter shouted back. 'We're reporters!'

'Don't shoot! We come in peace!' Amos held up his hands.

Belinski nodded at the officer, who directed them to move away and to one side.

'What's happening?' Peter asked him.

'Stay here until they're brought out.'

The motel manager was already handcuffed and a policeman was leading him away. Two others were poised with a door ram outside one of the rooms.

Belinski moved forward, his pistol drawn, and shouted, 'Open up. It's the police.' He waited for a response. When none arrived, he ordered, 'Break it down.'

The officers smashed the ram into the door, splintering it and tearing it away from its hinges. As they stepped away, other officers swarmed into the motel room. Above the shouts of the police, Peter heard girls screaming and men yelling. Bruce's camera whirred as they all ran forward.

'This is so exciting,' Amos said, pulling Peter along.

A sergeant turned and ran after them, catching them when they were level with the police vehicles. 'Stay here,' he snarled, 'or I'll frigging arrest the three of you.'

Moments later, five young women came out in handcuffs first, wearing little else. Belinski was as good as his word: the sight of the near naked girls followed by the men in various states of undress was dynamite. One of the girls was shouting in Spanish, *puerco*, while the rest were crying.

The two men had their hands cuffed behind their back. They dropped their heads down into their chest when they noticed Larry Bruce's camera.

'No photos or I'll break the fucking camera!' one of the men shouted.

'Yeah? How exactly?' Amos laughed as the sergeant pushed him away and told him to shut up.

A female police officer was attempting to pacify the women as they were directed towards a van. Bruce held his camera above his head and took several shots.

'Who are the guys?' Amos asked. 'I don't recognise them. Where's the host of the party?'

'I don't know them either.'

Two officers pushed the men into the back of the squad car.

Peter was hoping that the others hadn't escaped when two more men were brought out with their hands cuffed behind their backs. Both of them had towels over their heads.

'Bummer,' said Bruce. 'I can't see them. So are they...' He kept his camera raised but stopped shooting for a moment.

'Shit, you invite us to your party, but you don't entertain us,' Amos grumbled.

'We're missing the money shot.' Peter saw his headline disappearing fast.

One of the girls smiled at Peter oddly as she approached the squad car. He was wondering if he knew her from somewhere. As he was still trying to place her and drawing a blank, she swung herself around, executed a side kick and used her toes to pull the towels off the men's heads. Bruce whooped and Peter laughed. *That's it!* he remembered. *She's a Mexican wrestler!*

'Holy shit,' Amos shouted, 'the girl's an acrobat! Senator Richardson, you turn up in the best places, don't you? And I see you brought your best buddy with you.' He roared with laughter.

'Do you have any comment, Senator Richardson and Pastor Gatting? Do you know why you have been arrested?' yelled Peter.

There was no response. The girl was led away while Bruce continued to shoot and someone eventually replaced the towels.

Belinski came up to them. 'A great result, Jerry,' Peter said.

'Make sure you thank your informant, Raoul,' he said. 'We'll be able to get them on a few charges; soliciting and pandering prostitution, sex with a minor, bringing in illegal immigrants and drug use.'

'Drug use?' Peter asked.

'We found a bag of cocaine in the room.'

'That's heavy shit,' Amos said, 'but I'm sure Gatting has a passage from the Bible to justify it all to his parishioners.'

'Well, for the moment, these men will have to justify it all to a judge in a Californian court of law,' Belinski said. 'Who might not be quite as forgiving.'

He walked away in Gatting's wake and got into his car. The squad cars were pulling away with the men, as three network vans tore into the motel driveway. Their crews jumped out and began to assemble their equipment.

'You're too late, boys,' Amos shouted.

'Don't rush, we've got it,' Peter added.

Chapter Twenty-Six

Daily offices.

PETER WAS BACK AT HIS DESK, TYPING UP THE STORY, WHILE BRUCE worked on the contact sheet. His gratitude to Amos's source was beyond anything words could express. *Another splash*. And what a splash! The whole office was buzzing with excitement. A television was on, blaring out the news updates about the motel arrests. Most of the staff were glued to it, including Stella and Frank.

'Will someone turn down the bloody TV, I'm trying to type up the story,' he shouted.

Someone decreased the volume but the chatter continued.

'Thanks.'

Stella came over to Peter. 'How's it going?' she asked.

'It's going to be ready to go for the afternoon edition. I'm pissed off that I can't cover what's happening down at the police station.'

'I've got Mulroy there right now. I'm assuming that Gatting or Richardson'll make a statement from there.'

'I should be bloody doing it. It's my story.'

'Well, you can't be everywhere at once.'

'Maybe you're right. For once.'

'Great job by the way. If this doesn't make us the number one newspaper in San Francisco, I'll walk naked in Union Square at lunchtime.'

Peter laughed. 'I might hold you to that, Stella.'

A reporter who was at the television shouted, 'Peter, you might want to see this.'

'Shit, I'm going to throw that thing out of the bloody window!'

'No, it's Senator Richardson. He's making a statement.'

Stella and Peter rushed to the television. Richardson was standing on the front steps of the police station flanked by his lawyer and his wife who was wearing large sunglasses. He held up a paper and read a prepared statement: 'Today's arrest of myself and Pastor Gatting was an immense travesty of justice. It has caused unnecessary stress to my family and my supporters, and any charges will be rigorously defended. These accusations are false and are part of a conspiracy by leftist elements to discredit me.

'We neither sought to nor did we procure women for the activities of prostitution as has been alleged. Pastor Gatting and I were, in fact, interviewing and counselling these women, who are refugees from war-torn countries. Our mission as Christians was to help them start a better life in the United States. As devout Christians I feel we are being persecuted for carrying out the teachings of God. That is all.' Richardson folded the paper and stepped back as his lawyer moved forward to take questions.

'I will only answer three questions.'

'Why isn't Pastor Gatting here?' Mulroy asked.

'He is being treated at the moment.'

'What for?' another reporter questioned.

'That's private information but this event has caused a great strain on Pastor Gatting.'

'He's not dying?'

'No. No more questions,' the lawyer said.

Peter chuckled. 'Well, I'd like to find out how Pastor Gatting will react,' he said as he walked away from the television, Stella following closely behind.

'What are you thinking?'

'I want to go back to the church.'

'I don't know about that. They seemed suspicious of us last time we went.'

'I want to get their reaction to all this.'

'I won't authorise it,' Stella replied.

'Does that mean you're not coming with me?'

'Yes. Neither should you go.'

'I have to. I won't feel like I've done my job otherwise.'

'I'm not sanctioning it. You do what you think you have to do, but don't complain to me when they beat you up.'

'I'll take my chances.'

'Don't die for a story, Peter,' Stella said.

Peter laughed. 'That's funny coming from you.'

'Shut up. I'm talking to you as a friend. This isn't Australia, or England for that matter. Things can really get out of hand in this country.'

'Thanks for the advice.'

'It's water off a duck's back, isn't it, Clancy?'

'Probably.'

CHAPTER TWENTY-SEVEN

Diamond Heights, San Franciso.

'HE OPENS THEIR EAR TO INSTRUCTION, AND COMMANDS THAT they return from evil,' the woman said aloud, as she gestured for the boy to kneel next to her.

The boy was probably in his mid-teens and unexceptional in every way. There was a faint stubble around his chin where he hadn't shaved for a while. Together, they kneeled on the lounge-room floor in front of a wooden cross screwed to the wall and repeated the phrase over and over. *He opens their ear to instruction, and commands that they return from evil.*

They shut their eyes and bowed their heads and the repetition continued until the meaning fell away and all that was left was a pattern of sounds. Then the woman instructed the boy to stop and they stood up.

'You know that we have been called upon to remove evil from this earth.'

'I know,' he said.

'You know the task that we have been given.'

'I know,' he repeated.

'Are you willing to join me in a glorious life everlasting?'

'I am.'

'I am proud of you, son. It is a great honour to be chosen.'

'I know, Mama.' He took hold of the woman's hand.

'Soon, we will go into paradise together, where we will see the face of God and hear the song of angels. We are among the righteous. The righteous will be given all that they crave on earth and in heaven. We will never be alone.'

Chapter Twenty-Eight

The Ten Commandments Church.

Screening procedures for visitors entering The Ten Commandments Church had tightened since the motel incident. Peter noticed the difference as he pulled into the church carpark. Also new was the media contingent parked out on the sidewalk. The solitary parking usher had been replaced by four burly men with truncheons, wearing paramilitary uniforms.

'You're a worshipper?' one of them growled at him as he pulled up beside them. The guard pressed his face against the passenger window and looked inside.

'I am.'

The other checked the car number plate against a clipboard. 'Where's your wife?'

'She had to go back to Australia. Her mother was taken ill.'

'Pop the trunk,' the guard ordered.

Peter got out of the car and opened the trunk. The guard followed him while the other took the opportunity to look inside the car.

'What are you looking for?' he asked.

'None of your business. You got any cameras? Weapons?'

'This is a place of worship. You won't find anything on me,' Peter replied.

'Good, because we don't want to bust any heads today,' the guard sneered.

The guard pulled up the trunk flooring and searched the wheel well, then closed the trunk. 'Okay. You're fine to go.'

Peter took a deep breath as he returned to the driver's seat.

He faced another interrogation before he entered the church; the same questions to which he gave the same replies. Unlike the last time he had attended, the parishioners' mood was different; anticipation had been replaced by tension.

He found a seat two rows back from the stage. Because of the delay getting in, the music had already started. He watched the band and the singers closely, taking note that they were more subdued than last time. Then he focused on the woman playing the piano. He remembered the last time he had been here; she had been beaming but now she wiped the tears running down her face as she played.

She played two songs before the lights went down. When they went up again, Gatting and his wife were walking hand in hand onto the stage, followed closely by Senator Richardson and his wife.

The congregation stood and cheered for around five minutes before Gatting motioned the congregation to sit. Peter expected that the crowd would have jeered him off the stage but he was wrong; *Teflon Preacher* popped into his head as a potential kicker for his next story on the church.

Gretchen stood beside Gatting and stared adoringly into her husband's face as he pulled a handkerchief out of his coat pocket. Gatting and Gretchen slowly knelt and Richardson and the congregation did likewise.

'Let us pray,' Gatting said. 'I have only done Your work, oh Lord. I have only sought to help those who need Your spiritual guidance and Your charity. You told me that those poor, unfortunate Hispanic girls needed our help; those poor unfortunate girls who had been raped and tortured in their Catholic countries. Yes Lord, You knew our church unreservedly provided charity to these girls.

'You know what we did was good and it was not meant to be for the pleasures of the flesh. You know that we did not ever—not ever—want to indulge in sexual relations with these poor unfortunates.'

Gatting started to sob into the microphone. Gretchen leaned towards him and she and Richardson hugged him. 'Oh God, I despair for the wickedness of people who seek to destroy this great church. If You have provided this to me as a test of my devotion to

You, I am only human. I need Your help to help me fight this eternal wickedness. Please Lord Almighty, give me strength. Give this church and the servants within it the strength to fight the devil and his disciples. We need Your help. We need Your strength, oh Lord.'

The congregation repeated, *We need Your help. We need Your strength.*

Gatting wiped his face with the handkerchief. 'Let us fight the devil who resides in those who oppose our teachings: the faggot activists, the unholy press and the communist supporters of the faggots. Let them burn in punishment because they are the face of the devil on earth. Not only are they are inflicting their evil on the outside world, but the devil is among us right now. We ask this in Your name, God smite them this instant!'

The congregation gasped as they looked at each other. The woman next to him stared at Peter. He looked back at her. The words, *I don't have horns, lady, or 666 burnt on my forehead, do I?* nearly came out of his mouth.

Gatting and everyone else on the stage rose to their feet, imitated by the congregation. *Thank God*, Peter thought; his knees were aching.

Gatting paused for a glass of water and then his sermon began. 'By now, you have all heard about that travesty of reporting that led to the vile accusations made against me and Senator Richardson here. Well, that got me thinking, who told the police and the reporters where we hold our counselling sessions with those poor, unfortunate girls?'

He strode to the back of the stage. 'So I asked the Lord to show me who had betrayed us so foully and the Lord replied to me. He told me that the devil lives amongst us. Satan's disciples walk freely without challenge in this house of worship and have done so for a long time. The devil rejoices in the attacks on our great name.'

The congregation gasped again. Gatting started to criss-cross the stage. His voice rose to a shout. 'You are here. You are here, Spawn of the Devil, Judas of Evil! The Lord has given me the special powers to see you. Your days are numbered and you will be punished.'

He walked up to the pianist and stopped in front of her.

'Everyone, behold the Evil One!' he cried. 'We trusted you as a friend, Jackie Hamel, and were inspired by your songs of devotion. We welcomed you into our inner family and you have betrayed us. Of all the people I thought would do so. Doing this gives me great pain. Oh Lord, You have ordered me and I must obey.'

He placed his hand on Jackie Hamel's head. She tried to pull away but he pressed his hand harder into her head. It now dawned on Peter that Jackie Hamel must have been Amos's informant. She could be in danger. He had to get her out of here before she was harmed. But how?

'You know I love you and Mrs Gatting. I am a loyal friend,' Jackie stammered.

'Judas betrayed with a kiss,' Gatting replied coolly as two men standing at the back of the stage moved forward.

'It isn't me, Pastor Gatting,' she cried. 'I am not a disciple of the devil. I am innocent. I beg you.'

The men grabbed Jackie Hamel by the arms and dragged her to the edge of the stage.

'In times past, we would burn you in the cleansing fires of God.'

'Burn her, burn her, burn her,' a few in the crowd shouted.

'But we have to obey the laws of our land. We don't burn evil people any more, regrettably.' Gatting laid his hands on her. 'Instead you shall be cast out of the protection of this church to dwell amongst the idolatrous and the devil worshippers. May the Almighty have mercy on your pathetic soul.'

'I was trying to save the church,' Jackie screamed, 'to save it from your corruption.' Her knees gave way and she crumpled to the stage. Her head lolled backwards and forwards as the ushers lifted her up.

It was then Peter saw a boy aged about fifteen, running towards the stage.

'He opens their ear to instruction, and commands that they return from evil,' the boy shouted.

Only when the boy ran up the steps to the stage did Peter notice that he was holding two pistols. The men lay Jackie down again. One of the security guards ran forward to tackle the boy, but he fired at the guard. The crowd shrieked.

The guard tumbled forward, the wound to his head dripping blood as if a tap had been left open. Most of the congregation fell to the ground, while a few headed for the exit. Gatting and the others bunched themselves together near the piano. Jackie Hamel still lay on the stage.

Peter stepped over the people crouching beside him and crawled along the aisle towards the stage. He pulled out a small camera that he had been able to hide in his crotch. He managed to take a shot of the stage. The boy shot indiscriminately again and Peter dropped to the floor.

'I know you,' said Gatting as he held out his hand to the boy. 'You're David Merrell. Don't shoot, son. Let me hear your pain. You are hurting, David. I can help you.'

Another guard approached the boy from behind. A woman holding a revolver jumped up from her seat and ran up the aisle towards the stage, stepping over Peter. 'Behind you, David,' she yelled.

David spun around and fired two shots into the guard when he was nearly on top of him. The guard collapsed on the stage, shot twice in the chest.

'He opens their ear to instruction, and commands that they return from evil!' the woman screamed, climbing onto the stage.

'Leah, we are here to help you. Don't do this. Remember that this is a place of God,' Gatting pleaded.

'You destroyed this church. You and your whore wife are nothing but worshippers of false idols. You must die. You must all die.'

'No!' Gatting fell to his knees. 'Save us, Lord!'

'Your blood will cleanse the church. In the name of God, you must die!'

It sounded like dozens of fireworks exploding, as David and Leah directed their fire towards Gatting, Gretchen, Richardson and his wife.

The stage was now awash with blood and brain tissue. Peter kept crawling towards the stage. He really didn't know what he was going to do—save Jackie or get the hell out of there. While he was deciding, he took another photograph of the carnage.

The main entrance door opened and two more security guards

rushed up the aisle, firing as they ran. David and Leah squatted behind the piano and fired back. Peter started to worry he might be caught in crossfire, so he rolled into a row where a group of people were praying.

Leah Merrell leapt from behind the piano and fired at the guards. They shot back, wounding her in the arm and leg, but she kept firing, oblivious to the pain, until the guards both fell. Then she crawled back to her son.

Peter slithered back into the aisle and edged slowly towards the stage. He could see Jackie Hamel dragging herself through the blood to the edge of the stage. She caught sight of him.

'Help me. Help me, please.'

Outside, the police sirens blared. Peter moved closer, almost close enough to touch Jackie's hand. He wondered if he could pull her off the stage.

Leah Merrill had righted herself. 'David,' she shouted. 'You hear me? Soon it will be time to die for God.'

'Mama,' said her son, 'someone's moving.'

Leah wiped her hand on her skirt. 'Jackie Hamel. Of all, you are the most evil. You must die, too.' She took one of the pistols from David and fired into Jackie's back. Jackie's limp arm was draped over the edge of the stage. Satisfied, Leah returned to her son's side, replaced the clip and dropped his pistol.

Peter reached up and grabbed Jackie's hand and tugged, but she hardly moved. He wiped the blood off his hand and took a better grip of her hand. He tried to pull her motionless body off the stage. An elderly man took Jackie's other hand and pulled with him, as Leah Merrell picked up her revolver again and fired wildly into the congregation until it ran out of ammunition. As she picked up the other pistol, a SWAT team crept into the church in a tight phalanx formation.

She glanced at them for a moment and cried aloud, 'It's our time to enter the Kingdom of Heaven.' She placed a pistol against David's head.

'I love you, Mama. I'm waiting to go to heaven. I'm ready,' he said as he gazed at his mother.

Mrs Merrell kissed him on the forehead and pulled the trigger. His head blew apart, spattering brain tissue and blood all over her.

'I commend unto you, dear God, my beautiful son!' She crouched over him and hugged his lifeless body.

'Let's get the bitch!' The old man tapped Peter on the shoulder.

Without considering the consequences, Peter got to his feet and followed the man onto the stage. All he knew was that Leah Merrell was a monster and he had to stop her. She looked at them running at her. She held up the pistol to shoot them. The old man and Peter dived to the stage. Beyond them, she saw the SWAT team.

'I hear you, David. I'm coming, too,' she cried out as she placed the pistol under her chin.

Peter was going to tackle her, but she pulled the trigger before he could get to his feet. She dropped lifeless, next to her son's body, her head shattered from the impact of the bullet. A piece of her jaw flew at Peter and lacerated his cheek.

He wiped the blood from his face with the only part of his shirt that was still clean, pleased to find the cut on his face was little more than a nick. 'I don't know why I did that,' he said between breaths.

'That was pretty brave,' a police officer said. He looked at the elderly man who was struggling to catch his breath. 'And you too, sir.'

As Peter and the old man descended the stairs from the stage, a lieutenant moved forward. 'You two will need to stay here for a while. We'll need to speak with you.'

Peter tried arguing, but they wouldn't let him leave. If he could get out of here, he could ring Stella on the cell and then go into the office to work on the story. Now, he would be here for hours. Furtively, he tucked the camera in his pocket.

Jackie Hamel was barely alive. The paramedics intubated her and took her from the church to hospital in a helicopter. As the forensic team moved in, the uniformed police assisted people out of the church.

Peter was there for two hours before he was allowed to leave. He ran to his car and called Stella. A convoy of television vans were parked along the road. Two television helicopters hovered overhead.

'Stella,' he said.

'You know this is Sunday,' she replied.

'Of course I bloody do. There's been a shooting at the church.'

'You're okay?'

He glimpsed his face in the rear-vision mirror. It was smeared with dried blood. 'Yeah.'

'I'll meet you in the office as soon as I can,' she said.

'That's where I'm headed as soon as I change my clothes.'

'How bad was it?' she asked.

'Bad. Very bad. It was bad enough to make the paper number one again.'

'You saw it?'

'I was there, in the middle of it.' He heard Stella gasp at the other end of the line. 'But even better than that,' he added, 'I have pictures of the whole damned thing.'

CHAPTER TWENTY-NINE

Daily offices.

AT LEAST SEVEN DEAD IN TEN COMMANDMENTS CHURCH MASSACRE including Senator Terrence Richardson and his wife. A deranged mother and son who were members of the church are believed to be the shooters.

Peter exhaled loudly as he looked at the front page of the *Daily* which was entirely devoted to the church shooting. Three of the photographs taken from his small camera covered half of the front page, a little blurry but clear enough to convey a little of the horror of the experience.

He hadn't had the luxury of thinking about the incident; he'd had a piece to file. Like the other experiences he'd had, they'd revisit him when he least expected it, usually at night and often with a suffocating feeling of imminent death. For the moment, it was all about the story.

'I only wish I could have taken better photographs,' he said.

'You should be happy that they were the only ones of the shooting,' said Mulroy. 'That's an exclusive.'

'No shit, Mulroy.' Peter mused that if he ever got over his habit of stating the bloody obvious, Mulroy might make a great crime reporter. Nothing fazed him. He was completely devoid of sentiment.

'Peter,' Stella called from the doorway of her office, 'can you come in here for a moment?'

'Don't forget to ask her for a pay raise,' said Mulroy.

Stella closed the door behind Peter and returned to her desk. 'Are you okay?' she asked.

'A little shaken up, but that's the danger of going undercover.'

'The cops questioned you?'

115

'Of course. Belinski was there. It wasn't that bad.'

'Well, everyone knows who you are by now. You won't be going undercover there anymore,' she said. 'Or anywhere else for a while.'

'The church is pretty much finished. Now that the Gattings are dead…'

'Hmm, you'd think so, wouldn't you? Well, I've just got off the phone from a spokesman for The Ten Commandments Church. He says they'll rise from this again, bigger and stronger.'

Peter sniggered. 'Good for them. I think they should think about screening all their parishioners for mental instability and ignorance, as well as weapons, in the future.'

'That would reduce their congregation to around ten people, I imagine. The spokesman's a spinmaster all right. He says it's all due to the gay activists brain-washing the Merrells.'

'How did he figure that exactly?'

'David Merrell was sexually ambivalent, he says. That's why he and his mother joined the church. They attempted to straighten him out, as they say. He says they were both receiving counselling from a gay psychologist in recent times. Outside the church.'

'Well, they can spin it any way they want to, but the Merrells were crazy members of the church who went on a killing spree.'

'That's wasn't the end of our conversation. He wasn't happy with our coverage of the shooting. He thinks it was exaggerated.'

Peter laughed. 'The church incited violence, I heard it, you heard it. I was there. How can you downplay a bloody massacre?'

'Nup. Apparently, we exaggerated it so we'd sell more papers. And you're actually a government agent who has infiltrated the church so the government can take away their constitutional rights.'

'Okay. My head is spinning.'

'I think that's around the time I said I had to go.'

'Why did you give him any phone-time? I don't envy your job.'

'And you don't know this either. The police department has recommended you for a bravery award. You and a guy named Jack Hartman, for saving Jackie Hamel.'

'There was an old guy there. That must be him.' He shook his head. 'But I can't accept it.'

'Why? You saved her life.'

'What I did wasn't brave. My motivation was purely self-interested. I was really only there to get information on the church. I was only trying to save Jackie Hamel because she was our informant. If I had wanted to be a real hero, I would have tried to save Gatting, his wife, Richardson and the security guards.'

'Geez, Peter, I have news for you, mate: Superman you're not! You're beating yourself up because you didn't stop the bullets? You could have stayed under your seat, protecting your own sweet ass and nobody else's, just like all the others. The way I see it, Jackie Hamel wouldn't be alive if it wasn't for your actions. Plus, there's another splash in it.'

'I dunno.' He sat silently for a while. 'How is she, anyway? Any update on her condition?'

'She's critical but stabilising. She's still in ICU,' she replied.

'I've been trying to ring Raoul, but he hasn't returned my messages.'

'I've tried too. I've had no luck either.'

'I'm thinking of going to his office or the hospital and seeing if I can catch him there.'

Stella's desk phone rang as he spoke. She lifted the receiver and pressed it against her chest while she replied, 'Good idea.'

CHAPTER THIRTY

PETER ASKED FOR AMOS AT THE *BAYSIDE JOURNAL* BUT THE receptionist informed him that Mr Amos was busy and, besides, he had no wish to see anyone from the *Daily*. He noticed that the Mustang wasn't parked in its usual place, so he decided to head to the San Francisco General.

He talked his way into the ICU waiting room but no further; he said he was a relative of Jackie's. He asked the nurse if she could relay a message to Amos and then, not expecting a quick reply, sat down to read the paper. He decided to give it two hours before he'd quit waiting.

It took over an hour to prove his hunch right. Amos walked past the open doorway of the waiting room. Peter dropped the paper that he had read through several times.

'Raoul,' he called quietly. 'How is Jackie?'

Amos kept walking. Peter caught up to him as he was pressing the button on the elevator. He looked like he hadn't slept in days.

'I've been trying to catch you. How's Jackie?' Peter asked again.

'What do you want?' Amos pressed the button repeatedly.

'I'm wondering if Jackie's okay.'

Amos spun around and pushed Peter backwards. He fell against the opposite wall.

'You've really got a hide coming here. What do you want? Another frigging headline for your ass-wipe paper?'

'I can understand you're…' Peter tried to step forward but Amos pushed him back.

'You hung her out to dry.'

'Let's talk, Raoul. We'll just end up getting thrown out of here.'

Amos lowered his voice. 'I'm going to insist our readers boycott your frigging paper. That's just a start.'

'Come on, Raoul. We can be reasonable here.'

'I'm thinking of running a cartoon of Stella Reimers stepping over dead bodies as she reaches for another journalism award. Maybe I could add you in, too. How would you like that?'

'We didn't know this tragedy was going to happen. How could we have predicted that?' Peter argued.

'You pushed her too far. She took too many risks because of you. You did everything but identify her in your desire to claim glory. Anyone would have worked out who the informant was.'

Peter scoffed. 'Anyone? Well, I didn't! You never told me and I only worked it out when Gatting was standing over her calling her the devil. Can we go somewhere and talk calmly about this? I'll meet you at Shotguns for a drink.'

'I've declared war on the *Daily*. We're going to do your paper a lot of fucking damage.'

'I didn't set her up as an informant. You did that. You can't blame yourself for letting this happen.'

Amos spun around. 'You don't know what I'm feeling.' He kept punching the button repeatedly. 'What in the hell is wrong with this? Has it died or something?'

Peter thought for a moment what to say next. 'You know I was there, don't you?'

'Of course I do. I read the article. So what? I'm supposed to feel grateful? Where were you when she was shot? Why wasn't it you? That would have made a great deadline. Even stone-dead, you'd have loved it, I can see the headline: *Reporter Goes Down in a Blaze of Glory.*'

The elevator doors opened and a crowd of people slowly emerged.

'You don't know, do you?' said Peter shaking his head.

'Leave me alone.' Amos pushed through the crowd.

'Another man and I saved Jackie's life. We grabbed her after she was wounded and pulled her off the stage. Everyone else there died,' he called.

The elevator door closed. 'Frigging elevator...' Amos spun around. 'I didn't know that. Are you bullshitting me?'

'Honest truth.' He crossed his heart. 'You probably didn't think reporters like me would ever risk their lives. We're supposed to be scumbags. The scum of the earth, until one of us gets nominated for a bravery award.'

'Really? You saved her?' Amos looked unsteady on his feet. 'Don't go thinking that's a game-changer or anything. You still put her life in danger.'

'Well, let's not go there.' Peter pressed the elevator button. 'I feel like a drink; a real heavy one.' He glanced at Amos. 'How is Jackie? I'm really concerned.'

'Looks like she'll be out of ICU soon.'

'That's great,' he said as he wiped away a tear.

CHAPTER THIRTY-ONE

Pop's Bar, Mission District, San Francisco.

PETER ORDERED TWO BEERS AND ONE WHISKY CHASER, AND JOINED Amos, who was sitting in a booth.

'I thought you were having something heavy,' he remarked as he watched the solitary spirit arrive.

'I had second thoughts. I thought that if I have something heavy, I may not stop.'

'Have you always had a problem with booze?' Amos asked.

'Only when I wasn't drinking it. Cheers,' he said as he held up his glass.

Amos clinked his glass against Peter's. 'Yeah. Cheers.'

'To Jackie's recovery.'

'To Jackie. Best woman I've ever known,' Amos continued. 'I'll requalify that. Best person I've known.'

'Brave woman. Very brave. We wouldn't have got inside without her help.' Peter took a long draught from the glass.

'You know, I knew I was gay before I married her. I don't know why I didn't just walk away when we were dating. I thought I could stick it. Boy, did she hate me when I finally left.'

'She probably felt betrayed.'

'Despite what happened in the past, we eventually put the past behind us. Of all the straight people I've known, she was the only one who totally accepted me. She could have really hated me forever for what I did, but Jackie eventually understood what it meant for me to be gay.'

'It's not like choosing a footy team or a car. From what I've heard, you're born that way. The churches can go on about how sinful it is, but we've just busted a pastor for committing sex acts on underage girls. Doesn't that sound a lot like hypocrisy?'

'True. Very true,' Amos replied. 'So, where to from here?'

'I guess after the obituaries, we move onto something else. What else is there to report? Maybe Jackie will be interested in telling her story.'

'We'll see. It's early days yet.'

'I guess I'll do the crime beat again.'

'You know, this church isn't finished,' Amos said.

'How can they continue? Their pastor is dead.'

'They'll replace him with someone who is equally hateful. Extremists never sleep, they just regroup.'

'How do you know this?'

'I just know how these people work. I've noticed that hatred can only be leaderless for a brief moment. Hatred loves a leader; the loonier the better.'

'But what about the peacemakers?'

'Well, they usually get killed, don't they? When the powers-that-be think they're too dangerous or bad for business.'

Peter smiled. 'And I thought I was cynical.'

'Cynicism was once idealism that ran away from home to fuck strangers and take shit-loads of drugs. When idealism woke up from the haze, all that was left was cynicism and regret.'

'Yes. I guess I'm a cynic most of the times. Today I feel idealistic because I've done a great investigative story. I've always thought that the right story can make the world a better place. On the other hand, I've done stories about the abnormal sex lives of vacuous celebrities and that doesn't help the world one bit.'

'Well, you have to cross over to the dark side sometimes. You know that the church is blaming us for the shooting. This shit never stops, but if you don't fight it, you risk losing everything you believe in.'

'Do you ever worry about being killed?' Peter asked.

'Does it worry you?'

Peter sniggered. 'I've been threatened, shot at and watched people die in front of me.'

'And you haven't even been a war correspondent.'

'I say, you don't have to leave home to be in the action. If I thought about it too much, I'd give it away.'

'Yeah.' Amos nodded. 'I'd get bored sitting in an office pushing paper. Changing lives and hunting down gay-haters gives me purpose.' He finished his beer in one gulp.

Peter pushed the chaser towards Amos, held up his half-empty glass of beer and thought about ordering another. 'Here's to living dangerously,' he said.

CHAPTER THIRTY-TWO

Daily offices. 1975.

FRANK STYLES OCCUPIED THE DESK BESIDE ESTELLE COHEN. Not that she was often at her desk. He was sure Estelle had worms, although she said she was away from her desk so often because she was following up leads. It was extraordinary therefore that she was there when the deputy police chief walked into the editor's office.

'Help me,' she pleaded. She knew that it was going to be about her. Like every other investigative reporter in San Francisco, she was fascinated by the seamy underbelly of the city. Unlike most other investigative reporters in San Francisco, there was no limit to the lengths she would go to get an exclusive.

'What's wrong?' he said, glancing up from his typewriter.

'They're coming for me. I have a bad feeling, a really bad feeling.' She gulped down her coffee. 'I need a cigarette.'

'You don't smoke, Estelle.'

'I'm starting today. I'm already becoming a hard-core alcoholic. Drugs are next, I think.'

'You'll be fine. What could a girl like you have possibly done anyway?'

'I went too far, Frank. I wanted to get the inside story and scoop everyone else. I've screwed up.'

Frank pushed himself away from his desk. 'So, what did you do? Infiltrate the SFPD?'

The editor's door opened. A rotund man wearing a crumpled suit and almost no hair stood in the doorway. He waggled a finger at Estelle.

'Calihan wants me.'

'You'll be fine. You're getting worked up about nothing.'

She swallowed hard and walked towards the door as Calihan retreated into his office. 'Sir?'

'The deputy chief wants to talk to you. Be on your best behaviour,' Calihan replied curtly.

Deputy Chief Ahearn looked like he meant business: he wore his dress uniform and his face was flushed. He was known as a proponent of police anti-corruption. He was almost fanatical about it.

She tried to focus on his protruding nostrils hairs but for once her sense of humour failed her. 'Deputy Chief Ahearn?' She offered her hand. 'A pleasure.'

'Let's not beat around the bush. Deputy Chief Ahearn's here to talk to you about your conduct, Miss Cohen.'

She swallowed hard.

'There's a matter I want to raise with you,' Ahearn said.

Estelle remained mute. The less she said, the better.

'It concerns your relationship with Inspector Braun.'

'Inspector Braun? I know him. He's a friend of mine.'

'I have been informed that you were using your relationship with Inspector Braun to obtain confidential police intelligence from him.'

Estelle laughed.

'I'd keep quiet if I were you, Miss Cohen.'

'We had an intimate relationship, yes, but surely that's not a crime.'

'That may depend on the pillow talk. It appears that you wanted information on some murders in the city.'

'He was good in bed. That's all. Everything else I write about I work out by myself.'

'Is that so? Well, Inspector Braun was suspended today pending further investigations.'

'You're kidding?' She put her arm on the chair for support. 'But...' She took a deep breath. 'So what's going to happen now?'

Calihan sighed. 'The *Daily* has a reputation to uphold. We value our relationship with City Hall. I took a chance employing a girl for the news desk and I'm sad to say that our methods and yours are obviously incompatible. I'm terminating your employment as from this minute. You have time to clean out your desk. If you go quietly and don't stir up trouble, you'll receive a favourable reference,' he said. He didn't look the slightest bit sad.

'Wow. As Lee Harvey Oswald once said, I was the patsy.'

'Good day, Miss Cohen.' He went to the door and opened it.

Estelle composed herself and followed him. She turned around and squared up to him. 'One day, Mr Calihan, I'm going to come back here and sit in your office, and make this paper the best on the entire west coast, instead of the perennial bridesmaid it's always been,' she said as she stood in the doorway.

'I wouldn't count on that,' he replied. 'You'll be lucky to get a job in the mailroom.'

'We'll see.' She turned to the deputy chief as she left. 'A real pleasure. Honestly. Seeing justice in action.' She returned to her desk, trying to control her anger. She lashed out at her pen holder, scattering pens over the floor.

'It didn't go well, then,' Styles said as he stopped typing.

'Would you believe it? I've been fired, Frank.' She sat down at her desk and held her head in her hands.

'You want to talk about it?'

'Not now. We'll have a drink sometime.'

'I'm really sorry to hear that.'

'What am I going to do for a job? I just know Crusty Calihan will give me a bad reference.'

'Well, I know someone at the *New York Post*. I'll put in a good word for you.'

'I don't want to leave San Francisco. My family are already ashamed of me because I don't want to settle down with some schmuck, raise children and be a good Jewish housewife. Now this?'

'The change will be the making of you. I think this place is too conservative for you. New York will understand you,' he replied.

She stood up and embraced him. 'I'll repay you one day, Frank.'

'Just be true to yourself. That's your gift, Estelle. Don't take any *caca* from anyone.'

'You're the only person in the world who could say that and get away with it. You're too nice to be a reporter.'

'I'm probably too idealistic, that's true, but who else is going to tell the truth?'

She smiled and continued to empty out her desk. She then noticed an envelope lying on the keys of her typewriter. 'What's this?'

'It was dropped on your desk when you were in Crusty's office.'

'Could you...'

He slowly tore open the letter, pulled out the contents and looked at them briefly. 'What a sick, sick...' Frank dropped a photograph and covered his mouth.

'The son of a bitch! It must a victim of the Slasher. Good God, his...' She looked at the accompanying letter. 'He says that he'll kill and mutilate me if I continue to pursue him and criticise him publicly.'

'*A Christian soldier just doing God's work...* What a whacko,' Frank said.

'Maybe it's a good thing that I've lost my job,' she replied. 'I've been getting threats for a month, but nothing like this.' She put down the letter. 'You're right. Relocation may be the best thing for me. This guy means business. I don't think I have a choice.'

Chapter Thirty-Three

Estelle Cohen's house. 1975.

SOLOMON COHEN WAITED UNTIL EVERYONE HAD BEEN SERVED BY his wife Miriam before he spoke at dinner. He devoted each Sabbath to God, but Wednesday night was family night. Tonight's dinner was a family favourite: kosher corn brisket, cabbage and potatoes. Miriam's table was heavy with meat, pickles, salads and bread. She uncorked the wine and left it in the centre of the table.

'Solomon, the wine...' she said. 'Estelle, please serve the wine first.'

Their children, Aaron, Estelle and Nathan, sat patiently.

'Of course,' Solomon sighed. 'You tell me when you think I should talk.'

Estelle passed around the bottle of kosher wine. Once everyone had filled their glass, Solomon stood up. His speeches covered a variety of topics, anything from unfolding events in Israel to the increasing price of groceries. Sometimes the speeches drew on written notes, sometimes ad lib, but they often lasted ten long minutes, or until Miriam told him that dinner would be too cold to eat.

It had also become tradition that the children would try to guess what the topic would be. Usually they were wrong but tonight, as Estelle looked at the solemn look on her father's face, she could tell what tonight's talk would be about. Not even her mother would look at her. Solomon rose from his chair and talked about the importance of family values in society, working for a living and respecting those in authority, *yada, yada, yada*. After a few minutes, he took the bottle and topped up his glass.

'This has been a big week for our family. Congratulations, Nathan, for doing so well in your medical examinations. Soon you will be a specialist in paediatrics. *Mazel tov.*'

'Thanks, Pop.'

Solomon raised his glass. After repeating *l'chayim* everyone took a drink.

He continued. 'Aaron. Congratulations that you made partnership at your law firm last week. We are so proud of you. And soon you will be married too. *Mazel tov.*'

'Thanks, Papa.'

Solomon sat down. 'I'm hungry. Let's eat,' he said.

Everyone started to eat except Estelle, who finished off her glass of wine. 'And how did I make you proud this week?'

'At your age, you should have your own family already. Be quiet and eat,' he replied.

Estelle watched her father look past her when he reached for the bowl of pickles. She knew that he knew she'd lost her job. In his eyes, unemployment was shameful.

'Who told you?' she asked.

Miriam sighed.

'Don't worry about it, Mama,' Estelle replied, 'I'm over trying to impress my father. He doesn't notice.'

'Yes. We don't need to talk about it,' Solomon said.

'No. We don't, do we, Papa?'

'Not now, Estelle,' Nathan grumbled, taking a heap of potatoes.

Estelle put down her knife and fork. 'Why don't you shut up, Nathan? I'm sick of you always telling me how to behave. All I've heard all of my life is don't swear, don't drink, don't go out with people we don't approve of. Oh yes, and be quiet.'

'Don't talk to your brother like that. You should respect him,' said Solomon. 'After me, he is the head of the house.'

'Why? Because he's male? Or because he's a doctor and I'm not?'

Solomon stood up.

'Solomon, please,' said Miriam. 'Sit down. Eat.'

'You,' he said to Estelle, 'are a disgrace to this family.'

'Am I? Really?' she replied. 'Yet, I always thought I was just in the way—an inconvenience—because I wasn't born a boy.'

'You brought disgrace on this family when you decided to be a trashy reporter. All you do is mix with criminals and prostitutes.

And you write lies about decent people. It is an unworthy occupation.'

Estelle laughed. 'Funny, you can't go a day without reading a newspaper.'

'I read only good, honest newspapers, written by good, honest journalists, not the *Daily*. Did my daughter get a job in a good, honest paper? No. She gets a job with imbeciles and criminals. I said, it is not a job for a well-brought-up girl, but your mother insisted. Now I've been proved right.'

'I always did well at school and university. I was the first female reporter at the *Daily*. Did any of you ever congratulate me?'

'It is not your place to be congratulated,' Solomon said.

'Only Mama did. Did you ever toast me, Papa? Never. Poor Mama.' She sat down and blew her nose.

Solomon placed his hand across Miriam. 'You will leave her alone.' He turned to Estelle. 'I told you that becoming a reporter would only end in dishonour, didn't I tell you that?'

'Okay, so I was asked to leave the *Daily*.'

'Asked to leave? You were fired. None of our family has ever been fired. Not ever. How do you expect me to show my face at temple again?'

'That is overstating things, don't you think, Solomon?' Miriam cut in. 'The Goldsteins have a son who is a drug addict and they still go to temple. Estelle's not a drug addict.'

'Be quiet, Miriam. That is the Goldsteins, not us. We are a family of intellectuals, doctors, rabbis, lawyers. We have always been respected. My daughter can't even keep a job at a trashy paper. It's shameful.'

Estelle poured herself another glass of wine.

'Shameful Estelle, that's me. Then there's Nathan, always the good son. And Aaron, who really wanted to be a film-maker but bowed to the pressure.'

'Why bring that up?' Aaron replied. 'I only thought about it when I was fifteen. There's no future in films. Ask Papa.'

'I'm sure Francis Ford Coppola heard the same speech from his dad.'

'Enough!' Solomon shouted. 'All of you!'

Estelle rose out of her chair and drained the remainder of her wine. 'You all live according to Papa's rules. You don't agree with them, but you still live by them. Mama plays the piano at a concert in Munich before she meets Papa, and then, poof, suddenly her career's over. Ever asked yourselves why? Because Papa didn't approve. All artists are criminals and prostitutes.'

'That is not true, Estelle,' said Miriam.

'Poor Mama. You've always tried to make a life for Papa, but never for yourself.'

Solomon wiped his face with his napkin, rose out of his chair, walked down the end of the table and pulled Estelle out of her chair. 'Your mother and I survived the holocaust so we'd make a better life, a better life for our children, and this is how you repay us.'

'Not that again. I didn't cause the holocaust, remember? I'm not going to live my life according to what happened in the holocaust and what the Nazis did to my family. I am not going to wear that burden.'

Solomon raised his hand and slapped her across the face. She stood rigidly and rubbed her face as Miriam averted her eyes.

'This is not the first time you've hit a woman in this house, is it?'

'You're nothing but a troublemaker. No wonder you became a gutter reporter.' Solomon raised his hand to hit her again. Estelle stared at him and prepared herself for the impact but Aaron grabbed Solomon's arm before he brought it down.

'No, Papa,' Aaron said as he led his father away. 'Enough!'

Solomon pulled out of Aaron's grip and confronted her again. 'Get out of here,' he roared, 'and don't come back here until you learn some respect. This is my house. I decide who lives here.' He looked around the table with fire in his eyes. 'And the same will happen to anyone else here who disobeys me.'

'Fine. I'm moving to New York anyway, so you'll never have to see me again.'

'What are you doing, Solomon? How can you throw out your own daughter?' Miriam reasoned. 'Estelle, sit down!'

'Watch that you don't go too far, Miriam,' said Solomon. 'I do this for her own good. How else will she learn respect?'

Miriam turned to Estelle. 'Papa's a good man, really. I'm sure it's not too late for you to apologise.'

'For what? For being true to my dreams? Or for his foul temper?'

'Once you go through that door, you are dead to us from that moment on.'

'Fine with me. Don't bother tearing your clothes to mourn me.'

Estelle ran upstairs to pack. From below, her father yelled that she did not own even the clothes on her back. She put back the suitcase and picked up an overnight bag and her pocket book instead. Moments later, her mother appeared at her bedroom door.

'I'm sorry for your father. He'll cool down soon, he always does.'

'Mama, you might be able to put up with him but I can't. He's an ogre and I just can't stand him anymore.'

'He's your father,' Miriam said, dabbing her eyes.

'That's an accident of biology. This was coming; we both know that. It was only a matter of time before I left.'

'Yes, but not like this.'

Estelle threw her makeup, a change of clothes and some documents in the overnight bag and zipped it up. 'You and the boys can keep making excuses for him, but I can't. Be well, Mama. Don't take any more shit from that man.'

'I love you, Estelle,' she replied. 'Be safe and write to me. I'll send your things when you're settled. And wherever you go, make sure you observe Shabbat.'

'I love you too, Mama,' Estelle cried, 'but I can't live with him—with them—any longer.'

She ran down the stairs and stood at the door. 'See?' she said. 'I've taken nothing but what is mine.'

'Nathan, open the door!'

Estelle watched her brother do as he was told. He disgusted her. They all did. Solomon took hold of one of her arms and flung her outside, slamming the door after her.

She brushed the dust off her skirt and looked at the hole in her stockings. 'I'll prove I'm better than all of you,' she whispered as she slowly lifted herself up. 'One day.'

Chapter Thirty-Four

Stella's office. 1993.

'So, what's the news on Jackie Hamel?' Peter asked as he watched Stella mop up the coffee she had spilt all over her desk.

'Shit! I've become so clumsy lately.' She bent over to get a tissue out of her bag and teetered. She took a deep breath. 'She's improving all the time. She's out of intensive care now.'

'Great news. Do you want a hand?'

'No. I'm fine. Thanks for making peace with Raoul. Have you ever thought of going into the diplomatic corps?'

'I couldn't do the sucking-up-to-tyrants stuff.'

'Neither could I. Journalism was my only option.'

'He obviously still loves Jackie,' Peter said.

'Hmm. So where are you at with the church investigation?' She sat down and sipped what was left of her coffee.

'I'll flick the funerals to Mulroy. I don't think I could stand it. I'll follow what's happening at the church.'

'You won't get anywhere near it.'

'You know, I have my ways of getting around that.'

'You want a break from the crime beat?'

'No, I'll stick with it. I'm following up some contacts. The porn industry counts as crime.'

'Where angels fear to tread, Peter Clancy likes to dive straight in and swim around.' Stella put down her cup and rubbed her head. 'My head is really hurting, Pete...' She grimaced as she spoke. The words had barely left her lips when she slumped over the desk.

'Stella!' He rushed around the desk. 'What's wrong?'

She raised her head and blinked. She rubbed her eyes. 'I can't see! Peter, I can't see.'

Peter flicked the button on the intercom. 'Beverley. Quick. We need an ambulance. Something's wrong with Stella. She's in a bad way. An ambulance. Now.'

Stella sank to the floor. 'Help me. Mama?'

He knelt down and rolled Stella onto her side. 'Stella! Stella!' He shook her. He felt for a pulse. 'Why didn't you go to the bloody doctor like I told you to?'

Chapter Thirty-Five

UCSF Medical Center, San Francisco.

The neurological ward at the UCSF Medical Center at Mount Zion was entirely soulless. There was nothing in the waiting area for Frank and Peter to look at other than each other, and they'd already spent half a minute doing that. Peter was bored and anxious. His anxiety made him even more bored. He'd shared the last of Frank's mint candy, and now there was absolutely nothing for him to do.

Frank reached into his pockets, looking for a diversion. 'Do you think she's going to be all right?' he asked.

Peter was about to say, *how the fuck do I know? Do I look like a neurosurgeon to you?* but he curbed his tongue. 'I hope so. It's going to be a lot quieter at the office, if she decides to leave us.'

Frank smiled. 'Yes, Stella has always written her own tunes.'

'Do you know if she has any family? She said she was brought up here, but I've never met her family. Are they dead?'

'I don't know. I always got the feeling that there was some bad blood between them. I've known Stella forever. I've known her since she was Estelle Cohen.'

'Estelle Cohen?'

A nurse swept into the waiting room. 'Are you Peter and Frank?'

'Yes,' said Frank. 'Yes we are.'

'If you follow me, you can see Ms Reimers now.'

'Is she okay?' asked Peter as he followed the nurse along a corridor, Frank trailing behind him.

'She's fine. She asked to talk to the two of you.'

Stella was cursing at the television when they entered her room. She elevated her bed when she saw them and gave them a lopsided smile. Peter noticed she looked pale.

'Thank God you're here,' she beamed. 'There's nothing on television and they don't serve booze in this place. I've only been here half a day and already I'm bored shitless.'

Peter leaned over to kiss Stella on the cheek.

'What are you doing? You never kiss me,' she laughed.

Peter straightened up. 'I was being polite.'

'I've noticed that you only get kisses when someone wants something or you're ill.'

'So, no flowers?' Frank looked around the room.

'I hate flowers. They die and mess up the place. Take a seat.'

They grabbed two chairs and sat close to Stella's bed.

'So, what's happening?' Frank asked.

'I had a CAT scan. Peter, did you bring your flask?'

Peter patted his coat. 'For all emergencies and situations that require alcoholic sustenance.'

'Well, get it out. I need a drink. I've been through shit today.'

Peter glanced at Frank, who looked like a he was about to run away and confess to the contraband scotch.

'Why are you looking at Frank? He's not going to tell anyone.'

Peter took out his silver flask and poured small amounts into three plastic cups.

Stella took a sip first. 'I needed that.'

Frank took the cup but didn't drink.

'Oh, for fuck's sake, Frank, I know what you're thinking,' said Stella. 'No, I probably shouldn't, but this isn't going to stop me having one. When have I ever listened to those in authority?'

Peter downed his in one, while Frank sipped slowly. Peter couldn't tell if he was savouring the liquid or forcing it down.

'So, what did the doctor say?' Peter asked.

Stella took another sip. 'Oh, nothing much. He said I have a brain. Which, as you can imagine, came as a great relief to me. Oh, and he said I also have a small brain tumour,' she added softly.

'What?' said Peter. 'Is it malignant?'

'Possibly.'

'That explains the headaches you've been having. Shit, I wish you would've checked it out earlier.'

'Okay. Stop riding me. I have a life here and a job to do. There's more to my life than a frigging brain tumour.' She finished her drink. 'Barman. Another one. Neat. Stat.'

Peter poured Stella another.

Frank looked at his hands. 'So, what's the prognosis?' he asked.

'I need an operation fairly quickly.'

'And?'

'They give me six months if I don't have it,' Stella replied.

'So, you're going to have it, right?' Peter said.

'Well, the operation has a lot of negatives attached to it.'

'Like what?'

'There's a good chance I'll have a speech deficit or I won't be able to walk properly again. That's if I survive the operation.'

'I think you should have it. What's it matter if you can't talk? At least we'll be able to get a bloody word in,' Peter grinned.

'We support your choice and we're here to help you with whatever you need.' Frank finished his drink. He put out his cup. 'Another little one.'

Peter raised his eyebrows and refilled all three cups. 'So, when do you have to decide by?'

'I've already decided,' said Stella, toying with her drink. 'I'm not having the operation. I'm getting out of here tomorrow whether they like it or not, and I'm coming back to work. I'm going to work for as long as I can. Okay with you, Frank?'

'Sure. Of course. For as long as you can.'

'This isn't going to get in the way of us shooting for number one.'

'Stella, you drive me nuts sometimes. Just have the operation,' Peter said.

'Hey, we're all going to die so get used to it,' Stella said as she shifted up the bed. 'Isn't it sort of good to know when? You can make plans. To paraphrase Woody Allen, I'd just rather not be there when it happens.'

'I have to give it to you, you're the gutsiest person I've ever known,' Frank said.

'Are you going to tell your family?' Peter ventured.

'My family and I parted ways long ago. I haven't spoken to them or seen them in decades and I wouldn't even know if they were still alive. The *Daily* is my family and you two guys are my brothers. Let's leave it at that.' She took a drink.

'The other day, in your office...' Peter began.

'What about it?' Stella snapped back.

'I heard you call out to your mother for help.'

'I don't remember. I haven't had anything to do with her for a long time.' She sighed. 'There are important things to do. So much to do, so little time.'

A nurse came into the room and looked at them. She placed her hands on her hips. 'What do you think you're doing? You're not allowed to drink alcohol in the hospital!'

Stella sized her up, drained the cup and snapped it back onto the table. 'It's self-initiated medication for those who are about to die. So piss off,' she snapped.

CHAPTER THIRTY-SIX

The Ten Commandments Church.

PETER PARKED THE CAR ACROSS THE ROAD FROM THE TEN Commandments Church. He reached into his cunning-kit bag, and pulled out a wig and a moustache.

'What the f...' Mulroy exclaimed when he noticed Peter slipping the wig onto his head.

'Well, it looks like they're having a party in there, so I'm going to it as a porn star.'

'You look more pinhead than porn star. You enjoy looking like a fool?' Mulroy suppressed a laugh. 'I think a Van Dyke would look better on you.'

'And with glasses and a white wig, I'd look like Colonel Tom Parker. I'll remember that for next time.'

'Why don't we just try going as reporters?'

'If you had your brain switched on, Mulroy, you'd remember that I went to this church. I don't want to be recognised.'

'So then why don't you let me ask the questions and you stay here? That seems the easier option.'

'You're the protégé and I'm the teacher. Why would I do that?'

'I thought we were colleagues. I've been in this game nearly as long as you.'

'This isn't the time for artistic differences. I'm ready.'

'Great. So what's your porn star name?' Mulroy chuckled.

'I'll ask the questions. Ted Shaftstein sound like a good porn name to you?'

'I was thinking Fabian Fellatio. More Italian, less Semitic.'

Peter laughed. 'You're clear on the brief? What are their reactions about the massacre and are they going to open the church again.'

'Sounds good.'

Peter darted across the road and walked towards the heavy metal gates which protected the church complex, closely followed by Mulroy. A crowd of parishioners were huddled there, praying aloud. A boy aged about fifteen with white-blond hair led the prayers. Peter recognised him as the Gattings' son.

Mulroy and Peter stood away from the crowd, listening to them pray for the reopening of the church. One woman fainted during the prayers and two men carried her away to a car. As they passed, one of them glanced across at them, as Peter pretended to fiddle with his cell phone. A beefy man walked up to them.

'What's your business here?' he barked.

'I'm Peter Clancy and this is Chad Mulroy from the *Daily*. We just want to ask about your recovery from the shooting.'

'You have no business here.' He pushed Peter backwards.

'Hey, hey. Back off. We're from the press. Don't touch us!' Peter returned like with like.

'You've got no right to come near us,' the man shouted.

'Okay, no problemo. We'll leave as soon as we get an answer. Is the church going to reopen?' Mulroy asked the man.

'Leave us alone,' he shouted, as he continued to shove Peter. 'You've brought the devil with you.'

'Come on, Mulroy, let's get out of here,' said Peter.

The boy looked at the developing melee and frowned. 'Brother Thomas,' he called as the crowd parted to let him pass.

Brother Thomas obeyed and stood aside, head bowed slightly.

The boy approached Peter. 'I'm Elias Gatting. I'm the new pastor of The Ten Commandments Church.'

'You're the son of Zachary and Gretchen Gatting? My deepest sympathy,' Peter replied.

'That's very thoughtful, but there's no need for grief. My parents are now in eternal peace enjoying the bounty of a kind and loving God.'

Peter thought that the boy was either well-schooled or simply regurgitating his father's favourite platitudes. 'You're pretty young for a preacher, aren't you? A little soon to be assuming leadership of the church, I would have thought. Shouldn't you be going to school?'

'Not when the Lord tells you that you have to take the reins and lead your people. How old was David when he slew Goliath? Sadly, my parents were assassinated, but now they dwell in the house of the Lord.'

A few in the crowd shouted, 'Amen.'

'And the Lord has called on me to carry on their great work. Their work must continue.'

'So, the church will reopen?' Mulroy asked.

'Yes, it will. The Lord has told me that it will open in the next month.'

'Won't it be sad to go back into that church? A lot of pain there, isn't there?' Peter asked.

'There are no bad memories in the house of the Lord. The death of my parents was ordained. It is only a tragedy to us here on Earth; it is how the Lord planned it. They have been sacrificed, but their message will be stronger.'

'What do you think of the Merrells?'

Elias turned away and Peter thought he wiped a tear from his eye. When he turned back, he was coolly composed. 'The Merrells were sent by the devil and evil, anti-God, gay lovers. They thought they could wipe us out but we are stronger now. The devil's work will not conquer us,' he shouted. 'Amen, God!'

'Amen,' the crowd replied.

'The Merrells are burning in hell right now and will be burning for all eternity.'

A man wearing dark glasses and a suit pushed quickly through the crowd towards them. He was tall with a crew cut. 'Brother Elias,' he snapped, 'why are you talking to the media? You have specific instructions not to talk to the media. I'll handle that.'

'Yes, Brother Alexander,' Elias replied softly as he retreated back into the crowd.

'I'm Peter Clancy and this is Chad Mulroy. We're from the *Daily*. Who are you?'

'I'm Brother Alexander Shafer, communications officer for the church. You should have contacted me for comment.'

'Is that so? We were just passing and saw the crowd outside the church. Well then, Brother Alexander, have you any comments about the church's reopening or about the Merrells?'

'The *Daily*? As I said to your editor... What was her name? They were part of a conspiracy of homosexuals to wipe us out. What they have done has only made us stronger. These gay activists will be judged not only in heaven but also on earth.'

'How do you intend to fight back?' Peter asked.

'I have no further comment. If you think we're going to lay down and die, you're very wrong. You and your faggot friends are in for one hell of a fight. Now you can leave the premises or I can call the police.' Shafer removed his sunglasses, signalling the end of the interview and for two brutes to move towards them.

'Nice talking to you.' Peter took hold of Mulroy's arm and pushed him behind. 'No need for the rock apes, by the way. We're on public property.'

'You shouldn't be here, Mr Clancy,' Shafer said. 'Anything could happen. No one would even know you're missing.'

One of the thugs swung at Peter and connected just enough to knock him off balance. He fell on one knee. Mulroy took hold of Peter and pulled him towards the road. The thug swung again and hit Mulroy in the neck. Dazed, he and Peter scampered towards their car.

'You don't want to upset my friends, Mr Clancy,' Shafer called after them.

Peter unlocked the car and they fell into the front seats, locking the doors behind them.

'These people are really wired up differently, aren't they? Bunch of thugs.' Peter flexed his knee. 'That hurts. Pricks.'

'I don't really feel like dying for a story, though,' said Mulroy.

'See,' said Peter, swinging his legs around to take the pressure off his knee, 'that's the difference between first and third, average and exceptional, you and me.' He doubted Mulroy would ever make the grade. He didn't have enough mongrel in him. 'You have to be prepared to take risks. While you're sitting there licking your wounds, I'm already planning my next stoush.' He took out his cell and punched in Amos's number.

Chapter Thirty-Seven

Bayside Journal offices.

AMOS HUNG AROUND THE OFFICE FOR ANOTHER HALF AN HOUR before deciding to call it quits for the day. There were still two staff members there besides Clyde, an African American security guard. Clyde had become a permanent fixture in the office ever since the demonstration. He was big and fearsome, and the best defensive tackle since Joe Greene.

'Time to go home, everyone,' Amos called. 'Even dedication has an end.'

'Do you want to be escorted to your car, Mr Amos?' Clyde asked.

'Not tonight. Although the others may,' he replied.

'Well, just call out if you see anyone suspicious.'

'If I see anyone, I'll scream like a banshee.'

'Mr Amos, you're always good for a joke,' Clyde chuckled.

Amos turned down an alleyway after he left the office, heading towards a secure carpark where the Mustang was parked. He had only gone a short distance down the laneway when he saw two hooded men striding towards him. One was carrying a metal bar.

'This isn't the fucking time, boys,' he said as he turned around. 'I've had a long day at work and I'm not in the mood.'

Two more hooded men confronted him as he tried to head back to the street. These two were both carrying metal bars. As they moved towards him, Amos pulled out a can of mace from his jacket and held it in his outstretched hand. 'Give it your best shot,' he yelled at the men as they ran at him from both sides. One of them swung his metal bar and knocked the can of mace out of Amos's hand. Another one swung and hit him across the back. He fell to the ground.

'Die, faggot,' one of them shouted, lifting the bar over his head. 'Time to die.'

'I hope you pricks catch AIDS from me,' Amos slurred. He braced for the impact. He knew this was probably how it would end. He closed his eyes and held his hands over his face and waited. It felt like ages had passed when he heard the first gunshot, followed by another. He opened his eyes just as Clyde fired a third into the air. He lifted himself up on one elbow and saw the men running down the alley, with Clyde in hot pursuit. Clyde followed them just far enough to see them disappear and then he returned to Amos, who was trying to get to his feet.

'Are you hurt, Mr Amos?'

'Of course not. If those cowards think they're going to stop me getting out the message, they're very, very wrong.'

'Did you recognise them?'

'Yes, didn't you? They're the ignorant and the scared. You remember them, don't you?'

'Remember them? They never go away. You and me, Mr Amos, we're the same, only different. Folks like us just want to live our lives in peace, just like all the other folk. I wish we could consign men like them to history.'

Amos took Clyde's hand and struggled to his feet. The bruises would heal. 'Well, it's up to us to make it happen, Clyde. If we all sit on our hands and wait for Superman to come along, cowards like those, they only grow stronger.'

Chapter Thirty-Eight

Daily conference room.

Peter pulled out a chair for Stella as she entered the conference room on Frank's arm. She had her game face on, even if her gait was still a little unsteady.

Shapiro came forward to give her a bunch of flowers, while everyone else stood back and watched. She threw an incredulous look around the room and placed the flowers on the table.

'What in hell's name is this all about?' she asked. 'Did I wear my frigging tiara to work again?'

'Well, you're just out of hospital and we're making things nice for you,' Shapiro said.

'You usually do all this for me?' She sat down at the head of the conference table. Peter pushed her chair in as she scowled.

'No but...'

'Then enough already. And you go back to your seat, Peter.'

Frank cleared his throat. 'As you all know, Stella has been in hospital and is...' he began.

'It's all right, Frank. Stop fussing. Here's the lowdown. I've been diagnosed with a terminal brain tumour. What does that mean to you and the paper? Nothing really. Work goes on as usual and don't expect me to give you an easy ride. That ain't gonna happen. The only thing that you should worry about is the fact that we're still number two in circulation.'

'Surely that'll go up because of our coverage of the church massacre,' said Mulroy.

'We can only hope, but I wouldn't count on it. There was a lot of national attention from the television networks. That would have splintered the market. Anyway, the figures come out in another month.'

'Since we're talking about The Ten Commandments Church, I have to report that there have been more developments within the church,' Peter said.

'I've just got off the phone from your dear Brother Alexander,' Stella said, 'and he's not a happy man.'

'He wanted to let the dogs loose on us the other day.'

'He called to tell me that you and Mulroy assaulted some of the church members.' She added, 'No doubt, he was hoping we'd back off if he pushed hard enough.'

Peter laughed. 'Oh yeah? We were assaulted and we have the injuries to prove it. I hope you told him he'd receive no mercy.'

Stella looked at Peter, stony-faced. 'Actually, I told him that our reporters will leave the church alone.'

'You didn't!'

She flexed her fingers and glared at him. 'My call, Peter. And yes! I did! Where are we going with this, Peter?'

'Well, there's the Gattings' kid, Elias, who has come forward as the new preacher. That seems a little freaky to me,' he continued.

'He's young, I agree. That's not that unusual in a church of this type,' Frank rejoined.

'He incited the faithful to violence and then Raoul was assaulted last night. You think that's a coincidence?'

'I think you're fishing for a story,' Stella said.

'There's a link. I know it,' Peter said. 'I think Jackie Hamel might know more. I say we wait until she's talking, and then we give her an incentive payment.'

'Look, there was a story in it. You got two really strong pieces out of the church but that's that. Sadly, it ended in tragedy. Everything's been said and people are moving on. It's time we did the same.'

'You think that if we delve any further into the church, we could appear unsympathetic and jeopardise our readership and Raoul's cause. I say you're wrong.'

'I think you need to get yourself some respect and a strong cup of coffee,' she responded. 'Now, drop the church.'

He got up from his chair. 'I get it. Apparently upsetting people comes at a cost you're not prepared to pay.'

'That's enough, Peter,' said Stella. 'Take a break.'

He picked up the phone the moment he got back to his desk and called Amos. He respected Stella but he wasn't the kind of reporter to ignore a hunch.

'So kind of you to call,' said Amos. 'You heard about last night's fracas?'

'You're okay?'

'Well, I've had worse. This isn't going to slow down Raoul Amos.'

'That's good.' Peter scratched his head with the end of his pencil. 'I'm going completely off-piste here, and this is between you and me for the moment. I want to keep looking into what's happening at the church.'

'You're on the same wavelength as me. Finally.'

'Have you ever heard of Alexander Shafer? He calls himself the communications officer for the church.'

'No, I haven't.'

'He's never called you?'

Amos laughed. 'Churches like that don't call us. They just put rocks through our window or wait for us in dark alleys. They would never talk to us. Why are you interested in him?'

'He's a sinister character. He doesn't mind unleashing the dogs on you and he loves running to the media.'

'I suppose that's his job. He's sounds no different from Gatting. I wonder if they poached him from another church to get them back on their feet.'

'I thought The Ten Commandments Church was Gatting's baby. Is it part of a network?'

'Gatting was connected to an affiliation of churches with their own television channel, their own publishing house et cetera.'

'Where did Gatting figure in the affiliation?' he asked.

'He was a minor preacher. The major preachers got airtime. Apparently Gatting was pretty pissed off that he wasn't at that level.'

'This is what Jackie told you?'

'Well, she was a trusted insider.'

'Do you think she knows anything else?'

'I guess you may have to ask her that once she's fully conscious.'

Peter broke the pencil clean in half and threw it into the waste-paper basket. 'You know her. Do you think she'd do an interview?'

'We'll see. She's been through a lot so it's tiny steps at the moment. Who knows what she'll remember.'

'You'll let me know when she comes around?'

'I don't know if I should, Peter. She's been through enough shit.'

'I accept that but...'

Amos hung up. Peter replaced the handset on the receiver and looked up to find Stella hovering over him.

'Sounds to me like it didn't go so well with Raoul.' She grabbed a chair and sat next to Peter. 'I think you're pushing this too hard at the moment. Just back off until things settle down. What's the hurry anyway?'

'I want to destroy this church.'

'As I suspected, it's personal. You know better than to let your feelings affect the story.'

'Not my feelings. I don't like organisations that impose their views on others or force people to believe them.'

'That's coming from someone who was raised Catholic?'

'It's not that. I firmly believe the church is planning a big come-back.'

'I think you'll find that they are finished. Alexander Shafer is all smoke and mirrors.'

'Do you want to make a bet on it?'

'I don't bet, Peter, because I'm usually right and I hate taking money from friends.'

'Okay. We'll see.'

Stella smiled. 'Do you want a few days off? Explore California. The only sights you've seen are the office, the church and your apartment. You'll love Napa. How about it?'

'No. I'm fine. If you can work in your condition, I'm right.' He waited for Stella to go on the attack. Instead, she placed a hand on his shoulder.

'I'm scared, Peter.'

'I know. What can I do to help?'

'You said I called for my mother. I'm still thinking about that.'

'Maybe it's time to make peace with your parents?'

'You didn't with your mother.'

Peter took her hand and patted it. 'And that's precisely why I want you to.'

CHAPTER THIRTY-NINE

Dragon's Den.

JERRY BELINSKI SCORED THE TABLE CLOSEST TO THE DRAGON'S Den's kitchen so he wouldn't miss out on his favourite dim sum. He smiled when the tiny straw basket arrived on the table and the waitress lifted off the cover. Once the steam evaporated, he pulled the basket towards him and peered in. The dumplings snuggled together, all plump and satiny white, like the sweetest triplet babies.

'I've been waiting for these all week.' He tucked into his second serving of shrimp *fun gao*. 'How's it going with you?'

'Well I'm still investigating The Ten Commandments Church but I'm not really getting anywhere.' Peter aimed his chopsticks at a pork bun and speared it. He lifted it back into his bowl.

'I thought you'd be done and dusted with that.'

'It ain't over until the drunk reporter sings.' Peter took a sip of his beer and a bite of the bun. 'I think they're planning something. Everyone at work says I'm wrong but I trust Raoul's judgement and my hunch.'

'We have no intel suggesting that. We've spoken to Elias Gatting and he just wants to get the church back on its feet.'

'Strange kid. Looks like he overdosed on too much crackpot religion.'

'We're still piecing together the events leading up to the shooting.'

'Was David Merrell or his mother gay?'

'Not as far as we can tell.'

'Do you think they acted alone?'

'They appeared to have a plan, but as for others being involved, I don't think so. It's hard to understand why a devoted son and mother would decide to go on a shooting spree,' Belinski replied.

'I met some weird people there. Weird people do violent things sometimes. Then the church blames the gays. Go figure.' He dissected the rest of his bun to allow the pork to cool. 'So you'll be wrapping it up soon, I expect?'

'I'd say so.'

'I'm wondering if you can do me a favour?' he asked.

'You want me to look up someone's file, don't you?'

Peter smiled sheepishly. 'I'm wondering if you can find anything on Alexander Shafer? He's the new church spokesman.'

'Yeah, I've talked to him. He was with Elias Gatting during an interview. Military type, not particularly friendly. He calls himself a close friend of the family.'

'I'd like to know a bit more about him,' Peter said.

'I guess I could do an inter-agency search and see if anything comes up.'

'Thanks. I owe you one.'

'You owe me lots, buddy,' Jerry replied. He waved the waitress down and asked for some green tea. 'I was looking at the Slasher files again.'

'With everything that's been happening, I'd almost forgotten about that.'

'I had another look at Anthony Mayberry's statement.'

'The guy who survived?'

'This Susan Banks he met in the club called herself a private investigator,' Jerry said.

'Working for a wife checking on a gay husband? But kind of obvious, isn't it, going into the club? Don't they usually take photos from a car outside?'

'Precisely. So, I looked up an old directory. Her name wasn't on it. Not anywhere. Plenty of Susan Bankses, but no such PI.'

'She wasn't a private investigator and Susan Banks probably wasn't her real name,' Peter reasoned.

Jerry took a sip of the tea and winced. 'Man, that's hot!' He shook his head. 'I can't figure out why Susan Banks followed Mayberry and this Richard guy outside.'

'Unless she had a suspicion that Mayberry was in danger.'

'Or she wanted to kill two gay guys?'

'Which really leads us nowhere, doesn't it? What about this guy, Tony Mayberry?'

'He called himself a travelling salesman on his statement. Said he had no next of kin. He really didn't say anything.'

'You looked him up?' Peter asked.

'There wasn't any such name on our records. Unless we get a death-bed confession or some ground-breaking new information, we stay at first base.'

Peter sniggered. 'And I could see a book in this.'

'Yes, I know you're keen to solve it.'

'I'm keen to solve everything, but lack of information just keeps getting in my way.' He pushed his bowl away and wiped his mouth. 'You still have an open file on the Zodiac Killer, don't you?'

'Of course.'

'Well, I'll leave it as an open file then,' Peter replied. 'Further enquiries pending.'

CHAPTER FORTY

Daily offices.

PETER KNOCKED ON STELLA'S DOOR. WHEN SHE DIDN'T ANSWER, he opened it a crack to check that she was okay. The light was off and the office was empty. As he closed the door again, Frank Styles walked by.

'She won't be in until around lunchtime,' he said.

'She's okay, isn't she?'

'Stella had to go to a specialist appointment.'

Peter looked uncomfortable. 'Can I have a talk to you, in private?'

'Yeah. Sure. Do you want to get a coffee first?'

'Sure.'

Peter had never been in Frank's office before; he only ever saw him in Stella's. Sometimes he wondered if Frank even had an office of his own. Frank's was typical of an editor's office anywhere: a large, heavy wooden desk covered with pieces of paper, family photographs and awards. On the wall were framed photographs of Frank with various celebrities and politicians who had passed through San Francisco over his career.

'You've certainly had an interesting career, Frank,' Peter remarked as he looked at a photograph of Frank shaking hands with Ronald Reagan alongside a beaming Nancy.

'Journalism has been good to me. I have no regrets. You must have picked up a few souvenirs in your time,' he replied. 'Take a seat.'

'I've moved around so much lately that I think I've lost most of it. Maybe I need to get a job that comes with an office, but I'd sooner just have a desk and be out on the road getting stories.'

'Don't be scared of promotion. Imagine all the experience you could pass on,' Frank replied. He took a quick glance at a stack of papers on his desk.

'Imagine all the stress,' said Peter, as he followed Frank's gaze.

'So what did you want to talk to me about?'

'Well, you may think I'm meddling, but I think it would be good for Stella to see her family again. I want to find them for her.'

'Have you asked her?'

'She's receptive to it.'

'Receptive? That's a little vague, isn't it?'

'I think she should see them before she... It would be good for her to make peace with them,' he replied.

Frank looked shaken. 'She's been a good friend in a profession where you don't make many friends. I don't want to think about losing her.'

'Nor do I. I'm hoping that they will be able to persuade her to have the operation,' Peter added.

'Now I see where you're headed. But she hasn't seen or spoken to them in years. It may not be a happy reunion.'

'I'd like to try.'

Frank was silent for a moment. 'I'll tell you what I know but it's up to you from there on. I don't want to be in the firing line if it doesn't work out. You know how Stella can get.'

'She'll only yell at me until she runs out of breath. Do you know who they are and perhaps where they live?' Peter asked.

'I met them only once. She took me home for dinner. Her parents' names were... Let me think... Abraham? No, Solomon. Solomon and Miriam Cohen.'

'Stella and you weren't...?'

'What? Stella and I? No. Never. Always good friends. Even if we were dating other people we'd go out on the town together. She was always a lot of fun.'

'So you went around to their house.'

'Back then, she called herself Estelle Cohen. Reimers was her husband's name.'

'Stella was once married? It boggles the mind.'

'The Cohens were a prosperous family in the nice part of San Francisco. Her dad was an investment banker, mom stayed at home, and her two brothers, well, one was a doctor and the other was a lawyer. They were all there. It was awkward. Her father was very strict. Orthodox Jewish. Old school. Authoritarian. I couldn't say what he made of me. To be honest, I couldn't wait to get out of there.'

'I find it hard to imagine Stella having a normal upbringing.'

'I don't think it was really normal, not as we imagine normal. Her father was very disappointed that she had decided to become a reporter. He likened it to prostitution.'

'Only we get paid less,' Peter chuckled.

'Apparently, they had lots of arguments over it.' He continued, 'Stella was very close to her mother. She had a lot of time for her mother.'

'So what happened to bring it all to a head?'

'She lost her job at the *Daily*. The editor...'

'Crusty Calihan?' Peter asked.

'You've heard of him?'

'She's mentioned him in passing.'

'He didn't like her methods and he didn't like women, period. So he fired her.'

'Like that?'

'Stella was always ambitious. She rubbed Crusty and his band of chauvinists up the wrong way a few too many times.' He cleared his throat and took a drink of coffee. 'It was different times then. After that, she went to New York.'

'No wonder she's tough. And you stayed in touch with her after she went to New York?'

'Always.'

'So where do I start looking for her family?' Peter asked.

'The Cohens were a prominent family, so you can probably start at B'nai B'rith. They may be able to help you,' he replied.

'Great. I'll do that.'

'Don't get your hopes up and don't mention to Stella that you've talked to me.'

'Will do.' He caught sight of a small framed photograph of a girl next to a picture of Frank and his family. 'That's not a photo of her, is it, when she was young?' He laughed as he picked it up.

'I'm surprised you could recognise her. That's a long time ago.'

'Her face hasn't changed but I'm glad she got rid of the Afro.'

'It was all the fashion back then,' Frank replied.

'Is that you with her?'

'Yes, fifty pounds leaner and with fifty per cent more hair.'

'But there are different names written here, on the photo...' He took a closer look. 'Thompson Trembath?'

'That's me. It was a joke between us. They were our joke aliases; in case we ever got into a tight situation... I was quite a bit older than her, you know, but we were both still young and stupid back then...'

'And she was...' Peter squinted to make out the scrawl. 'Is that an S?'

'That's right. I think you'll find it says—'

'Susan Banks?'

'That's right,' said Frank as Peter felt for the chair. 'She was Susan Banks.'

CHAPTER FORTY-ONE

THE RECEPTIONIST AT B'NAI B'RITH WASN'T GIVING PETER ANY information about the Cohens, despite his sob story about being a long-lost relative from Poland. Maybe his Eastern European accent wasn't that good. Maybe he should have practised his Polish when she decided to take him on, instead of feigning deafness and hanging up in her ear.

His bigger concern at that moment was to learn what Stella knew about the Slasher. Why hadn't she ever told him about it? He was distracted, and so he fluffed around and drank two more coffees while he waited for her to return to the office. It was nearly midday by the time she returned. He jumped out of his chair the minute he saw her and headed towards her.

'I'm too busy to talk right now,' she said as she opened her office door. 'I've got a bad headache and I'm not in the frigging mood to talk to you.'

'But you don't even know what I'm going to say.'

'Let me guess. If it's about my family, forget it. I don't interfere in your private life, so don't interfere in mine.' She attempted to shut the door on Peter. 'Have you been talking to Frank?'

Peter prised open the door and said nothing.

'Shit, Peter, where do you get off? Don't take liberties with me; I'll still fire you if I have to.' She went to her desk and sat down.

He remained standing, as she poured herself a glass of water and pulled a bottle of pills from her bag.

She grimaced. 'What is it then? You've got five minutes before I throw you out.'

He cleared his throat. 'Okay. I've been looking into finding your family.'

'Which means you've been talking to Frank,' she said.

'He told me about them,' he replied.

'I'm going to have a word with him.'

'Come on, Stella. We're only trying to help.'

'You can help by butting out,' she fumed.

'Okay. I'll drop it but don't chew Frank out.'

'I want you to stay out of my private life. Okay? Can you do that? I know you mean well but I have to deal with it by myself.'

'All right. I'm sorry. I won't pry anymore.'

'Good. Now you can get out,' she said as she put down the pills, and picked up a ream of documents and started to sort them.

Peter didn't move.

'You're still here. What the hell is wrong with you today? You definitely need to get laid. You're acting really weird.'

He cleared his throat again. 'I was looking at the Slasher case again.'

'I think you have too much free time on your hands. What's happened with the porn industry story?'

'It's stalled. My main source murdered his co-star in a drug-induced rage on the set of their latest movie.'

'That's an obit I'd love to read,' she replied.

'I think the Slasher killings are more important.'

'You think so? I don't. I'll have to organise a foreign assignment for you.'

'I didn't think we did foreign assignments.'

'I'm thinking of sending someone to Mexico to research illegal immigration into the United States. Would you like that? You can use the moustache from your dumb kit and go undercover, which means we'll save on accommodation expenses.'

'Not really. I don't speak Spanish and Mexican food gives me wind.'

'Then enough of the Slasher stuff,' Stella replied, 'or I swear to God I'll do it.'

'I know you were close to catching him,' he said quietly, 'Susan Banks.'

Stella didn't answer immediately. 'How did you know that? If it's Frank, I'll frigging kill him.'

'It's not Frank. I read your statement after the shooting. You called yourself Susan Banks, private investigator. I was in Frank's office this morning, asking about your family, and I saw a photo with your aliases written on it. I connected the dots.'

'That fucking photo,' she growled. 'I think I need a drink.'

'Do you want me to get my flask?'

'No, no. Don't worry about it. I shouldn't be drinking anyway.'

She rocked in her chair and massaged her face. 'Why did you have to bring that up? I've done my best to forget it.' She took a deep breath. 'I feel like I'm having a flashback. I want it to go away.' She took several slow breaths. 'It's horrible. It was a horrible time. I wanted to stop thinking about it.'

'Why are you so secretive about it? You should be happy you nearly caught him.'

'I'm not as tough-assed as you think. Give me a moment.' She stood up and looked out the window.

'I'll go and get the flask. Sorry, I didn't realise it would bring back bad memories. I won't be long.' Peter turned to leave the office.

'No. No. I guess I'll be dying soon, anyway. I can deal with it.' She turned around and returned to her chair. 'You read the statement. So you know what happened?'

'More or less. You're lucky to be alive.'

'I survived but I lost my job.'

'I know, you've mentioned it before. Frank says you didn't get on with the editor.'

Stella laughed. 'Well, I didn't tell him the part about me going undercover in a gay club, did I?'

'But Frank is one of your best friends.'

'Yes, but I still saw him as competition. Remember, he went after the Zodiac Killer. I didn't want him to steal my story.'

'You haven't told him since?' he asked.

'As from that time, I never told anyone. I buried it in the attic. Trust you, Clancy, to bring it up again.'

'Why is it still so raw? Is it the fact that you nearly became a victim of the Slasher?'

'It's that, and it's also the death threats.'

'From whom?' Peter asked.

'Not sure but I have my suspicions. I was getting inside information from an inspector I was screwing at the time. When I started turning up at the crime scenes, the death threats started arriving on my desk. Horrible stuff. I was afraid to open my mail after a while... Pictures of the victims... I feel sick thinking about them.'

'I've seen them too. Beyond evil.'

'And they were always signed as *On Behalf of Concerned Christian Soldiers* or *Christian Warriors*.'

'Christian, huh? I think they were working for the other side.'

'I always felt that it was a religious nutter within the police department itself. That was always my theory.'

'So you were probably glad when you left San Francisco.'

'In a way, yes, I suppose I was. I genuinely believed that my life was under threat and it wasn't an idle threat. On the other hand, I always had unfinished business with this place.'

'Do you want to solve it?'

'No. Not now. I think it would be impossible to solve now. It belongs to the past. The past belongs to historians.'

'Maybe if we could find this Tony Mayberry character. That isn't his real name by the way.'

'Of course not. Would you give your real name if you were leading a double life? He disappeared into the ether or he died or the AIDS epidemic got him. That's black humour by the way,' she said.

'Can you remember anything that Mayberry said to you in the club?'

'Not really.' She sat back and sighed. 'You know, since this tumour shit happened, my old memories seem brighter somehow. My brain's on overdrive. Wait... I remember that Mayberry said he once worked for a record label in the sixties,' she replied.

'Okay. Did you believe him?'

'Not really. He probably believed me as much as I believed him. You didn't tell anyone who you really were in that place... He introduced the attacker as Richard.'

'Do you remember what Richard looked like?'

'I'd recognise him now if I saw him. He was tall and muscular.

161

He also had a chiselled face and the most lifeless blue eyes I've ever seen.'

'Anything else?' he asked.

'Mayberry said that this Richard was in the military. No, he had just gotten out of the military.'

'Or at least, that's what he was told.'

'It's just all bullshit stuff. I think it's time you dropped it and moved on, Peter.'

'You're right. I'm just wasting time. Porn town, here I come.'

'What are you doing tonight?' Stella asked.

'Do you want to go out for a drink? Are you up to that?'

'Not going out. I've been invited over to someone's place for dinner.'

'Who? Someone I know?'

'You may have heard of them.'

'Okay. You don't want to tell me?'

'You'll find out. I'll pick you up at five-thirty. And wear something decent for a change.'

Chapter Forty-Two

Sea Cliff.

Stella steered her car up the sweeping concrete driveway that led to a large mock-Mediterranean villa. It was terracotta and Tuscan ochre under a waning Californian sun. Two other cars were already there: a BMW 750iL and a Porsche 911. From the top of the driveway, Peter watched the imminent sunset glowing orange over the Pacific Ocean.

'Is this Sea Cliff?' he asked as he looked around. 'I've heard of it.'

'That's right. You know your geography.'

'A nice view of the ocean,' he remarked as he looked out.

'One of the best views I've ever seen,' Stella replied.

He looked up at the mansion. 'These people must be made of money. Pardon me for sounding common. How did you say you knew them?'

'I'd thought you'd like it.' She parked her Mazda MX5 behind the Porsche and grabbed the bottle of wine from the passenger footwell.

'Anyone I know? Is it the home of a celebrity, Courtney Love perhaps?' Peter said.

Stella chuckled. 'You'll find out soon enough.'

He looked at the bottle of wine and back at the house. 'Shouldn't you have brought something more expensive to go with the house? Something French maybe?'

'What's wrong with American wine? And since when have you been taken aback by wealth?'

'I may be liberal, but I like to be stylishly liberal.'

'Hurry up. They're waiting for us.'

Peter followed her along a path framed by California roses. Beyond the path, two people were standing in front of a large, wooden entrance door. One was a young man dressed in a suit and the other was an old woman holding a walking stick.

Peter looked at Stella. 'Now I get it. You cunning old fox.'

Stella waved at the woman and young man. 'Mama.'

'You beat me to it!' he exclaimed.

'Well, you prompted me.'

'And you never told me?'

'I don't have to tell you everything.'

'Have you told them about the brain tumour?'

'Let's just enjoy tonight, okay?' Stella waved again. 'You may have to speak loudly, my mother is hard of hearing.'

Stella kissed her mother and her nephew, Sam, before they were bustled inside.

'Quickly, inside,' said Miriam, grabbing Stella's arm. 'It's almost sunset.'

Peter darted in before the door slammed behind him. He found himself in an enormous beamed entrance hall. The house was lit up like Macy's department store.

'And this is my colleague, Peter Clancy,' Stella spluttered. 'I've told them all about you.'

'Good to meet you, Mrs Cohen,' Peter said loudly.

'So, why are you yelling? Are you deaf?' Miriam smiled.

Peter blushed. 'Sorry. Stella told me that you…'

Miriam laughed.

'She wanted me to play a joke on you. Nothing wrong with Mama's hearing.'

'Good joke,' he smiled. 'I can see where your daughter got her sense of humour from.'

'And what a handsome man you are. Do you have a girlfriend?'

'No. I don't, Mrs Cohen. I'm between girlfriends, you might say,' he replied.

'Maybe you and Estelle? There's an age difference and you're a *goy*, but I'll talk you into converting. Age doesn't matter these days, so long as you're happy.'

164

'Mama, please,' Stella mumbled, 'stop match-making.'

'You're right. Come. It's nearly time for Shabbat.'

'Yes, it's Friday night. Very special. I'm sorry, Mama… I haven't been…' she began.

'Estelle, you never forget your heritage. Have you heard of Shabbat, Peter?' Mrs Cohen asked.

'Of course. I read all Leon Uris's books.'

Miriam looked at Sam and shrugged her shoulders.

'Come on, Buba. It's nearly sunset.'

'Yes, we must hurry. The family is waiting.'

Sam held out his arm for Miriam and they walked away.

'Family?' Peter whispered. 'Are you all right about that?'

'That was what Mama wanted. It will be good to see everyone,' she replied. 'My two brothers, their wives and their children are here. My father died two years ago.'

'Sorry to hear that.'

Peter and Stella followed them down a wide hallway, into the bowels of the house. It was huge.

'I was angrier with my father than the rest of my family,' Stella continued, 'but it's all about forgiveness and moving on. I should have done something about it earlier. How long can you stay angry for?'

'People can stay angry until they die. You can take anger to the grave. It seems pointless to me. At least you didn't wait until it was too late.'

Eventually, they entered a large dining room with a heavy oak table as its centrepiece and decorated with family pictures and china ornaments. It was rather too baroque for Peter's taste.

'Everyone, this is Peter. Make him welcome. You can all introduce yourself to him during dinner,' Miriam said to the many adults and children who were standing around the table. She took hold of Stella's hand. 'Come, Estelle, let's light the candles and pray together.'

'Yes, Mama. That would be nice.'

Mrs Cohen lit the seven candles on the silver menorah and they began the prayer to welcome the arrival of Shabbat. *Baruch atah*

Adonai, Eloheinu, melech ha'olam... When she took her hands away, Peter noticed that Stella had tears in her eyes as she recited the prayer with her mother.

They then sang songs, welcoming the two Shabbat angels into the house and praising Miriam for all the work she had done over the past week. After more blessings, Nathan lifted the challah and prayed over the wine, and they all sat down at the table.

'Thanks, Mama,' said Stella. 'I feel like I never left.'

'You didn't leave, my darling. You were always here,' Miriam patted her chest. She then rang a bell near her. Shortly afterwards, two middle-aged Hispanic women came into the room with serving platters full of food.

'I hope you like brisket, Peter. It's our family favourite.'

Peter looked at the platter of meat. It looked familiar. He took a piece and tasted it. 'Corned beef? I was raised on it.'

'Really. Was your mama Jewish?'

'Not as far as I know. My family were all Irish.'

'Oh, yes,' Miriam laughed, 'Jews with booze.'

Peter raised his glass.

'Shabbat Shalom.' Miriam raised her glass.

'Shabbat Shalom!'

Over the next few minutes, Peter felt he'd met every Cohen in existence and his head swam. He downed his wine in a single gulp.

Aaron Cohen stood up. 'I like to say a few words.'

'There goes the next thirty minutes,' Nathan grumbled.

'Sit down, Aaron, and you, Nathan, be quiet,' said Miriam. 'Estelle, welcome home. The family has missed you. No one made us laugh or told stories like you did. Even Papa said that.'

'He said that?' Stella was incredulous. This wasn't the Solomon Cohen of her recollection. She loaded her plate with all the flavours she'd missed over the last seventeen years.

'Congratulations on winning the Pulitzer Prize,' said Nathan. 'If Pop was still here, he would have been very proud. He would have wanted to put it in his trophy cabinet. And welcome to our family, Peter. Shabbat Shalom.'

'Shabbat Shalom.'

166

'That brisket is beautiful,' Peter said to Miriam, helping himself to another slice.

'I'm glad you like it, Peter. You know you are always welcome in our house.'

He turned to Stella who was sipping wine. 'You're okay? Not overwhelmed?'

'I'm fine. I'm glad to be here. It's like all of the pain has disappeared.'

'Yes. I told you that you'd feel a lot better once you reunited with your family,' he replied.

'Always trying to get the upper hand, aren't you?'

Nathan stood up and shouted. 'Estelle, tell us a story.'

'Yes,' said Aaron, 'tell us the one about Papa and you going to the Grateful Dead's house.'

'You mean, the Jefferson Airplane story?'

'Jefferson Airplane?' Peter was in awe. 'You met Jefferson Airplane?'

Stella put down her glass. 'Well, I'm going to have to tell you a censored version, seeing as we have children present.'

'Disappointed,' said Sam.

Stella shifted in her seat and cleared her throat. 'Two of the members of Jefferson Airplane used to live nearby. I think it was Paul Kantner and Grace Slick. They used to have the wildest parties, lots of loud music, and you know what else. The parties weren't held that often, but often enough to annoy our parents. It used to drive Papa crazy. We didn't mind, though I was more a Led Zeppelin fan.'

'I remember, the music sounded like someone was screaming in pain and all of the instruments were loud and distorted. Too loud. That music would send you *meshuge*. It was always the same old process, Papa would call the police, they'd come and nothing would happen,' Miriam interrupted.

Nathan tittered and Stella continued. 'This time Papa was going to sort it out himself. He was furious. I was going to college at the time. So, he grabs me and says to me, "You come with me so you can interpret."'

Everyone laughed.

' "Papa, they speak English," I reply. "Well," he says, "if it's English, why can't I understand it?" So, we go to the house. There are hippies going in and out of the house. Some are smoking joints. We walk straight into the house. Then Papa sees naked men and women walking around, getting into the pool or lying on the floor. We don't know where to look. Papa sees me looking at a man and a woman lying together. He covers my eyes. Papa says, "What have I done? We've walked into an orgy. I've corrupted you." '

She paused to take a drink. 'So Papa starts to leave, covering my eyes as best he could. Paul Kantner sees us and comes up to us. "Hey man, you're Mr Cohen, aren't you?" he asks Papa, "Do you want a drink or a joint?" Papa looks shocked. "How do you know who I am? I've never met you." Paul Kantner then says to Papa, "Your wife bakes us cookies every so often. We love them." Papa looks so shocked that he can't answer immediately. I'm thinking, he may pass out.'

Peter looked around the table. Aaron and Nathan were crying with laughter.

' "Is the music too loud? Is that why you're here?" Paul asks. Papa says, "Maybe, if you could just turn it down a little." Poor Papa, for once he's lost for words. We leave soon afterwards. When we get home Mama asks where we've been and Papa points to the Kantner house as he pours himself a straight scotch. Mama says...' Stella spluttered with laughter. 'Mama says, "What a nice couple, though I don't much agree with their taste in music." ' Still laughing, she sat down.

It was a great story. Peter wished he'd been there. He was still chuckling when one of the maids rushed into the dining room.

'There's a telephone call for you, Miss Estelle.'

'No phone calls on the Sabbath,' said Miriam. 'It is forbidden. Take a message, Maria.'

'Miss Estelle, he said it was very urgent.'

'Did he say who it was?' Stella asked.

'It was Frank Styles.'

Stella began to get up. 'Okay. I'm coming.'

'No! It is forbidden. Estelle!'

Stella turned to Peter. 'It's not forbidden for you. Would you?'

'Of course.'

'You work too hard, Estelle. Doesn't she, Peter?' Miriam said as he was leaving the room.

'She never stops. I'm sure she works in her sleep.'

'Her father was the same. He always had to prove something. I don't know why. Estelle and her father had the same personality. That's why they clashed a lot.'

Peter followed Maria across the hallway to the telephone. He picked up the receiver. 'Frank?'

'Peter? What are you…'

'I'm here with Stella and her family. It's the Sabbath, Frank. Stella can't take the call. What's wrong?'

Frank hesitated. 'It's Raoul…'

'What's happened?' he asked.

'He's been shot.'

He felt his dinner rise to his throat. 'Is he dead?'

'I don't know. He's been taken to hospital. We have to get down there.'

'Yes, of course. I'll go but I'll leave Stella here,' Peter replied. 'She doesn't need to know about Raoul yet. I'll make an excuse. Let her enjoy the Sabbath.'

'Sure.'

The sound of laughter echoed along the hall. He returned to the dining room with a heavy heart. He looked at Stella's beaming face. 'I'm really sorry to do this, but Frank wants me to cover a shooting.'

'What? Now?'

'I'm afraid so.'

'What did he want to talk to me about?' asked Stella.

'He was trying to track me down and thought you'd know where I was. You stay here and enjoy Shabbat with your family. Maria's calling me a cab.' He looked around the table. 'I want to thank you all for this wonderful dinner and your fabulous company. I'm afraid I have to leave.'

'So soon?' said Miriam.

'Thank you, Mrs Cohen.'

'But you'll come again, Peter?'

'Of course. It's just the life of a reporter, you understand.'

'You work too hard, too,' said Miriam, giving Peter a kiss on each cheek.

Chapter Forty-Three

Seven pm, the same evening. *Bayside Journal* **offices.**

Amos was walking through the office saying goodbye to everyone. These people were his family and his life; he sometimes wished he could stay at work permanently.

'I'll see all your sweet selves in the morning,' he said.

'Wait for me, Mr Amos, I'm escorting you to your car,' Clyde said as he put on his coat.

'Sir, can't I have a night off? I've been a very good boy.'

'I'm sorry, Mr Amos, but after last time… I'm not taking any more chances.'

'Have you been reading my fan mail again?' he joked.

'I have. I'm sure you get more death threats than the President,' Clyde replied.

'And you get to be my own secret service agent.'

'I'm just trying to be careful, Mr Amos.'

'Okay but you have to call me, Raoul, just Raoul. I feel so old when you call me Mr Amos.'

'Of course, Raoul. I can do that.' Clyde smiled.

'Okay. Let's go.'

Amos and Clyde walked out of the front door and headed down the alleyway that led to the lock-up carpark. It was just on sunset. Clyde looked around as they entered the alley. They walked together until they reached the garage.

Amos unlocked the garage door. 'I should be fine from here,' he said as he swung open the metal door.

'I better come with you. You can't be too careful.'

'If you must. All of the people that use this carpark are honest folks.'

'I'm sorry, Raoul.'

He laughed. 'I know, you want to check out the Mustang, don't you?'

'No, it isn't that. People can probably still get into the carpark if they try. I've checked it out during the day. This place isn't totally secure, if you know where to look.'

'Are you sure you're not secret service?'

'I was a cop once.'

Amos continued into the darkened interior of the carpark. Clyde flicked on his flashlight. 'I don't know how you see in here, Raoul,' he remarked as he scanned the carpark.

'I've always regarded myself as a nocturnal creature.'

They continued towards the Mustang. Amos grabbed Clyde by the arm.

'There's something wrong.'

'What is it?'

Clyde stopped and shone the flashlight beam around the carpark.

'I can't see anything.'

'Look, look. The car looks different.'

'Stay here,' he replied. 'I'll check it out.' He moved closer to the Mustang. 'The tyre is down,' he called out.

'Be careful,' Amos called back.

Clyde pulled his pistol out of its holster and shone the flashlight around the carpark again.

'Is the car open?' Amos asked.

Clyde walked around the car, checking each lock. He called out when he checked the driver's door.

'It's open.'

Amos then saw a shadowy figure coming from behind Clyde. 'It's a trap, Clyde. Get out!'

Clyde spun around and raised his pistol to fire. One shot rang out around the carpark.

'I'm hit,' Clyde screamed as he fell onto the bonnet of the Mustang.

'I'll get help,' Amos yelled. He heard movement behind him.

'His ministers are a flaming fire,' a male voice muttered.

Amos turned around slowly. 'You guys, again. This fag isn't going without a fucking fight,' he yelled as he jumped towards the voice.

Two shots sounded. Amos fell to the ground. 'Jackie. Jackie,' he whispered.

Another shot rang out. Then silence.

Chapter Forty-Four

UCSF Medical Center, San Francisco.

Frank was already sitting in the waiting room when Peter got there. He stood up when he noticed him. 'I shouldn't have called you. You could have stayed with Stella,' he said. 'I could have taken care of this.'

'How could I? What's happening?'

Frank looked at a pale man in his twenties who was standing nearby. 'This is Paul Schultz. He's the sub-editor of the *Bayside Journal*. He'll be able to fill you in a bit more.'

'What happened?' Peter asked.

'Raoul and the security guard were ambushed in the carpark when Raoul was going to his car.'

'How are they?'

'The security guard was shot in the leg but Raoul is touch and go. They're operating now,' Schultz replied. 'I think it was the same people who attacked him a little while ago.'

'I have my suspicions, too,' Peter said. 'I reckon it's someone within The Ten Commandments Church. They have the most motive.'

'Hmm,' said Frank. 'Does Raoul have any family?'

'He has, but he's been estranged from them for years. He always puts me and his ex-wife as his next of kin.'

'No partner?'

'Not lately.'

'And Jackie is still in a coma,' Peter observed.

They sat in the waiting room, trying to find something to occupy their minds. There was a television in one corner of the room, which no one was watching. *Why are the chairs always so damned uncomfortable?* Peter had just settled when the surgeon appeared. He noticed the resigned look on the surgeon's face. *Not a good sign.* They all stood up.

'Paul Schultz?' the surgeon said as he walked into the waiting room.

'I'm Paul Schultz. How did the operation go?'

'Not as well as we'd hoped. He'd lost a lot of blood. We tried but...'

Schultz started to weep and fell into a chair behind him. Frank rested his hand on Schultz's shoulder.

'The wounds were too extensive and there had been so much blood loss, his heart gave up. There was nothing more... I'm sorry.'

Peter fumed, 'I need to get hold of Jerry Belinski. This is personal.'

'Listen, Peter, this isn't your fight. Let the police get them,' Frank said. 'Look at what happened to Raoul. You're only supposed to report the facts, not solve the murders.'

Peter glared at Frank. *How old are you? Fifty?* Frank spoke of retirement, but surely he wasn't nearly old enough to have lost all his purpose. 'Is that what you were thinking when you went after the Zodiac Killer, Frank?' he snapped back.

'You could be putting your life at risk,' he replied.

'No shit. I'm not prepared to sit around and hope it all falls into my lap.'

Frank took Peter aside. 'This is no time for heroics or anger, Peter. Stay out of it.'

'I'm already in the firing line. Remember, I helped expose Gatting too.'

'Then, I think you should be put under protection. If they shot Raoul, they could possibly have you in their sights.'

'I don't want any protection. In our line of work, Frank, there are always risks. You know that. A few low-lifes have tried to put me away. I accept that risk. What I don't accept is that they think they can get away with it.'

'Just because you think The Ten Commandments Church members are strange and they roughed you up a bit, doesn't make them the murderers. Raoul made himself a few enemies in his lifetime. I'm sure that some people in the gay community didn't even like him.'

'Give me a week to prove it,' Peter replied.

Frank sighed. 'I want strong evidence, not just hunches, in the next two days,' he replied.

Peter called Belinski on his cell the moment he left the hospital. 'Where are you?' he asked. 'I've just left the hospital.'

'At my desk. I just heard that Raoul Amos died on the table.'

'Yes. It's awful. Any suspects yet?'

'Too early. By the way it played out, it looks like it was a professional job.'

'How's that?' Peter asked.

'They lured the security guard away from Raoul and shot him when he was alone. The shots weren't wild, they were very well-aimed, like an execution.'

'I think The Ten Commandments Church is behind it. They had the greatest motive.'

'Yeah, that's what I thought too, except they've been in disarray since the massacre. I don't think they could organise such a calculated killing, even if they wanted to.'

Peter glanced at his watch. 'Can I meet you at the station? I want to run a few things by you.'

'I don't know. I've been at work since this morning. I'm beyond all reason right now.'

'All right. How about you meet me at the Merrells' house first thing tomorrow? That's where I'd like to start.'

'The Merrells? If you're looking for clues, we searched that place with a fine-tooth comb.'

'I'll talk to you more when I get there. How early can you get there?'

'Make it seven. The address is 1018 Duncan Street, Diamond Heights.'

'Sounds good. See you then.'

CHAPTER FORTY-FIVE

Seven am, next morning. Diamond Heights.

PETER CREPT ALONG DUNCAN STREET, LOOKING FOR HOUSE numbers. He counted in any he couldn't see, and figured that he must have reached the Merrells' house. He pulled up adjacent to the driveway of a two-storey wooden duplex that looked like it needed a paint job ten years ago. He got out of the car and walked to the porch. Police tape still sealed the front door.

He tried to look through the front window but it was covered by a thick curtain. He walked around the small front yard and looked up at the closed windows. Funny, he thought, you can never profile a psychopath or a mass murderer by the house they live in, the job they have or the car they drive. In his experience, murderers were nondescript on the exterior but a mass of demons inside.

He waited a full fifteen minutes before Belinski arrived alone in a squad car.

'Sorry, slept in,' Belinski apologised when he got out of the car holding a cup of coffee.

'I should have got you to get me one,' Peter replied as he looked longingly at the steaming cup.

Belinski leaned into his car and took something out. 'Donut?' he said, inclining a paper sack towards Peter.

'For breakfast?' *I'll never understand the Yanks' desire for sugar, starch and fat first thing in the morning.* 'Sure.' *What the heck.* He was hungry: he'd already missed breakfast. Even so, he ditched it after the first mouthful.

'So,' said Belinski, taking a bite from a glazed donut, 'you brought me here for a reason, I suppose. It better be good.'

'I don't think the Merrells acted alone and I have a feeling there may be something in this house to confirm that,' said Peter.

'That's it? I'm here because you have a feeling?'

'They never steer me wrong, you know. I trust them with my life.'

Belinski took another bite and chuckled. 'I don't why I'm going along with it, my colleagues would think I'm crazy. If we go in there and don't find anything, promise me you'll stop riding me about it?'

'Yeah, all right.'

He took a set of keys out of his jacket pocket and inserted them into the front-door lock. He fiddled with the lock several times and then bent to take a closer look. 'Someone's tampered with it. It's all scratched.'

'Neighbours?'

'Who knows. This isn't a classy neighbourhood.' He persisted and, after a lot of jiggling, he was able to insert the key into the lock and turn it. 'I have to warn you. It doesn't smell too nice inside.' He slowly opened the door.

'Shit, that reeks.' Peter grimaced as he caught the first whiff. 'Did someone die in there?'

'Twenty cats lived here, no joke. Some were already dead when we went through the place. The rest went to the animal refuge. You don't want a cat, do you?'

'Not me. Not a fan. They're smelly and arrogant; they remind me of some bosses I worked for.'

Belinski swung the door wide open and stepped into the hallway. Peter took a small jar of Vicks out of his pocket, scooped a wad of the ointment and smeared it under both nostrils. 'Want some?' He held out the jar. 'It's a trick I got from the cops in Australia.'

'I'm fine. I've smelled worse than this.' He continued along the dark hallway.

'Me too, but I haven't had a proper breakfast yet. I don't want to spoil it.' Peter attempted to turn on the light.

'We've switched off the power. So what exactly are we looking for?'

'I don't know yet,' Peter replied as he looked around. 'Something out of place. Or something so unobvious that it's obvious.'

'That's not filling me with confidence.'

Most of the furniture had been overturned and the contents of a cabinet had spilled out onto the floor. All of the videos had been removed from the television cabinet, opened and scattered about. One section of the wall had been removed, exposing the studs underneath.

'What happened here?' Peter asked.

'There was a bulge in the wall. We thought it may have been a cache of weapons and ammo. There was nothing there, in the end.'

He noticed the phone. 'Did they have an answering machine?' he asked.

'The machine and the tape are in the properties department.'

'Did you listen to the tape?'

'There was a month's worth of messages there; just people from the church mainly, plus a loan company chasing a debt.'

'Did you call them?' Peter asked.

'Yeah but it rang out. Leave a message, we'll get back to you stuff.'

'I guess where they were going, their debts weren't going to follow. Do you remember the name of the loan company?'

'Carmel Ridge Loans,' Belinski replied.

Peter made a mental note to look them up when he returned to the office. He and Belinski continued into the kitchen. Again, the cupboards were empty and the contents removed. The refrigerator door was open, empty except for a rotting head of lettuce and several soda cans.

'So, has anything caught your attention?' Belinski asked.

'That lettuce looks suspicious.'

'Nah. It's all right. We ran a polygraph test on it, kept saying I'm innocent, lettuce alone.' Belinski laughed. 'Get it?'

Peter ignored him. 'I got it. Can we check the bedrooms now?'

'They're in the same state.'

They climbed up a narrow staircase and entered Leah Merrell's room. The mattress had been removed and lay cut open on the floor.

'You guys are thorough, aren't you?' Peter remarked as he stepped over a pile of clothes and shoes.

179

'That's what I keep telling you, but you don't want to believe me.'

Peter moved towards a dresser next to the bed. He picked up a bible lying on top of a lace doily and flicked through it. 'Parts of it have been underlined,' he said as he browsed.

'I guess that's what they did in their church. They probably did it as part of their Bible studies.'

Peter looked in a drawer and laughed. 'Bloody hell! There's a black dildo in there. I bet she didn't tell anyone at church about that.'

'I should have warned you. I get the feeling she was a lonely and repressed woman.'

The ceiling above his head had been torn down. There wasn't enough light to see into the roof cavity.

Belinski followed Peter's gaze. 'Before you ask, we didn't find anything up there either.'

'What did the neighbours say about them? Did they have any visitors?'

'The neighbours barely heard from them or saw them. The curtains were always drawn and no one ever visited. Occasionally they said you'd hear her singing religious songs or loud arguments between her and the son. It was usually David yelling at Leah. Why do I have to do this kind of stuff, why is this happening, that kind of thing,' Belinski replied.

They walked across the hallway into David Merrell's bedroom.

'Same again,' Belinski yawned.

Once again, the bed had been turned over and the mattress pulled apart. Books, clothes and tapes were scattered across the floor. Peter noticed a bible opened on a shelf.

'He had one too,' he said as he picked it up and flicked through it. 'I guess.'

He opened the cupboard door and peeked in. 'Porn magazines?'

'Gay porn. I reckon the old woman took him to the church to make him straight.'

'Hmm. I've heard of some churches doing that. I don't hold with that shit. It's not as if people wake up in the morning and say, "Hey, you know what? From now on I think I'll be gay." ' Peter went to the book shelf and picked up the bible again. 'Can I keep this?'

'You want to know how it ends? Watch the movie... Shit, I shouldn't have said that. My Polish parents wouldn't be thrilled with me.'

'Catholic doctrine, making people feel guilty for two thousand years. Me too. We band of brothers...' He slapped Belinski on the back. 'Mind if I take her bible too?'

'We have no further need for it. Go ahead. Do you want to check the garage for anything?'

'I'm sure you've gone over it but I'll have a quick look anyway.'

They walked back down the stairs and through the back door. Belinski took off a padlock and opened up the garage door. The garage was nearly empty, except for two cardboard boxes.

'What's in them?' Peter asked.

'Old newspapers. Do you want to take them too?'

Peter shuffled through the bundle. 'Why would someone keep old newspapers, especially from Albuquerque?'

'Leah Merrell came from there.'

'That's in New Mexico?'

'It is. You should go. You might like watching the desert sunsets.'

Peter rolled his eyes. 'Too close to home. I did many years of it back in Australia, before I moved to the city. That was enough dirt and dust for a lifetime.' He put the papers away. 'I don't know why she bothered. Looks like it's a place where the biggest news is the rain.'

'You can have them.'

'Thanks.' He placed the bibles on top of the papers and closed the boxes.

'Well, that's it. Tour's over. Don't be disappointed.'

'I've got two days to find something or I have to drop it. If I can't prove this, it goes to the same place as the Slasher killings.'

'In the too-hard basket?' Belinski asked.

'No, nothing is too hard. No, I'd have to put it in the one that says breakthrough-pending-don't-tell-the-boss.'

'I sympathise with you, buddy. Come on, I'll buy you breakfast.'

They picked up a box each and walked out of the garage.

'Got any information back on Shafer?' asked Peter as they passed through the house on their way out.

'Soon.'

'And did Leah Merrell have any financial statements? I'd be interested to see what was going in and out of her account.'

'Me too. Her bank didn't want to play ball. We had to get a court order to get them,' Belinski replied. 'I'm sticking my neck out here, only because I think we can help each other. I'll let you have a look at them and we'll see what you make of them. I don't want this getting out. You find anything, you call me first, right? I don't want to be reading about it over my morning coffee along with Joe Public, you got it?'

'Fine. Great. Now, come on. I'm dying for a coffee and some real food,' Peter said. 'I'm starting to get a headache.'

CHAPTER FORTY-SIX

Same day. *Daily* offices.

PETER WAS CARRYING THE TWO BOXES OF PAPERS OUT OF THE elevator when he bumped into Mulroy, who pretended not to see him. The corner of the bottom box was digging into Peter's wrist and he was five seconds away from dropping the lot.

'Mulroy,' he said through gritted teeth, 'can you give me a hand?'

'Are you moving in?' Mulroy took hold of the top box.

Peter flexed his wrist. 'Hilarious. It's called research. You like doing research, don't you?' He steered Mulroy towards his desk and stacked the boxes on the floor.

'Not really.'

'Good. You can help me, then. You haven't done much investigative reporting, have you? Just so you know what to expect, we'll be trawling through a mountain of mundane looking for a single, tiny gem. Stuff like bank records, medical records, property details, even old newspapers. I've even sifted through trash looking for the dirt on someone—literally.'

'That stinks.'

'You're on fire today, Mulroy. What really stinks is when all you find is kitchen waste. But some stuff, like used nappies and empty bottles of wine, can be gems.'

'Did you say gems or germs? Anyone I know?'

'From analysing a particular Australian celebrity's trash—and I won't name names—I was able to write a piece about how she was neglecting her child because she was pissed all the time.'

'That's harsh. That sort of thing can destroy a career.'

'It did. But it also just happened to be true, and it probably saved her son's life and possibly even hers. Celebrities are fair game to me; they're overpaid, overexposed and overrated.' He picked up the top box and handed it to Mulroy. 'That's yours. I want you to read through every one of those papers and look for anything related to the Merrells.'

'The Merrells?'

'Try and frigging keep up, we're on a deadline here, the mum and son shooters. Apparently Leah came from Albuquerque. They're hers. She must have kept these old papers for some reason, and I want to know why. There may be something I can hang my hat on.'

Mulroy sat down at his desk and spread one of the newspapers across his desk. 'This is going to be so much fun,' he grumbled.

Peter smiled, took the lid off the box and took out the two bibles. He sat down and opened them up at the same page. 'Do you know anything about the Bible?'

'Only what I did at Sunday school. I wasn't really religious. My parents were. My father was a pastor.'

Peter picked up the bibles and gave them to Mulroy. 'Excellent. You're close enough to a theologian. You might enjoy looking at these as well.'

Mulroy placed the bibles side by side and opened one up, while Peter opened a directory looking for a listing for Carmel Ridge Loans. There was none, but he found a listing for The American Loans Association. He picked up the phone and dialled their number.

'Hello, my name is Peter Clancy. I'm a reporter from the *San Francisco Daily*. I was just wondering if you have Carmel Ridge Loans on your books?' He waited while the receptionist went to check. 'Anything?' he said as he looked across at Mulroy who was scanning both bibles at the same time.

'They've underlined the same passages. So far, all of the passages are from the Old Testament. Here's one about Sodom and Gomorrah; something about divine retribution.'

'I heard they were great places to visit in the summer,' he laughed.

'And get turned into salt.'

'David Merrell was most probably gay. He may have been undergoing conversion therapy… We should check that out.'

'Conversion therapy is…?'

'Hold on… she's back.'

Mulroy continued to flip through the bibles.

'What did you find for me, miss?' He picked up a pen and scrawled, *Carmel Ridge Loan Agents. Maybe based in Albuquerque.* 'That's very interesting. Do you have an address? 556 Talavera Road. Tijeras. Phone number? 5052789766. Thanks.' He wrote down the details. 'Before you go… Was there a name of a director, manager, whatever you call them?'

Mulroy stopped reading to listen in.

'Al Margulies… an office in Geary Street… that's here, isn't it?' Peter signalled his amazement to Mulroy. 'Can you tell me why there are two addresses? No… you can't… Okay. Thanks for that. Much appreciated.' He put down the phone. 'Mulroy, look for anything about Carmel Ridge Loans in those papers—advertisements, whatever,' he called as he bounced the pen off the desk.

'Now I'm interested.'

'I think someone has created an elaborate web. I'm going to give Carmel Ridge a call and then try and track down Al Margulies.'

'What about the bibles?'

'Once you've finished with them, have a look through the papers.'

'Okay. There must be about two years of newspapers in these boxes.'

'Whatever it takes. We don't have a lot of time.' He picked up the phone receiver.

'You said this kid was probably gay? If he was undergoing conversion therapy…'

'Sorry, I'm going to give this phone number a call.' It went straight to a message, and Peter waited for a beep that never came. Instead, the tape cut out. He hung up and replaced the receiver.

'Do you know much about conversion therapy?' Mulroy asked.

'Not a lot. That's where people use quack science to make people straight. It's bullshit. Did you…'

'It was never an issue in my family and, besides, my parents didn't believe in it. They were more liberal in their views.'

'What do you know about it?'

'Well, some of the more conservative churches still think homosexuality is a mental disorder. They use aversion therapy: electric shocks while showing them homosexual images, that kind of thing.'

'What I thought. Do they lobotomise people too?'

'I don't think it goes that far. They do use hypnosis and intense Bible study to convert them to heterosexual,' he replied.

'And this is legal?'

'In some states.'

'All it's going to do is alienate people and make them feel like they're sexual deviants. Life's hard enough without adding shame and guilt to the mix. Let people live their lives, I say.'

'My uncle's gay. I guess he may have influenced my father's thinking, too,' Mulroy remarked. 'There was never a minute when my father wanted him to change. He just lets him be what he is.'

'So, you've looked at a fair number of the passages by now,' said Peter. 'Is there anything special about them?'

'I can't find the common thread, but I haven't found any passages about homosexuality yet,' Mulroy replied.

'Okay. I'll try to chase down Carmel Ridge Loans.'

Stella walked up to Peter's desk and rapped on the credenza. 'Have you forgotten? Raoul's memorial service is in thirty minutes time.'

'Shit, I was busy on this… Okay, I'm going.' He grabbed his coat and notepad.

'It's at The Transfer on Church Street.'

'I'm on my way,' he said as he swept past Stella.

'I'll keep going on this then,' said Mulroy.

'Do that, and give that number a call again.'

'Carmel Ridge Loans?'

'Yep. That one.'

CHAPTER FORTY-SEVEN

The Transfer, Church Street, San Francisco.

THE CROWD WAS ALREADY SPILLING OUT ONTO CHURCH STREET by the time Peter arrived. The Transfer had been one of Amos's favourite clubs, so it was fitting that his memorial should be held there. Peter didn't have a hope of getting in. That didn't really deter him; funerals and memorials usually ran according to the same template: songs, prayers, praise, sorrow. The difference was that this one didn't have a burial or cremation at the end. Amos's body was still with the coroner.

Peter didn't figure Amos for a big memorial sort of guy, but Peter suspected that he'd never discussed it with anyone and hadn't anticipated going in such a dramatic fashion. Amos had been so vigorous as a gay rights campaigner, he probably couldn't have got away with a small memorial anyway.

Peter decided he would look for an angle for his piece out here on the street. He noticed a few police officers blocking a small group of anti-gay demonstrators who were yelling insults at the crowd and holding up placards and pushed his way towards them.

The group consisted of about six people: four middle-aged women and two men in their thirties. The police had it contained so, other than a brief mention in the write-up, that was a non-story.

The demonstrators looked disappointed and one of the men was doing his best to rally them. They must have thought the TV networks would have cameras on them, but the networks were nowhere to be seen. Typical media; they had turned up for Amos's murder but not for his memorial.

Peter headed back to the front entrance. He was able to get close to the front door by telling people he was a close friend, but no further. The double doors had been opened to allow people to look in.

He only barely made out the mayor of San Francisco's eulogy and then Hank Wilson went to the podium. Although Peter had no hope of hearing most of it, what he could hear of Hank's eulogy was very emotional, and at one point Hank had to brush away his tears. The mourners were already weeping by the time four African American women stood up to sing a gospel song, and Peter even found himself crying.

The papers had already covered everything publicly known about Amos's murder, but, as clinical as it sounded, Peter knew covering the memorial would add more colour and depth to his story. It wasn't worthy of the front page but it would sit well on page two or three.

An hour later, the crowd started to disperse. Peter overheard someone say that once his body was released, Amos was going to be cremated and the ashes were going to be scattered in the bay. He followed the crowd along Church Street. The demonstrators had already left, probably due to lack of interest. It was then he spotted Belinski who was shuffling away just ahead of him.

Belinski must have sensed Peter watching him, and turned around. 'Just paying my respects.'

'You're not looking for anyone?'

They continued to walk. 'Well, I don't know what I'm looking for.'

'I've heard that murderers like to go to their victim's funeral. I guess that also applies to their memorials. Spot anyone?'

'That would be handy if I knew what they looked like,' Belinski replied.

'Has the security guard told you anything?'

'We interviewed him. This is off the record. I can't let you publish this during the investigation.'

Peter took a deep breath. 'Okay. Tell me anyhow.'

'Clyde, the security guard, said it was two males. They had their faces covered. They were tall, well-built. It was dark. It was quick.'

'Nothing else?'

'Someone saw two people running from the carpark on the night. It was dark, they couldn't make out any faces. Ballistics didn't show up anything remarkable, no fingerprints. It was a professional job.'

'Which could point to...?'

They both stopped walking. 'You're thinking of that church again? I can't believe a religious organisation would be associated with organising a murder.'

'That's probably what people say about the Vatican, too,' Peter ventured.

'Hey,' snapped Belinski, 'watch it! I'm a practising Catholic, don't bring my religion into it, all right?'

'Sorry, I just thought because of your comments at the house that you had given up on the church.'

'Not that it's any of your business, but I didn't throw the baby out with the bath water.'

'Point taken. I guess I'm one of those Catholics who thought it was already too late to save it.'

There was a brief silence. 'Off the record, have you ever thought that one of Raoul's associates at the newspaper might be a suspect? We've started interviewing them and I get the feeling that one or two of them weren't happy with the direction the paper was going in.'

'Surely, that's not enough to kill someone?'

'So, you don't think newspaper folk kill each other?'

'I guess they might but...'

'When you find you've hit a dead end let me know,' said Belinski, 'and I'll buy you a drink so you can drown your sorrows.'

Peter stopped when they reached Belinski's car. His own car was parked in an adjacent street. 'I called Carmel Ridge Loans,' he said.

'And?'

'I left a message. Could it be bogus?'

'Maybe, maybe not. Innocent until proven guilty.'

'The nominee is based here. Some guy called Al Margulies. The address is in Geary Street,' Peter said.

'Al Margulies. I've heard of that guy,' Belinski replied. 'He's an attorney. I came across him once. He was representing some low-life drug dealer. Margulies got him off but the prick was guilty as sin. Like most attorneys, he'd represent the devil himself if he could get a high enough fee.'

'I should go and have a talk to him,' Peter rejoined.

'Good luck with that. Lawyers aren't exactly liberal with the truth, are they?'

'I can only try. If I don't push against the door, it isn't going to open, is it?'

Belinski chuckled. 'What if you're pushing against the wrong door?'

Peter laughed. 'No stuff back on Schafer or the bank statements?' he asked.

'I don't think it's far away. You know, bureaucracy works in another time zone.'

'More like little wheels grinding away. Give me a call when you get them.'

'Peter, don't let your past experiences and your bitterness towards Christian churches influence your story.'

'I'm not bitter towards all churches. I have a hunch about this one and I'm sticking to it.'

'If I'd relied on my hunches, I would have been kicked out of the police force by now.'

'That's why I'm a reporter and not a cop.'

CHAPTER FORTY-EIGHT

Daily offices.

MULROY WAS STILL LOOKING THROUGH THE BIBLE PASSAGES WHEN Peter returned to his desk. He was scribbling notes as he read, and hardly seemed to notice his return. His face was stony.

Peter threw his coat over his chair and sat down. 'Got a headache yet?' he asked. 'Any luck with Carmel Ridge?'

'I called them three times but there's just an answering machine. How did the memorial go?'

'I guess he had a good send-off. He would have loved the entertainment.' Peter turned on his computer and started typing. 'So, where are you with the bibles?'

'Well...'

'Keep talking. I'm not your normal guy; I can listen and type at the same time.'

'There are passages in here relating to the sin of homosexuality.'

'Yes, anything else?'

'Mum and son really got stuck into the Book of Revelation. You know that book?'

'Doesn't he write about seven seals?'

'He does, but what's interesting is that it seems the Merrells were only interested in four of the seals.'

'Meaning what?' He stopped typing and pushed his chair next to Mulroy's.

'See,' he pointed.

'They've marked the passages in black, but I still don't get it.'

'Got time for me to explain it?'

'I need a coffee first.'

As he looked up, Shapiro was walking past the coffee machine.

191

'Shapiro. You're headed that way. Can you get me a coffee, mate?'

'Haven't you got two legs?'

'Yeah, but they're both needed here. Go on, be a sport.'

'Okay. But just this once.'

'Thanks, I owe you one.' He looked closely at the Bible passages. 'So they marked out the four horsemen of the apocalypse. What do these passages mean?'

'Well, they can be interpreted in different ways. The first one is the white horse. It could be interpreted as the Roman Empire's conquest, or Christ, or infectious disease, or as evil.'

'That's pretty wide. What's the infectious disease interpretation?' he asked.

'Book six, chapter one, verse two. Read it, if you're interested.'

'Not really. Read it out for me. The simplified version.'

'Well, this dude's on a white horse, he's wearing a crown and using his bow and arrow to spread pestilence throughout the land. That's about the sum of it.'

'Right. Moving on,' Peter said.

'The red horse signifies war.' Mulroy read out, *'When He broke the second seal, I heard the second living creature saying, "Come." And another, a red horse, went out; and to him who sat on it, it was granted to take peace from the earth, and that men would slay one another; and a great sword was given to him.'*

'Okay, although your version's more succinct. Next.'

'The black horse is about famine or Empire oppression. You want my version or the King James version?'

'I can see our deadline on the horizon.'

'Okay. So the next rider's carrying a set of scales and weighing out basic food for inflated prices. It's costs twenty dollars for a Big Mac, only no one can afford it.'

Peter leaned back on his chair and rubbed his hands over his temples. 'I don't get any of this. Is it just something related to their Bible study?' he asked. 'Maybe it was nothing more than that.'

'Could be. The fourth horse is pale, and signifies death.'

'Maybe along with physically planning the shooting, they were spiritually preparing for it.'

'I feel like I've wasted time reading these passages. It's easy to read things into the Bible that simply aren't there.' Mulroy stood up and stretched.

'Go get yourself a coffee. And while you're at it, you might as well see where Shapiro's gone with mine.'

Mulroy returned with two cups and handed one to Peter. 'Couldn't find Shapiro.'

Peter took a gulp and stretched out. 'Where would you have Armageddon if you were planning it?'

'Somewhere out in the desert. It's quiet, no interruptions, no complaining neighbours. You could just go for it. But I think the location has already been chosen. It's Israel.'

'Thanks. Where else would the world end?'

Mulroy looked defeated.

'Have a look through those newspapers,' said Peter. 'Tell me if you see anything about Carmel Ridge Loans.'

'While I was reading the Bible I was thinking about the name and wondering if it was a Biblical reference, like Mount Carmel, or am I reading too much into it?'

Peter rocked back and forth on his chair for several minutes. 'Possibly. Although how that connects to Albuquerque, I wouldn't know.'

Mulroy shook his head. 'I don' think they have anything to do with each other.'

'I think I'd better go have a talk to Margulies. Maybe he'll be able to tell me about the activities of Carmel Ridge.'

CHAPTER FORTY-NINE

Margulies's office, Geary Street, San Francisco.

AL MARGULIES'S LAW PRACTICE REEKED OF WEALTH, FROM THE heavy, double-glass entrance door to the original artwork, leather sofas and teak table in reception. It was furnished with a disregard for expense and a keen eye for elegance. It was appropriate that his receptionist would also be stunning. Peter was taken aback by her beauty; she was tall, busty and exotic. Her dress straddled the border of good taste. She had the warmest brown eyes fringed by the longest lashes. His last love, Ruby, a blonde, had been beautiful too, but in a very different way. It wasn't Peter's fault if his taste in women was eclectic.

He stared at her for several minutes until she stopped typing and looked up.

'I hope you weren't waiting long. May I help you?'

'I was just admiring your typing,' he said. 'You're fast. You must be typing over a hundred words a minute.'

'One-eighty. You know about typing?' she smiled.

'My name is Peter Clancy, I'm a reporter from the *San Francisco Daily*. I know a little about typing but I'm always looking to improve. You don't run classes do you?' He handed her his business card.

'No, I don't. Do you have an appointment?' she asked brusquely.

'No, but I would like to see Mr Margulies if at all possible. I just want to ask him a few questions.'

Her face softened. 'I'm trying to figure out where you're from...' She wrinkled her nose as she searched her mind. Peter found it alluring. 'Not Boston...' She stiffened again when she heard a male voice calling out.

'Claudia…'

'What does it pertain to? Mr Margulies is very busy.' She snapped back to attention.

'I'm doing a story and I just have some background questions on a company he represents. I'm no expert so I need a little help with it.'

'Just take a seat, Mr Clancy. I'll see what I can do.'

Peter retreated to the waiting area, picked up a *Time* magazine and pretended to read. He could hear Claudia talking on the phone to someone, presumably Margulies. By the look on her face she was getting a blast from the other end. He looked up when he noticed Claudia standing over him.

'He'll see you between appointments. You may have to wait a while.'

'That's okay. I'm in no rush.'

He went back to pretending to read the magazine. Every now and then he would find himself drifting away from it to look at Claudia. He imagined her swimming in the Mediterranean. *That's precisely where a woman like that would fit in.* Then he imagined himself swimming in the Med with her. That kept his mind occupied for a while. After that, he stopped imagining. It wouldn't do him any good to take the affair too far, even in his head.

Claudia stopped typing and stepped around to the other side of the counter and started arranging flowers in a vase. Her dress was definitely a size too small. Peter was mesmerised.

'You were wondering about my accent,' he said. 'I was wondering about your heritage.'

'Half Italian, half Spanish, a hundred per cent American.'

'I thought so,' he said. 'I'm a hundred per cent Australian. My accent, that is. Everything else is Irish and who-knows-what else.'

Claudia smiled and the office lit up. She reached up to place the vase on a shelf.

Peter shot up. 'Can I help you?'

'Oh no, I can manage,' she replied. Her dress rose as she stretched. Her legs were long, lean and tanned.

Peter sat back down again and admired the view. *It's been too long…*

An office door opened. The sound of conversation in the corridor shocked Peter out of his daydream.

'Mr Clancy,' Claudia called. 'Mr Margulies will see you now.'

Peter looked at his watch. Two hours had flown by. He jumped out of his chair and headed down the corridor as two stony-faced men in dark suits headed towards him from the other end. He brushed past them and walked into Margulies's office. Before he could close the door, he heard, *You're a persistent fuck, aren't you? I was hoping you would give up.*

Margulies was in his sixties; short, rotund, his dyed black hair slick with gel and his face viperous.

'We haven't met, I'm Peter Clancy from the *Daily*. I just have a few questions.' He held out his hand, which made Margulies laugh.

'Shake hands with a reporter? I'd rather piss on my hand.' Margulies poked his finger into Peter's chest.

Peter could feel himself getting angry. 'You represent companies?'

'That's nothing to do with you,' Margulies said as he returned to his desk and sat down. Peter began to follow suit when Margulies barked, 'Don't fucking sit down. I don't expect you to be here very long.'

'I read a newspaper promotion saying that you did.'

'If it was in the article, then I must. You can believe everything you see in print, can't you?' He poured himself a glass of something from a crystal decanter. 'Tell me what's this really about. You wanting background questions about companies sounds like bullshit to me.'

'Have you heard of Carmel Ridge Loans?' Peter asked. 'Or Alexander Shafer?'

Margulies didn't answer immediately. 'I've never heard of them. Where did you get your information? If it was fucking Claudia, I'll fire her. She may be pretty but she isn't the sharpest knife in the drawer.'

'No, it wasn't her. I found your name in a business directory. You're listed as the nominee of the company. Do you know anything about that?' Peter asked.

Margulies tapped his hand on the desk before answering. 'Carmel Ridge Loans? I've never heard of them.'

'But your name is listed…'

'Well, it's fucking wrong, isn't it? Now get the fuck out of my office before I call security.'

Peter didn't move. 'What do you know about The Ten Commandments Church massacre?'

'I told you to get out.' Margulies picked up his phone. 'Claudia, get security,' he shouted.

Peter sat down in a chair.

'The police are looking at a connection between the church massacre and Carmel Ridge Loans? Do you know anything about that?'

'Get the fuck out,' Margulies yelled as he reached into a drawer and pulled out a 45-calibre pistol.

Peter held up his hands. 'Don't shoot, I'm a member of the press, remember.'

'So? They'd never convict me.'

Peter stood up as a security guard came rushing into the office. He grabbed Peter by the arm.

'Get him out of here,' Margulies shouted as he waved the pistol around.

'Think about what I've said, Mr Margulies. Do you want to be connected with these activities? It could jeopardise your licence to practise.'

Peter was manhandled back into the corridor. 'Nice meeting you, Claudia,' he called as he was dragged past Claudia's desk.

'It didn't go so well,' she said, shaking her head.

'It's just an unfortunate part of the job. Call me if—' he managed to say as he was pushed out the door.

CHAPTER FIFTY

Daily offices.

BACK AT WORK, PETER HAD TO ADMIT TO HIMSELF THAT HIS meeting with Margulies hadn't quite gone as planned, although he hadn't really formulated a plan to begin with. It wasn't a complete loss: he got to meet Claudia. The deadline was now looming large and he was running out of ideas.

'You got nothing out of Margulies,' said Mulroy, without looking up from his screen.

'How do you know?' Peter muttered.

'I can tell.'

'The prick pulled a gun on me.'

'You make an easy target.'

'I'm thinking that's pretty extreme, what's he hiding?'

'Hmm. So, where to from here?' Mulroy asked. 'I've looked through most of these papers. There's nothing in them related to Carmel Ridge Loans. And no mention of the Merrells.'

'Shit. I need a drink.' He got off his chair and headed towards the vending machine. He turned around when he heard his phone ring.

'It's Jerry Belinski, Peter. You might want to take this,' Mulroy called out.

Peter rushed back to his desk and snatched the phone off Mulroy. 'What have you got for me?' he asked as he sat down at his desk and picked up a pen.

'We got the statements from the bank,' Belinski replied.

'Anything interesting?' Peter put the receiver into the nape of his neck and grabbed his notepad.

'Yeah, it's interesting in that she seemed to be financially secure.

She only had five hundred dollars in the bank but she didn't owe money to anyone and she owned her house outright.'

'What about Carmel Ridge Loans?'

'Nothing. They're not on the statements. We had a real close look,' Belinski replied.

'Could Carmel Ridge Loans be a front company?'

'I've only seen that with organised crime but they'll have a legitimate business like a building construction company, or a restaurant to launder money from their illegal activities.'

'Is it possible that a religious organisation could be doing the same thing and Margulies is fronting Carmel Ridge Loans?' Peter asked.

'If they wanted to keep some of their activities under the radar. Perhaps.'

'Which brings me back to Margulies. I had a talk to him this morning. He pulled a gun on me and kicked me out.'

Belinski laughed.

'Not funny, Jerry.'

'I'll put some pressure on him. I'll go and have a talk to him.'

'Good. Hang the slimy little shit out of the window if you have to. I'm going to talk my boss into letting me go to Albuquerque.'

Stella was unambiguous about her thoughts on Peter's pursuit of Carmel Ridge Loans all the way to New Mexico. Everyone in the office heard her shout and slam her fist down on her desk. Her response wasn't measured; Peter had always known she was a firebrand, but he struggled to recognise her these days.

'I'm convinced that Carmel Ridge is a front company for The Ten Commandments Church,' he said.

'Yeah? I'm convinced that Santa is alive and well and coming to my house this Christmas with a cure for me. You've got nothing and I'm sick of hearing about it. You got nothing out of Al Margulies. And even if I thought there was some evidence to back your hunch, I would still ask one of the reporters in Albuquerque to check it out.'

'Shit, Stella, you're letting your position cloud your judgement. I bet if you were in my shoes, you'd already be there,' he responded.

'You think you know everything about journalism but, from where I sit, you know shit. Have you failed to notice that The Ten Commandments has gotten a lot of public support because of the shooting? If we go after this church for no good reason we'll be crucified, not only by the other media outlets but by the church's lawyers too.' Stella picked up a newspaper. 'In today's *Chronicle*… Elias Gatting is on the front cover talking about his pain on losing his parents. That's a story we didn't get because we've fallen out with the church.'

'Are you blaming me?' he asked.

'I'm blaming the fact that we were overzealous after the shooting. We should have treaded more carefully. We should have been a little more sensitive.'

'Well hey, I was the one roughed up by them without any provocation. Pick me.' He held up his hands.

'The public love this stuff, Peter,' Stella said as she pointed at the paper.

Peter grabbed the newspaper from her and scanned the article. 'They're still going on about the Merrells being victims of gay activists.' He threw the paper back on the desk. 'Don't you get it? The shooting serves the church's purpose.'

Stella took a deep breath. 'I think you've lost your judgement. I'm giving you some time off. I don't think you've been the same since the shooting. I'm giving you five days off.'

'That's fine by me.' He turned around and headed for the door.

'And think seriously about whether you want to continue at the *Daily*,' she continued.

'Are you firing me?' Peter said as he spun around.

'No, just think hard about whether you still have what it takes to do your job.'

'I never thought that those words would ever come from you. I really thought we had a close working bond as well as a close friendship. Some old hack told me during my cadetship days, "Don't trust anyone you work with, son, they either want your job or they want to steal your lead. And worst of all, the bastards never shout at the pub."'

Stella was shaking her head 'It's not that.'

Peter left, slamming the door after him. He went back to his desk and grabbed his coat. He called out, 'I'll see you when I get back,' as he walked away.

'Where are you going?' Mulroy called back.

'Apparently, the Rio Grande is lovely this time of year.'

'You're going to visit the Carmel Ridge office? The boss agreed for you to go to A—' he began.

'Of course not. I just thought I'd go sightseeing for a few days,' he said as he headed to the elevator.

CHAPTER FIFTY-ONE

Albuquerque, New Mexico.

PETER DROVE OUT OF ALBUQUERQUE INTERNATIONAL AIRPORT following the map he had spread out on the passenger seat. Except for the high mountains in the distance, he might have been in inland Australia. It had the same dry heat, the same absence of greenery. The sunlight was different, though. It wasn't as blindingly white as the Australian sun. And the cars travelled on the wrong side of the road.

He had been expecting to see Pueblo buildings scattered everywhere, but Albuquerque generally looked like just another city. Hopefully, this was a city that was going to provide answers.

He pulled over by the side of the road to check the map again. The address was near Tijeras, a small town high up in the Sandia Mountains along Interstate 40. He estimated that the address he was searching for was about twenty miles away from the city centre. He thought it was interesting that a business address should be that far out of town. He accelerated back onto the highway and headed east.

Talavera Road was a turn-off onto a dirt road just before Tijeras. For a moment, Peter felt like he was back in the Australian bush. Truthfully, the vegetation bore little resemblance to home, so it must have been the dirt road that felt so familiar. He travelled about three miles before he saw the first signs warning against trespassing onto the Carmel Ridge Ranch. He stopped the car and checked the property number against the address for Carmel Ridge Loans. It was the same.

He drove on slowly until he came upon open grassland. He looked around and estimated that it stretched for at least one hundred acres. A compound of ten outbuildings was situated a hundred or so yards away from the road, dominated by an enormous, two-storey ranch house built out of logs. The entire compound was surrounded by high mesh fencing.

Peter stopped the car near a set of towering spiked wrought-iron gates which dominated the entrance. There was a sign stuck on one of the gates with *No Photographs Permitted* and *No Trespassing* written on it. Clearly, whoever was inside either valued privacy very highly or had something to hide. He tried the gates, but they obviously operated remotely.

Near the gate was an intercom with a buzzer, but without identification or instructions. He pressed the buzzer and, when there was no response after a few minutes, he pressed it again. This time the response was immediate.

'State your business.' The voice was clipped, calm and male.

Peter was tempted to pretend he was from a government agency but he changed his mind at the last moment. People with seven-foot fences were unlikely to take him at face value and he'd left his cunning kit behind. 'I'm Peter Clancy from the *San Francisco Daily*,' he said. 'I have some questions about the Carmel Ridge Loans Company. Could you assist me?'

The man didn't answer immediately and for a moment Peter thought all communication had stopped.

Three minutes later, the voice resumed. 'If you wait by the gate, I'll send someone down to assist you.'

Peter returned to his car and sat down. He pulled out the same camera he'd taken with him to the church service and furtively snapped several photos of the complex. A full fifteen minutes passed before he saw an open-top Jeep containing two men descend the gravel driveway. The driver looked like a security guard and the passenger was an older man, probably in his sixties. Peter got out of the car and walked to the gates as the Jeep pulled up on the other side.

The security guard wore a pistol in a shoulder holster on the outside of his shirt. He climbed out of the Jeep and then helped the older man out.

'Hi, I'm...' Peter began.

'Yes, son, we know who you are.' The older man was tall with greying hair and walked with the aid of a cane. He smiled. 'You've come all the way from San Francisco to ask me questions about some company called Carmel Ridge Loans?'

'I didn't catch your name.'

'That's because I haven't pitched it to you yet. I'm Joshua Mason and this is my employee, Robert.'

'Mr Mason. Is this your place?'

'I'm the caretaker of this beautiful piece of serenity.'

Peter thought that Mason seemed totally unsuited to the role he claimed to play. *He can barely take care of himself, let alone a ranch.* 'Can you tell me who actually owns it?' he asked.

'I'm not at liberty to provide you with that information.'

'Is this a ranch?'

'It is a place that provides all our worldly needs but, most importantly, it provides all our spiritual needs,' Mason replied.

'It's like a spiritual retreat?'

'Oh, that and much, much more. But enough of that, what's this about Carmel Ridge Loans?'

Peter shifted feet. 'Have you heard about the church shooting in San Francisco?'

'I have heard about it. A very tragic event. Is this pertaining to the shooting?'

There was something about Mason that didn't sit well with Peter. He was a little too controlled, his responses too studied. It made him uneasy. 'In a way. Do you know David and Leah Merrell?'

'Why, yes, I believe I do. What an unfortunate episode. I can confirm Mrs Merrell borrowed money from Carmel Ridge.' Mason suddenly seemed forthcoming.

It took Peter by surprise and he hadn't quite formulated his next question. 'You loan money to people?' he asked.

'Loans are available for those who are members of our congregation only. We loan money without interest to our members.'

'You can confirm that she was a member of your congregation, then?'

'She was. Mrs Merrell and her son left us about a year ago to live in San Francisco.'

'Do you know why she left?'

'She and David chose to leave. Please don't get the wrong idea about us. No one is prevented from leaving here whenever they please. Since they are no longer living, I betray no confidence when I tell you that there were problems with David and Leah Merrell. They weren't totally committed to our church and our ideals,' Mason replied.

'Does that have anything to do with David's... sexuality?' Peter waited for a reaction but Mason was inscrutable.

'I have no knowledge of that.'

'I take it that Mrs Merrell still owed Carmel Ridge Loans money, and you were chasing her for it.'

'Mr Clancy, like all organisations, we have our business obligations. Our loans are exactly that. It's a pity that some folk confuse "loan" with "gift". We are totally self-supporting but we still need to account to our members. We did have financial difficulties with her. We simply wanted her to pay back her debt.'

'Did you ever go to San Francisco to see her personally? Did you ever counsel Mrs Merrell about her son? Did you know Pastor Gatting?' Peter fired out the questions.

Mason looked uncomfortable. 'I think I've told you all I can. I have no further comments to make, Mr Clancy. Enjoy your stay in New Mexico. I have work to attend to. Good day.'

Robert took hold of Mason's arm and led him back to the Jeep as Peter returned to his car. He waited until the Jeep had moved away before starting the car. He drove back along the dirt road and turned onto the road leading to Tijeras. He pulled the car over in front of a diner and got out. The village was quiet except for a pick-up driving along the street and a couple of people looking at a street stall selling fresh produce.

Peter went inside and sat on a stool at the counter. A waitress in a striped apron approached him within ten seconds. She looked fresh out of central casting, from the pencil behind her ear right down to her comfortable shoes. He ordered a coffee and a piece of apple pie.

The waitress didn't bother to write it down. The place was empty except for the two of them.

She brought out his order a minute or two later, and then returned a few minutes after that. Peter had only just taken a sip of his coffee and a mouthful of pie.

'How do you like it?' she asked. She was probably in her forties, but she retained a girl-next-door prettiness.

Peter swallowed. 'It's very good.'

'You're not from around here are you?' she asked.

'I'm from San Francisco.' She watched as he took another bite. 'Did you make this pie?'

'I did. I always get compliments for it.'

'It may very well be the best I've tasted,' he remarked.

'Thank you.' The woman blushed. 'Brenda. I'm the owner.'

'Pleased to meet you. I'm Peter. Is it usually this quiet? I'm surprised this place isn't packed.'

'During the week it is as quiet as a tranquil sky... Are you here on vacation?'

'No. I'm a reporter from San Francisco.'

'This isn't a place reporters usually come to, and I know everything that happens here. Has something happened that I haven't heard about?' she asked.

'I was out at the Carmel Ridge Ranch.'

Brenda's eyes widened. 'What have they done?'

'Nothing. I'm doing a story on religious retreats. Do you know much about them?'

'They keep to themselves. If one of them came in here, I wouldn't even know who they were.'

Peter finished off his coffee and pie, and Brenda bent down to collect them. 'I like a man with an appetite. Another coffee, Peter?'

'Yes, please.'

She sauntered off towards the counter, and returned with a fresh cup moments later.

'So, have you heard anything about the ranch?' Peter asked.

'I know they don't like people snooping around their place. I heard that some local kids went out there once, looking around. The

206

crazy kids got under the fence, but they soon went back through it when they had shots fired at them.'

'Wow, that's extreme. They clearly value their privacy.'

'I always say, leave folks alone who want to be left alone, but I don't think you should shoot at people. I think you should take that as a warning, in case you're planning on crossing those folk. '

'You've obviously figured I'm not a travel writer. That said, I always go through the proper channels. I'm a reporter, not a commando.'

'Preservation is better than expiration, I say.' Brenda chuckled.

'Did the kids ever complain about the shots to the local sheriff?' Peter asked.

'Not as far as I know.'

Brenda took away Peter's empty cup and wiped down the counter top.

'Did they ever tell anyone what they saw when they got inside?'

'I heard they saw RVs with spotlights coming towards them. Then they were shot at and they were out of there.'

'Thanks for the information, Brenda.' He reached into the pocket of his jacket, pulled out his card and handed it to her. 'If you come across any more information about the ranch, can you give me a call?'

'Sure. I want to know what's going on there as much as the next person.'

'Well, no reason to suspect that it's anything illegal. I'm just interested to know what motivates people to go there and why these places are around. Thanks for the coffee and pie.' He handed her a twenty-dollar bill. 'Keep the change.'

He climbed back into the car and drove into Albuquerque, and stopped near the old town historic district. Since he had to kill time before catching the flight back to San Francisco, he figured he might as well look at the attractions. He'd lived in a lot of places but he almost never took the time to see the sights.

He got out of the car and crossed the road but the pavement was thick with tourists and souvenir stands. Some were selling silver turquoise jewellery, others Navajo crafts. He retreated back to the hire car. It was now dawning on him that the trip, at his own expense, was probably a waste of time. As he considered how best to fill in time, his cell phone rang. The voice at the other end was Belinski's.

'I called your office,' he said. 'Mulroy told me you were on vacation.'

'A work-imposed vacation—if you could call it that. It's more like, go away and think about your future at the paper.'

'We call that stress leave. So where are you having your vacation?'

'In Albuquerque. Where else?'

'I could think of lots of other places to go. Tell me you're not checking out Carmel Ridge Loans.'

'Okay, I won't. But I drove by there today and turns out it's a well-guarded, very private religious commune out in the middle of nowhere. Doesn't look like any loans company I've ever seen.'

'It probably caters to an exclusive clientele. By the way, I got back Alexander Shafer's records,' said Belinski.

'Does he have a criminal record?'

'He assaulted a couple of tourists a year ago who were taking photographs of—'

'Not the Carmel Ridge Ranch.'

'You got it. He stated that his position was Director of Security, Carmel Ridge Churches.'

'Well that's interesting.'

'So, he was a member of Carmel Ridge, but I'm not sure of any connection between him and the Merrells. A bit too coincidental that they turn up in San Francisco and at the same church.'

'They're dots that just have to be connected.'

'I also had a talk to Al Margulies. Nice-looking secretary, by the way.'

'Yeah. She's a babe. Still waiting for her to call me.'

'Well, Margulies didn't pull a gun on me, but he wasn't giving out any information about Carmel Ridge Loans.'

'That guy is as tight as a fish's arse.'

Belinski laughed.

'I wonder if the Merrells and Shafer knew each other?' Peter asked.

'They probably did. When are you headed back here?'

'I might go out to the ranch and have another look,' he replied. 'I'll be back tomorrow on the first flight.'

'Are you crazy? Leave that stuff to the local police.'

'Well, I'm not going to go in there and bust the place open.'

'Stay away from the place, Peter. You don't want to mess with religious fanatics. Things can turn ugly on a dime.'

'Fine, if you insist.' Movement further along the street caught his attention. A parking attendant was slapping a ticket on a car windscreen three cars away. He didn't want to add any further expense to the growing tally. 'Sorry, Jerry. Got to go. The meter's just run out.'

Chapter Fifty-Two

PETER CHECKED INTO A CHEAP MOTEL NEAR THE AIRPORT AND waited until five o'clock. He debated whether he should risk going back to the ranch, but the temptation to blow open the story was greater than any concerns he had about his personal safety. He'd already taken on the underworld and survived; Joshua Mason was hardly in the same league. After changing into a pair of old jeans and a dark t-shirt, he headed back up to Tijeras.

It was getting onto dusk when he hit the dirt road. It might have been a beautiful sunset in the mountains but Peter wasn't there for the peace and tranquillity. He parked the car about a mile from the ranch, just off a side road that he had spotted earlier.

He knew that he would only alert them to his presence if he went anywhere near the front gate. He had seen the closed circuit TV cameras there when he had last visited. Instead, he crossed through a forest of juniper and oak, until he reached the boundary fence. He searched for cameras along the perimeter, but couldn't see any. They probably didn't need them; the fence looked like it was impenetrable. There was no hum and no transformers. At least it wasn't electrified.

In the distance he could hear the sound of rapid gunfire. He surmised that the ranch must have a gun range. Much closer to his location, he could hear people singing.

Having grown up in the bush, Peter knew that fences weren't infallible. He doubted that there would be alarm sensors along the fence, since it was likely that wild animals pushed through it on occasion. He was also hoping that the odd small breach in the fence might have gone unnoticed. He waited for the dark, and then he took a penlight out of his pocket and crept towards the fence. If he couldn't find a gap in the fence, he was going to call it a night.

He followed the fence for about two hundred yards until he found a gap where the wire had come away from the post and lifted out of the ground. Part of it had rusted so he bound his hand with his tie and pulled it out further, just far enough for him to squeeze through. Despite his usual diet of booze and takeaway, he was still pretty slender. He looked around and listened for any activity. The gunfire had now ceased. Apart from the distant sound of music, it was deathly quiet. The air had filled with the smell of ozone, and he wondered if a storm was brewing. He took a deep breath, made a mental diagram of his location, and crawled through the gap. If he couldn't find his way back, he'd be stuck out on a limb, relying on the mercy of the members of Carmel Ridge.

He inched along the ground until he found a solitary oak growing in a paddock. Nearby, a small mob of cattle scattered as he approached. He stood up behind the tree, and massaged the blood back into his legs. His shirt was covered in dirt. He listened to the unfamiliar sounds of the Sandia countryside and a distant rumble of thunder, and estimated that the singing he could hear was coming from a large hall a couple of hundred yards away from him.

The small camera was still in his pocket, but Peter didn't take it out. To use it would only expose him. He shaded the penlight with his palm and slinked towards the hall. Over the thunder, he could hear the growl of an RV coming in his direction, driving slowly along the boundary fence. A spotlight attached to the roof shone along the fence and out into the forest beyond. He dropped to the ground, hoping that the shrubbery would provide coverage. The spotlight continued to illuminate the fence and passed over Peter. He breathed a deep sigh of relief.

As he moved forward again, a flash of lightning illuminated the sky and was soon followed by a thunderclap, much closer than before. He raised the collar of his shirt and waited for the inevitable downpour of rain. He was drenched in seconds, but at least he wasn't cold. It wasn't nearly as warm as the summer rain in North Queensland, but it certainly wasn't cold Melbourne rain either.

The RV turned off its spotlight and high-tailed it back to the complex of buildings. Peter felt the dirt turn to mud under him and he raised himself onto his hands and knees and kept crawling.

It was as if the whole of the year's rain had decided to fall on one night: the night Peter had chosen to infiltrate the ranch. The rain was dense and blinding as he headed towards the light of the hall. It streaked down the windows on the southern side of the building. It was so heavy that anyone looking out wouldn't see him.

He reached a wall of the hall and leaned against it. He felt like cursing the weather. He wiped the water from his eyes and looked about him. Not far from him was a large window on the lee side of the building. He checked it. The rain had hardly touched it. From his vantage point, the window allowed him limited visibility of what was going on inside, without him being seen. There were some fifty adults in the hall, with a small group of children seated at the front.

Joshua Mason was standing on a platform but Peter couldn't make out what he was saying. It looked like he was delivering an impassioned sermon, judging by his flamboyant gestures and the movement of his mouth. In the centre of the stage stood an altar, covered only by a white cloth.

An enormous portrait of a man with long, white hair dominated the stage. He would have looked like a Hindu guru if he'd been Indian. What was most notable about him was his pallor; his skin was almost translucent. There was a slight bend to the corners of his mouth, as if he was about to smile.

Mason turned to the portrait every so often, as if he was venerating the man in the portrait. Peter found it disturbing. He doubted that he'd be able to gather any information but, if he could take a photograph of the portrait, he might find out who this guru—this prophet—was. He pulled the small camera out of his pocket and held it up to the corner of the window, confident he couldn't be seen by the congregation. He felt like blessing the weather. He waited. Lightning was still flashing intermittently across the sky.

Then there was an ear-splitting strike. He seized that moment to take two photographs. The strike was so close that he could smell sulphur. Some of the children were crying and looking to their parents for reassurance. Peter slipped the camera back in his pocket and headed out again into the torrential rain.

He scrambled across the sodden fields to the gap in the fence and back to his car. He thought about peeling off his muddy clothes and throwing them in the trunk of the car, but he was too cold and too jubilant to do that. He started the car and slowly drove back across the muddy road, feeling like he might have finally opened a crack in the investigation.

He returned to the motel, shedding his clothes at the door. After a hot shower and a stiff scotch, he changed into a sweatshirt and track pants, and crawled into bed. He checked the time. It was nine o'clock.

He reached for his flask of scotch and poured out the last of the contents. He then picked up the phone and called reception. The surly girl at the desk agreed to bring him a bottle of Johnnie Walker Black for a price he was willing to pay, just to forget about the night.

He hung up the phone and lay back on the bed. As he waited for the liquid anaesthetic to arrive, his earlier optimism began to wane. *All this effort and what have I got? I've got nothing.* He closed his eyes and considered going back to Australia and forgetting any of this had happened. Working at the *Wagga Wagga Chronicle* had its appeal. As he imagined himself driving up the Newell Highway, his cell phone rang.

'Yeah, Peter Clancy here but I don't feel like talking to anyone right now.' He was about to switch off his phone when he heard a voice say, 'It's Claudia.'

He sat upright. 'Claudia! Oh, right! Sorry about that. I've just had a bad day. How are you?'

'However bad yours was, I bet you haven't had one as bad as mine,' she replied.

There was a knock on the door. He got off the bed and opened it to the receptionist with the bottle of scotch.

'Are you on assignment?' asked Claudia.

Peter took the scotch, paid her the agreed amount and tipped the girl a dollar. She frowned and slammed the door as she left. 'Yeah, kind of,' he continued. 'I'm in Albuquerque right now but it was pretty bleak until you called. So, what happened to you?' He unscrewed the bottle and poured himself a glass.

'That asshole of a boss fired me today.'

'You were right. That trumps my day. I only met your asshole of a boss once, but seems to me that Al Margulies is a dickhead of the first order. I'm sure he didn't deserve you working for him. You deserve much better.'

'He was always feeling me up. I got tired of it and I told him so. The past is the past. I moved on and he didn't.'

Peter spluttered. 'You had a relationship with him?'

'No, not a relationship. It was never that. I guess I was going through a bad time and he took advantage of it. It was just a fling, that's all, but he wanted to set me up, make me his mistress…'

'And you?'

'I'm no home-wrecker. So I said no, I wouldn't do that to his wife. He said I already did it and what was the difference? I told him sex was sex, but a relationship was cheating. So he got all angry and he threatened me, but I said no again and that's when he fired me.'

'Are you okay?'

'Sure. Thanks for asking.' She was quiet for a moment. 'The main reason I'm calling is that you seemed pretty interested in Al Margulies, and I know a lot about Al Margulies. I think you'll be very interested in what I have to say.'

'About Carmel Ridge Loans?'

'That and other information besides. But not over the phone.'

'I'll be back in San Francisco tomorrow morning first thing. Can I meet you somewhere?'

'And the other thing is… I don't know how to say this…'

Peter was revelling in the moment. *It's a booty call! She wants me. I can tell.* 'Go on.'

'I want five thousand dollars for the information.'

He gulped. 'Five thousand dollars?'

'If you can't pay me, I'll go somewhere else,' she replied.

'I'll have to ask my boss tomorrow about it. You don't want to go anywhere else right now. Five thousand dollars is a lot of money. Give me something to take to my boss.'

'I don't really want to do this over the phone.'

'The phone's not bugged. No one's gonna deal with you without knowing what you've got first.'

'Oh, well then, maybe just a little…' She huffed. 'I overheard you ask Al about Alexander Shafer. He used to visit the office… often. He always brought a briefcase. I have proof about stuff. That's all I'm saying right now. Remember, I want the money before I tell you all I know.'

'Where do you want to meet?'

'Meet me at Devine's at eleven tomorrow morning.'

'The coffee shop? Okay. Fine. Tell me, why'd you phone me?'

'I felt sorry for you the other day and I trust you. Besides, I don't know any other reporters.'

Peter wasn't sure what to make of her. 'Thanks, Claudia. Five thousand's a tall order but I'll do my best. Tomorrow at eleven.' He hung up the cell phone and punched the air. He dialled Belinski's number.

'Do you think you could possibly get that answering machine out of properties for me?'

'Why?'

'I want to have a listen to the tape.'

'No way. It's evidence.'

'But you let me have the bibles.'

'The bibles were nothing. I checked them over. They were clean.'

'Yeah,' said Peter. 'But the phone messages are evidence, are they? Of what?'

Belinski thought for a while. 'I don't know exactly.'

'Well, let me listen to them. Maybe I can give you a hand with the tape. I've got an interview at eleven but I'll be back in the office by two.'

Belinski didn't reply straight away. After a while, he said, 'I'll think about it,' and hung up.

CHAPTER FIFTY-THREE

Next day. *Daily* offices.

STELLA WAS BACK IN HOSPITAL AFTER HAVING COLLAPSED AT work again. Peter was a hair's breadth away from cancelling his meeting with Claudia and forgetting about the whole thing, but the newshound in him simply wouldn't let him. He wasn't a doctor and he knew that there wasn't anything he could do medically for Stella. If she had been well, there would have been no way on earth she would have countermanded his story. So, after sending his photos down to the lab and wresting Mulroy from his desk, he really didn't feel bad taking it over Stella's head to Frank.

Frank, his eyes shut and his hands gripped behind his neck, listened to Peter describe the events of the previous night.

He opened his eyes but his face betrayed no emotion. 'How much does she want?'

'Five grand.'

'That's a lot for a possible dead end. Let's negotiate.'

'No. She said she'd go to another paper if I didn't come up with the money.'

'Another paper... Yeah? Maybe we should let her try to find another paper with deep pockets who'll trust her. Then she might negotiate.'

'I'm meeting her at a coffee shop at eleven. The story has legs, I promise.'

Frank leaned forward and tapped his left hand on the desk several times before replying. Peter checked the clock on the wall; it was ten thirty.

'If this doesn't go anywhere,' said Frank, 'I'll be put in a position where I'll have to fire you and sue you for the five grand. Are you prepared to take that risk?'

'I'm prepared to take that risk.'

He reached into a drawer and pulled out a cheque book, pen poised. 'What name?'

'Claudia. I don't know her last name,' Peter replied.

'Shit, Peter, you don't even know her full name?' He sighed. 'Can I trust you to fill that part in?'

'You can. And leave the amount blank. Her story may not be worth what she's asking.'

Frank sat forward and began to write. 'You remind me of myself when I was younger, except I was only willing to go to the edge of the cliff to get the lead, where you're willing to walk right up and look over it.'

'The massacre wasn't just about a crazy lady and her son, it was planned by people outside the church. There was a wider involvement.'

'How sure are you about this?'

'Sure as a fart after eating a can of beans,' he replied.

Frank endorsed the cheque *not over five thousand dollars* and handed it to Peter. 'Just make sure, when you peer over that precipice, you don't fall in.' He smiled. ' 'Cause no one will be able to rescue you.'

CHAPTER FIFTY-FOUR

Devine's coffee shop, San Francisco.

CLAUDIA WAS WAITING AT A TABLE AWAY FROM THE WINDOW when Peter arrived at eleven sharp. He went straight to her and, for a moment, he couldn't help getting caught up in her appearance. She was something to look at.

'Before you sit down, have you got the money?' she asked.

Peter tapped his breast pocket. 'Of course.'

'Okay.'

He sat down, took out the cheque and showed her. 'I just have to fill in your surname.' He took a pen from his pocket. 'And the amount.'

'Alvarez. My name is Claudia Alvarez. I thought we agreed about the amount.'

'I said I'd do my best. If your information is as good as you say, you'll get your five thousand. If not…' He filled in her name and slipped it halfway across the table. She glanced at it, and reached forward.

He slid the cheque away from her. 'Uh uh. Not yet. You don't buy shoes without trying them on, do you? I've shown you mine, now you show me yours.'

She frowned and reached down for her bag. She took out a piece of paper and unfolded it. She pushed it across the table.

Peter read the piece of paper and smiled. 'From Carmel Ridge Ranch? Not Carmel Ridge Loans.'

She nodded then slipped it into her handbag. 'No. They're separate companies. I have more of those and others, besides.'

'Linking—' he began.

'Ssh.'

218

A waitress appeared to take their order.

'Large coffee, no cream,' she said, looking past the other patrons and out the window. 'You?'

'Same.'

The waitress left.

'So what have you got on Al?' he asked.

Claudia looked away, past the other patrons and towards the window. 'This was really dumb,' she replied. 'I've just had a change of mind.'

Peter searched her face for a clue. She looked frightened. 'Is your life at risk?'

'I don't know what he will do. Al Margulies is a violent man,' she whispered.

The waitress returned moments later with their coffees. He watched as Claudia pouted her lips and blew on her coffee.

'That's why you should expose him,' he replied.

She put down the cup. 'I don't know if I can.'

Peter was angry. He felt like he'd been led to water and not even allowed a single sip. 'If you're not going to give me any information, I'm going to tear up the cheque. Say bye-bye to five grand and hello to the unemployment line.'

Claudia broke into tears. She dabbed her eyes with a tissue.

'We had a deal, Claudia.' He followed her line of sight as she looked out the window again. 'Do you think you were followed here? You keep looking out of the window.'

'He threatened to kill me on the phone this morning and then he said he loved me. The guy is crazy. My mind has been all over the place since then. I don't really know what to do.'

Peter reached across the table and took hold of her hand. She pulled her hand away. 'Do you want to know why I've been chasing The Ten Commandments Church?'

'Someone has stolen a lot of money from the church and laundered it through Al?'

'You know about the shooting at the church?'

'Of course I do.'

Peter lowered his voice. 'I'm certain that the shooting wasn't an act of madness, it was organised. For whatever reason, someone wanted to kill the pastor, his wife and the senator.'

'But weren't other people killed also?' she asked.

'I think that was collateral damage.' He took a sip of his coffee. 'I'm certain of a connection between Margulies, Shafer and Carmel Ridge, and the Merrells. Would I have put myself in harm's way by going to Al Margulies otherwise?'

'Well...' She reached across and patted Peter's hand. 'I think I get it now.' She kept her hand on his. 'You know about Alex Shafer... the woman...?'

'Leah Merrell? You know about her? What do you know?'

Claudia flinched when she heard a car backfiring. 'Enough for now. Can we go somewhere else to talk? Somewhere more private?'

'I have an apartment not far from here. I live by myself.'

'Can I trust you?'

'Promise I won't lay a finger on you.'

'It's not that...' she began.

'The money? Of course you can.' He tapped his chest again. 'You saw the cheque. I can go up to five thousand dollars. For the right information.'

CHAPTER FIFTY-FIVE

Peter's apartment, Dogpatch, San Francisco.

CLAUDIA'S GAZE FLITTED AROUND THE APARTMENT WHEN PETER opened the door to let her in. She looked dumbfounded. She stepped over a pile of papers just inside the door.

'So this is how a reporter likes to live? You live like a college student,' she said as she looked the apartment over again.

'The maid couldn't make it today. Wait here.' Peter went over to the kitchen bench and threw all of the pizza boxes and empty beer cans into a trash can. He gathered all of the dirty plates and cups and put them in the sink. 'Better.' He went over to a window and pulled back the curtain.

'I can see why you live by yourself.'

'I like it that way. You have no one to blame for the mess but yourself.' Peter started to fill a kettle. 'My work takes up most of my time.' He opened up the refrigerator briefly. 'Hungry?' he asked. 'There's not much there.'

'You have eggs, some tomatoes, milk, a block of cheese. I'll make lunch. I have a feeling that I'm probably the better cook.' Claudia smiled.

'I have a feeling you probably are. Another coffee?' Peter asked.

'Have you got anything stronger?'

'I've run out of beer but I do have red wine and a bottle of scotch.'

'A glass of wine sounds fine to me,' she replied.

He switched off the kettle, reached into a cupboard and pulled out the bottle.

'You've got wine glasses? Please tell me that you don't use jelly jars.'

Peter reached into another cupboard and pulled out two long-stemmed wine glasses. 'I may be a bachelor but I'm not a barbarian.'

He poured out two glasses and handed one to Claudia. 'Cheers, to a better future,' he said.

'Cheers.'

They chinked glasses and took a drink. He watched Claudia open and shut each of the kitchen cupboards, pulling out plates, a bowl, a whisk and a frying pan. Her shoulders jiggled as she beat the eggs and grated in the cheese. She was smiling as she cut up the tomatoes and fried up the lot. It was as if she was letting go of the day's worries. She piled the omelette and tomatoes onto two plates, grabbed a couple of forks and returned to the sofa, where Peter sat patiently. She kicked off her high heels when she sat down.

'You don't mind, do you? My feet are aching.'

Peter took his plate and tasted the omelette. It was rich and cheesy and good. 'Delicious.'

'Really? You like?' He watched her cool the eggs with her breath. With lips like hers, he doubted he'd ever tire of watching her do that. 'Mmm,' she said.

He waited for her to take another mouthful. 'Do you now want to talk about what you know?'

She took a deep breath. 'You're not going to record me, are you?'

'My five thousand. For that, I need you on the record, it better be outstanding and I need all the documents you've got, or it's no deal.'

She was mulling it over. 'Do you have to write down my name when you write the article?'

'I can use a fake name.' He paused. 'We do this?'

'Yes, that's fine.'

Peter took a Dictaphone out of a drawer and returned to the couch. He clicked it on and asked Claudia to identify herself. He could see she was uncomfortable, but she complied.

'Go on.'

'Alex Shafer used to bring a briefcase full of money into Al Margulies's office every week.'

'How do you know the briefcase was full of money?' Peter asked.

'I had to take it to the bank.'

'How long was this happening for?'

'Six months,' Claudia replied. 'About that.'

'How much was it?'

'It was a lot of money. I've taken copies of the bank statements. It was millions.'

'Have you got them on you?' he asked.

'No but they're in a safe place.'

'You have to get them to me. So, what made you take copies of the transactions?'

'I knew Al was into some illegal activities. I'm doing the books, but I don't want to get into trouble if the Feds or the IRS turn up, so I figured I may need to keep records just in case,' she replied. 'I don't know why I kept working for that bastard. The money was good, I guess. He was pretty generous, too. Once, he even bought me a car.' She finished her glass of wine and waited for Peter to refill her drink. 'Al was also laundering money for a South American drug cartel. But that's another story.'

'I'll keep that in my back pocket. What do you know about Alexander Shafer?' he asked.

'Have you met him?'

Peter nodded.

'He's a creepy guy, isn't he? He used to look at me like I was on the game and he was a narc, or something.'

'Shafer would stone people if he was given the chance. Did he talk to you?'

'Only to ask for an appointment, or to complain that he had been waiting too long.'

'So, not much interaction.'

'That's the way I liked it. He's creepier than the drug cartel people. Some of those guys are very polite.'

'That's nice to know. Where do you think Shafer was getting all the money from?' Peter asked.

'From The Ten Commandments Church. The one where all of the people were shot.'

'How do you know that?'

'Al told me,' Claudia replied. 'He trusted me. I think he probably loved me in his own weird way. He said that we'd end up together after he got rid of his wife.'

'Margulies was going to kill his wife?' Peter shook his head in disbelief.

'I don't know about that. She was going to disappear. But you don't want to know about that, do you?'

'I'll store that up for later too.'

When they had finished their eggs, Claudia lay back on the couch and rested her legs on the coffee table. She grinned. 'I caught you peeking. You're a leg man.' She yawned then shut her eyes. 'I couldn't sleep much last night. I like your voice, it's relaxing.'

'Thanks. When I get out of journalism I'll do meditation voice-overs.' He noticed she had finished her second glass of wine. He was hoping he'd be able to get all of the information out of her before she was too pissed. 'Do you think Shafer was skimming off the top?'

'So Al said. Shafer was in charge of that area at the church. Al thought it was funny.'

'Why?'

'A church that preached Christian values and one of their leaders was stealing from them.'

'So, if he got caught out, maybe he got the Merrells to shoot the Gattings and the senator. But why would he get Leah and David Merrell to do it? What a piece of work he is.'

'Evil.'

'Which brings me to what you were going to say at the coffee shop.'

'I saw her,' Claudia said.

'Leah Merrell?'

'I did.'

'Are you sure?' Peter asked.

'Of course. I recognised her photo in the newspaper.'

'Where did you see her?'

'She used to come in with Shafer sometimes. I don't know why, but he always let her carry the briefcase.'

'Do you think they were a couple?'

'I don't think so and, if they were, they didn't show it. They didn't talk to each other much. It seemed more like she was working for him,' Claudia replied.

'Which ties in neatly with the pay slip you showed me at the coffee shop. Shit. Leah Merrell was on the Carmel Ridge Ranch payroll. What a revelation. I get it. She was an employee following instructions. That, or she was brainwashed,' he said.

'She brought in the briefcase by herself one day,' she said.

'Shafer trusted her?'

'She didn't say much. She didn't seem like she was on this planet.'

'Did you see Shafer after the shooting?' he asked.

'No, I didn't. Someone else brought in the briefcase after that.'

'You know who it was?' Peter asked.

'A guy. He looked like a goon… I think his name was Max. Do you think you got your money's worth from my information?'

'Not yet. And I need all the documents to back up your story before I pay you. Here's the deal. A thousand now and the rest when I get everything. Deal?'

She closed her eyes again. 'I trust you. One now and four later.' She sounded half asleep.

Peter clicked off the Dictaphone, closed his notepad and finished his wine. 'I have a bed you might like,' he remarked.

Claudia's eyes snapped open. 'Excuse me?'

'I mean, you may feel more comfortable if you go to sleep on my bed. I promise, I'll leave you alone.'

'I'm really tired of being scared. I could lay low for a few days here. Where's your bed?' She peeled herself off the couch and picked up her high heels.

'Follow me.'

'Are the sheets clean?' she asked. 'I don't want to lay down in someone else's…'

'That's the one thing I'm careful of.' He swung open the door. 'Make yourself at home. I have to go back to work.'

She looked around the room and nodded her approval. 'Thanks. You don't mind?'

'If you crash here for a few days? No. The couch isn't the most comfortable, but I'll manage.'

She dropped her shoes and began to unzip her skirt. 'Who said anything about a couch?'

Peter smiled. He filled out the cheque for one thousand dollars and placed it on the bedside table next to her. Then he turned around and shut the door behind him, and returned to the kitchen to wash up. He had a pressing appointment in thirty minutes with the SFPD.

CHAPTER FIFTY-SIX

Daily offices.

BELINSKI WAS SITTING AT RECEPTION, PRETENDING TO READ A paper. He put it down when Peter stepped out of the elevator. 'You said you'd be back by two. You're late,' he said.

Peter smiled. 'That's rich, coming from you.' He checked Belinski's hands. They were empty. 'I was hoping you'd bring the answering machine with you. I thought I made out a good case for it.'

Belinski leapt to his feet. 'Don't flatter yourself. Got anything for me?'

'Mind if we talk somewhere more discreet?'

'Sure.'

Peter led Belinski to the conference room and shut the door. They both remained standing.

'So what did you find out?' asked Belinski.

'That going all the way to Albuquerque was a waste of time.'

'I see. Nothing else?'

'Nothing much yet. The Carmel Ridge Ranch looks more like the headquarters for a cult than a loans company. They seem to venerate some guy with a long white beard.'

'Yeah? Don't we all?'

'Not that guy. Someone else. Al Margulies is an enabler. The minute I have anything concrete you'll be the first to know.'

Belinski's gaze lingered on Peter as if he was trying to size him up. 'As far as everyone's concerned, I'm only here because I'm following up a lead on Al Margulies. You never received this from me and I have no idea how you got it, right?' He tossed a mini-tape on the table. 'It's a copy of the one in the Merrells' answering machine. You can play it on any mini-recorder.'

'You copied all of it?'

'It's all there.'

Peter picked up the tape and turned it over in his hand. 'Thanks, Jerry.' He looked at it. 'I'm following up a lead at the moment. I'll let you know how I go.'

Belinski nodded. 'If you make anything of that,' he said, pointing at the tape, 'let me know. I like conspiracy theories almost as much as you do. I'm betting that the Merrells didn't shoot up The Ten Commandments Church for no good reason, and I want to get whoever's really behind it.'

'So do I. I want to break the story and I want you to put them away. Deal?'

'Deal.' He moved towards the door. 'I'll catch up with you later. See what you think.'

Peter walked Belinski back to reception and then returned to his desk. The tape fit neatly into his Dictaphone. He clicked play and leaned back in his chair. The first message came from a member of The Ten Commandments Church discussing a meeting.

Mulroy peered around the partition that separated his desk from Peter's. 'Is that what I think it is?'

Peter hit pause. 'Possibly.'

'The answering machine?'

'Yep. The Merrells'. But you can't breathe a word about it.'

'Sure.'

He clicked it back on and listened to another message about another meeting. 'Boring, next,' he said.

The messages continued. *'Hi, it's Gretchen Gatting, here. Don't forget it's bake-a-cake week at the church, Leah…'* Message after message, they were the kind anyone might expect a church to leave. Nothing stood out. Then one came from Carmel Ridge Loans. *'Mrs Merrell, this is Pastor Mason,'* the voice began.

Peter leaned forward and paused the tape. 'That's Joshua Mason. I talked to him when I went to Carmel Ridge Ranch. He told me that they had loaned her money.' He turned it back on.

'You owe Carmel Ridge Loans six thousand, one hundred and two dollars, Mrs Merrell. Please pay as soon as possible.'

That was followed by another message from Joshua Mason. *'May I remind you that you borrowed six thousand, three hundred and four dollars. This must be repaid at the end of the month or we will commence legal action.'* Then there were more mundane messages from the Gattings and their entourage.

'There must be dozens of messages here,' Mulroy remarked.

Peter sped the tape up. Joshua Mason's voice cut through, even when everyone else sounded like chipmunks. It was the depth and timbre that made it stand apart from the rest. *'We wish to remind you that you now owe six thousand, five hundred and six dollars. We demand your immediate attention...'*

'That's a different amount every message,' Mulroy said. 'I've written them down.'

'It's not interest. Sometimes it's a bit more, sometimes less,' Peter remarked. 'Always a threat, but no follow up, it seems.'

'I wish to remind you that we are forced to commence legal action, Mrs Merrell. You now owe six thousand, seven hundred and eight dollars.'

Then there were no further messages.

'I'm surprised they didn't get rid of this,' Mulroy said.

'Maybe there's nothing to hide. Who has time to erase an answering machine tape anyway?' Peter responded. 'I have a hunch.' He opened up one of the bibles.

Mulroy peered at the opened page. 'Why are you looking at the Bible?' he asked. 'This isn't the time to be reading the Bible. Focus, man.'

'Divine inspiration? What if the amounts of money refer to passages in the Bible?'

'That's it, that's it!' Mulroy exclaimed. 'Remember what we found about the horsemen?'

'White meant evil or infectious disease. Red meant war. The pale horsemen meant death. Something like that,' Peter replied.

Mulroy read from his notes. 'Six thousand, seven hundred and eight dollars was the last amount Mason mentioned.'

Peter flipped pages until he found Revelation six, verses seven and eight. 'It's the passage about the pale horseman.' It was underlined. 'The one about death,' he said. 'And it was the last message.'

Mulroy asked, 'Did he mention a date?'

Peter rewound the tape and replayed the last message. He checked the date it was recorded. *August second.* 'That's the day of the shooting.' He slumped back in his chair. 'Mason was delivering the signal to shoot up the church. And they thought they could disguise it all in code. I'm going to pay Al Margulies another visit. I think he's the weakest link in all of this.'

'Really? I thought you'd go to Shafer first.'

'I've been interviewing his PA about Margulies and she had lots to say. She was too scared to go home, so I let her stay in my apartment. I'd better get back there now,' Peter said as he grabbed his coat off his chair. 'Can you tell Frank I'm at my apartment looking after someone, if he asks? Okay?'

'Do you want me to start writing up anything?' Mulroy asked.

'Not yet. We haven't connected enough dots.' As he moved towards the elevator, his cell phone rang. It was Belinski.

'I've got bad news and good news, which do you want to hear first?' he asked.

'Okay, I'll bite,' replied Peter. 'Give me the bad news first.'

'We're going to have to find somewhere else to have dim sum from now on. Tommy Lee's been arrested.'

'What did you arrest him for? Passing rubber bands as abalone?'

'Hilarious. Not me, the Feds. Turns out he was a big-wig in the Triad's local chapter. He was doing it right under our noses. Who knew?'

'That's going to be an enormous loss. I really liked his Peking duck,' Peter mused. ' So, what's the good news?'

'Jackie Hamel's out of her coma,' Belinski said. 'She's woken up but she isn't talking yet.'

'And now what?' asked Peter.

'The waiting game begins. It's almost as bad on the nerves as being shot at.'

CHAPTER FIFTY-SEVEN

Peter's apartment, Dogpatch.

PETER FELT A LITTLE JUMPY AS HE WAITED FOR THE ELEVATOR TO take him up to his apartment. He had found himself looking over his shoulder several times on his way home. He had the feeling he was being followed, but he saw nothing unusual and no one on his tail. Still, he had a weird sensation that wouldn't quit, and for most of the journey, he felt as if his head was on a swivel.

He knew better than to ignore his feelings—they had saved his life more than once before—but this time he employed logic. Who'd want to follow him and what for? Albuquerque was a long way from San Francisco and, besides, Claudia aside, all his enquiries had resulted in not much to date. Why would anyone care about a journalist at a second-string paper on a fishing expedition?

He felt confident that Claudia would never tell anyone about her location or his involvement. That would be counterproductive. He had a good cache of alcohol in the apartment to keep her focused. She would be waiting for him and they could continue where they left off.

He knocked several times then opened the door with his key.

'Claudia, are you here?' he called as he wandered towards the bedroom.

He could smell Claudia: a mixture of perfume and sensuality. He opened the bedroom door slowly. She was lying there asleep with the sheet over her and his eyes lingered on the gentle curves of her body. Her head was cradled in the crook of her arm and her hair was a tumble of dark curls. There was an innocence to her as she slept that wasn't evident when she was awake. Obvious differences aside, she had something of Marilyn Monroe about her. He had to leave the room.

She woke with a start when he opened the bedroom door to leave.

'I didn't mean to scare you,' he apologised.

She swivelled to look at him. 'Oh no, it's all right.' The sheet pulled down to her waist as she moved. She was topless.

He tried not to look, but she seemed unconcerned. She either didn't care about her nudity or she was doing it on purpose, he couldn't figure out which. Even lying down, her breasts were glorious.

It had been such a long time between drinks. 'I'll leave you alone,' he said, fighting his every instinct.

'Please don't.' In a single gesture, she pulled the sheet away. She was completely naked and he couldn't look away. 'I hate to be in bed alone.'

He lay down beside her and she turned her body towards him and kissed him hard. Her hands flew down the buttons of his shirt to the buckle of his belt. In a moment, she'd unzipped his trousers and pulled them off. He cupped his hand gently around one of her breasts and started to kiss her nipple. He did the same to the other breast. She moaned and pulled off his shirt.

She caressed his erect penis. From under her pillow, she brought out a condom. She had evidently been planning her conquest, but he didn't care. He was lost in the moment. She stroked his penis several times more and then slipped on the condom.

'I want to ride you, baby,' she said as she tossed back her hair. She mounted Peter and slowly moved up and down.

'Yes,' he groaned, fondling her breasts and sitting upright to kiss them.

She held his shoulders and kept moving faster and harder until they both cried out and then she fell back onto the pillow.

'Oh God. That was amazing,' she said. 'I want to do it again.'

Peter rolled on his side and kissed her on the mouth. 'You're so beautiful,' he said as he rested his head on his arm. 'And funny.'

'Guys have called me sexy plenty of times. Some have even offered me large amounts of money to sleep with them, but few have ever said I was beautiful, and only you have ever called me funny.'

'Well, you are.'

She rolled away and sighed. 'I wish I hadn't got caught up in this mess. If Al hadn't been such a bastard I'd still have my job. The cops will want to know everything and I'll have to be put into witness protection for the rest of my freaking life.'

'I'll help you,' he said.

'No, you won't. Even if you wanted to, they wouldn't let you. Isn't that the deal for spilling your guts? Say goodbye to everything and everyone in exchange for locking up the bad guy. Great reward. You won't stay, and that's cool. Most men leave, anyway. They go after you like you're a prize and when they've screwed you a few times, they move on to the next prize.'

'Not me. Besides, there's something about you, your honesty,' Peter said.

Claudia stroked Peter's face and then kissed him. 'You don't know a damn thing about me.'

'I know you're special. You're totally crazy but you're special, pleasant on the eye and, what we just did, was great. And nice eyes and a sexy accent.'

'Would you come into witness protection with me?' she asked.

'I'd try.'

There was a knock on the door. Peter slid off the bed and put on his clothes. 'Timing,' he said, 'is everything.' He sidled over to the door. 'You could have taken your time, Jerry,' he shouted as he opened it.

As the door swung open, Margulies stepped forward. He was dishevelled and wild-eyed. He pointed a gun at Peter's head.

'Margulies?' Peter held up his hands. 'If you'd told me you were coming I'd have invited the SWAT team over for coffee.'

'Shut up, you pathetic sonofabitch. Get inside.' Margulies shuffled forward, still pointing the gun at Peter, and slammed the door closed with his foot. 'Where is she?'

'I don't know who—'

Margulies pushed Peter backwards. 'Claudia? You here? I know you're in here. Max saw you at the cafe and he followed you here.'

233

Margulies moved forward until he had Peter pinned against a bookcase.

'She left. I don't know where she went,' he said, 'so why don't you chill out? What do you drink?'

Margulies clicked back the hammer of the gun. 'I should kill you right now you smart-assed schmuck. Where the fuck is she?' he yelled. He pushed the end of the gun into Peter's temple. 'I'll blow your brains all over your crappy apartment. Tell me where she is.'

Claudia emerged from the bedroom. Peter was relieved to see that she was dressed. 'I'm here, Al,' she said softly.

'Claudia? Claudia, why did you hurt me?' Margulies lowered the gun but kept Peter pressed against the bookcase.

'I was wrong to go, Al.' She moved towards him. 'I'm sorry, baby.'

'Have you been fucking this cocksucker?' he asked as he raised his gun again and pointed it at Claudia.

'Him? No. I was lying down, that's all. I have a bad headache.'

'You're not lying to me, are you? I'll know if you are. I couldn't take it. I love you, Claudia. Come back to me.'

'I wouldn't sleep with him, baby. Are you crazy? Look at him. He's young and good-looking but he's got no class.' She held out her arms. 'He's not my type. You're my type, baby.'

Margulies lowered his gun to his side and snuggled into Claudia's neck. 'I miss your smell. I miss sleeping with you.' He sniffed her.

Claudia pulled away. 'He gave me a thousand bucks for information on the church, but I fed him a lot of bullshit,' she said. 'I'll go get the cheque and show you.'

'You sure he wasn't paying you for a piece of your ass? You shouldn't have gone to the papers,' Margulies yelled. 'Don't I provide for you?'

'I know, baby, I know. I didn't tell him anything truthful. Trust me,' she said as she glanced at Peter. 'Money for nothing, that's all.'

Peter looked around for anything that he could hit Margulies with. There was nothing close by, other than a few books.

'I want you to come back to me.'

'I will, baby. I just want to think things over.'

'I'll give you anything that you want. If you want a house, I'll buy you the best house.'

She held out her hands. 'Come on, baby. Let's go back to your place. I'll make it all right again.'

'That would be so good. You know that I love you, Claudia. I always have.' He smiled and dropped the gun to hold her hands.

Claudia glanced at Peter, took Margulies' hands in hers and twisted them backwards. 'Peter! Now! Hit him!' she screamed.

'That hurts. What are you doing?' Margulies tried to pull away.

Peter threw himself forward and punched Margulies hard to the side of the face, and followed up with his elbow to the bridge of his nose. Margulies pulled out of Claudia's grip, staggered and then fell heavily to the floor. He lay there, unconscious.

'Have you killed him?' Claudia cried.

'No, it was just a good punch.'

'He could have killed us. Fucking asshole,' Claudia screeched. 'I hate you. I hate you. How dare you threaten us?' She started to kick Margulies' prone body until Peter took hold of her.

'It's okay. It's over. He isn't going to hurt us.' Peter picked up the gun with a tea towel and moved it to a shelf beyond Margulies' reach. As he returned to comfort Claudia, he noticed Margulies stirring. Peter jumped on him, twisted his arms behind his back and tied his hands and feet together with the belt from his trousers.

'Last time I did this was when I was a kid out on the cattle station, tying up a young steer.'

Claudia looked perplexed. 'Cattle station?'

'Never mind. You go and call the police and I'll keep an eye on Al. Here's the number. Ask for Inspector Belinski.'

CHAPTER FIFTY-EIGHT

IT TOOK BELINSKI NO MORE THAN TEN MINUTES TO GET TO THE apartment, lights and sirens blazing. The paramedics had already arrived but hadn't gone upstairs. Peter had poured out two large whiskies and cajoled Claudia into drinking one. She sat in a corner shaking, while he tried to console her.

Margulies had come to, but he was too groggy to struggle. He was muttering something no one could understand. The paramedics gave him a sedative and wheeled him into the hallway. Belinski took one look at Peter and Claudia and shook his head. He took Peter aside.

'What the fuck were you doing, man? Al Margulies' girlfriend?'

'I was interviewing her, that's all. She's probably implicated in Al's grubby scheme, but she's ready to turn State's evidence.'

'You mean you were screwing her and taking advantage of the pillowtalk. Then you hog-tie Al Margulies. You're fucking mad.'

'He threatened to kill us, Jerry. The gun's on the shelf. I didn't wipe it. It should have his prints all over it.'

'Heck, I'd threaten to kill you if I caught you porking my girl-friend. You're just lucky he didn't deliver on his threat.' Belinski returned to Claudia's side. 'You'll have to come with me for an interview.'

'Can I at least call my parents? Let them know I'm okay?' she said as she dabbed her eyes with a tissue.

'Of course you can, Miss Alvarez, but don't tell them anything else,' Belinski replied. 'We'll arrange somewhere safe for you to stay.'

'I wish you were coming with me, Peter,' she cried.

'If Margulies spills his guts, you shouldn't be in a safe house for long,' Belinski stated. 'I just want to make sure you're safe while we sort this out.'

Belinski glanced at Margulies as the paramedics prepared to take him down the elevator. 'What did you hit him with, Peter?' he asked. 'A chair?'

'A forearm jolt to the nose. He was threatening Claudia. What else could I do?' Peter embraced Claudia then kissed her on the forehead.

'Chivalrous is not a word that comes immediately to mind when I think of you, but I've got to hand it to you,' Belinski said as he shook his head. 'It was funny, though, seeing him all trussed up like a Thanksgiving turkey. I've wanted Margulies locked up for a long time.'

He glanced at Claudia and Peter. Their eyes were locked on each other. 'I hate to break up the party, but we have to be on our way to the station.'

'I'll see you soon,' Peter said to her. 'Call me when you get out...'

Claudia managed a smile. 'I will. I promise.'

Peter followed them to the door. He touched her hand as she went out and then she was gone. He closed the door and locked it. He was missing her already. The incurable romantic in him had been let out of the bag. Again.

He slept fitfully for a few hours and then rushed back to the *Daily* offices. As he came out of the elevator, he noticed that Stella's office door was open. He also noticed Mulroy sitting back in his chair drinking a cup of coffee.

'Mulroy,' he barked as he approached.

Mulroy spun around. 'You're back.'

'Time to pull your finger out if you want a byline on this story.'

'You're giving me a byline?'

'I'm feeling generous, but your name will definitely not be ahead of mine.' Peter threw his coat over his chair in the usual customary fashion. 'Start writing.'

'What have you got?' Mulroy poised his fingers over his keyboard.

'Gangland lawyer, Al Margulies, arrested after tense hostage drama. *Daily* chief crime reporter, Peter Clancy, disarmed Margulies who was armed and dangerous...'

Mulroy typed. 'You disarmed a gunman?' He stopped typing. 'And you're here? I'd be a nervous wreck just being around the guy.'

'I didn't have a choice. He was in my apartment.'

'Holy shit. That's what I call gonzo journalism: real Hunter S Thompson stuff. Are you all right?'

'Yeah. No time to think about what happened. You work on that while I go and see Stella.'

'I forgot to tell you that she's out of hospital.'

'I know.'

He darted down the corridor and knocked on the open door a couple of times.

'Come in, Peter.'

He entered Stella's office. 'I'm glad you're back. Are you feeling okay?'

Stella was seated looking at the pile of papers in front of her. He noticed she looked gaunt and pale. 'I'd feel a lot better if I didn't have all of this shit in front of me. Take a seat.'

He did as he was told. 'Are you having the operation?'

'My brother the doctor says I should get a second opinion. I'll decide after I see another neurosurgeon. My brother knows a guy. He says he's the best in the States.'

Peter took a deep breath. 'I want to apologise for what happened last time we saw each other.'

'We've had our moments but we'll always be mates.'

'I never want to lose your friendship, Stella.'

Stella's eyes misted over. 'Don't go all sensitive on me. I've been trying to be mad at you.'

'Frank brought you up to speed on my activities since you've been gone,' he observed.

'He certainly did. I'm surprised he gave you the money.'

'I gave him a good reason. But I didn't pay her the lot at once.'

'Please tell me this woman didn't string you along. Tell me she knew more than just the brand of Al Margulies's sexual perversion.'

'Claudia was at my apartment.'

'Of course, she was. Claudia? Nice name. Last I heard, you were celibate. So, was she there for security reasons or was it more personal?' Stella said as she shook her head. 'What did I say about sticking your pecker in other people's business?'

'Isn't that what we do for a living? Can't sell papers keeping to yourself, you know. For the record, I was just trying to keep her safe, but Margulies broke into the apartment and threatened to kill us. I disarmed him.'

'You're the real action man. You save Jackie Hamel and now this. Have you ever thought of joining the secret service? Where's the girl now, by the way?'

'Claudia is in police protection.'

'Is that to protect her from you or Al Margulies?' Stella laughed.

'Funny. Belinski thinks he'll be able to get Margulies to grass on his clients. He'll keep us updated.'

'So you're doing a holding story?'

'Mulroy and I are working on it right now. The main story won't be far away.'

'When you have more on Carmel Ridge?'

'Yeah. I was able to get photos of a large picture of an old guy in the Carmel Ridge Ranch. It's some kind of church—a cult, really. The people seemed to treat the guy like a prophet.'

'America is full of them. They're as common as Elvis impersonators. I'm sure they cross over sometimes.'

'I want to find out more about this guy. I'm thinking he may have a connection to The Ten Commandments Church massacre.'

'If it was a picture and he wasn't there, maybe he's dead and they like to worship him?'

'That's something I have to find out.'

'Good. I'm giving you free rein on this, Peter, but I want regular updates.'

'Will do, Stella,' he replied. 'I'm glad you're back.'

'I think you're onto something. I should have trusted you on this one,' she said.

'I knew you would eventually, I just had to keep working on you,' he smiled.

'Apart from being full of shit, you have great intuition, Peter.

Keep up the good work but try not to become part of the story. You'll end up in hospital. Or worse.'

He turned to leave Stella's office.

'Wait.'

He turned around.

'I can see a spring in your step and a sparkle back in your eyes. I'm glad you're over Ruby.'

'So am I.'

Mulroy was still typing when Peter got back to his desk. 'Back in the boss's good books?'

'None of your damn business. Where are you with the story?'

'We need more background on Margulies.'

'Get hold of the press clippings. Belinski said Margulies was involved in representing a major drug dealer a few years ago.'

'I'll get onto that. By the way, Belinski called,' Mulroy said.

'Is it about Margulies?'

'No, he wants to meet you at the hospital. Jackie Hamel is talking, but she isn't making much sense. He said you may be able to help.'

Peter grabbed his coat off his chair. He then realised he hadn't had breakfast and, worse still, he hadn't yet had a coffee.

CHAPTER FIFTY-NINE

San Francisco General Hospital.

BELINSKI AND A NURSE WERE IN JACKIE'S HOSPITAL ROOM WHEN Peter walked in. Jackie was sitting in a chair trying to read a book aloud with the assistance of the nurse, who was sitting beside her. She faltered on several words, but was right most of the time. She didn't look like the same energetic woman that he had seen in the church: her hair was almost white. She now looked like a crippled old woman.

'How's she going?' he asked the nurse quietly. 'Sounds like progress is slow.'

'She knows her name and where she is, but doesn't know the time or the date. That's understandable,' the nurse continued. 'Day and night don't exist in ICU.'

'So you've finished interviewing Margulies,' Peter remarked.

'Not yet. Jackie Hamel is a higher priority.'

'Has he cracked yet?' he asked.

'He thinks he's tough, but we're working on him. Margulies says he wants police protection before he gives out any information.'

'It must be nice negotiating with an oxygen bandit,' Peter replied.

'All part of the game. Do you want to talk to Jackie? She was asking about Raoul before,' Belinski said.

'Did you tell her?'

'Not yet.'

'Should I?'

'The doctor said it probably won't sink in. If she finds out here, they can give her any help she needs. I'm leaving it to you.'

'Thanks.' He moved towards Jackie. 'Can I have a brief talk to her?' he asked the nurse.

'I know you need to know vital information but don't stress her too much. I'll have to stop you if Jackie becomes too distressed. She's making great progress.'

The nurse got out of her chair to allow him to sit beside Jackie. She stopped reading and looked at Peter. 'Are you a doctor? Can I go home now?' she asked.

'Unfortunately I'm not a doctor,' he replied, 'I'm Peter.'

'I can't remember if I ever swore but I'm going to swear now... Shit.'

He smiled.

'Do I know you?' Jackie asked vaguely.

'We've met. At church.'

'You have a nice smile.'

'Thanks.'

'I used to like going to church. I think I used to play piano once.' She stroked imaginary keys on her bedside table. 'Yes. I played piano. But that was a long time ago.'

'You did play piano beautifully and you will again when you get out of here,' Peter remarked.

Her fingers stopped playing. She returned to her book. He glanced at what she was reading.

'*Moby Dick* by Herman Melville,' he said.

'It was the first thing I remembered when I woke up. I remember my mother buying it for me when I was a teenager.'

'Do you like the book?'

'I do, but I'm sure I've read this many times. I have a feeling that I know how it ends.' Jackie sighed. 'Sad. I wish everything could end happily.' She closed her eyes and took a deep breath. 'My mind is so scrambled now. Nothing is in order.'

'It will come back. Your brain is just reprogramming itself,' Peter replied.

The nurse glared at him. 'Perhaps the prognosis is better left to the medical staff.'

Jackie ignored the nurse. 'Like a computer?'

'I guess.'

She closed her eyes again and drifted off to sleep. Moments later, she woke with a start, clutching the edge of the bed table with her fingertips. She raised her hands to her ears. 'Make it stop!' she cried. 'The gunfire and people screaming. It won't stop.'

The nurse leaned over her. 'Jackie, dear, it's all right. You're safe now. No one will hurt you.'

'I can see a guy standing off stage. Alex...' she continued.

'Alex Shafer?' Peter exchanged glances with Belinski.

'Alex Shafer. That's him.'

'What do you remember about him?' Peter asked.

'I'm not sure. I remember some things but not others. I'm tired. I just want the noise to stop.'

'That's enough,' said the nurse. 'Come back in an hour or two.'

'No, no, it's all right. I see things when it's quiet or when I close my eyes.' She sighed. 'Maybe I'll feel better if I tell someone. I remember that Alex came to Ten Commandments from some-where else. Pastor Gatting always looked to him for advice, I don't know why.'

'You said that Shafer was off stage when you last saw him,' Peter said.

'Yes, he was standing there doing nothing. While...' She wiped her eyes with the corner of the sheet. 'She shot everyone.'

'Leah Merrell?'

'Yes, her. Leah Merrell thought she was special; superior, even. I didn't like her.' Jackie shuddered, took a deep breath and contin-ued. 'She was always with Alex Shafer. He acted like he was the boss and she played along.'

'They were a couple? They lived together?'

'No, but I saw them kissing once. She followed him everywhere. She and her son thought Shafer was an angel. They said so.'

'What do you mean by angel?' he asked.

'Abaddon,' she replied.

Peter looked at Belinski. 'Who is Abaddon?'

'The Destroyer... a devil.'

'Do you remember what he was doing during the shooting?'

She shut her eyes. 'He was pointing...' Her brow furrowed. 'I can see it. He was signalling... To that woman and her son.' Jackie turned her face into her pillow and wailed. She wept inconsolably, rocking backwards and forwards.

Peter moved towards the bed but the nurse intervened. 'She's distressed,' she said. 'Please. Leave the room!'

'We'll come back another time,' Belinski said.

Peter was reluctant to leave, but the nurse was gesturing for him to go with one arm, while she comforted Jackie with the other. He eventually followed Belinski down the hallway. Belinski was deep in thought. He turned around near the elevator lobby.

'I'm heading back to the station,' he said

'What about Shafer?' Peter asked. 'It's clear that he was no innocent bystander. He obviously planned the massacre.'

'I want to find out exactly how much Margulies knows. I'll take it from there.'

Peter shook his head. 'What are you waiting for? Shafer could be preparing to unleash hell again on some other poor victims as we speak. It could be the whole gay community next.'

'Listen, I'm not a reporter, Peter. I can't go off like a firecracker whenever I get a tip-off or based on someone's version of the truth. I'm an inspector, that's all. The DA and the Commander have a say in what happens. Jackie's just come out of a coma, she's confused. It's not enough. Shafer has rights, you know, and men like him aren't afraid to remind you of that.'

'Rights? According to Jackie, he's the devil. The devil has no rights.'

'Piss off. Talk to me once you've settled down.'

With that, Belinski walked away, leaving Peter standing alone in the lobby.

CHAPTER SIXTY

Daily offices.

BY THE TIME PETER RETURNED TO HIS DESK, MULROY HAD finished a draft of the piece he'd been tasked to do on Al Margulies. He was standing next to his desk, hopping from foot to foot. Peter thought it was undignified for a man in his thirties. At least it showed him that Mulroy was enthusiastic. It was pathetic that his enthusiasm played out publicly in a jig.

He rushed past Mulroy without commenting on the dance he'd just witnessed. He called out *coffee* as he passed, so that no one would impede him. Mulroy nodded. He wasn't quite as addicted to the stuff as Peter, but he understood what it was to be facing midday without any caffeine on board. Peter returned a minute later with a jug as well as a cup. He pushed aside some notes to make space for them on his desk, and sat down.

'Jackie Hamel is out of her coma,' he said, pouring some coffee out of the jug into the cup. 'She said that Shafer directed the massacre.'

'Shit. Are they going to arrest him?'

'Not yet,' he replied, taking a swig. He smiled as the caffeine filtered through him. 'Now I can see shapes and think in the abstract again,' he said. From the bundle of notes, he picked up an envelope addressed to him and ripped it open. 'More fan mail. I hope it's not from the turd burglar.'

Mulroy took a step backwards. 'So, what do we do?' he asked.

'Do we sit here like stale bottles of piss or do we see what Shafer is up to?' Peter pulled the letter out of the envelope and read it aloud. *Your end is soon. Prepare for your death and that of all the unbelievers.* It was signed, *From the Flamekeeper.*

'That's a death threat,' said Mulroy.

'Really? I didn't think it was a frigging astrological reading.'

'Are you going to tell anyone?'

'What for? You get this sort of shit every now and again. You put up with it. I usually treat them as encouragement. It means we're getting too close to the fire. Besides, Margulies already tried and failed. Perhaps this Flamekeeper told Al to kill me.'

'You should be careful all the same, don't you think?'

'Careful? That's for the faint-hearted. We're investigative reporters, not wimps.'

Mulroy shook his head. 'I don't know if I'm up to this.'

'Of course you are. In fact, you're doing well. As that old hack said to me once, if you think you're going to piss your pants, wear an extra pair of undies.'

'Undies?'

'Underwear. Y fronts. Tighty whities. When are you going to learn to speak Australian?' He finished his first coffee of the day and refilled the cup. He offered Mulroy what was left in the jug. 'What do you make of the name "Flamekeeper"? You're the Bible guy.'

Mulroy upended the jug's contents into his own cup. 'I don't know. I haven't heard of it.'

Peter sat back and sipped his coffee for a while, as he read Mulroy's draft. He was marking it up in red ink when his phone rang. The voice at the other end seemed familiar.

'Mr Clancy.'

There were only a select few who had ever called Peter 'Mr Clancy', and most of them were long dead.

'Yeah, this is he.'

'I hear that you've been asking after me.'

'Is that so? And who might you be?'

'Alexander Shafer.'

Peter nearly dropped the phone. He was playing it ice cold. 'So sorry, I didn't catch your name,' he said. 'What did you say your name was?'

'You know exactly who I am. You want to know something about me? So, why have you gone around asking whores, invalids and third-rate lawyers? Why don't you just ask me? I'll be at The Ten Commandments Church compound for the next hour. Come alone. I think you'll find what I have to say most interesting.'

Peter was stunned by the call. He immediately leapt out of his chair and grabbed his coat and was heading towards the elevator when something made him turn around.

He went back to Mulroy's desk. 'I just got a call from Shafer. Are you coming?' he asked.

'Where are we going?'

'If the heart of the story won't come to us, we go to the heart.'

'Should we let someone know?' Mulroy said as he slid out of his chair.

'Leave a note. And we'll grab Larry Bruce on the way out. He may be able to get some good pics.'

Mulroy hesitated. 'I'm not sure about this, Peter.'

'Fine. I'll go by myself,' he replied. 'We haven't got all day. If you want to share the byline you have to step out of your bloody comfort zone.'

'Okay. Let's throw caution to the wind. Let's go.'

CHAPTER SIXTY-ONE

The Ten Commandments Church.

'I ALWAYS HAD A FEELING THAT WE'D END UP BACK HERE,' MULROY said as he wiped his sweaty forehead with a handkerchief. 'A bad feeling. A real bad one.'

Larry Bruce was puffing nervously on a cigarette in the back of the car while he set up his camera. Peter pulled the car up fifty yards from the driveway, got out and strode up to the gates. They were closed but not locked. He peered past them, but saw no one. He had expected someone—Shafer even—to have met him there.

He returned to the car. 'That's strange. There doesn't seem to be anyone around.'

'I'm taking it as a sign that we should leave.'

'We're not leaving. Shafer called me here for a meeting. Maybe he's waiting for me in the church. I figure that Shafer is feeling the world closing in on him. Margulies and Jackie Hamel are both talking about him. He must be wondering who's going to rat on him next. He may be about to spill the beans. He's under siege.'

'You know Shafer's dangerous, and still you agree to meet with him. You're outright crazy,' Bruce remarked.

'He called me. Whether he's here or not, something's going on and I mean to find out what that is. Do you want in on the story or don't you?'

Mulroy and Bruce looked at each other. 'Nope.'

'I'm staying here,' Bruce said as he slung the camera strap over Peter's neck then lit up another cigarette. 'You're on your own.'

'Same here,' Mulroy added.

Peter laughed. 'Fine. I'll go it alone. You wait for me here and I'll check things out first. If I don't come back and give you the all clear in a couple of minutes, call Belinski. If there's any sign of trouble, call Belinski.'

He continued to the front gate while the other two stayed by the car. He rotated the enormous handles, pushed the gates open and walked up the driveway towards the church. It was very quiet. He could see eight cars in the carpark but nobody seemed to be around. *Maybe Shafer's in church, praying. Begging for God to save his sorry arse.* He stopped when he reached the steps of the church and listened. Silence. It seemed odd. He went around the back of the church and listened for a while longer. He could hear people inside, and a woman whimpering.

He opened the door. It was dark except for a few candles in a stand.

A male voice at the back of the church said, 'Help us. Are you the police?'

'Mr Shafer?'

'Who are you?'

'I'm a reporter. I'm here to see Alex Shafer.' He moved slowly down the aisle. It was as if nothing had ever happened. Everything had been repaired and painted, but Peter was finding just being back there overwhelming. He took a deep breath and closed his mind to everything other than the task at hand.

'Please, don't get too close,' a woman spoke softly. Her voice quivered.

'Why?' He stopped and looked around the church, along the balcony and up at the ceiling. 'Is Alex Shafer here?'

There was a sob in her throat. 'There's a bomb under the altar. He said it's going to go off in another hour. He said if we move too much, it will go off.'

Peter looked at his watch and inched closer. A few minutes had already passed since he left the car. 'Who did this to you?'

'Shafer. You can't touch us. We've been tied to the altar. Please get help.'

Three women and two men were sitting in front of the altar, tied together by a thick rope that ran around their waists several times. One of the men was slumped over and three of them still had tape across their mouths. The two who had spoken to Peter had worked the tape loose. It clung to the corners of their mouths. On top of the altar lay another man. He wasn't moving.

'Are you okay?' Peter asked.

'Elias Gatting is dead. Shafer killed him and put him on the altar. And Mark's in a diabetic coma. Please, we need help.'

Peter took his cell phone out of his pocket.

'There's no coverage in the church,' said the man. 'The Gattings fitted a device to disrupt calls to avoid any interruption to the services.'

'No matter,' said Peter. 'I'll go outside and try again.' He retraced his footsteps and tried the door. It had been locked behind him. He returned to the side of the stage. 'Is there another way out?'

'There are another four exits,' said the man.

Peter darted around the perimeter of the church, trying each of the exits. They were all locked.

The woman started to cry. 'We're going to die. Please, I don't want to die.'

Peter called. 'What's your name, ma'am?' he asked.

'Katherine.'

'I'm Peter. And you, sir?'

'Tobias.' The man was obviously in discomfort but resisting the urge to wriggle.

'You're both doing very well. Stay calm, Katherine. I have two colleagues just outside. The police are on their way.' He hoped that Mulroy had taken the initiative.

'I prayed. I knew God would send us help,' said Tobias.

'Where's Shafer? Is he here?' Peter asked.

'Shafer left with his men and all the others.'

'Do you know where they went?'

'He didn't say. He just said that it was time to rise up and prepare for the end of days.'

'Prepare for what?'

'The end of days. He kept repeating that, and something about it happening on the Sabbath. He said it was the signal from the Prophet for all believers to rise up and kill all of the unbelievers, the sinners and the sodomites.'

'The Prophet?' Peter asked. 'Who is the Prophet?'

'He's… He's their prophet. He calls himself Moses.'

'And then he left you with the bomb?'

'We were elders of the church. We didn't agree with what Shafer was doing to the church, and we told him so. He did this to us. Please, we need help.'

Peter crouched down next to Katherine. He could see a package behind the altar, but he had no idea what it was. 'I'll wait right here next to you, until they come. I'm not leaving you.'

'You have a kind heart, Peter,' said Katherine. 'We're good people, really. We're not full of hatred. We never wanted to harm anyone. After the Gattings died, we found out that Shafer had been stealing from the church, and then he tried to take us over. Then he started preaching that all homosexual people in San Francisco must die. He said that it was our duty to kill them. Now, we all know that sodomy is a sin, but we wouldn't go along with killing anyone.'

'Our church would never stand for that. I believe the devil came to us and he was in the form of Alexander Shafer,' said Tobias.

Peter was praying inwardly that the police would arrive before anything exploded. He didn't have a death-wish, but he couldn't leave them alone. His ears pricked up when he heard sirens in the distance.

'Is that the police?' said Tobias. 'Thank the Lord.'

The sirens stopped. Hardly any noise infiltrated the church, but a minute or so later, two shots rang out loudly just outside the main entrance. Peter turned around and ran back down the aisle towards the door as it opened. Just in front of it lay a man dressed in combat fatigues holding a pistol. Blood was seeping from a chest wound. Beyond the man were several police officers. Peter raised his arms above his head.

'Don't shoot! There's a bomb inside,' he called to the police coming up the stairs, 'under the altar. There are five hostages. They're tied to it.'

'He's the only gunman?' asked one of the officers.

'As far as I know. The bomb's expected to go off in another forty minutes or so.'

251

The officer moved to escort Peter outside. He shrugged him off. 'Katherine's scared. I promised them I'd stay with them.'

'Are you Peter Clancy? Inspector Belinski warned us about you. I'm sorry, but you have to leave and that's an order.'

'But...'

'Outside. Now. We've got it from here.'

'Fine.' As he turned to leave, he became aware of the camera weighing heavily around his neck. He hadn't taken any photographs. Suddenly, the journalist in him took over. He switched on the motor drive on the camera and took whatever he could before he was ordered to stop.

Outside, the police were out of their cars with weapons drawn. He tried to change the roll, but his hands wouldn't work. He looked down at them. His hands were shaking. He was led away from the church to a waiting ambulance. He sat by a paramedic and let her wrap a blanket around him. He watched and waited.

The bomb squad truck arrived but from where he now sat, he couldn't see what they were doing. He noticed Mulroy and Bruce talking to a police officer at the gate. They came up from the car and stood next to him.

'You okay?' asked Mulroy.

'Fine,' said Peter.

'Then why the fuck aren't you taking photos?' Bruce took the camera from him and began to load a new film.

'I did, but now I can't,' he replied.

'What do you mean you...'

Peter raised his hands chest high straight in front of him. They were shaking so badly, it nearly threw him off the stool. 'Strange, I don't know what's wrong with them.'

Mulroy looked aghast. 'Nothing wrong with them, mate, nothing at all. They're beaut. See, just so happens that I've been studying how to speak Australian.'

Peter appreciated the sentiment. They all sat there until the deadline for the bomb to explode approached. Bruce snapped off roll after roll, and tried to get as close as he could to the church. Peter checked his watch. Then he said the *Our Father* and a *Hail*

Mary for each of the hostages.

'I think they're out of danger,' Bruce said as he kept snapping.

'Are you sure?'

'Look, the cops are calling in the paramedics. That's got to be a good sign.'

Paramedics were moving up to the church pushing six stretchers in three two-person teams. A man in a bomb suit emerged slowly from the church, carrying a defused bomb in his gloved hands. He handed part of it to another colleague in a bomb suit. The two moved slowly down the stairs and then well away from the church, where they placed the bomb parts on a sheet on the ground. Other members of the bomb squad joined them and Belinski rushed over.

'Six stretchers?' Peter observed. 'There's nothing they can do for Elias Gatting, except to put him on the stretcher and cover his body. Poor kid.'

Bruce glanced at the reporters further away on the street. He laughed when he saw how far away from the action they were. 'You've got yourself another exclusive, Clancy,' he said. 'That surely must be pissing off the TV networks.'

'I feel like a stiff whisky,' he responded.

'I think I may have pissed myself, but I'll check later,' Bruce added, 'but at least I got some great pictures.'

Peter assured the paramedic that he was fine. He felt in control again and was aching to meet the deadline. He took off the blanket and he, Mulroy and Bruce headed back to the car. He sat in the front passenger seat and closed his eyes.

Belinski opened Peter's door. 'No doubt about you, if you can't find a frigging story, you'll create it, Peter.'

'I did what anyone would do. Was it really a bomb?' Peter asked.

'For sure. There was a quarter pound of C4 attached to a timer under the altar. It would have killed everyone tied up at the altar and you as well.'

'Shit.' He reached into his coat and pulled out his trusty whisky flask. His hands still shaking as he attempted to screw off the lid.

'Here, I'll help you.' Belinski took the flask out of Peter's hand, unscrewed it and gave it back to him. Peter took a long swig.

'Don't expect me to call you a hero,' Belinski said, 'but what you did in there...'

'Don't talk shit, Jerry. That line's straight out of *Top Gun*,' Peter said dryly. 'We were just in the wrong place at the right time and we did the decent thing.'

Belinski's cell phone rang.

'Excuse me,' he said to Peter.

Peter listened in but couldn't quite hear what was said. 'Good news?'

'Margulies is starting to crack. Right now it's imperative that we find Shafer and his henchmen ASAP. We're combing the city for them as we speak. We've posted police at gay centres like the Ambassador Hotel and the *Journal* office. We have to catch them, Peter.'

As Mulroy tried to drive away, he was surrounded by a throng of reporters. A woman with blood-red lips and a blonde pageboy haircut tapped frantically on the window. Mulroy stopped the car.

Peter partially unwound his window. 'What's wrong?'

'You're Peter Clancy, aren't you?' she whined above the gaggle of voices, all yelling at him and thrusting their mikes towards him.

'I am.'

'Peter, can you tell me what happened? We heard that a reporter was killed, but the hostages are okay?'

Peter laughed. 'You'll have to read about it in the *Daily*. Now, excuse me, I have to get back to the office.'

'Peter, please. Give us something,' another reporter yelled.

'Mulroy, just go. They'll get out of the way,' said Bruce.

Mulroy threw the car into gear and reversed slowly.

The blonde was still yelling at him, as she attempted to run after the car in a pencil skirt and stilettos. 'Don't be a sonofabitch, Peter. We can work together on this. Call me. I like your style. I'm Naomi at TVN.'

They laughed when she jerked to a stop as her microphone lead ran out.

CHAPTER SIXTY-TWO

Daily offices.

'HOW THE THREE OF YOU DIDN'T GET YOURSELVES KILLED IS beyond me,' said Stella. 'Peter, you have to slow down or you're going to die before you get anywhere near forty.'

He was sandwiched at his desk between Frank and the wall, while Mulroy began writing the copy. Peter was itching to take over and he wanted the inquisition done with. 'I will, Stella, I promise. When this is finished...'

Frank piped up. 'You say that Shafer has gone somewhere to prepare for Armageddon. Got any idea where that might be?'

'I could think of a few places in Australia which would be the perfect setting for the end of days, but my hunch is he's heading back to Carmel Ridge Ranch. Belinski thinks they're going to target gay facilities in the city but I'm not so sure of that.'

'And what do you know about this guy they call the Prophet?'

'You said you got a photo of him,' said Frank. 'I'd like to take a look at it.'

'Yeah, I got two, but I haven't seen them. They must be back from the lab by now,' he said. He looked around his cluttered desk until he found a manila envelope from the photo laboratory. 'It's been here for a couple of days. Shit. I need to clean up my desk.'

He tore it open and took out two photographs. He held them up and frowned. 'I shot them through a window, so they're not the best quality.'

Stella took one out of Peter's hand and peered at it. 'So this could be the Prophet.'

'Apparently he's called Moses.'

'Moses? Not very original,' she rejoined.

'His portrait was hanging up at the back of their altar, so it's probably safe to assume he's the Prophet. They were praying to him. But I couldn't see him there.'

'Could he be dead?'

'One of the hostages, Katherine, said that Shafer and his cronies left to join the Prophet, so I guess he's still alive.'

'He's possibly in his fifties, although looking at the hair, he could be older.' Frank chuckled. 'He's doing his best Charlton Heston impersonation, isn't he? It's the chiselled face and the eyes.'

Stella kept staring at the photograph. 'You wouldn't have...' She took the other photograph from Peter. 'The lighting's better in this one. I can make out his face better... Strange. Very strange.'

Stella went back to her office and returned with a magnifier loupe. She cleared a spot on Peter's desk and lay the photograph flat. She passed the loupe over the surface. 'His face looks so familiar,' she mumbled. 'I can't place it.'

Peter tried to look at it, but she shrugged him away. 'It's the eyes. Eyes never change. Never.' Suddenly, she put down the loupe and staggered backwards.

'What's wrong Stella?' Peter asked. 'Are you okay?'

'I'll call the paramedics,' said Frank as he shot up.

'No. I'm fine. It's not that. It's the man in the photo. I know exactly where I've seen him before.' She pushed the photograph and the loupe towards Peter. 'That man is Richard. Take a good look at him. That's the Slasher.'

'What?' Peter stared at Stella. She had turned deathly pale. 'Are you sure?'

'Yes, Peter. It's him. It's the bastard who tried to kill me and Tony Mayberry in that alley almost twenty years ago. I never forget a face and I've certainly never forgotten his. He may be older. He may have reinvented himself as a religious prophet, but the bastard still has those evil freaking eyes.'

Frank picked up Peter's phone. 'I'm calling the police. I think you need to talk to them. Maybe this time the idiots might do their job properly and put this psycho away.'

Jerry Belinski came to the *Daily* office thirty minutes after Frank called him. Frank had been waiting for him at reception, and he bustled him past everyone and into Stella's office, before Peter had an opportunity to say anything to him. Peter had taken over the piece from Mulroy and it was already proofed and ready to go.

He didn't want to start anything new but Belinski had been with Stella for almost an hour and he was thinking of calling it a day. He had hoped to catch him before he left. He leaned back in his chair and he must have dozed off. The next thing he knew, he was being jolted back into consciousness by a rap to the head.

'Hey,' he said. 'Oh, it's you, Belinski.'

'I see you're doing what you're best at. I've got some good news about Margulies.'

'Great. Tell me later.' He had pushed all thoughts of Margulies aside for the moment. 'So, what did Stella say?' he asked.

'She's adamant that it's him despite the years. She's pretty compelling, but we'll need to look into it. We'll have to establish his identity.'

'I can tell you where he is right now. He's probably getting ready for the end times in his compound in New Mexico. Does it surprise you that Richard the serial killer turned prophet?'

'Nothing surprises me,' said Belinski. 'Only in America... She said Richard may have been in the military in the seventies. Apparently, Tony Mayberry told her Richard had just gotten out of the military. I don't know if all of this is true, but he may have been based at the Presidio. Off the record.'

'You're alerting the police out in New Mexico?'

'I have already. I'm hoping the military will be able to give us an identity soon.'

'I don't know whether to hang around here or go to New Mexico to be there when they arrest Moses. Any signs of Shafer yet?'

'Nothing so far.' Belinski checked his watch. 'Better go. I'm going to the hospital to question the church hostages.'

'You're a busy man, Jerry.'

'Ever since you came to town things have been heating up, Clancy. I'm thinking of creating a task force to deal with your stories.'

Peter laughed. 'Routine is for retirees, Jerry.'

'That may be only three years away, if you don't cause me to go out on a stress pension first,' Belinski replied.

They agreed to meet up at a bar at six.

After Belinski left, Peter knocked on Stella's door, waited for her to respond and then entered. She had turned her chair around and was looking out at the San Francisco skyline.

'Everything all right, Stella?' he asked.

She didn't answer immediately. 'Do you ever get to a point in this job when you feel like you've reached saturation? You've seen too much?'

'Of course. I've seen a lot. I don't like to remember what I've seen. Maybe, that's why I keep doing investigative reporting: I'm trying to forget the previous story. And then I think, what would I do if I gave the game away? I'm not a mouse-on-a-wheel kind of guy. Are you worried about your health?'

'Not really. Everyone has to face that sometimes. Seeing what I saw all of those years ago nearly finished me off. I actually gave journalism away when I first came to New York. I lasted three months. I'd be bored working a normal job.' She swung her chair back. She looked exhausted. 'No, I feel like I need to have a rest. After I beat this tumour, I'm going to look after my mother for a while.'

'What about the hunt for number one newspaper?'

'That's for someone else to take on. I haven't told Frank any of this and I'm relying on your discretion. All right?'

'My lips are sealed.'

'You're always around, aren't you, Clancy? Watching my every move. I'm trying to make sense of all of this and then you appear like a damn fairy to share your wisdom and make everything all right.'

'Yeah, that's me. Just call me the Fairy Godfather.'

Stella grinned. 'So,' she sighed, 'let's get back to work. Where are you with the hostage story?'

'Done. Off stone.'

'Good. Great. That's quick.'

'When you're one of the eye witnesses, it cuts down on the interviews.'

'I've been wondering where we head after this. Do we send you back to New Mexico to follow the potential arrest of Moses the psycho prophet God knows when, or do you hang around here to see what happens with Shafer?'

Peter looked at his palms. 'I have a hunch about this.'

'And there's yet more from the soothsayer!' Stella groaned. 'I used to think it was just your gut making noises, but now I'm beginning to think that your hunches have some accuracy.'

'I want to go to New Mexico.'

Stella studied Peter's face. 'You look tired too, Peter. I could send Shapiro and you could direct proceedings from here.'

'I don't hold with the theory that Moses will be taking the long way home this time. I need to be there. It's been my story from the beginning. I want to be the one who wraps it up.' Inside he was fuming at the suggestion that Shapiro steal his splash. He thought he hid it well, but he could see she'd picked up on his mood.

'Okay. Calm down. Give me some more information and I'll think about it.'

Stella concluded the meeting by abruptly swinging her chair around again, and looking out as San Francisco went about its business below her.

Peter searched his desk for a piece of paper with Brenda the Tijeras diner owner's number on it and cursed his own messiness. He shuffled random bits of paper from one side of the desk back to the other without success. He couldn't recall the name of her diner, so looking it up in the directory wasn't an option. He finally found the number stuffed into an old coffee cup. Part of the paper had adhered to the dregs, but he managed to unstick it without losing any of the numbers. He dialled them up.

Brenda didn't remember Peter at first, but eventually his accent jogged her memory.

'Now I remember. Peter, the reporter from San Francisco. The cute guy with the gorgeous baby blues. Why didn't you say so from the start? You were out at the Carmel Ridge Ranch.'

'Yes, that's me. This isn't just a social call, Brenda. I was wondering if there was anything happening there? Have you noticed any unusual activity going on?' he asked.

'Well, I haven't heard anything really, although there seems to be more traffic than usual heading there. It may just be folks coming from other parts of America to spend time there. They get together and talk about, well, whatever they talk about. It happens every year.'

'Around this time?'

'I think so. Pretty much.'

'They don't stop at your diner?'

'Sometimes, but they don't say much. They're just here to buy themselves a drink or a meal, and move on.'

'Okay. Thanks for that. Can you let me know if you notice anything unusual?'

'I will. What's this about, Peter? Should I be worried?' she asked.

'Nothing to worry about, Brenda. I'm still trying to do a story on their leader. He's very elusive.'

'We've learned to leave them alone over the years and maybe you should do the same.'

CHAPTER SIXTY-THREE

Six pm. Saloon Bar, North Beach, San Francisco.

PETER SLIPPED INTO A BOOTH AND RAISED THE GLASS OF SCOTCH up to his lips. Normally, he'd have knocked it back in one, but this was smoky and peaty, a good single malt worth taking his time over. A warm glow came over him as he swallowed the first mouthful. He closed his eyes. *Meditation time.* All the cares of the world, washing away with every sip, at least for the moment.

He should have wanted to celebrate but he just wanted to unwind. He had another front-page story hitting the newsstands. The *Daily* had scooped everyone and his perspective was unique. It was a sure-fire number one. Now he just wanted to reflect.

In the background, an NFL game was playing on a screen above the bar. All of the patrons except for Peter were glued to every play. The Forty-Niners versus the Dallas Cowboys. Peter picked the Forty-Niners as winners. They were ahead. Maybe if they played Aussie Rules over here he would be watching too, but he didn't give a shit about gridiron. It wasn't football if it took a mathematical genius to work out the rules.

He felt like he had almost forgotten what an Aussie Rules game looked like but, thanks to a mate in Melbourne, at least he was up on the latest results. Collingwood had beaten West Coast in an away game by one goal point on the weekend. For the first time since he had been in the States, he felt homesick, he felt nostalgic, and he felt alone.

He sympathised with Stella. How much longer could he do this? He felt like he had finally arrived at the stage when he needed someone in his life. Someone permanent. Was he going to wake up old and alone one day, or wake up with someone beside him?

Headlines don't keep your bed warm at night and tell you they love you.

Belinski arrived just as the Forty-Niners scored a touchdown. Everyone at the bar was cheering and ordering more drinks.

'You look like you're drowning your sorrows. You should be celebrating; another headline story and the Forty-Niners way in front,' Belinski said as he fished in his pocket for his wallet.

'I'll celebrate when Moses and Shafer are caught. How about that?'

'I think it's my round. Another drink?' Belinski asked before he headed to the bar.

'Why not? I might feel like celebrating once I'm pissed. You know what I like.'

Belinski bought a beer and a scotch and slipped into the booth opposite Peter. He held up his glass of beer and said, 'Cheers.'

'Cheers,' Peter replied. 'So, give me an update.'

'We haven't caught Shafer yet,' Belinski muttered as he sipped the froth off his beer. 'But I think he hasn't left San Francisco yet.'

'I'd have known by the look on your face if you'd caught him,' Peter replied dryly. 'You know you're wasting your time.'

'Do you know something that I don't?'

'I told you, they've slipped out of the city and back to New Mexico. Katherine said Shafer told her that it was the end of days. The Prophet is gathering his followers for the end of days when they will rise up to kill the sodomites and the unbelievers. They will be doing it at Carmel Ridge, for sure.'

'Why there?'

'Of course they'll do it there. The Prophet lives there. The followers will want to be around him, won't they? All cosied up to each other as they play it out,' he reasoned.

'What? You think they're going to sit around and sing *kumbaya* on the designated day, roasting marshmallows over a roaring fire?'

Peter took a long drink of scotch. 'Of course not. One thing I've noticed about these guys is they're secretive to a point, but they want to broadcast their hateful message. So, they'll start something to attract the authorities and the media. The media will love it.

Moses'll want everyone to know about it. He won't want to go gently into that good night.'

'They've always sailed under the radar.'

'Not Shafer. And not the Prophet. Jerry, I've seen the place, they were practising at the firing range when I got in there that night. How many churches do you know that have gun practice before evening prayers? The place is like an armed camp getting ready for the enemy to attack.'

'Well, I've let the Albuquerque police department know about Moses. They're in the loop. I'm still working on getting a name for them to work with. Once I establish an identity, they'll want to interview him.'

'I thought you'd already know who he is,' Peter remarked.

'Priorities, Peter. We haven't been exactly sitting on our hands. We were combing the city for terrorists. A serial killer can wait a little longer.'

'I wouldn't fuck around with this, Jerry.'

'You're not getting it. Justice takes time. You get it wrong, the perp walks. So, Stella recognised someone she saw once twenty years ago in a nightclub, and who may have been the Slasher killer, from a grainy photo you took of the Prophet through a window. Can you see what I'm saying here? In my game, you can't let yourself be startled by all of the lights.'

'I don't want to tell you your job, mate,' Peter said after he finished his scotch.

Belinski drained his beer. 'Another one and a change of subject?'

'Yep, my shout.'

'Make it a scotch, too.'

Peter returned with two scotches. The crowd at the bar had grown quieter since the Forty-Niners had fallen behind. 'Not looking good,' he remarked as he placed the two drinks on the table and sat down.

'They're behind.'

'I think they got the collywobbles,' Peter laughed.

'Say what?'

'Aussie slang for letting victory slip out of your hands.'

263

'Well, it's not over yet.' Belinski's eyes lingered for a while on the game.

'I hear Margulies is singing like a canary.'

'With conditions. Off the record, right? We had to give him witness protection.'

'Well, when you decide to rat on a drug cartel, sleeping safely is a thing of the past. What's he saying?'

'Off the record—'

Peter interrupted. 'You know you don't have to say that all of the time. I understand your position and I'm a mate. I'm not going to put any of this in our paper.'

'Okay. Margulies was laundering money for the Carmel Ridge Church—Ranch—whatever, as he was for the drug cartel. He met the big players in Bolivia. He was wined and dined and had a good time there for a while. He developed an expensive cocaine habit which they gladly paid for. That and the expensive cars, girlfriends and houses. That's about it.'

'An interesting combination of clients. I wonder if the cartel and the church knew each other?' Peter smiled.

'I don't think so, although I did wonder how Shafer got hold of the C4 explosive.'

'I guess you can't pick it up from a local Walmart. Do you think he'll ever tell?'

'It's an ongoing inquiry. We have to devote limited resources to rounding up the members of this drug cartel. That will have to wait until all of this is settled.'

'I think you're going to be busy clearing up all of this until you retire.'

'It's massive.'

'How's Claudia?'

'She's fine.'

'Does she miss me?' Peter asked.

'Not from what I've heard,' Belinski replied.

'No mention of me, whatsoever?'

'No. I thought you'd be a no commitment, no strings attached, sort of guy anyway.'

'So, Claudia's probably moved on?'

'You know how women like that are. They're beautiful and they want a rich guy to keep them. That's why she worked for Margulies. She's not going to want you on your salary, is she?'

'You're right.'

'I've been married twenty years and I know what my wife wants. Happy wife, happy life.'

'I envy you in a way. I've occasionally tried to have a relationship but it hasn't quite worked out that way. In my life, there have been two women that I could have lived with, possibly three.'

'So, what happened?'

'One tried to kill me.'

'Wow, that would definitely make things awkward at breakfast. The other?'

'When I told her my real identity she tried to kill herself.'

'Real identity?' Belinski asked. 'I won't ask.'

'It's a long story. Maybe I should wear a warning label.'

He laughed. 'And don't forget what happened at your apartment with Claudia. Margulies tried to kill the both of you.'

'I think it was just me, but it's that pattern again. For safety's sake, all women should stay away,' Peter said sadly.

'You may be dangerous to be around but you're a real funny guy. There would never be a dull moment around you. And you're one hell of a reporter.'

'Funny and talented probably isn't enough.' He downed the rest of his scotch in one gulp. 'I need another.'

'Don't get down about it. There are going to be other women. I heard Naomi from TVN was chasing you the other day,' Belinski said.

'Her? I don't know about her. I think that was about information-sharing. Besides, she isn't my type. I don't have the ego or face for television.'

'I'm a guy, but you may be wrong about the face.'

Peter looked down at his empty glass. He needed a drink. 'I'm a good drinker when I get going. I can drink away all the troubles of the world. Come on, Jerry. Whose shout is it?'

Belinski got out of the booth. 'It's mine. I'll buy you one before I go,' he said as he checked his watch.

'The wife has got you on a curfew, my friend. Don't worry about buying me another one. I'll be able to take care of myself. I'll hang around here for a while. I don't mind drinking alone, you don't get in any arguments that way. But then again, you can't talk total bullshit to anyone either.'

Belinski smiled. 'Who said you would be drinking alone?' He looked towards the front door.

'What in the bloody hell are you talking about? If you've set me up with Naomi, I'm pissing off right now.' Peter quickly slipped out of the booth.

Belinski grabbed hold of his arm. 'It's not her, buddy,' he said.

The bar door opened and Claudia sidled in with a large smile on her face. Peter's jaw dropped. Around the bar, the Forty-Niners lost their appeal. Most of the patrons turned to look at her. She was beautiful as always, dressed in tight jeans and a blouse, hair tied back in a ponytail. Someone wolf-whistled as she approached.

'You said she'd given up on me,' Peter said to Belinski. 'You prick.'

'I know you'll get me back, but Claudia is now officially out of witness protection. No need for her to give evidence.'

Peter went to kiss Claudia on the cheek, but she turned her face at the last moment and caught his lips.

'It's so good to see you.' He was lost in her eyes. *No words.*

'It's good to feel you.' She giggled. 'Happy to see me?'

'My work here is done,' Belinski said as he walked towards the door.

'See you soon, Jerry,' Peter mumbled. 'Maybe tomorrow.' He turned to Claudia. 'I know a great place with food and wine, great atmosphere and attentive staff. It's not far from here and we won't have to make a reservation. I dine there a lot. I bet you can't guess. It even has accommodation.'

Claudia laughed as she took hold of Peter's hand. 'Back to your place? Great idea. I've been dreaming of your clean sheets since I left.'

CHAPTER SIXTY-FOUR

Peter's apartment, Dogpatch.

CLAUDIA MADE HERSELF RIGHT AT HOME FROM THE MOMENT SHE walked in the door. Before Peter even had time to switch on the light, she'd taken off her blouse, and her jeans were already around her knees.

'Wait!' she shouted. She pulled off her jeans, tiptoed barefoot to the window and closed the curtains. 'Now you can turn on the light.'

'I never took you for someone who'd be bashful,' said Peter.

'I'm not really.' She danced around him in her bra and panties. 'I just like to control who sees me. I hate clothes. They bore me. I really love being naked. If it was up to me everyone would be naked all the time. Naked, everyone's the same. It's so liberating. In fact, I may never wear clothes again.' She kicked off her panties and unhooked her bra. 'See? Better.'

She pranced around for a while, as Peter watched. *Everyone isn't the same naked. You're extraordinary.* He plainly enjoyed the view.

'Won't you join me?'

He didn't need a second invitation. In a few seconds, he was naked too. Claudia giggled, came close enough to him that he could feel the heat of her body and then ran to the bathroom. 'I need a bath,' she said flicking on the tap. 'Won't you join me?'

He poured two glasses of wine and retreated to the bath with them. He left them to one side and climbed into the tub, even as it was still filling.

Claudia looked down at him and laughed. His penis was surrounded by the rising water. It stood up like a mast on a sinking boat.

'I think I can help you with that.' She climbed in and strad-dled him as he lay back amongst the steam and the heat. The wine remained untouched. It was wonderful to feel her again.

They stayed in the bath until the water cooled and then they moved to the bedroom. She hopped into the bed and waited for Peter to switch off the light.

'Once more?' she said playfully.

'I don't know if I...' he began. 'Yes!' he proclaimed as she dis-appeared under the sheet. Old and lonely was banished forever. Tomorrow, he would be waking up in bed with a beautiful woman.

Peter felt as if he'd only just fallen asleep when his cell phone rang. Claudia was still fast asleep. He ignored it for several rings before answering it.

'Peter, it's Brenda. Brenda from the diner in Tijeras.' She was clearly agitated.

He got up and took the telephone into the kitchen. 'You sound distressed. What's wrong?'

'I was out at the ranch earlier.'

'You know you really shouldn't go near that place. I didn't mean for you to—'

'You're right. Well, I got curious and went out there. Although, I wish I hadn't.'

'Why? What happened?'

'These crazy people started shooting at me when I just went near the front gate. The place is armed like a fort and they're ready to fight. I'm only glad I got out of there alive.'

'You're okay?'

'A bit shaken up, that's all. Something's brewing at the ranch.'

Claudia drifted into the kitchen with the bed sheet draped around her. 'Everything okay?'

Peter turned to talk to her. 'I'm fine. Just work.'

'At this time of night? Tell them you have company.'

'I won't be long.' He smiled at her and touched her on the face. Then he returned to the call.

'I think you're right, Brenda.'

'Are you coming to see for yourself? There are people with guns all over the place, women and children, even. They even have an armoured car with a machine gun on it patrolling the fence.'

'It looks like I don't have an option.'

'I hate to ask, but do you think you could pay me for giving you that information? I wouldn't ask, only I risked my life tonight to help you out,' she said.

'Of course I'll be able to pay you.'

'But I don't want no photos of me in your paper. Okay?'

'Of course not, Brenda.'

'I kinda trust you. You got nice eyes. You can see the soul of a person through their eyes.'

Peter thought of the Prophet. 'That's for certain.' He looked up and caught Claudia staring daggers at him. 'I'll be there as soon as I can. I better go. You should call the police. They'll want to know about what happened.'

'Yeah. I don't know whether to call the police or the National Guard.' Brenda feigned laughter.

Chapter Sixty-Five

Carmel Ridge Ranch, New Mexico.

THE MAN THEY CALLED THE PROPHET WAS RESTING IN A RECLINER chair, watching a John Wayne movie on a large theatre screen. His two female attendants, Sister Abital and Sister Bihah, stood at attention behind his chair while Brother Joshua Mason sat at a small desk on the other side of the room attending to church business.

Brother Joshua was the only person permitted to sit in the presence of the Prophet. The door attendant, Brother Caleb, stood near the door. He was armed with an Uzi sub-machine gun which he had slung over his shoulder. Brother Caleb stirred when he heard the door buzzer ring and signalled to Brother Joshua by raising his right arm. No one was allowed to speak in the presence of the Prophet unless he spoke to them first. His two female attendants moved from behind his chair to ensure the Prophet was prepared for visitors by checking that all of his body was covered to the neck in a woollen blanket. No one outside this room was allowed to see the Prophet's withered body, only his face and that was largely covered with a head scarf. Only his eyes, the colour of glacial ice, and his voice continued to radiate any energy and authority.

The Prophet looked away from the screen to the door.

'Brother Joshua. He has come,' he croaked. He cleared his throat. 'Adjust the volume.'

Brother Joshua got up from his desk and moved to the centre of the room. He noticed one of the attendants reaching for the television remote.

'Sister Abital, I will attend to the volume,' Brother Joshua hissed. 'You are here only to serve the Prophet's personal needs.'

Sister Abital lowered her head by way of contrition, and kept her head lowered. 'Most humble apologies for my transgression. I will expect punishment from you at our service later tonight.'

'Yes, you will accept punishment which will be in the form of… ten lashes.'

Sister Abital became faint and unsteady on her feet. 'I gladly accept the sacred punishment; a punishment which is directly from the Prophet and God.'

'Now raise your head,' Brother Joshua ordered.

Sister Abital raised her head again and stood as if she was lined up on a parade ground.

Brother Joshua reached down to adjust the volume on the television remote. The Prophet suddenly broke into a coughing fit. Sister Bihah gently removed his oxygen mask so he could spit into a tissue she was holding. Sister Bihah gave him a drink of water from a straw in a glass and the Prophet's cough quickly settled.

When Sister Bihah had replaced the mask, she and Sister Abital lifted the Prophet's emaciated frame so he sat higher in the chair, and quickly covered him up to the neck again with the blanket.

After a quick inspection of the Prophet, Brother Joshua directed an order to Brother Caleb. 'Brother Caleb. The Prophet is ready. You may open the door but only slowly. The Prophet's eyes must not be hurt by the glare.'

Brother Caleb slowly opened the door. Alex Shafer marched into the room, fell to his knees and lowered his head, just short of where Brother Joshua was standing.

'You have returned from the city of Sodom,' Brother Joshua stated loudly, 'but your mission has failed, Brother Alexander. Why have you failed on your mission, Brother Alexander?'

Brother Joshua removed a small whip from inside his jacket and brought it down hard across the back of Shafer's shoulders. Shafer didn't flinch.

'I brought you a wealth of riches from The Ten Commandments Church and kept none for myself, exactly as you asked. I instructed them in your holy teachings, Prophet Moses, but they wouldn't listen. They have been corrupted by a campaign to destroy us…' Shafer began.

Brother Joshua cleared his throat.

Shafer continued. 'The church elders refused to slay the sodomites. I slew Elias Gatting in front of them, and yet still they refused. I have returned as you ordered, to prepare for the end day, as you have proclaimed it, here, three days hence.'

Brother Joshua mocked, 'But you are a former Special Forces officer and you say you were defeated by a handful of apostates and members of the communist, fag-loving, black-loving press? You disgust me.'

'The reporters from the *Daily* somehow found out our plans,' Shafer stammered.

'But you have failed to kill the sodomites and gather the masses against them. You should have completed your mission, even if you had to die there. When you die for the Prophet, you are received immediately into heaven. But when you fail him...' Brother Joshua slapped the whip down hard across Shafer's back again.

'I have returned as ordered for the end day. I follow your orders. If I must be punished, I will gladly accept it.'

The Prophet held up his shrunken arm and cleared his throat. He wrapped his spindly, spider fingers around the mask and attempted to remove it himself. Sister Abitah quickly intervened and assisted the Prophet in removing the oxygen mask from his head. Everyone in the room bowed.

'The Prophet is going to speak. Praise and listen to the Prophet's every word,' Brother Joshua announced.

'All praise and listen to the Prophet's every word,' the others said in unison.

'We are glad Brother Alexander has returned safely from his mission. He has not fully completed it, but yet we see it as a success,' the Prophet began in a faltering voice. The Prophet paused to take a deep breath. 'It is a success in that we have enlightened the masses to these evil sodomites and to their immoral ways,' the Prophet's voice grew stronger as he spoke, 'especially in Satan's city where sodomy is practised as if it were normal behaviour. It is a vile city, an abomination. You had a difficult mission, Brother Alexander. We have lived in the city of sodomites. They are as

272

filthy and as numerous as rats.' He paused again for breath.

'The Ten Commandments Church will henceforth under our guidance be seen as an example of goodness. It will be seen as the beacon of light that has tried to fight the darkness of Satan. The Evil One—that demon that comes in the form of the liberal, fag-loving press, fag-loving politicians and fag-loving intellectuals—must be stopped. Our message must rise above their message. Our message must be stronger. When our message is stronger, the masses will follow us and will cleanse all of the sinners from the earth.'

The Prophet paused to cough. Sister Bihah gave him a drink of water.

'Our message is strongest, because it is the message of God. Isn't it, Brother Joshua?'

'Yes, it is, Prophet Moses.'

'So, there will be no punishment for Brother Alexander. He is David, our warrior.'

'No punishment?' Brother Joshua queried.

'Such is the will of the Almighty. We have already witnessed these events unfold. This was meant to happen. The Almighty told us that warriors like Brother Alexander will be needed to fight on the end day. Soon, the world will listen and follow our example. Our strength will be imitated by others. The believers will gather here when the war against Satan begins. On the end day, many thousands of believers will gather here, on Carmel Ridge, with us, from all over the world. It is here, our forces will overthrow the evil infidels. Our deaths will cause the rise of the believers. They will fight off the forces of Satan. And at our deaths, we will be received as angels in heaven, and we will sit at the right hand of the Father. Now we will prepare. Are we prepared for the end day, Brother Alexander?'

'All of our congregation are undergoing weapons training, as we speak. The perimeter fence needs more reinforcing but we are working on that around the clock.' He gestured to Sister Bihah to wipe the Prophet's mouth.

'How many of the congregation from around America have answered the message to return to Carmel Ridge, Brother Joshua?' the Prophet asked.

'Two busloads came yesterday. There would be close to three hundred who have returned for the end day.'

'The place will be ready for when the soldiers of Satan come to battle our Christian warriors,' Shafer remarked.

'Well done, Brother Alexander. We have the utmost confidence that we will overcome the soldiers of darkness.'

The Prophet started to cough again and Sister Bihah gave him water then allowed him to cough into a tissue. Sister Abital then replaced his mask. Prophet Moses raised his hand then dropped it onto his lap in total exhaustion.

With that signal, Brother Joshua announced, 'The Prophet has spoken. All praise the Prophet's word.'

'All praise the Prophet,' the others repeated.

Prophet Moses managed to speak briefly again before closing his eyes, 'Now we must prepare ourselves spiritually.'

'Pray to the Prophet for guidance,' the others said in unison.

'You may rise and leave the room, Brother Alexander,' Brother Joshua said.

With that, Alex Shafer got on his feet, bowed to Prophet Moses, turned and left the room. Brother Caleb locked the door after Shafer had left.

'May I speak to you in private, Prophet Moses?' Brother Joshua said.

The Prophet slowly opened his eyes. 'Make it brief, Brother Joshua. We are drained of energy.'

'Everyone out of the room,' Brother Joshua ordered. He didn't speak until everyone had left. He then grabbed his chair and pulled it close to the Prophet. 'I am concerned for your health, Moses. Are you up to all of this?' He stroked the Prophet's hand.

'We are prepared for death. Our body may be riddled with cancer, but our spirit is glowing with holiness. It is for you to ensure the others are prepared also.'

'We will all follow you into heaven. We are not afraid.'

'That's reassuring. For a brief moment, you went above us when Brother Alexander was in the room.'

'Yes, I am sorry. I would have liked Shafer to have completed his mission. That city is foul with sodomites and their filth. There are so many of them and they seek out others to join their ranks. It disgusts me.'

The Prophet managed a smile. 'Remember, this is only the beginning. This is the spark that will become an inferno. The inferno that will engulf them all and cleanse the world. Can you see it?'

'Yes, I can see it.'

'You must never question us ever again,' the Prophet said.

'I will not question you ever again. I am prepared to die for you.'

'Good, you may bring the others back in,' the Prophet ordered.

Brother Joshua got off his chair and was returning it to his desk.

'The other thing.'

'Yes, Prophet Moses.'

'Put the television on again. We were almost up to the best part of *True Grit.*'

'As you desire, Prophet Moses.'

Chapter Sixty-Six

Daily offices.

Stella was already in the office when Peter arrived at eight am sharp. He knew she was in because he had seen Frank go past with two cups of coffee and a bag of bagels.

He made himself breakfast first—a much-needed coffee—before trying to call Claudia again. The night had not ended well. It had gone progressively downhill after Brenda had rung. The spectre of a lonely old age was once more clearly visible on the horizon.

Claudia had warned him that he shouldn't go to Carmel Ridge, as he would be risking his life. They had only just got back together and he wanted to run off to New Mexico to get a scoop and get shot at. He had tried to reassure her that it was going to be the last time he was chasing stories like this. After that, he wanted time off, he wanted to relax. Maybe, he might even write a book. Claudia hadn't bought his story and she had left in a furious mood. Thanks to his career, Peter was alone again.

He left her a message again, the third that morning. He gulped his coffee and reflected. Sex was sex; they both understood that. Time to move on. *No woman should get in the way of your career. From this day forward, my career is my mistress.* He was already having second thoughts when he noticed Frank had left Stella's office. It was time to sell Stella his idea.

He had rung Belinski already this morning to find out if they had caught Shafer and his gang overnight, but even he now agreed that they had almost certainly left the city and returned to Carmel Ridge. Peter felt like throwing his computer at a wall. *If everyone just listened to my theories, things would run a whole lot smoother.*

Now, he had to get to New Mexico pronto, before the action started and the media pack descended on Carmel Ridge. He knocked once and then entered.

'Can't I drink my coffee and eat my bagel first,' Stella complained, 'before I have to face you?'

'Don't let me interrupt you,' Peter said as he sat down.

'Thanks, I won't.' Stella bit into her bagel and had a sip of coffee. 'Until I say otherwise, you don't exist.'

Peter didn't say a word. He simply stared her down. It had worked before.

'I can't start the day without coffee and bagel,' Stella said, 'but you're even more annoying when you're silent. How is that possible? So, I give up, what is it now?'

'Belinski's now convinced that Shafer has left the city and returned to Carmel Ridge.'

'Is he? That's good. Maybe he's still here only they just haven't caught him yet.' She wiped her hands on a tissue.

'I'm convinced that he's back in Carmel Ridge getting ready for the end of days.'

'That again. What days are they again? I'll make plans to do nothing that day, just get drunk or get my hair done. When I meet the Big Boss, I want to look my best,' she laughed.

Peter rolled his eyes. 'You're a real comedian,' he said dryly.

'What makes you keep thinking that Shafer is back there with his bag of mixed nuts?'

'Brenda—the owner of the diner in Tijeras—called me late last night.'

'And?'

'She said the place was like an armed camp. Everyone she saw, including women and children, were armed and there were armoured cars patrolling the fence. Must cost the earth to fund. We can guess where The Ten Commandments Church's money went.'

'Hmm. So security's been stepped up since you went there?' She leaned back on her chair.

'For sure. I doubt I'd get in there now. I'd be riddled with bullets just approaching the fence. They're getting prepared.'

She thought for a while before replying. 'All right, I'm sending you back but you're also going with a photographer this time. If it all blows up, it's going to be very visual.'

'Can I take Larry Bruce? He kind of understands me.'

'Aside from a psychiatrist, he'd be the first. Heaven knows I've tried and failed miserably,' she said as she picked up the phone. 'I better call the lab and let Larry know he's on assignment. I'm sure he'll be thrilled. I know he likes mini bars and all-you-can-eat buffets.'

'I'll see if we can catch the next flight out,' Peter said. 'I'll grab him on the way out.'

'Aren't you going home to pack?' Stella asked. 'And Larry? Don't you think he'll want to take his toothbrush?'

'What do we need? We're boys. We just need a change of underwear and toiletries. We'll buy that stuff at the airport.' He turned and headed quickly for the door.

'Peter.'

He stopped and spun around. 'What,' he grumbled, 'can't you see I'm in a bit of a hurry?'

'Have you told your girlfriend?'

'Girlfriend? It was just a brief liaison, that's all.'

'Well, at least you have me to care about you. Be safe.'

'Thanks, Stella. We'll go out for a drink when I get back.'

'Yeah, we can celebrate that we survived the end of days.'

Peter's cell was ringing on his desk when he got back. It had vibrated itself to the edge of the desk and was about to fall off. He picked it up as he grabbed his coat off the chair. 'Yeah, it's Peter. What's happening?'

'Peter, it's Jerry Belinski.'

'You've got something big to tell me.' To be honest, he felt a little disappointed that it wasn't Claudia. 'I've noticed your voice gets faster and higher when you're excited.'

'There you go. You're right.'

'What have you got? I'm heading out to New Mexico as we speak.'

'We got the files from the Presidio just now.'

'And?'

'It seems Stella was right about the military connection. By the time he was discharged and by the sound of his physical description, it points to a guy named Gary Emmett O'Toole. He was a military psychologist who held the rank of captain on his discharge. He did two tours of Vietnam.'

'Is there anything in there about why he was discharged?'

'I thought you'd want to know that part,' Belinski replied. 'He received a dishonourable discharge for sexually assaulting a patient.'

The dots were finally connecting themselves. 'Male or female?'

'Male.'

'That's our man. Angry about his sexuality, he kills homosexuals. Angry about being gay and at God, becomes a self-appointed Messiah. His message is blaming homosexuals for the ills of the world. He attracts enough ignorant people—and God knows there are plenty of them around—to form a cult.'

'That's him, in a nutshell.'

'Have you notified the Albuquerque police?'

'I've just notified them. They said they'll go to Carmel Ridge today. I told them to expect a confrontation.'

'That means I haven't got much time to get there and settle in.'

'I'd be looking to extradite him. I'd like to be the cop who brings O'Toole back here for trial. I'll see if I can get there.'

'You're such a glory seeker, Jerry.'

'Right back at you. You'd better go.'

Peter slipped on his jacket and ran back to Stella's office. He barged in without knocking. 'I have a name for the Slasher killer. He's been identified as Gary Emmett O'Toole. The Albuquerque police are going out to Carmel Ridge today.'

Stella whooped. 'We've got him! Great work, Peter.'

'Great work in you identifying him.'

'A reporter should never forget a face. Fortunately, his face was particularly evil and unforgettable,' she said.

'Can you get someone to prepare a background story on O'Toole?'

'Sure.'

'Larry said he'd meet you in the foyer. Now go, off, before you miss something.'

CHAPTER SIXTY-SEVEN

Later that day. Carmel Ridge Ranch.

BY THE TIME PETER AND BRUCE ARRIVED, THE POLICE HAD already sealed off the road to the compound to a half a mile radius. Peter stopped the hire car in front of the New Mexico State Police roadblock before winding down the window.

'Peter Clancy, from the *San Francisco Daily*. What's happening, Officer?' He looked up when he heard a police helicopter buzzing overhead. In the distance he could see the compound. A salvo of shots rang out from it.

'You said you're Peter Clancy? You were mentioned in the briefing. You were working with the SFPD.'

'Yeah,' he replied. 'Me and Jerry Belinski.'

'You supplied the intel, so I guess it's all right... Two officers have been fatally shot as they tried to enter the compound,' the officer said in a distressed voice.

'Oh God,' Peter responded, 'they should have sent in a SWAT team.'

'Now, will you back up so we can have access for emergency vehicles. There's a small clearing—'

'I know,' Peter interrupted, 'I've been here before.'

'Right,' the officer replied with a puzzled look on his face.

Peter backed up along the narrow, dirt road until he reached the clearing.

'You've brought me to another frigging war zone, haven't you, Clancy?' Bruce muttered as he grabbed his camera bag from the back seat. 'If I'd wanted to be a war photographer, I'd have volunteered for Operation Frigging Desert Storm.' He then lit up a cigarette.

'It's our job. I never figured you for a sook, Larry.'

'I have no idea what you just called me, but I can guess. Unlike you, I've got plenty to live for. Let's get this over with and get home.'

Peter parked the car and hot-footed it out, with Bruce close behind him. He looked around. Aside from some reporters from the local rag, there was no media about. Everyone else there was attached to the operation.

'Okay. We go back to the roadblock and take it from there,' Peter said as he walked.

'That's good, for a minute I thought you'd actually want to break into the compound.'

'Well, if there's no action, we may have to.'

'You're crazy.'

'Can you get any photos of the compound from this distance?'

'I have a telephoto lens,' Bruce snapped. 'You take care of the story and I'll take care of the pictures, okay?' He slung the camera bag over his shoulder and followed Peter.

'Sure. No worries.'

When they reached the roadblock, Peter approached the officer who had stopped them earlier, and asked who was in charge of the operation, while Larry Bruce positioned himself further along the road and set up his camera.

The officer pointed to a captain standing next to an unmarked police car. He told Peter to wait at the roadblock while he checked if he had clearance to approach. Peter watched as the officer spoke briefly to a sergeant and then returned to the roadblock.

'Sergeant Kapinsky's taking it from here. You'll have to wait.'

He watched the sergeant wait until the inspector had finished talking to two senior officers dressed in sniper outfits. He and the captain then spoke briefly. The captain turned to look at Peter. Moments later, the sergeant trotted back to where Peter was standing.

'I'm Peter Clancy from the *San Francisco Daily.*'

'Sergeant Kapinsky. I'm told you've been studying the leadership of the Carmel Ridge Ranch and you've been cooperating with the SFPD. Captain Gordanis would like a word with you.'

Peter followed Sergeant Kapinsky closer to the compound and waited for the captain to finish his conversation on the radio. The captain was shorter than Peter, heavier set and bald. His eyes gave away the burden of his rank.

He turned to Peter. 'I'm Captain Jack Gordanis. So, you've come all the way from San Francisco, huh? This only began an hour ago.'

'I've been following developments here for some time.'

'Jerry Belinski told me you'd be coming. He seemed to think we might be of some value to each other. Just don't get in the way.'

'I'll do whatever I can.'

Gordanis shook his head. 'It breaks my heart when officers are killed. Breaks my heart,' his voice trailed off.

'So, this started when you tried to arrest Gary O'Toole, Captain Gordanis?' Peter asked. He turned around when he noticed that the shooting from the compound begin to slow and then stop.

He didn't answer. The helicopter made two passes over the compound before banking and leaving for the clearing.

'So, what are your plans?' Peter continued. The cooperation was only running one way.

A uniformed officer handed Gordanis a cup of coffee. He took a sip and put it down on the roof of the car. 'We're trying a police negotiator first. Apparently there are lots of women and children in there.'

'I was here a few weeks ago. I actually got in there at night and took a photo of the inside of their church.'

He had piqued Gordanis's interest. 'What are you, a frigging commando? You actually got in there?' As he spoke, a man carrying a loud hailer passed them, heading slowly towards the compound. 'How many in there? Can you break that down to men, women and children?'

'Well, at the time I'd estimate about fifty in there, and I noticed about thirty men amongst them. According to my local source, lots of cars and buses have passed by on their way there lately. So, I reckon it's now more like a few hundred.'

'And this O'Toole character. Have you met him?'

'He's a serial killer turned cult leader. He's everything that

Charles Manson wanted to be. My boss had a chance encounter with him in the seventies. He's remorseless and brutal and he knows how to play mind games to boot. O'Toole's someone you'd never want to meet. He's the Psycho Messiah.'

'Can you draw me a plan of the compound and show me where you got in?'

'Sure.'

Gordanis handed him a piece of paper and pen. As Peter drew, Gordanis grabbed a pair of binoculars off the hood of the car and stared at the compound. One of the officers was dragging himself back towards the nearest police car.

He darted forward. 'Stay where you are, buddy! Don't move, we'll get you. Stay there!' he yelled.

As he spoke, two officers rushed forward to grab the man, but they were stopped in their tracks by a hail of bullets. Peter heard three distinct shots. After that, the officer stopped moving.

Gordanis picked up his radio and barked into the mouthpiece, 'Christ. Pull the negotiator back. It's too dangerous. Everyone back to the roadblock.'

He lit up a cigarette. 'Shit. These people can't be negotiated with. They'll kill anyone within range.'

'Well, Captain,' Peter said as he handed the plan to him, 'from what I've seen I've realised that these people are prepared to die. To them, it's the end of days and they want to take as many of us as they can along for the ride.'

'You know when this end of days is?'

'One of O'Toole's henchmen, Alex Shafer, apparently said something about the Sabbath. Which Sabbath exactly, I don't know. Hell, I don't even know whether the Sabbath falls on a Friday night, a Saturday or a Sunday for them. Whenever it is, I know it can't be far away.'

'I'm not prepared to allow my men to die needlessly. Except for the children, I don't give a shit about any of these people.'

Gordanis signalled three other senior officers to join him. Together they studied Peter's map. He pointed to a location on Peter's drawing. 'Is this the place where you were able to get in?'

Peter glanced at the map. 'Yes. It was a break in the wire where an animal had probably crawled through. Fortunately, their spot-lights didn't quite reach that far. I guess that's why it was breached in the first place and why they'd missed it.'

'Can you take us there now?' Gordanis asked.

'No worries.'

Gordanis pointed out two police officers who were dressed in civilian clothes. 'Burns and Santos, Mr Clancy here is going to show you where we may be able to break in. Happy with that, Clancy?'

'Not really,' Peter said reluctantly as he looked at the two officers.

'I appreciate your help,' Gordanis continued. 'I'll give you tickets to the game and an exclusive once this is over.'

'Thanks,' Peter replied incredulously. 'Although I'd much prefer a bottle of scotch to go with that exclusive.'

CHAPTER SIXTY-EIGHT

PETER LET LARRY BRUCE KNOW WHERE HE WAS HEADED BEFORE setting off into the forest. A helicopter swooped low over the area as they were talking.

Bruce looked up. 'They're here,' he said. 'It's a TV helicopter.'

'The foot soldiers will be here soon,' Peter observed.

'You know what that means,' Bruce laughed.

'If Naomi from TVN is going to be here, I'm staying in the forest.'

A police officer tapped Peter on the shoulder. 'We're ready.'

'If I don't make it back,' he said sadly, 'let Claudia know that I was sorry.'

Bruce shook his head. 'You're so full of bullshit, Clancy. You'll be back. You're too much of an asshole to die.'

He backtracked all the way down the road, followed by the two officers, until they reached the clearing. To the left, the under-growth was thick but not impenetrable.

'Stick to me,' Peter said quietly. 'Into the woods we go.'

The officers drew their weapons but kept their safeties on, and followed Peter into the juniper forest. They were crouched low, stepping slowly and quietly through the undergrowth until they reached a row of oaks near the forest edge. They could now see the perimeter fence clearly.

'That's where I went in,' Peter whispered. He glanced at the fence. 'It wasn't like that when I was here. It's been reinforced.'

They heard a vehicle creeping along the fence. By the growl of the engine, it wasn't a Jeep. 'Down,' ordered one of the police officers.

They dropped onto the forest floor. The sun couldn't penetrate all the way down to the decaying leaves and it was still damp. Peter raised his head just far enough to allow him to see ahead. The vehicle was an armoured military type. One man drove while another stood out of a hole in the roof, operating a rotating gun turret.

'What the fuck?' Officer Santos swore under his breath. 'How the hell are we going to get in there?'

The vehicle slowed and then stopped. The driver got out of the vehicle and went to the fence to examine it, as Peter held his breath. He hadn't dressed for the occasion and hoped his sweater wouldn't stand out. The driver didn't seem to notice anything suspicious, and he got back in and moved on. Their eyes followed the vehicle until it disappeared.

'He touched it, so I don't think the fence is booby-trapped,' said Officer Burns. 'Or at least not here.'

'Let's see how often he comes around,' Santos replied.

Peter's chest was getting cold and he wanted to move away, but he kept the thought to himself. He rested his head on his arms. At least the earth smelled sweet and, unlike the last time he was there, Santos and Burns were welcome company. They watched and waited. The vehicle returned to their position again after ten minutes.

'These guys must be going around the fence continuously. Okay, we've seen enough.'

They retraced their tracks and returned to where Gordanis was positioned. Kapinsky and another sergeant stood near him. Peter's map was still sitting on the hood. From the compound, hymnal music was playing.

'Odd siege music. I'd much prefer to listen to Led Zeppelin, myself,' Peter said.

'You want a coffee?' Burns asked him.

'Please. Cream and sugar, thanks.'

'That music just started playing. Anyone got any theories why?' Gordanis asked the officers around him.

Peter had a thought. 'Motivational. A preparatory ritual, perhaps? I'm no expert.'

Gordanis stroked his chin.

'Sir,' said Santos, 'we won't be able to get in the way Mr Clancy showed us. I can't tell if the fence is booby-trapped but they have an armoured vehicle with a gun turret regularly patrolling the fence. Ten-minute intervals, from what I could tell.'

'Shit.' Gordanis turned to Sergeant Kapinsky. 'We have two choices. We bust in there and probably suffer lots of casualties or wait it out and see what will happen next.'

'I say we wait it out,' said Kapinsky, while the others nodded.

Peter interrupted, 'Would it help if you let the people in the compound know that their so-called prophet is a serial killer?'

Gordanis thought briefly. 'They're probably so brainwashed that they'll think his crimes were acts of heroism.' He paused. 'I guess there's no harm in trying. Okay. Get the negotiator here and find us a loudspeaker.'

Two media helicopters buzzed overhead. 'Is there anything we can do about them?' Gordanis asked Kapinsky. 'Call the Chief. Get them out of here.'

'Sure thing. We probably only have another two hours of light before they go anyway.'

Gordanis clapped his hands. 'Okay. Everyone back to work.'

Peter walked back to the clearing where Bruce was reclining in the passenger seat of the car dozing. He jerked open the door and Bruce woke up with a jolt. 'Who died? What's happening?' He looked at Peter. 'Oh, you're back. In the flesh.'

'Did you get any photos?'

'Yeah. The lens works a treat. Gets me right in the action.'

Peter looked around at the crowd of reporters hustling in on the scene. Unlike them, they were kept behind a cordon. He felt like laughing until he spied a blonde head bobbing up and down. A waving hand joined the bobbing head, and then a whiny voice. Naomi's voice.

'Peter! Peter! It's me. Naomi from TVN.'

Larry Bruce looked across and chuckled. 'She's tracked you down. I wouldn't tell Claudia, but I think she's got the hots for you.'

Peter ducked behind the car, but the whine continued. 'Peter, I'm glad to see a familiar face. Can you get me in there?'

'Now I know what it's like to feel besieged.'

Naomi squirmed to the front of the pack. 'I heard you were helping the police,' she yelled. 'Can you tell me what you know about this place and the sect leader? Why have the police come here?'

Peter strode up to the cordon. 'Are you interviewing me?'

'You can see I don't have a microphone. I just want to know. Once again, you have a head start on us. Tell me what you know, please.'

'Would you have done the same for me?' he asked moving along the cordon.

'Well, I like to collaborate with my fellow reporters,' Naomi said vaguely, trying to keep up in high heels and stumbling over a rock.

Peter sighed. 'You're such a bullshit artist, Naomi.'

'Come on, Peter, give me a break. We can work together on this. You know, our producer is keen to offer you a job. He's been calling you.'

'Is that a fact.'

'I bet you'll earn a lot more than you do now. And you'll get to work with me.'

Peter shook his head. He began to walk away. Then he suddenly stopped and turned around. 'Stay here.'

He had an idea, but he needed to clear it with Gordanis first. Things were looking desperate and Gordanis was keen to wrap things up as quickly as he could, before there were any more casualties. He listened to Peter's idea. He wasn't convinced at first. Finally he gave him the go-ahead.

A few minutes later, Peter was back at the cordon. 'You can do two things for me,' he said to Naomi.

'Sure.'

'Can you go on television and say that the cult leader is one Gary Emmett O'Toole? Say that he is wanted for a spate of murders that occurred in the nineteen seventies when he was in the Army. Say that he targeted gay men as he is believed to be gay himself. Can you say that?' he asked. 'I have a hunch that O'Toole's followers may like keeping people out, but they love hearing about themselves on TV. If they are watching the siege on television, maybe they'll have second thoughts about their Messiah after they've heard that.'

Naomi thought for a moment. 'I'll have to run it by the producer. What's the other request?'

'I need a drink and I forgot to bring my flask with me.'

'We should be able to find you some booze.'

'Do all of that and I'll be able to fill you in. But you have to mention it was sourced from me at the *Daily*, San Francisco. Got it? If you can't do that, there's no bloody deal.'

'I'll go and see.' She shimmied through the crowd to join her crew.

'It looks like we're here for the night,' Bruce said as he rubbed his hands together, 'and I forgot to bring a warm coat thanks to you.'

'Good. The cold will keep you awake.'

'Great.'

'Okay. I'll give you one of mine.'

'We'll also need food.'

'You can go and get some food from Brenda in the village, I have to stay here. Any more frigging requests?'

'I'm working on it.'

The gunfire had all but stopped, with the exception of the occasional burst from the armoured vehicle. Peter watched the setting sun cast a pink glow across the horizon and sipped the bourbon Naomi had sourced for him. He didn't much like bourbon, it was too sweet, but at least it was having the desired effect. A warm indolence was spreading over his entire body.

It might have been serene, except for the two loudspeakers blaring out from the compound and the negotiator attempting to be heard above someone reading from the Bible. The compound's spotlights had turned on, exposing two police officers who were dragging their dead and wounded to the relative safety of an armoured police van. A series of shots rang out from the compound, but no one was hit.

Peter nudged Bruce. 'They've got them out. We better get over to the roadblock.'

'Surreal, isn't it,' Bruce commented.

'I'm glad you think so, Larry. It all looks and sounds like the end of the world to me.'

Naomi returned to the cordon and called out to Peter. 'He'll do it as long as you're willing to do a live interview. He says it will have more gravitas.'

Peter thought about it briefly. It would be worth it if it saved even one life. He agreed to the interview and arranged for her to join him on the other side of the police cordon as the other reporters looked on enviously.

Naomi interviewed Peter live in front of the roadblock while Bruce snapped photos of the scene. It lasted for five minutes and, in that time, he kept debunking O'Toole's divinity. There was an earnestness about his style. He knew he could rely on good looks to catch a viewer's attention and after that his message had to be crystal. Prophet Moses was none other than Gary Emmett O'Toole, a ruthless serial killer. They had all been conned.

After the interview, Peter chose to ignore Naomi's attempt to give him a high-five. Santos bustled her back to the media pack and assigned a sentry.

'How did I go?' Peter asked Bruce.

'I can see why you went into print journalism.'

'Thanks for the compliment,' he said before tossing him what was left of the bourbon and walking away.

'Where are you going?'

'To the TVN tent. I'm sleeping somewhere warm tonight. Enjoy sleeping in the hire car. I'll bring you my coat after I've had dinner.'

'You're a real prick, Clancy.'

CHAPTER SIXTY-NINE

PETER'S CELL PHONE RANG AS HE HEADED BACK UP THE TRACK. It was Stella. She had seen the interview. He held his breath and waited.

'I thought it might be you,' he said. 'Are you mad?'

'No. I can see where you're headed with it.'

'Desperate times and all that… I don't know if Jerry Belinski will like it,' he replied.

'With any luck, he won't be able to reach you. Meanwhile, I'll see if I can smooth things over. He'll be fine with it.' She paused. 'I'm having the operation tomorrow.'

'Shit… With all of this, I forgot. I wish I was there with you.'

'The best thing you can do is get on with your job. Coincidentally, the circulation figures are also due out tomorrow.'

'All of the best with everything, Stella. I know you'll be fine.'

'Thanks. I'll….' The signal broke up.

Peter dived into the warm comfort of the TVN tent and caravan. He was ecstatic to learn that Naomi wasn't there—she'd taken a room in the village with a TV and a bath. Day one of the siege was over.

Back at the motel, Naomi was tucked up in bed with Chinese takeout, watching herself on television.

At the end of day one in this tense Carmel Ridge siege, two police officers have been fatally shot and two wounded. What tomorrow will bring is anyone's guess. We can only pray that there it will be no more tragedy. I'm Naomi Crabshaw from TVN News.

She tossed the container away and snuggled down for a good night's sleep.

CHAPTER SEVENTY

Five am, next day. Carmel Ridge Ranch.

LARRY BRUCE STIRRED FROM THE BACK SEAT AND TRIED TO release his five-ten frame from the foetal position he had been forced to sleep in during the night. He stumbled out of the car and stretched himself out. Everything hurt.

As he took a piss in the bushes, he was cursing Peter for having left him out in the cold. He winced as he attempted to straighten up his back. Feeling like he could now face the first part of the day, he grabbed his camera bag and headed back to the roadblock. A coffee and a bag of donuts would probably see him through to lunch.

Two State police officers were manning the roadblock, standing around an open fire drinking coffee. Bruce recognised them as the officers who'd gone with Peter the day before.

'That's what I need,' he said when he noticed the fire. 'I've had a shit night. I should have bunked down here.'

'There's a pot of coffee, there. Pour yourself one. It'll warm you up,' Burns said.

'Looks like we're the only ones awake,' said Santos to Bruce, as he poured himself a cup.

'What about the zoo inhabitants?' Bruce asked as he looked towards the Carmel Ridge compound. The compound was covered in fog except for the peak on the roof of the main building.

'Nothing, except for those patrol vehicles going around the fence all the time,' the officer said.

'We're going to be frying up some bacon and beans soon. Do you want some?'

'Sure. I'll go set up my camera before all of the network guys swarm in.'

'Remember, don't go past the line.'

'I won't,' he replied before wandering back to the position he had yesterday. He crouched down behind a fallen log and unzipped his bag and assembled his camera, attaching the telephoto lens. He looked into the camera. He noticed something moving.

'Holy shit guys,' he shouted to the officers, 'there's a bunch of people trying to get over the fence. I can see men, women and children.'

Burns ran to have a look through Bruce's camera, while Santos shouted into his radio. 'We need support immediately. There's a breakout from the compound.'

The compound loudspeaker crackled before a booming voice came over it: 'There is no escape. It is the end of days. Unbelievers who leave must die.'

The voice stopped and the silence was deathly. Suddenly, the sound of rapid gunfire broke out from the main building. Two of the armed compound patrol vehicles charged into the group of people, firing continuously from their gun turrets.

Bruce watched through his lens as the victims were mown down. He felt guilty as his camera whirred, but there wasn't anything else he could do. History needed a witness. Most of the people fell, but a woman and a man managed to scale the gate and run towards the roadblock. He could see that they were both wounded. They fell into the arms of the paramedic team.

Peter was running down the track towards Bruce just as Gordanis and his team arrived in a police car.

'Get the BearCat in there,' Gordanis ordered over the radio. He looked over to the compound. 'Break down that goddamned gate. We have to get as many out as possible. Now. Now. Now.'

'It's today,' Bruce shouted at Peter. 'The end of days. They're all going to die today.'

Peter watched the unfolding horror and wiped his eyes with his shirt cuff. 'They won't be able to save them.' He joined Bruce at the police cordon. No one said a word.

He watched the compound as Bruce reeled off more shots. At the other end of the cordon, Naomi composed herself for the camera.

The State police's BearCat armoured personnel carrier had arrived and gone through the roadblock. It immediately drew gunfire from the compound. The fog had now lifted, allowing the police and media to see the full horror beyond the fence. Behind the gate lay bodies of men, women and children—all dead. Some of them lay on top of each other. There were four dead bodies flopped over the gate.

Bruce lowered his camera. 'There must be at least twenty people there.'

The voice boomed again over the compound's loudspeaker. 'Today we will die and ascend to heaven where we will be greeted as heroes. For us, there is life everlasting. The unbelievers will perish in the flames of Satan.'

The compound's patrol continued to direct fire on the BearCat as it slowed down to push past the gate. It was indomitable. The metal slowly buckled underneath it and snapped apart.

Dozens of people ran towards the open gates, mothers clutching their children, men and women dragging others out of the main complex. As quickly as they could scramble away, so were they caught by the bullets raining over them from the patrol vehicles while the loudspeaker kept broadcasting.

The BearCat fired on the patrol vehicles but was unable to immobilise them. They continued to fire at the fleeing people. Then, as abruptly as it had started, the firing stopped. The gunfire in the complex also ceased.

'They're out of ammo,' Gordanis announced. 'Send the tactical team in. Let's wrap this up.'

Another BearCat came through the roadblock and headed towards the compound.

'I can see people getting out of the patrol vehicles,' Bruce yelled.

'Shit, are they giving themselves up?'

The gunfire started again.

Bruce turned away from his camera. 'They're frigging killing themselves! They're all kneeling on the ground and putting guns to their heads. Oh God. It's going to be a mass suicide. It's frigging Jonestown all over again.'

The loudspeaker could be heard above the gunfire. 'We will be in heaven today, and the world will be consumed in eternal flames.'

It was silent for a while, before the first of a series of bombs exploded. The earth shuddered under Peter's feet and the noise reverberated through his chest. Flames leapt hundreds of feet into the air. Then each of the remaining nine buildings exploded and, within minutes, the whole complex was engulfed in fire. The devastation was so sudden and so complete that there'd been no time to evacuate the compound. The BearCats reversed out of the grounds.

'Can you see anyone coming out of there, Larry?' Peter shouted.

'No. No. I can't see anyone... No, wait...'

One of the officers had climbed out of the BearCat and sprinted back towards the hall. He grabbed a child scurrying away from the flames. He threw his coat over the child to stop the embers, holding him tightly and running towards the paramedics. Tears were streaming down his face as he handed the child over. As he did so, his knees buckled.

'What's he doing? Is he praying?' Bruce asked.

Peter felt a tear splash onto his collar and realised he was weeping too.

The gunfire never resumed. The officers looked frantically for any other signs of life but there were no more miracles that day. As they came back out of the compound, the men wore their anguish like lead jackets. The lull after the storm was too awful to bear.

As Peter walked back to the car with Bruce, his cell phone rang.

'Peter, it's Stella.'

'I thought you were having an operation.'

'I'm at the hospital getting prepped. I can't talk long,' she said. 'Is everything there okay?'

'The siege is over. It hasn't been a good outcome. Very few survivors.'

'That's terrible.' Her voice faded away. 'And what about you? Are you okay?'

Peter hesitated. 'To be honest, I'm not really sure.'

'I called you because I wanted to tell you something, just in case

I don't get a chance to. After what you've been through, it seems a bit silly, really.'

'Yeah. I'm having trouble hearing… There were explosions, you understand. And there are lots of people around...' He moved away from the fracas that surrounded him. 'That's better.'

'Oh, okay. I'll be quick. I thought you'd want to know. The *Daily* is now number one again.'

The phone cut out. He felt numb. Now wasn't the time to celebrate.

He and Bruce flew back to San Francisco the next day. Even without a nip of whisky, he had slept through the entire flight and arrived groggy and unshaven. The end of days had come and gone. It was finally over and he was exhausted.

He looked at the faces of the people passing by him at the airport, at those saying goodbye and those hello, and he thought of those wretches who had lost people they loved all because of a psychopath. For them there would be no more hellos.

He switched on his cell phone the moment he reached the baggage hall, and found a message from Stella: *OP GON WEL*. She really wasn't that hot on the latest technology. He was about to delete it when the phone alerted him to another message. This time, it was from a number he didn't recognise.

Turn around.

He did as he was told. At the far end of the hall, right next to the baggage carousel, he saw someone waving. It was Claudia.

THE END

296